'Where on earth has this been?' said Griswold, waving the dust away from his nostrils.

'In a place where no creature has ever dared to venture. A place known only to one man and protected by the most awesome magical powers ever known. A place – '

'Under your bed,' said Griswold.

'Under my bed.'

The last shred of sacking slid off the table and floated to the floor, raising another small cloud. The men stared at the object.

'It's a sword,' said Griswold before he could stop himself. 'I already have a sword.'

'Thou dost not have *this* one,' said Merlin.

'I do not need *this* one,' replied Griswold flatly.

The scabbard under its layer of dirt and dust was about as commonplace as one could imagine. Fashioned from a grey leathery hide, it was quite featureless and appeared to be too large for the weapon. The hand-guard was made of grey iron and the hilt was deep black with a dull, rather grubby stone set in its end.

'What dost thou think?' asked Merlin. His voice was unusually quiet.

'Is there any soup left?' said Griswold.

Also by Collin Webber in VGSF

MERLIN AND THE
LAST TRUMP

Collin Webber

RIBWASH

VGSF

First published in Great Britain 1994
by Victor Gollancz
A Division of the Cassell group
Villiers House, 41/47 Strand, London WC2N 5JE

A VGSF paperback original

A catalogue record for this book is
available from the British Library.

ISBN 0 575 05830 7

Typeset by CentraCet Limited, Cambridge
Printed and bound in Great Britain
by Cox & Wyman Ltd, Reading, Berks

Acknowledgements

I want to thank Faith, a great editor who lived up to her name, despite all my attempts to shake it.

And I want to thank Mo for not saying, 'Oh, blimey, here we go again.'

'In the wake of the Last Trump, the people of Earth were thriving. Tales of great deeds, concerning Man's triumph over Evil, still echoed across the face of the planet.

'Life was not bad.

'Mankind slowly rebuilt his world, under the rule of King Uther Pendragon; not the wisest of kings, nor the most far-seeing . . . nor the most diplomatic . . . certainly not the most dignified.

'In fact, hardly monarch material at all.'

'Then, in AD 4096, just when the planet was getting back to its old ways, the miracles began.

'Once-deserted deserts flourished and grew green.

'Disease, famine and starvation vanished almost overnight.

'Wars began to die out.

'Mankind gasped in awe and thought of Messiahs and Second Comings.

'Uther was apprehensive. It was all too good to be true.

'He didn't mind coping with the Forces of Darkness again.

'He wasn't too happy about taking on God.'

PROLOGUE
AD 4096. Gnomedom

GNOMEDOM is a ghastly world in a gruesome part of the galaxy, two hundred parsecs and three or four Realities to the left of Mankind's homeworld, Earth.

Gnomedom was and still is one of the few completely ugly worlds in existence. Every world has, in theory, some redeeming quality, something that one can look at and say, 'That's not so bad', even if it's only by comparison.

Gnomedom doesn't.

Beside Gnomedom, Gormenghast pales to mere grotesquery.

By Gnomish standards, Hell is positively heavenly.

When one thinks of Gnomedom, one thinks of a gift shop. Looking in the window of that gift shop, one sees a range of dull, cast-iron characters, black and silver-grey, each one finding a pretentious reason for owning a multi-faceted artificial crystal ball.

Such is the common hue, minus the multi-faceted artificial crystal ball, of Gnomedom and of the gnomes, right down to the last man, woman and ghastly infant.

It is hardly surprising that the people of Gnomedom are coldly savage and evil to a degree that would embarrass the average demon from Hell.

There is never a trace of colour in their world, except during and in the aftermath of the 'squabbles', when blades flash, bodies are split open and steaming organs of a surprising variety of hues spill out to relieve the unremitting silver-grey of the cobblestones or the horizon-spanning granite-grey of the countryside.

The gnomes of Gnomedom would live for a thousand years, if it wasn't for the 'squabbles'. These involve batches of fifty to a thousand gnomes at a time and tend to shorten the odds against longevity to around three hundred years, unless, of course, one is a real gnome's gnome.

No one is quite sure why gnomes orchestrate their squabbles with such political precision or pursue them with such fascist vigour. Perhaps there is some survival value involved, although many a short-lived gnome would take some convincing.

Such is the attraction of Gnomedom that no one but gnomes will live there. Indeed, no one but gnomes is allowed to live there.

The gnomes see to that.

But there was one exception.

A sorcerer who, after a few centuries of tyranny and terrorizing the fairer worlds of Mankind, fell foul of the wrong man. Following a battle that had raged across the face of the Earth and had impinged on several local dimensions, the sorcerer was defeated and, since he had dealt in grim and ghastly dealings, his fitting punishment was to be banished to the grim and ghastly Gnomedom.

A lesser man would not have lasted a month. Actually he wouldn't have got through the first night without becoming even less of a lesser man, in terms of hands, feet and, probably, ears.

Grandeane, however, was made of stuff that was stern enough to ensure his survival on Gnomedom for over three thousand years.

Encyclopaedia Esoterica,
Revised edition, AD 4800

Things had been tough for Grandeane for the first two hundred years. However, with a rapidly growing trail of shrivelled, shrunken and shredded gnomes behind him and a rapidly growing reputation preceding him, he was soon allowed to go about his business in peace. Thereafter, Grandeane blended into the background like an amiable milkman who is known to teach karate on Sundays to the local police force.

In the year AD 4089, three centuries after the failure of the Last Trump to destroy Mankind, this man of magic was wandering through Gnomedom when a complete stranger passed him in the street. The stranger was squat, unbelievably ugly and festering with thoughts of genocide. Having nothing particular on his mind at that moment, Grandeane inadvertently picked up the other's passing thoughts. Stopping dead in his tracks, with something akin to the feeling one gets when one steps up to one's waist in volcanic lava, he snatched a breath, lost several seconds in wrestling with disbelief, then whirled around to find that the thinker had disappeared into the crowd.

Since the crowd was universally squat, unbelievably ugly and festering with thoughts not far removed from genocide, it was impossible to distinguish which of them had caught his attention.

'Sod,' said the sorcerer, for one word had distinguished this particular matrix of homicidal writhing between two large pointed ears from all the other matrices ever conceived on Gnomedom. 'I must find him.'

He dived through the crowd, which parted before him, partly out of deference but mainly because it made more sense than being parted *by* him at a molecular level. He glided unhindered across the cobbled street and, catching the faint scent of errant mind, he rounded a corner and sped through the packed square.

Ahead of him a squat, stocky-legged creature strode with grim purpose. While the rest of the local populace glared with the grateful resentment of those avoiding dismemberment only because they weren't important enough to warrant it, the figure ahead clenched and unclenched his warted fists, oblivious of both his pursuer and the rest of Gnomekind. The emotions boiling between those ears struck Grandeane like a blow from a writhing hammer.

His voice thundered across the square.

'YOU!' he roared. 'HOLD!'

The figure like everyone else, froze. Its fists balled into

two fissured clubs as it turned to face Grandeane with slow deliberation. Everyone else did, too, though not so slowly.

Although the sorcerer was used to being hated by now, even *he* hesitated before continuing. What he saw was hatred at sub-cellular level. It negated any fears its owner might have had and manifested itself in contempt on a cosmic scale. It was the sort of hate that would still reside in one's mind long after its owner was dead. It was the sort of hate that men would rather worship than kill, because it would be obscene to destroy such strength, no matter what form it took.

It was the sort of hate that was too good to waste.

'You, sir,' called Grandeane softly. 'You look like a man of compassion and understanding. Do you drink?'

A collective gasp went up and all eyes turned to the lone gnome. His own gaze narrowed noticeably. His body went rigid and his fingernails, long, sharp and diamond-hard, dug into his wrists.*

He stared at Grandeane with passion.

Twenty minutes later not a muscle, not a single cell had changed position. The conflict of opposing concepts sparking across the synapses of the gnome's brain was no more visible than the ponderous battle of two gargantuans deep beneath the glassy surface of an ocean. Neither had Grandeane moved, for that would tip the delicate balance of the conflict and he would be forced to destroy a potentially priceless ally.

The other gnomes stared carefully from one to the other. They didn't relish being caught in meaningless cross-fire and the sorcerer was known to exhibit a certain indiscriminate tendency when he wagged his fingers at people. If

---

* The structure of a gnome's hand prevents his clenched fingers from reaching his palms, so they dig into his wrists. No gnome has ever seen this as a viable method of suicide, since it doesn't include slashing out at anything in reach until one, both, or all of you are dead.

the lone gnome decided to take offence at Grandeane's first remark, ducking would be sort of academic.

The gnomes waited.

Carefully.

A tiny creak split the silence like a crack of thunder as the gnome finally turned his head. Several black hearts missed a beat.

The gnome gazed long and hard over his shoulder and the eyes of the other gnomes followed his own. The whole square stared towards the local inn, the haven of Gnome-kind's second love and obsession after squabbling. Grandeane, who had been holding his breath for the last twenty minutes, held it even harder. The gnome looked back at him with the gnome's version of a smile, which is to say his gaze relaxed to one of mere loathing. He pursed his lips, spat across the intervening space with sparkling accuracy between Grandeane's boots, then turned and strode towards the door of the inn, leaving two small pools of deep red blood to brighten up the cobbles.

Deep below the ocean's surface the two gargantuans declared an honourable, if temporary, truce.

The sorcerer relaxed his aching ribs and followed the squat figure through the doorway.

Grandeane sat back in the dimly lit alcove and watched patiently while the gnome drained his third mug of local ale. Two more mugs of the silver-grey fluid stood at hand and Grandeane's bag of silver coins lay open on the table to encourage a steady supply.

The gnome laid down his empty mug, glared longingly at the next one, remembered the gnomes' code of honour, which was roughly, 'Don't owe nothing to no bastard', and looked up. Grandeane leaned forward.

'So where did you hear of this word, "Earth"?' he said.

1

AD 570

The townsfolk of Camelot were very understanding.

Almost before Sir Lancelot du Lac's armoured body had clunked to the ground like a pile of tired engine parts, they were smiling philosophically and turning to wend their way back to the village.

One or two murmured contentedly, 'Nice one, Griswold.'

Up on the grandstand a perplexed Queen Guinevere stared down at Lancelot lying dead on the tournament green.

One is supposed to feel distraught when the love of one's life lays slain, she thought, so why does one feel so relieved?

She hoisted her dress clear of her slippered feet and tripped daintily down the steps to the divot-sprayed turf, where the survivor of the joust was walking round in circles and peering at the ground.

As she crossed the green, the twenty or so castle guards ambled towards Lancelot and his opponent with a view to carting one away and congratulating the other. Guinevere, for some reason, had other ideas.

'Two of you will do,' she called, shooing the rest away with a flick of her fingers. The soldiers looked at her, at each other, then shrugged and wandered off after the villagers.

'See thee later, Griswold,' they called.

The knight known as Sir Griswold des Arbres gave a vague wave of his hand and continued pacing. The remaining soldiers bent over Lancelot and each grabbed a foot.

Ignoring them, Guinevere glided across the green.

'Sir Griswold,' she called. 'Thou fought well,' which wasn't actually true, but Guinevere was a romantic at heart.

Griswold's voice answered from behind his visor, muffled and distorted.

'*Fank you, your majesty,*' and 'For thee, my queen,' he said.

Simultaneously.

'Sorry?' said Guinevere.

'*Ahm?*' and 'Er?' said Griswold, simultaneously.

His helmet wavered thoughtfully and a little disjointedly from side to side, then his head dropped and he resumed his wandering, his eyes fixed on the ground.

Guinevere gazed about her. Somehow this was not the way that tournaments between valiant knights were meant to turn out. There should be cheering and flags waving and herself tying her scarf to the lance of the victor. Instead, the king's favourite knight was being dragged away by his heels and his opponent was wandering round like a goat on a tether.

Guinevere's lower lip drooped.

'Griswold,' she hissed.

'*Wot*/yef?'

'What are you *doing*?'

'Finger. Loff my finger.'

Griswold held up his left hand for her to see. Guinevere frowned uneasily. Where there should have been either a mangled appendage or a small fountain of red there was, simply, a clean smooth stump. And the knight's hand had a distinctly odd appearance. Very . . . solid.

'How?' she said.

'Know not/*Not sure. One second,* there; the next . . .'

Griswold's armour creaked as he shrugged his massive shoulders. Guinevere cast an indifferent glance at the prostrate Lancelot. The soldiers had stopped dragging him

16

across the green and were discussing relative modes of transportation.

'See? Armour's not designed for dragging around by the ankles. It just gouges into the ground. Stops thee dead,' said the one sitting on Lancelot's chest. 'Got to be head first. Get thy breath back and grab an arm.'

Guinevere's indifference was interrupted as Griswold sidled blindly towards her and stepped on her foot.

"Sooth. Pray forgiv—/Woopf. Forry,' said Griswold.

'It might help,' snapped the queen, 'if thou took thy helmet off!'

In the absence of a fanfare, a knight-kissed hand and the clamour of a loyal populace, she considered a little tetchiness to be more than acceptable.

Griswold stopped his pacing and squinted out through his visor.

'Mmm/Ay,' he agreed and raised it with a flick of his wrist.

He gave her a wistful smile.

Queen Guinevere stared into the darkness of Griswold's helmet and, with a strangled gasp, a waft of flimsy gauze and her headdress slipping over one eye, slid to the ground in a dead faint.

Griswold was used to women going weak when they first met him, but he and Guinevere had known each other for over twenty years.

Perhaps she was a bit peeved about Lancelot.

With the unaccustomed effort of one who has just lost one's little finger, he removed his helmet and dropped to one knee beside her. His armour seemed to weigh a ton. Behind him the two soldiers, who had turned round at the gasp, stared with some interest at Griswold's bare head. Then one of them doubled over and threw up his breakfast, while the other, who obviously had the stronger stomach, simply went into a kind of mild shock.

Sir Lancelot lay where he was, which he would, of course.

'Guinevere/*vere*,' said Griswold in stereo. 'What ails thee/*thee*?'

He took her hand in his good one and patted it uncertainly. He was all right at strapping up broken bones or stemming the pump of blood from a man's gaping limb, his own included, but he wasn't too hot with fainting women. He looked around for help. The only two people within hailing range seemed to be preoccupied. He sighed the calm sigh of a warrior, gathered up the queen in his arms and staggered to his feet.

By the gods, she *is* a lump, he thought. She doesn't look it.

Then he realized he didn't know the way back to Camelot Castle, which was odd because he had only come from there half an hour ago. What's more, the mist that had covered the landscape as soon as he'd removed his helmet didn't help.

Bit odd, this mist, thought Griswold. Lovely sunny day, nice and dry, yet the air is full of heavy vapour.

He looked down at his armour. Not a dewdrop in sight. He glanced at Guinevere. Her lovely face with its prominent teeth and over-slender neck wavered and superimposed before his double vision.

Ah, he thought, I know an addled brain when I have one. By which he meant concussion, which it wasn't.

Still, he went on, my duty is clear.

His survival instinct, which was more or less limitless, brought animal faculties to the surface of his mind. He remembered that the castle was sunwards of the tournament ground at this time of day. Therefore it had to be on the other side of the forest to his right. He turned and trudged towards the trees.

His armour really was *incredibly* heavy.

By the time the spires of the castle had appeared through the trees, Griswold was almost on his last legs. His vision was more blurred than before. His feet dragged across the grass and his queen was sliding gracelessly from his drooping arms. He sank to his knees, laid Guinevere gently on the ground and remained where he was, head bowed and gasping for breath.

Only one thing for it, he thought. Got to get rid of this armour. Come back for it later.

Griswold was not stupid. In fact, some would say that his brains probably overqualified him for the job of Round Table knight and protector of the realm. But he was deficient in one or two areas. Certain synaptic pathways had long since atrophied from lack of use or been over-grown by the dense foliage of duty. One of these led to the sign saying, 'Give up'.

Although he was exhausted, and Guinevere was in no danger, it didn't for a second occur to him to rest.

He fumbled at the straps of his armour, his teeth clenched with the effort. His muscles were burning as he dropped the last plate of metal to the ground and fell on his face, gasping. Before he could gather his resources, he gave a huge sigh and tumbled into a profound sleep, one arm draped across Guinevere and his nose buried deep in the grass.

2

Guinevere's piercing scream, slicing through both the forest and Griswold's brain cells, brought him to his feet, grabbing for a nonexistent sword before his mind had caught up with his reflexes. He twisted round, peering into the shadows.

The forest was empty. He turned to the queen and his

head exploded with pain, threatening to blow his eyeballs out.

'Curses/*Dammit*,' he said, grabbing his head in both hands. After a few seconds he was able to turn it without worrying that it might come off in his hands. As he did so the pain vanished and in seconds his sight and his brain were as clear as a crystal stream.

He closed his eyes and gave his head a tentative shake. No pain. No blinding light. Perfect. Most odd.

He opened one eye, then the other. Guinevere was still lying where he had left her, but she was staring at him in horror.

'What afrights thee?' he asked.

Her mouth opened and closed but no words came out. Her eyes, which had a tendency to converge, giving her an optimum focus of around twelve feet, followed a parallel path until they met his with the fascination enjoyed by a frog six inches from the jaws of a cobra. Griswold, whose relationship with Guinevere had encompassed many emotions, none of which had ever resembled stark horror, was confused.

'Am I bleeding?' he said. 'I don't feel wounded.'

By a remarkable feat of coordination, Guinevere managed to shake her head from side to side while her eyes remained rigidly fixed on his.

'Am I dead then? A phantom, perhaps?'

Guinevere frowned. The eyes, glad to be relieved of the unaccustomed effort, slid gratefully towards each other and stared at a point twelve feet ahead as she considered the question.

The gaze that she returned to Griswold was perplexed.

And parallel.

'No,' she whispered. 'Quite the opposite.'

Squeezing through the treetops, little beams of sunlight threw dancing dapples across her face.

'What art thou?' she asked in a trembling voice.

The answer, ominous if rather ill-informed, came from the shadows.

'Easy meat, that's what ye are!'

Four men came into view. They were vulgar, aggressive and they carried clubs, which made three mistakes apiece. Four, if you consider attacking a knight of the Round Table with only a club to be a viable proposition.

Guinevere gave a gasp and stood up, and Griswold moved between her and the newcomers. His eyes scanned the ground for a weapon of some kind.

His armour, lying close by, was all the forest floor could offer.

Oh well, he thought, If needs must/Better than a poke, etc.

'Can we talk about this?' he asked.

'Not with our tongue cut out and shoved up our arse, we can't,' said the largest man. He was grossly overweight and greasy-haired and carried two daggers in sheaths on his belt.

And, thought Griswold, at least two more hidden about his person.

Impressed by their leader's scintillating wit, the other men sniggered happily and tossed their clubs from hand to hand. Griswold glanced at each in turn. If he'd had a choice right then he would willingly have given each man a sword in exchange for Guinevere's absence even though it might have meant him fighting his last fight.

But he didn't have the choice and her presence was a real handicap.

'What dost thou want?' he asked.

'Well, it's not thee, that's for sure,' roared the leader, sending the others into fits of loyal hysterics.

'Gods, Hector, th'art a veribitable jester,' snorted one who prided himself on his education.

It's surprising how many mistakes some people can make in one day. When one of those mistakes consists of upsetting the Queen of England, the maker clearly qualifies for some sort of prize.

Hector was about to get his.

Hauling up her skirts, Guinevere stepped out from behind Griswold with a face like thunder. Before he realized what she was doing, she had marched up to Hector and thrust her face to within six inches of his.

'DOST THINK FOR ONE INSTANT I'D ENTERTAIN THY FOUL OBESITY ANYWHERE NEAR ME?!' she screeched.

The silence that followed told everyone that a slight shift in the balance of power had taken place. Hector wasn't quite sure if he could cope with it.

'I'm not obese,' he protested weakly. 'I'm well-rounded.'

'Oh? Well, get thyself round this!' snarled Guinevere.

Her foot swung back and everyone knew that the next few minutes would be ones of rich and varying experiences. Four men winced in anticipation, while one whose build allowed him no chance of avoiding the inevitable rose as high as his toes would allow, with his face contorted in terror, before the royal foot ploughed home.

With a sigh of admiration Griswold strolled forward, caught up the club that Hector had decided to discard, along with his consciousness, and addressed himself to the matter in hand.

The gloom of the forest prevented Hector's men from seeing what Guinevere and her guards had seen when Griswold had taken off his helmet, so they could not appreciate that two cracked skulls, several broken ribs and some unusually sinister dislocations were to be seen as 'getting off lightly'.

Griswold suffered from a splinter in the finger when he snapped one of their clubs in two with his hands.

'I cannot imagine how thou didst that,' said Guinevere as they strolled towards the castle. 'Thy strength is awesome.'

'It appears so,' agreed Griswold. 'Though my body feels as heavy as it did with my armour on. 'Tis most odd.'

The queen glanced at him sideways. 'Dost thou *feel* odd?'

'Tired. 'Tis all.' He returned her gaze. 'Do I *look* odd?'

She looked up into his dark eyes. In their depths lay a quiet, but smouldering intensity, and the pulse in her throat thumped.

'Thou looks more alive, more . . . real than any man I have ever known.'

Which was a pretty fair description.

3

The year is still AD 570.

In the valley below us, the village of Camelot bustles with market stalls, creatures bleating and crowing, farmers clinching deals with spit-wet handshakes and traders selling the more appetizing parts of warm dogs, technology not yet being ready to take the blame for electric hot plates.

Across the valley stands Camelot Castle, home of King Arthur, Queen Guinevere, assorted knights, troops, a jester and a handful of upwardly mobile courtiers to whom 'a stab in the back' means something more substantial than the odd inter-departmental memo. The geriatric castle lazily suns its old grey stones, unconcerned about the turmoil within.

We, however, are outside a cottage, in which any reprisals are confined to mental self-flagellation when the occupant feels that he has failed himself, or his monarch, or Mankind in general. This aspect is another infinitely

23

complex story that may become clearer as the tale grows. Or not.

The cottage has a thatched roof, a doorway that most men would find a bit of a squeeze, and Disneyesque flowers that swarm over its walls. They do this throughout the year, defying all natural laws because the source of their existence is . . . extra-natural.

That source is, in fact, only a moment away. In the next dimension but one, actually. The door to that dimension is located at a point three and a half feet above the ground. It is a tiny black spot, no more than a pin-hole. We see the spot and the air for several feet around it as though we are looking through a sheet of stretched clingfilm which is being sucked in at the middle.

For a while nothing particular happens.

Then the air creaks, just like stretched clingfilm.

A foot appears.

It pokes out of the spot, twitching, and the leg attached to it disappears hideously into the pin-hole. From somewhere on the other side of the foot comes a tiny screech, not so much of anguish as of intense irritation, and a voice as thin as a pipe stem cries out, 'Oh, crudthirtle and garnish!'

The creaking increases to thunderous proportions and, with an ear-cracking SPLOP, a figure explodes from the the pin-hole, hurtling end over end in a flat trajectory that would, on level ground, have carried him at least fifty feet through the air before allowing him to land amidst flailing limbs and with multiple but healthy curses.

But we are on a hill. Steep. One in six. By the time he starts to descend the ground is eighty feet below him. He plummets, his pale cloak, as wispy as his long white hair, flapping wildly about him with ever-increasing urgency.

We wince and our scrotums, or whatever, squirm in anticipation of a deathly thud spiked with calciferous cracks and the sight of a body reduced to angularities for which it was never designed.

However, we are not watching an amateur conjurer here. This is no back-street sleight-of-hand merchant with three little cups and a black-eyed pea. We are talking top of the range, state-of-the-art wizardry. A destroyer of demons, a creator of kings, harbinger of history, that sort of thing.

He also does things with herbs.

We are talking Merlin the Enchanter.

Some ten feet from the earth he twists, cat-like, and drops feet first, stopping six inches above the lush grass where he bounces gently on to a yielding cushion of magic. The arched white eyebrows relax with languid satisfaction.

'Heh, heh, heh!' The figure sneers. ''Twill take more than that to keep me out.'

He cocks an eye towards the sky and the cosmos in general.

'D'ye hear?' he shouts. 'It'll take more than a wart on the skin of Reality to stop me!'

He straightens up to his full five feet and strides through the air towards his cottage. His cloak, not listing precognition among its magical powers, fails to avoid his descending boot and its hem is squashed into a Reality still six inches above the ground.

The cloak does not have much life of its own, but what there is is guarded by a desperate survival instinct.

It jerks itself free, breaking the Enchanter's concentration and allowing him to demonstrate a perfect one-and-a-quarter back somersault on to the hard, unyielding earth.

Merlin untangles himself, rises to his feet and grabs the folds of his cloak by the throat, his fingers twitching in a manner that makes those who know him dive for cover behind the nearest heat-resistant object. His blazing eyes have abandoned their normal ice-blue colour for more sinister multi-flecked hues. In fact, it might be better if we left him to it and came back later.

4

S ir Griswold des Arbres awoke with a start, puckered up his lips and sent them searching for the trembling neck of his queen. When they came back alone he frowned and opened his eyes.

In the gloom of the bedchamber he saw nothing but his own chandelier above, its three small candles trailing smoky flames behind them as they swung gently to and fro in the early morning draught.

He pursed his lips again, this time in concentration.

'I'd have sworn that only last night I was bestowing my favours on Guinevere to the point where . . . but clearly I couldn't have been.'

He was right on both counts.

He swung his legs off the bed. They didn't seem as heavy as they were yesterday.

Must be getting my strength back, he thought, though how and where he had lost it he really could not remember.

He opened the wooden slats in the window. The summer sun poured happily in, warming his limbs and making him squint. He looked out across the rolling green hills and woodlands of England and smiled.

It is good to be back, he thought.

Not that I've been away, he added.

Have I? He frowned. A faint wisp of memory drifted over the terrain of his mind and dissolved into the sky of his unconsciousness.

He wondered where Merlin would be that day.

That thought also fled as the bustle of early morning activities rose up from the courtyard to meet him. Arthur's soldiers were doing soldierly things such as drilling, sharpening their swords and trying to terrorize the villagers. The villagers walked around them, selling livestock, buying vegetables and enjoying the sunshine.

They didn't appear too terrified.

Griswold nodded with approval.

'Everything seems normal enough. I must have been dreaming a singularly fanciful dream,' he said aloud.

He pulled on the tunic, boots and leggings that knights of the Round Table wore on their days off, left the room and padded down the stone passages of the castle until he reached the courtyard. Wandering out into the open air and the hum of activity he cast his eyes around at the familiar scene. Among the crowd a juggler was juggling. Bony dogs were creeping around looking for scraps and a small group of sheep were waiting patiently to be slaughtered for the evening meal.

Griswold took a breath of clean, fresh air into his lungs. Even though 'clean' and 'fresh' meant 'only reeking of stale cabbage today because the breeze was blowing the unrelieved pungency of the nearby stables in the other direction', he heaved a sigh of contentment.

Watching the everyday bustle of village folk, he felt again as though he was seeing it afresh after being away for months.

''Mornin', sir knight,' said a voice at his side.

Cedric Holgrass was one of the more successful farmers of the area, a man whom Griswold knew vaguely and with whom he'd exchanged the occasional pleasantry. Cedric might have been tempted to exchange some more heated unpleasantries had he known of Griswold's more than vague knowledge of Cedric's daughter.

'Nice mornin',' he added. He sniffed the air. 'Well, would be if 'twere not for the cabbage.'

'Indeed,' replied Griswold. *'But at least it lacks the noxious smog of horseless cart fumes.'*

Cedric knew his place. It was several rungs below that of

a knight of the Round Table. Most rungs, actually. If a chap who travelled around on crusades and such likes to talk a bit foreign at times, who was Cedric to pass judgement?

Besides, the knight was looking remarkably solid.

Cedric nodded sagely and said something rather interesting.

'Ye're right there, Sir Lancelot. Small mercies, eh?'

5

AD 4096. Hell

Archeous the demon strode bandily along the highway to Hell Central, pausing only long enough to reply to a request from an obvious newcomer to the Netherworld.

'Excuse me,' said the stranger, blocking his path. 'Can you tell me which side the Ministry of Evil and Unholiness is on?'

'Ours,' Archeous replied and walked on.

He was plump; five feet four inches of human lineage with three strands of hair brushed across his wide scalp, and he wore a permanent frown even when he smiled. His naked skin bore the fading suntan that he had arrived with two thousand plus years ago. In the normal light of his home world he would have appeared pale-nut-brown and wrinkled. In the constant flashing reds and oranges filling the local sky he resembled an irritable satsuma.

He crossed the road, avoiding the onrush of pulsating peak-hour vehicles by dodging round whichever dimension they were passing through, and paused on the other side to get his breath.

'Maniacs,' he snapped without heat and set off on the last few hundred yards to the steps that led up to the palace. On either side of him the lurking spires, buffeted by Hell's equivalent of high winds, i.e. passing Realities, wavered and reeled, disappearing out of sight into the black and red cloud-thundered skies above him.

'When I'm ruler, I'll put a stop to all this ridiculous meteorology. Far too melodramatic.'

He put his head down and strode on, oblivious of the reflections of purple and blood-pink clouds on a pavement that had been polished to mirror smoothness by the passing of doomed feet over a thousand millennia. He heard neither the constant howl of the blistering hot winds nor the molten rumbling deep beneath the ground, nor yet the tormented screams therein. Only the acrid sting of sulphur niggled at him.

'That'll go too,' he murmured. 'Pretentious rubbish!'

He reached the steps and clambered to the top, passing through the great shimmering iron doors into the vast entrance hall of Hell Central. The torturous cacophony of the streets ceased as the doors clanged shut behind him and the cool, air-conditioned room echoed to the sound of his feet tapping across its marble floor. Archeous had rarely made concessions during his lifetime and he had no intention of changing his habits since dying, but cloven hooves and furry legs carried considerable credibility with the masses, not to mention a long history of association with young maidens, so he had condescended to undergo the relevant changes. He drew the line at horns, though, which he considered undignified.

And the fur had to be fire-proof.

He reached the far side of the hall and went up more steps circling the high marble walls and flanked by massive marble pillars. Through the windows the thriving turmoil of fruitless purgatory continued in silence before his eyes. He clopped on, passing other creatures, occasionally either acknowledging their presence with the merest nod or ignoring them altogether. As he approached the main office, the slightest tremor of apprehension rippled through him. He wasn't completely above fear, particularly in the presence of Lucifer. It was just that his fears, like most of his negative emotions, had long been submerged beneath the heaving tides of ambition.

The main office was full of creatures coming and going about their business through different doors and dimensions, appearing from nowhere and vanishing into nowhere, correction, somewhere else with clipboards and briefcases and . . . correction, somewhere and/or somewhen else with . . . anyway, they came and went, looking as though they would be quite at home in three-piece suits, if they had needed to wear clothes at all. Humanity, demonry, bestiality, gnomery and several other ys trotted hazily through each other's personal space, superimposing a constantly shifting kaleidoscope of bodies.

How they ever get anything done with this sort of organization, God knows, thought Archeous blasphemously, although the admin section of Hell Central was more efficient than anything that Man could knock together. It *did* have a million years of experience behind it, of course, but there was always room for a bit of pruning.

Amidst the living turbulence, sitting serenely behind her fiery red desk, the duty receptionist, young, positively angelic and wearing only a pair of blue horn-rimmed spectacles, was doing receptionistic things. She looked up as Archeous approached and gave him a professional smile.

'Hello. Can I help you?' she said.

Probably, thought Archeous.

'You're new here, aren't you?' he said.

'I've been here two weeks, yes.'

'I have an appointment with Lucifer.'

'Name?'

'Archeous, née White,' he replied.

One day, he thought, it'll just be Archeous and everyone will know exactly who I am.

The receptionist was glancing through a scroll, her full

lips pursed in concentration. Archeous' own lips twitched and he shifted from one hoof to the other.

'Ah, yes,' murmured the girl. 'Here we are.'

She gave him a moist smile that made him think of a sunlit iceberg on the verge of melting.

'Please go straight in,' she said. 'It's—'

'I know the way.' He frowned at her spectacles. 'Why blue?' he asked.

'I like to stand out.'

'You can stay,' mumbled Archeous.

'Pardon?'

'Never mind.'

Archeous stood before the smouldering oak door and gave his version of an offhand knock.

'There's no need to break it down,' called Lucifer, Prince of Darkness. 'It's open.'

'It's not,' said Archeous.

There was a pause which seemed to have a slightly confused air about it.

'Oh.'

The door dissolved into flames and vanished. Archeous stepped through the gap and into the room. With a quiet *whoomp* the gap filled with flames and the door reappeared.

'Sorry,' whispered Lucifer. 'I was miles away. Part of me, that is.'

'And has that part returned?' asked Archeous tonelessly.

'Partly. Not to worry. It'll come back when it's ready.'

'Good.'

'Sit down, old man. Make y'self comfortable. Wine?'

The Prince of Darkness looked like an incredibly old young man. In cosmic terms he was quite young, only having been around since the beginning of Man, but one doesn't live for that long without incurring a few lines and the odd grey hair along the way.

Lucifer's mouth twitched and his eyes creased, momentarily adding half a million years to his age. Then his beautiful blue-grey eyes lit up and his brilliant white teeth glinted as he threw Archeous the sort of grin that would stop a raging bull at fifty yards. The curly blond locks that framed his bronzed face bobbed and danced in time with his laughter. He gathered his massive white wings about him and sank gracefully into a nearby bean-bag.

'By God, Archeous, you're an ugly little sod, but it's good to see you again. Did you say yes to wine?'

'No. Thank you.'

'Do you mind if . . .?'

Archeous waved his consent and the Prince of Darkness slopped amber liquid into his goblet.

'Been busy?' he asked.

'Very,' said the demon carefully. 'But the work is rewarding, so I've no complaints.'

Lucifer grinned. 'Ambitious old bugger, aren't you?'

'I aim to serve,' said Archeous.

"Course you do. That's why you're here.'

He took a slow drag at his wine, giving Archeous a bright smile over the goblet's rim.

Archeous smiled back thinly.

One day, he thought.

Lucifer drained his wine, plonked the goblet on the floor and settled back with a thoughtful look in his eyes.

'Ever thought you'd like *my* job?' he murmured.

'That's an academic question, surely?'

The Prince of Darkness shrugged. Then he said 'Damn!', flickered and, with a crackle of mute thunder, vanished into a rapidly diminishing whirlpool. Before Archeous had time to lose his patience, Lucifer reappeared, hazy, distorted and spread all over the room. Quickly drawing himself together, he flopped on to the bean-bag, resignation etched into his handsome features.

'Sorry about that,' he gasped between breaths. 'Bloody Cygnus Minor again. Every two or three thousand years the dozy bastards set up a revolution against Evil, drag in exorcists and priests and such and generally make a sodding nuisance of themselves. Would you believe, after all this time, I'm the only one who can handle them? If I didn't know better, I'd swear they had the blood of Mankind in their veins.'

He gave Archeous an embarrassed glance.

'No offence, old chap. Anyway, it goes with the territory and it keeps me in shape.' He leaned towards Archeous with a conspiratorial air. 'You can't beat Power, eh, Archeous?'

Archeous was no fool. He could smell an offer through ten layers of Reality.

'Why did you ask me here?' he said, conveniently forgetting that he had not been asked, but commanded.

Ignoring what would normally be an unforgivable lapse, Lucifer rose to his feet, gave his wings a shake and headed for the door.

'Come with me,' he ordered.

The room was not quite a room. It was an absence of outsideness. The corridor that they were walking through ceased to exist at that point and, on the far side of the 'room', Archeous could see other corridors and floors leading towards him from all sides. They led into nowhere before they reached him. The nothingness seemed to have some rather effective underfloor lighting, not easy when there is no floor. In the centre stood a glass-like cylinder, perhaps twelve feet high, radiating a warm green light.

Inside the cylinder was the figure of a man.

'Come,' said Lucifer quietly.

As they approached the glass Archeous could see that it was not so much a man as the remnants of one. It sat cross-legged with its hands resting on the floor, shoulders slumped, its chin sunk deeply into its shrunken chest. Two flaccid slugs that had once been a demon's vibrant horns hung from its temples. Two eyes that had once glittered with devilish zeal lay white and rotting in their sockets.

When a man dies he usually dies a bit at a time. Whether

a blow from without or a cancer from within, the untouched parts of him still exhibit a healthy impression to the eye.

'What on Earth . . . what the devil happened to him?' asked Archeous. 'He seems to have died . . . all at once, right down to his last cell.'

'Ever heard of a chap called Merlin the Enchanter?' said Lucifer.

'Of course. He was known throughout the world in my time. Some mythical Welshman.'

'Welsh, English, whatever,' said Lucifer vaguely. 'British anyway. Like you, I believe?'

Archeous nodded stiffly.

'And, like you, he was a real, living human. Half human, actually.'

'Really.'

'Mmm. Lived around the time of a chap called King Arth—'

'I know the story.'

'Sorry,' said Lucifer. 'Well, this Merlin got wind of my plans to stamp out the last outpost of Mankind which, as it happens, was the planet Earth.' He glanced at the demon. 'No offence. Business is business and all that.'

'Of course,' said Archeous. He pointed his chin towards the glass. 'And what had—?'

'Nemestis.'

'What had he to do with this?'

'He was meant to be the organizer and executor of my plans. Would have succeeded, except along comes Merlin, shows up at the last minute and blows my plans right down the pan.' He nodded towards the glass. 'The Enchanter did that, too,' he said simply. 'And Nemestis is not dead. He still lives. Inside that crumbling husk. That's the punishment for failure.'

'Whose punishment?'

'Merlin's,' said Lucifer. 'And mine. When it came to the

crunch, Nemestis let his emotions get the better of him. That was the cause of his defeat, I understand.'

In the light from the cylinder, Lucifer's wings and white robes glowed pastel green. His reflection stared back at Archeous.

'It's not a weakness I suffer from.' He smiled.

Lucifer's smile was as bright as the light of which God said, 'Let there be . . .' It was also as cold as absolute zero. Despite himself, Archeous gave a shiver, although it was not completely without a twinge of anticipation.

'Why am I here?' he whispered.

Lucifer put a powerfully muscled arm round Archeous' shoulders and raised his other hand towards the remains behind the glass.

'Because he is there,' said the angel.

6

AD 570 again

The villagers of Camelot were becoming less understanding by the minute.

Lancelot was beginning to make a prune of himself. He had obviously got a crack on the head when he clashed with that foreign pansy, wotsisname, Griswold des Arbres, the one whose neck he broke in the tournament.

You could understand how Lancelot felt up to a point, and a bit of remorse is the sign of a gentleman. But it was too much to go around saying that the bloke you killed is you and that you're him and how can anyone who's known you both for the last fifteen years say any different, and you're all bloody *bonkers*.

What's more, you don't endear yourself to Camelonians

by getting stoned out of your head and wrecking the local inn and everyone in it.

Or challenging the other knights to take you on when you can't stand up long enough to get your sword out of its sheath.

Or trying to bed every woman from Guinevere down when you can't stay awake long enough to . . . well, long enough to.

'Lancelot,' said the villagers, 'will get kicked out on his ear when Arthur returns in two days' time. And,' they added knowingly, 'Guinevere doesn't seem too inclined to do anything about it.'

Which just went to show how much of a pain Lancelot was becoming. The villagers were not stupid, were they? They were well aware of what had been going on between Lancelot and Guinevere for years. In fact, they'd be very surprised if half the kingdom didn't know about it. The only one who appeared to be in the dark was King Arthur, but then his head was always in the clouds.

Anyway, Lancelot was going too far this time.

'*You* saw when I god dis one,' snarled Griswold. 'Twelve yis ago, tournamen' wiv S' Percival. H' nearly beat th' hell outta mi, sliced m' leg open, took sis months to heal, Lanz'lot wasn't even in the country then!'

What he actually said was far more alcoholic, but it doesn't make for easy reading.

'Look a' this,' he snapped. 'Imogine's husban' gave me this one withis sickle, you mus' remember this one!'

He was standing, swaying actually, on a hay wagon in the market place with a flagon in one hand and an accusing finger extending from the other. It was pointing at his rump which gleamed in the afternoon sun. A short but deep scar broke the smooth whiteness of his powerfully muscled buttock with a dash of pale purple.

Two days ago the villagers would have roared with approval at the memory of Griswold leaping from Silas Fairweather's bedroom window with the old man's sickle firmly sunk into his buttock. The men would have slapped their thighs and said, 'He's a one, that Griswold,' and the women would have gone prune-lipped with jealousy, or smiled secretly.

But not today.

Today he was Sir Lancelot du Lac, Arthur's favourite knight, 'secret' lover of Guinevere, destined for immortality, and he was standing blind drunk amidst the straw on a trader's wagon.

For a bunch of yokels the Camelonians had an extraordinary sense of history. Perhaps it was because Merlin had told them almost daily for the past gods-know-how-many years that they were part of it. The Camelonians were very proud of their 'history', whatever that meant. They were certain that this wally was doing things that were definitely unworthy of history.

'Get down, Lancelot, and put thy clothes on,' snapped the owner of the wagon. He reached for Griswold, then quickly lost interest in the matter.

'Touch me not, Master Baines/*Shove off, ayehole*,' snarled Griswold, tossing the remnants of his shattered flagon into the crowd and reaching into the straw for a full one. The villagers watched grimly.

'There'll be hell to pay when Arthur returns,' said one.

'There'll be more than hell to pay when Merlin turns up,' said another.

'If,' corrected a third.

'Gods only know where *he's* been these past days.'

'Saving the world from Evil, I expect,' sniggered the first.

'. . .' said the second.

'What on Earth's the "world"?' asked the third.

Before an out-of-depth philosophical discussion could ensue, Griswold attracted everyone's attention by toppling out of sight and clambering to his feet, spitting straw.

The villagers took several steps backwards. They weren't completely certain that they had seen what they had seen.

Perhaps this was understandable for it's not every day that you see a man rise to his feet and . . . rise to his feet again and sort of . . . merge with himself and suddenly appear very, very solid.

It wasn't particularly dramatic. Just an impression of two Lancelots, one displaced from the other by a mere hairsbreadth, as if he had temporarily slipped slightly out of his rightful place in space, or Time, or perhaps both. Many of them had seen worse at closing time on a Saturday night.*

They considered giving a collective gasp of horror, but as the memory was washed instantly from their minds and Lancelot was standing there looking his normal embarrassing self, they said, 'He's certainly a one, that Lancelot.'

And the women went prune-lipped or smiled secretly.

7

Merlin growled irritably and concentrated fiercely for the third time that morning.

The sun shining in at the wizard's window was trying valiantly to forge a path through the drifting motes of dust in the room, but it was on to a loser. You don't just shove aside dust floating about in wizards' cottages. Weight for weight, each mote had soaked up more of Merlin's residual magic than any other entity, except other motes. When things tried to penetrate the dust, the motes simply ignored them. By walking through Merlin's cottage, you didn't

---

* This is a strictly metaphorical concept. Saturday night hadn't been invented and closing times didn't dare show their faces in the Dark Ages.

invade the dust's personal space. You allowed it to drift through yours. While you were still in it.

The sun bounced haphazardly off the motes and veered into every nook and cranny, lightening the dark, herb-strewn beams, the ancient buff-coloured parchments and the little glassily imprisoned life-forms with gold-tinged pastel hues. It glimmered through Merlin's flimsy cloak, outlining the sparse limbs in their baggy trousers and tunic with a halo of iridescence. It shone through his ears, making them glow pink and highlighting a myriad of tiny red veins.

Merlin raised his arms and hummed a wavering falsetto hum. The volume of the hum increased. The dried herbs shook and the seeds rattled in their pods. On the cupboard mystical instruments and dirty crockery rocked gently. With the air shimmering about him, the Enchanter slowly brought his hands together, touching thumbs and fore-fingers to make a diamond shape before his eyes. Staring through the diamond, he created a picture within the fleshy frame.

A woodland path.

A procession of familiar figures on horseback, tramping along and led by King Arthur. The picture became clearer and sharper until each tiny figure appeared quite solid and recognizable to the Enchanter. Merlin smiled with satisfaction.

Then he did a simple trick.

For the unmagical amongst us it has its equivalent, which goes something like this:

Wrap your left hand round your right thumb so that the tip of the thumb pokes up out of your hand. Whip your right hand out from under your left hand. Grab your right thumb with your right hand before it, the thumb, vanishes.

Simple.

All Merlin had to do was to leap through the hole framed by his fingers and enter the forest. Then he could quietly guide the forces of destiny along the paths that he had spent so many years in creating and nobody would be any the wiser.

Except Griswold. Merlin wasn't looking forward to explaining himself to Griswold.

The Enchanter took a breath, rose up on his toes and leapt.

This time he got further than on his previous attempts.

Surfacing from beneath a pile of fallen herbs, he untangled himself from the legs of the table and scrambled to his feet. The glowing frame and the woodland scene within it faded, leaving him with just the sunlit motes floating lazily in the air.

'Gods, how I would love to trade places with thee,' he told them.

With a wave of his hand he sent the herbs floating up to the beams. He snapped his fingers and his cloak flapped briefly, flicking the dust from its folds on to the floor where it belonged.

It was his own fault, of course.

'Have no fear, Arthur,' he had told his monarch. 'While thou art away, thee and thy men will suffer naught from demons, black alchemists or any form of inhuman evil. Thou needs only defend thyself from the attacks of men, for that accords with the way of things for mortals.'

And, so saying, he had cast a spell around the king to ensure Arthur's complete protection, supernaturally speaking.

There was just one wrinkle in his plan.

'Fool, fool and thrice fool,' he muttered.

He glared at the granite toad sitting on the window sill. The toad was one of the least magical things in Merlin's cottage. Its magical value was marginally less useful than that of legs on a rock and everyone, including itself, wondered why the Enchanter bothered having it around.

'Because it lacks the dependence of a dog, the disdain of a cat and it doesn't talk back,' Merlin would tell them.

The truth was that, when verbal self-flagellation became

too much to bear or too frequent to be effective, Merlin could swear at the toad.

'What sort of creature art thou,' he snapped, 'that lets me cast my spell without making due allowance'. . . his arched eyebrows drooped with bushy contempt . . . 'for my being the very type of creature that it is designed to repel?'

His eyes bored into those of the toad.

'Hmm?' he demanded.

The toad gazed back.

Stonily.

Merlin went to the table and plumped himself down with his chin in his hands. His chair just managed to slide under his descending bottom by a hair's breadth.

'A hundred and fifty years is too long,' he mused sadly. 'My powers are still potent, but my earthly faculties are long past their peak. Certainly my memory is.'

As usual the Enchanter was being overly harsh on himself, but this was a habit that had lasted him a lifetime and had ensured that his lifetime had lasted as long as it had.

On the other hand the part of him that was Man wasn't quite the man it used to be. This was the second time in two days that he had concocted a spell and left out a vital ingredient.

A knock on the door interrupted his gloom. It was a knock like any other knock, but Merlin knew that it belonged to only one person. Two things told him this. One was his innate sensitivity that could perceive and distinguish the auras of any one of his thousands of acquaintances, human and otherwise, as clearly as if he could see them. The other was the creak of the straw above the doorway. The only man who ever leaned his arm on Merlin's thatched roof when he knocked at the door was Griswold des Arbres. It was the knock that Merlin had been dreading for the past two days.

'Come in,' he said.

As the door opened and the figure filled the doorway,

Merlin's heart sank. Griswold was smiling. The Enchanter recognized complete trust when he saw it.

"Morrow, lad,' he said. 'Art thou fit after thy little scrap?'

'Lost a bit of weight, but otherwise perfect,' said Griswold. 'And thee/*What about you?*'

The last words juggled for Merlin's attention like a chaotic bundle of puppies.

And they got it.

'Oh, Lord,' groaned the Enchanter.

Griswold sat himself down at the table and leaned on his elbows.

'*May I ask a question?*' he asked.

The smile disappeared as he spoke and the jagged scar that ran down his right cheek and under his black beard sprang into vivid relief.

'Of course,' said Merlin. 'Ask what thou wilt.'

'Why has everyone started calling me Lancelot?'

Some time later, Merlin stared with admiration and some relief at the remains of his kitchen table. It was . . . had been good solid oak, the top three inches thick. A half-hour stint with a fair-sized axe *might* have achieved what Griswold had just managed with one blow of his fist, but Merlin had his doubts.

He looked out through the door which was managing to hang on by its one unbroken hinge. Griswold was striding down the hill towards the valley. His normally placid manner was no longer evident. The shoulders were bunched in fury, the fists clenched and his stride had a dreadful purpose about it.

Merlin had never heard the phrase, 'Bluddipistoff', but the manner in which it was punctuated by the thunder-crack of splitting oak had left little room for misinterpretation.

'Methinks the next few months will be a shade fraught,' he mused, giving the table an absent wave.

The table stood up with some difficulty and attempted to seal itself together, but the smaller shards of wood, cowering in different parts of the room, weren't too keen on risking another bashing.

The table had been hewn, in its hundredth year, from an oak planted on the day of Merlin's birth. Apart from the odd nick, caused by some sharp instrument hurled in frustration, its top had been worn as smooth as a mirror over the past fifty years. Now a jagged split ran across its width.

'I shall needs be careful not to lean too heavily,' mumbled Merlin. With another wave he gathered up the scattered shards and stood them in a vase by the toad.

The significance of the split was not lost on him.

'I fear it shall be a long time before the lad sees sense and the rift is healed between us,' he said to the table. 'Till then thou canst remain thus, to remind me that, for one such as I, the needs of history must come before friendship, and those who are unfortunate enough to be my friends must be so on history's terms.'

The table sagged perceptibly. It already had its own history and it didn't need to be lumbered with Man's, especially a man like Merlin.

Just because the rosy history that Merlin had created for Arthur had been skewered when Griswold had stepped in and slaughtered that poncey Lancelot in combat. And then Merlin had dragged Griswold off into the future on some ludicrous errand and returned him two days *earlier* into the place he'd already occupied and now there were literally two Griswolds in the place of one.

And the new one had brought back a head full of half-memories from that future.

And the two of them were seeing the world from two different relative space-time matrices, which made everything look like double vision shrouded in mist.

And on top of that the dozy knight had made the same mistake as he had the first time, killed that idiot Lancelot *again* and put any possibility of redressing Arthur's spoon-fed reputation right out of the question.

The table had certainly learned a lot about magic over the years and it had heard a load of twaddle talked across its mirror-smooth top about the importance of Man as opposed to men, but frankly it had every sympathy with Griswold. It didn't see why he should have his identity swapped with Lancelot's by that ridiculous mass-hypnosis nonsense, just so Merlin could maintain Arthur's holier-than-thou image through the centuries for the sake of 'Mankind' (in inverted commas, no less). If Arthur couldn't make a decent name for himself without the help of Merlin's magic, he should give up monarching and be a pig breeder.

Personally, the table thought that Griswold would make a better king any day.

He packed a hell of a—

'Scurrilous lackey, pull thyself together!' hissed the wizard, bringing the table back to the present with a creak. 'As I am condemned to serve Man, so thou art to serve me. Straighten up. I have need of thy . . . tableish qualities.'

The table straightened and, after a few moments of rummaging through his cupboard, the Enchanter came back and slapped a pile of parchments down on it.

'Since I can't get to Arthur, I'll just have to wait one more day until he returns to Camelot. Until then my time will be best spent in seeking a cure for two men sharing one sickness.'

For the rest of the day he pored over the parchments, tracing the paths of words beginning with the letters 'schizo . . .' By evening he reached the conclusion that he should be looking under '. . . ozihcs'.

8

AD 4096 again. Hell

Although the onslaught of Earth by the Forces of Evil failed to destroy Mankind, no immediate attempt was made to finish the job. Since the end result of the conflict was that Man, having defeated the most thoroughly executed invasion in His history, had proved that He was a worthy child of the cosmos, the reason for Lucifer's tardiness is a mystery.

Encyclopaedia Esoterica,
Revised edition, AD 4500

(And a frustrating one at that, not that Man was complaining, but blank pages do tend to grate.)

Editor, Enc. Esot.

Archeous was old for a demon. Not because he had been one all that long, but because he had become one late in life, in his eighty-sixth year to be precise.

He had died in moderately unusual circumstances, exactly thirty minutes after announcing, 'Yes. I'd sell my soul for half an hour with her.'

Thirty-one minutes later he went to Hell, contented on two counts, one smugly and one grimly.

In his earlier lives his occupations had included royal executioner, witch finder, raper and pillager, slave trader and grave robber, to mention some of the more savoury ones. His soul agent, being shady to the point of pitch-black, had always managed to see him right, but somehow Archeous had missed out on the biggy. What with the various superstitions and religions impinging on his lives, he invariably managed to finish up repenting to the current

45

deity, or else some pious idiot would come along and *forgive* him.

He had been a victim of his times.

Then, in the early twentieth century, his agent found him a job that was highly respectable but was clearly destined to become, over the next fifty years, an immensely powerful, disreputable and corrupt occupation.

Archeous, née Walter White, became a banker.

Thus he earned himself a pole position in the rat race, and brought himself to the attention of the people who really mattered in the power stakes, i.e. the forces of Evil.

Having joined a profession that embraced the twin gods, Money and Power, both of which were unrepentant and unforgiving, he cleverly managed to forgo the danger of reprieve at his last breath. There had been another god in Walter's childhood that had threatened to scupper his future, but this one, named with startling originality 'God', had rapidly become outmoded during the mid-twentieth century, and Walter White managed to escape with his soul intact and unblemished by Goodness.

So, when, in the evening of his years and under the guise of succumbing to Man's eternal weakness, he offered his soul up for grabs, Walter was approached by the local area rep and willingly enrolled into the most exclusive club in Eternity.

Now, Hell is really *the* place to be if you are upwardly inclined, mobilewise, and have the balls to go for gold. Not everyone's ideal choice, of course, and, as in the banking business, those at the top are few and far removed from the masses. By the same token, however, they are usually set up for Eternity, even when they make the most appalling mistakes, like subsidizing notorious cowboy out-fits or asking customers what they think of the service. The only really bad mistake they can make is to get on the wrong side of the top man. As Chief Managers go Lucifer was fairer than most, having no vested interest in the financial aspects of his business, but he was infinitely more ruthless.

Archeous was now one of the few at the top, which meant that he no longer had to work a seven-day week in scorching conditions, shovelling and raking to keep the home fires burning. By a combination of bribery, threats and the occasional swing of an eighty-pound shovel, he had, over little more than two thousand years, carved a path through the dense jungle of demonic hierarchy to the sunlit clearing at the top of the mountain, and now he sat at Lucifer's right hand.

But that was not enough for Archeous. Although he was confident that he would never slide down the slippery slopes of Hell again, he still wasn't satisfied.

He wanted to be Number One.

Nevertheless it was one heck of a shock when he was actually offered the job.

'When the inhabitants of Earth were decimated,' Lucifer was saying in an irritatingly sing-song voice, 'I was certain the survivors would resort to fighting amongst themselves and so prove to the cosmos in general that they weren't worthy of recreating. So for the last three hundred years I've left 'em to it. Had enough to do, keeping the Path of Unrighteousness clear of clowns like the Cygnions and such. You cannot imagine how many half-baked attempts there've been to spawn some sort of . . . Master Race, some pinnacle of piety in order to maintain cosmic order in the face of that old Black Magic that I wea—'

In the wake of Lucifer's monologue, which had lasted for an hour and a half, Archeous' look of polite concentration had become glazed.

'Ah,' said the angel. 'I can see I'm losing you, old chap. Suppose I'd better get to the point. Anyway, leaving them to it was a bad mistake. Somehow, somewhere, some remarkably adept chaps crawled out of the woodwork and forged the remnants of that pious bunch into a cohesive, survival-oriented society. And now they've begun to progress down paths that we had managed to obscure very nicely over the centuries. Do you understand what I mean?'

'A unilateral monetary system?' murmured Archeous.

'They are about to spread to the stars,' intoned Lucifer.

'You mean they've achieved space travel?' exclaimed Archeous.

'More than that,' said Lucifer. 'They are about to discover magic.'

He gave the demon a meaningful nod.

'The White sort,' he added.

Grandeane stared in amusement at his drinking companion. The gnome's enormous grey eyes slid out of focus and his head bobbed drunkenly. The pile of coins on the table was almost gone and the sorcerer's question remained unanswered. A dozen empty mugs were piled up in three precarious tiers on the table's sodden surface. The only thing preventing the gnome from sliding under the table was his compulsion to complete another tier before the money ran out.

Grandeane watched him carefully. The merest awareness of a possible upgrading in the sorcerer's destiny, the tiniest drop in temperature towards that of ice-cold ambition about to be realized, was lurking deep within the sorcerer's eyes. He leaned across the table to give the creature a nudge, thought better of it and slid another mug under the pocked strawberry nose.

'We were talking about Earth, remember? How is it that you come to be drinking ale at my expense and trembling with fury every time you think about the home world that I miss so dearly?' he whispered eagerly.

The gnome gazed vaguely in Grandeane's general direction and let out a long and noisy belch. For a moment the space in front of his face shimmered. The gnomes behind him warped into living mirages before the late contents of his lungs dissipated in the hot, heavy air of the packed inn. Grandeane sighed impatiently. With only three hours to go before closing time, the atmosphere was becoming noticeably tense. Soon the place would be alive with squabbling gnomes. There would be much gouging of eyes and splitting of skulls. Within minutes every appendage would bear bloody teeth marks. After all, this was Gnomedom, not some medieval outpost in the galaxy where Saturday nights were strictly metaphorical.

Grandeane stood up.

'I think you'd better come back to my place,' he said and beckoned with one finger. The gnome also rose to his feet. His chair tipped over and landed with a crash as he continued to rise until he was floating three feet from the floor. Grandeane turned and walked towards the door. The gnome closed his eyes, gave a contented snore and, grabbing instinctively for the last mug of ale, drifted across the room after the sorcerer. The other drinkers stared uneasily. They wondered briefly if the gnome would wake up to find himself trailing behind the sorcerer like a lost dog. Then they downed their drinks, rolled up their sleeves and forgot about him.

Stepping out into the early evening air, the sorcerer strode across the square with the gnome floating dreamily behind him. He took the path up through the forest and continued at a steady pace towards the top of the hill in which was buried his cave.

Fortunately they passed nobody on the way. Gnomes don't have much going for them, but what they do have is straight, wholesome Evil, untainted by religious or political pretensions. Because of this they maintain a high degree of dignity. Rumours of a gnome floating through the air, on his stomach, trying, in between snores, to pour a mug of ale into his upturned mouth, could spark off an impromptu squabble.

Impromptu squabbles really *are* undignified.

*

Grandeane entered the cave and paced along the tunnel towards his cavern with the gnome trailing after him, arms and legs dangling from his snoring carcass. The tunnel dutifully lit up as the sorcerer strode through and dimmed behind him. His dwelling was surprisingly uncluttered by the sort of unspeakable beings that are usually employed to protect villains' lairs from the Forces of Good or from other villains. Grandeane felt, quite rightly, that his reputation was protection enough.

However, he was quite keen on tradition. He waggled his fingers and two smallish wisps of smoke appeared. By the time he had reached the interior two small, unprepossessing trolls squatted at the doorway, gazing disinterestedly into the dark Gnomedom sky.

9

AD 570

Have you ever noticed how a cat will stay just out of reach when he doesn't want to be picked up? You amble towards him and, as you are about to make a grab for him, he'll be a couple of paces on, not seeming to have used up one iota more of energy than he needs to avoid you.

Don't you just hate that?

Dogs have a marginal degree of expertise, but cats have it down to a fine art.

Griswold had several things in common with cats, tomcats anyway. He loved to fight. He normally sublimated this particular urge in the cause of king and country, except when the call of mead-soaked revelry demanded a natural decline into manly hostilities. He loved to 'love'. This pastime, while having no strong survival value for him personally, often obliged him to acknowledge the value of a powerful survival instinct in the face of irate husbands, fathers and fiancés.

Had Griswold been a tom-cat he would undoubtedly have sported at least one torn ear, various facial scars and a roving, probably battle-whitened, eyeball.

At the moment he was engaged in remaining just out of Merlin's reach. Down the corridors of the castle, across the courtyard Merlin strode, trotted and scampered behind him, alternately pleading and commanding. Griswold ignored him. Merlin nearly had him and then, with deceptive ease, Griswold simply disappeared round a corner.

Irritably Merlin sat himself down at the base of the castle wall and pondered.

Until I can catch up with the pup and make him see sense, he thought, Arthur's reputation will remain in jeopardy.

He snorted with impatience.

'Tis hardly the end of the world, having to change one's name in the interests of one's monarch and of Mankind.

It didn't help the Enchanter to know that he had only one day left to persuade Griswold to agree with his mass-deception before Arthur's return. If Griswold *did* go ranting the truth all over the countryside, nobody would actually believe him, but myths and inconsistencies would still spring up like dandelions. When *they* took root and spread their seeds across the centuries, who knew what flora might emerge to choke the roses of English legend that Merlin had planted?

He had to come up with something rather sharpish and it wasn't a gardening hoe.

What do I offer a tom-cat to bring him to me? he wondered. The immediate and most obvious idea flashed through Merlin's mind, but he hastily pushed it aside. There had to be a less distasteful way of attracting Griswold's interest.

*

51

Griswold wasn't at all convinced that his monarch and Mankind were worth what he was being asked to put up with right now. He was as loyal as the next man and he had the scars to prove it, *but* he was Griswold. Sir Griswold des Arbres, Sir Griswold of the Trees, a name he bore proudly because his father was a common woodsman. Griswold had shown those 's'not what you wot, it's *who* you wot' merchants just what a lad could achieve with only guts and loyalty to drive him. He had defied the laws of ancestry to rise through the ranks and become one of Arthur's closest and most trusted knights, second only to the adulterous moron whose name he was meant to adopt. Lancelot might have been Arthur's most trusted knight, but he was by no means the most trustworthy. Griswold did not want to be linked with a name like that. Merlin had often told Griswold what history had in store for Sir Lancelot du Lac and now the wizard was asking Griswold to become a part of that very history.

'Hogscobblers,' said Griswold as he loped away from the castle and down the hill towards the woodland. He was keeping out of Merlin's way until Arthur returned and then he was going to kick up hell. He wasn't taking the arrows for Lancelot's lust and Merlin's vanity. He picked up speed and started to jog. He was becoming used to the heaviness that had first come upon him after the joust. In fact, he was beginning to feel strong enough to cope with it. Very strong, in fact. He broke into a sprint.

Overhead, the sky began to darken.

In the great courtyard of the castle Merlin the Enchanter was addressing the courtiers, knights and ladies who strolled idly by in the sunlight.

'Dost not feel it? Can'st not sense this feeling of foreboding? There is Evil afoot. Trouble ahead. Danger at hand.'

Merlin had been around longer than any of them could remember. Not once, to their knowledge, had he ever cast a worthwhile spell. Not that they *would* remember, he had seen to that. Therefore their faith in his predictive powers was understandably limited. They strolled on. Merlin sniggered to himself.

Evil afoot, he thought. Trouble ahead—

Nearby two ladies-in-waiting smiled at him tolerantly and walked past.

Silly old fool, he thought. The silly old fool of Camelot. So be it. Let the silly old fool fall foul of the denizens of Hell. Let the silly old fool be powerless against their evil designs. All the better. The scene is set. The audience is arrived. Let the farce begin.

He cocked an eye towards the sky. Beneath his cloak his fingers fluttered unseen. Under his whiskers his lips moved silently.

> *From the smoke of the woodfire*
> *I mould thy frames*
> *From the breeze through the trees*
> *I fashion thy screams*
> *From the screech of the ravens*
> *I carve thy anguish*
> *From the heat of the sun*
> *I fire thy dreams*
>
> *Thine nebulous forms are mine to command*
> *The motives that drive thee obey my demands*
> *And when I am done with thy services, then*
> *Thou'll return to thine elements ever again.*

Merlin walked to the centre of the courtyard, gathered his cloak about him and sat on the ground.

Overhead, the sky began to darken.

At the first crack of thunder, Griswold slowed down and glanced into the blue. There was not a cloud in sight. A mere handful of birds graced the higher reaches of the sky, gliding dots a lifetime away.

Griswold stopped. All was still, and yet Griswold . . . felt . . . the pull of forces within his own body, a mere stirring that threatened a greater turbulence outside the gentle drift of submarine life that speaks of the storm churning the sea's surface. He had never sensed such signals before.

Just as he wondered if he was coming down with something, the signals grew stronger. He spun round and stared at Camelot Castle. His eyes narrowed. Above the battlements hung a blackness, not quite a cloud, not anything living, but something in between. It boiled and rolled around itself, quietly rumbling and crackling. A louder crack of thunder split the air and the formless mass jerked as it was pierced with lightning. It grew, shadowing the battlements and towers and spreading down over the moat that skirted the castle walls.

Griswold began to run towards the castle. Common sense alone would have told him that it was no ordinary storm building up. Now the senses inside him positively clamoured their warnings.

He was weaponless and without armour, but it was clear that Merlin and the people of Camelot were under threat. Wasting no time in wondering at his new-born 'sixth' sense, Griswold sprinted faster up the hill.

Beneath the cloud the people in the castle scattered for shelter or stared up in horror, unable to move. Merlin smiled coldly, barely able to suppress a chuckle.

Serve thee right. Do thee good. Milksops and courtesans, he thought. Soon thou'll see some action to enliven thy miserable lives.

He wondered how long it would be before Griswold showed up, flashing his sword and strutting before the ladies of the court. He glanced idly at his fingernails.

Shouldn't be long now.

*

Although it was over a mile to the castle, uphill all the way, Griswold was not even breathing hard as he reached the drawbridge. If he was amazed at this he didn't show it, but then he had been rather busy trying not to crash into anything. When your vision is still a little on the 'double' side and you are running faster than any earthly man has ever run before, any lapse in concentration could result in an abrupt halt with your arms and legs wrapped round a tree trunk and your nose squashed into the insect-infested bark.

The cloud had changed drastically. From the billowing mass strange shapes were forming and dispersing into separate entities. Massive hideous creatures with strong-muscled necks and thighs lurched through the air on leathery blue wings. They dropped from the sky, lashing their snake-like tails and screeching so loudly that they could be heard above the crashes of thunder echoing from the cloud. A score of them plummeted towards the grounds of the castle. As Griswold raced across the drawbridge and under the portcullis they landed, some skilfully, some crashing on to the stones then picking themselves up and turning their cavernous snouts to sniff at the panicking crowd around them.

Griswold drew abreast of two castle guards standing with their mouths agape. Grabbing the nearest one by the arm, he snatched the man's sword from its sheath and hissed, 'Call out the troops. Now!'

Then he turned and ran towards the creatures. His alarm gave way to horror when he saw Merlin surrounded by the monsters and attempting to fight them off. Spears of light burst from the Enchanter's fingertips, piercing the glistening skins and erupting out of the creatures' backs in showers of oily blue fluid. Some of them staggered and fell, but some relentlessly bore down on him with talons outstretched and fanged jaws drooling. The Enchanter was retreating. Everyone else had vanished into the shadows and corridors of the castle from where they peered with terrified eyes. Only Merlin and Griswold remained.

Sparing a valuable second to see if the guards were obeying him, Griswold leapt towards Merlin with his sword singing. His blade bit deeply into a smooth, round belly, evoking a scream of agony from its owner. The creature's claw whistled towards Griswold's head. He ducked and it passed harmlessly over him, but as he rose the demon reversed its blow and sent a back-hander crashing into Griswold's face, which had him rolling across the stones. He came to his knees with the sword still in his hand, thankful that he had been spared the talons, but as he moved forward again two of them blocked his path. He thrust and hacked at them, barely avoiding their blows in his desperation to reach Merlin's side. The howls of the demons and the hiss and spit of Merlin's fire split the air around them. For a few seconds Griswold completely lost sight of the little wizard, but still the eye-wincing flashes from Merlin's fingers bounced off the stone walls and the alien skins as he continued to deal out his unique method of destruction.

Then the lightning ceased.

Griswold cut his way through the walls of ghastly flesh, showing no signs of tiring though he should have been gasping after a mile's run and frantic hand-to-hand combat. As the demons fell beneath his blade he saw Merlin stumble and four of the creatures pile on top of him. His sword rose and fell with unbelievable power. His eyes glowered with an intensity equal to that of the eyes around him. Amidst the splash of alien fluids, an arc of red sprayed into the sky, sprinkling bodies and stones. No earthly cry came from beneath the unearthly bodies, but all movement stopped. Griswold and demons alike were motionless. Then the thundering power of Griswold's battle-cry resounded across the courtyard, making the creatures jump. With his limbs trembling Griswold raised his sword once more, but before he could strike the creatures leapt out of reach. Then they did something silly. Snarling, roaring and screaming, they fell upon each other. They appeared to be wrestling. Griswold, whose only concern was to dig Merlin out from under the pile, leapt in again and hacked about wildly, but now his sword passed harmlessly through them. No fluids and viscera followed the path of his blade. Instead blue-grey smoke trails poured from the bodies and swirled about him. Still brawling, as if trying to retain their solidity by devouring each other, they began to dissolve into one shapeless, cloudy mass. Their screams faded. A small, rather tinny rumble of thunder emerged from the cloud as it drifted into the sky. Beneath it, seated on the ground, Merlin gazed impassively up at Griswold.

'Thou hast a powerful pair of lungs on thee,' murmured the Enchanter. 'One couldst never accuse thee of subtlety.'

The clang of Griswold's sword shattered the silence as he flung it to the ground.

'*I thought you were dead,*' he whispered. '*You bastard,*' he added.

Through eyes clouded by double vision and tears of rage he saw the Enchanter rise to his feet and come towards him. The porcelain features that were so familiar to him were unharmed, the robes unbloodied, the old limbs intact.

'Now thou knowest that I am not,' sang Merlin, 'perhaps thou'll listen to what I say.'

The clattering of troops pouring down from the battlements interrupted them. The men reached the courtyard, looked around and, seeing no reason for being there, stood toying with their swords while the knights and ladies emerged from their hiding places. For a brief moment eyeballs swivelled in confusion. Nobody was quite sure what they had seen. Merlin had done something that, of course, he was totally incapable of and Sir Lancelot had spent the last few minutes fighting with a bonfire. Merlin flicked his fingers through the air and the Camelonians resumed their strolling. Unnoticed, the cloud rapidly dispersed above their heads. The guards sheathed their swords, assumed their habitual arrogance and went off to look for the dozy twit who'd called them away from their cribbage.

Griswold glared at Merlin.

'What sadism is this that thou visits upon me/*What sort of moron are you?*' he growled.

'The sadism of a father whose child will not listen to reason. The sort that does not intend to chase thee all round the countryside to make thee see sense,' hissed Merlin.

He wasn't enamoured with trying to answer two questions at once whenever Griswold opened his mouth.

'*I've seen your kind of "sense"*,' said Griswold bitterly. '*Look at me.*'

He held a bare fist under the Enchanter's nose. It glistened dully.

'Listen to me,' he gritted hollowly. '*I'm . . . I'm . . .*'

Merlin studied the massive fist in front of him.

Invincible, thought the Enchanter.

'Thou art *here*,' he snapped. 'And here thou'lt remain until I've said what I have to say. Sit down.'

The dark eyes before him blazed for a second then softened. Griswold's face lit up with a grin as he sank to the ground and sat on his haunches.

'*Next time you pull a trick like that don't expect me to come and get thee out of trouble, understood?*' he said.

'Understood,' said Merlin.

10

It is two a.m. 13 January 1987 and James Dimmot can wait no longer. He feels somehow as if he's been waiting for centuries for something to give his life a purpose.

He sits on the snow-swept parapet of Tower Bridge, slippered feet dangling over the Thames. Below him assorted blocks of ice flow down to the sea, bobbing and chuckling amid the effluence, for it is the worst and the coldest winter for many decades.

The grey gabardine raincoat that is his only other clothing does less to protect him from the icy blizzard than does the lethally high alcohol content in his bloodstream.

The chimes of Big Ben begin to sound the hour, a vaguely familiar death knell.

But James Dimmot is unconcerned. In a few moments he will have consigned his body to the deep and it will all be over. He flings back his head and, with a peculiar feeling of déjà vu, simultaneously drains the last dregs from the bottle and topples backwards into the drift of snow piled high against the balustrade.

With his feet lodged on the rail above his head and the snow soaking through his splayed raincoat, he lies there for some time, thinking.

Well, fantasizing really. He drags his body painfully to its feet, wondering how it could have got so bruised and battered by falling into a snow drift. He pauses, squinting into the blizzard, as if trying to remember . . . anything.

With a shrug and a grunt, he weaves a purposeful path

back to his empty flat, leaving, as the only sign of his passing, a thin layer of skin from buttocks frozen to the unfeeling ironwork.

Behind him a minor disturbance caused by an object falling from an unbelievable height and crashing into the frozen surface of the river goes unnoticed. Ice bursts asunder and sprays into London's night sky, mingles with the swirling snow and, glinting in the riverbank lights, falls back to Earth with a concerted phlatter and splash.

For yards around the river rolls in protest, tumbling its glassy-grey charges over and about before returning morosely to its accustomed slide down to the sea. The assorted ice blocks settle back comfortably, unconcerned as to whether they will find themselves rewelded to their companions or adrift in some alien sea.

The sky is quiet beneath the whirl of silent snowflakes, save for the creak of the ice and the whisper of the wind. It remains thus for perhaps ten minutes or so.

Then, with a thrashing of limbs and a spluttering of lungs, the subject of the disturbance elbows its way to the surface and crawls on to the smashed iceflow, its eyes ablaze with cold fury. It, he, glares at the blocks and pebbles of ice, daring them to drift apart and send him slithering back into the water.

The blocks and pebbles know better.

He glowers up at the night sky at any gods that may be looking down, challenging them to mock him.

Any gods that may be looking down wander off whistling casually.

He tosses a surly snarl at the snow, but the snowflakes, being innocent and devoid of malice, don't recognize total Evil when they see it. They romp playfully around him like puppies, licking at his nose and tickling his eyelids.

Looking towards the riverbank, he sees the lights which spell out 'Mankind'.

He totters with ruthless dignity across the frozen terrain towards the shore.

Snuffle.

11

AD 4096. Hell again

Imagine yourself in the midst of a churning ocean of molten lava, mountains of the stuff crashing down on your splintering bones, the sulphurous pink-hot wind howling across the waves to scorch your eyeballs and shrivel your tongue into a parched husk in your mouth. A hundred million creatures tumble about you, their limbs smoking, their body fluids escaping in short-lived puffs of steam from their ears, their noses and their cracked, gaping skins. The creatures that are screaming non-stop are new here. Those whose raw, bloody throats can only manage the odd croak have been around for some time.

You are all being tossed about ruthlessly, endlessly, relentlessly, and every other-lessly you can think of because you have been damned for all Eternity . . . and nobody cares.

Six hundred feet above the boiling pit, two figures wandered along an endless and very narrow footbridge. From below they looked tiny to anyone with the inclination and enough eyeball left to look up with. One of them strolled casually since heights held no fear for him while the other one clopped carefully along at his side, acutely aware that the bridge had no guard-rail to compensate for the gusting winds. He studiously avoided looking down.

'Call it what you like,' Lucifer was saying. 'Evolution. God's will. The long and short is that Man was designed to evolve out of adversity, and the greater the adversity the faster will Man develop. The progress of his evolution was stifled by Nemestis for nearly a thousand years. After that he came within an ace of being totally wiped out. Can you imagine how that can speed up a species' development?'

Archeous stared back coolly as if the question didn't merit a reply. Lucifer smiled and went off on a different tack.

'The Last Trump did us more harm than good, once word got round the galaxy that Man had survived. All manner of enslaved species have been plucking up the balls to jump on the riot wagon ever since. It's only a matter of time before they gain both the courage and organization to do it.'

A geyser of hissing lava burst into the sky high above the bridge before plummeting its cargo of twitching bodies back into the depths.

Lucifer smiled appreciatively.

'Isn't that a wonderful sight?' he said.

Archeous gazed briefly into the blood-red sky and said nothing. Lucifer stopped and turned to the demon with a faintly quizzical frown.

'God help us, pardon my language, if all the bolshie races decide to revolt at the same time. We'd have a right job on our hands. That's why we must destroy Mankind once and for all *and* as spectacularly as possible. Shining example and all that.'

'Is there any reason to think that a galactic revolt is imminent?'

'Well, not really, but they won't hang about for ever. They're bound to spill over sooner or later. 'S the way of things.'

Of all Lucifer's irritating traits, his vague generalizations got up Archeous' nose most.

'Well, how long *have* we got?' he asked icily.

'Ah, now there's the rub,' said Lucifer. 'If we're going to destroy Mankind once and for all, before he starts becoming too clever on the magical front . . .'

'Yes?'

'. . . we'll have to do it within the next hundred years.'

Archeous stared long and hard at Lucifer. The angel's wings arched high over his shoulders and swept down behind his back. His bright golden gaze appraised the demon casually. His sturdy legs and powerful arms glistened in the blood-orange glow of the lava below and dimly reflected the turbulent purples and scarlets of Hell's evening sky. He looked, and was, invincible.

'May I ask a question?' asked Archeous in the sort of tone that says, 'I am observing a formality under considerable sufferance, since I have every intention of asking it anyway.'

'Of course, old chap,' said the angel.

'Why have you waited so long before doing something about it?'

A bleak silence ensued. It was broken only by the distant sounds of suffering. Then the angel spoke.

'Fact is, old chap, I've not been completely honest with you.'

'Oh. In what way?'

'Commitment.'

'Pardon?'

'Lack of.'

'I don't understand.'

Lucifer wandered to the side of the bridge and leant on the nonexistent guard-rail. Angels can do this. Lesser beings tend to fall off things. He gazed down at the heaving mass of melted rock and humanity far below.

'Do you know how long I've been doing this job, Archeous?'

'Some considerable time, I understa—'

'Considerable! Apart from a temporary stint with my rival's firm, I've been employed here since Man first walked the Earth.' He squinted over his shoulder at Archeous. 'My heart's not in it any more.'

'And?'

'I'm thinking of asking for my old job back.'

'You mean you want me to take over when you've gone?' said Archeous.

'Correct,' replied Lucifer. 'But it's not that cut and dried. Mankind has to go first. You get the job when you've proved you're up to it.'

Archeous had succeeded in the banking world by making use of his two strongest assets: his obsessive ambition and his astuteness in taking advantage of a bent deal when he saw it. He had controlled the first and honed the second to gain him a top, highly prestigious position in the banking world by the time he died.

Now his ambition, which was red-hot you might say, was about to bind him to a deal that was not only bent but bent double.

'Get it right,' murmured Lucifer, gazing into the distance, 'and you get to be the ruler of Hell. That *is* what you want, isn't it?'

Archeous shrugged as casually as he could manage and spent several seconds trying to unstick his tongue from the roof of his mouth. When he finally managed to speak in a nonchalant squeak, he asked, 'What do we do first?'

Lucifer smiled his brilliant smile.

'First you receive some enlightenment. Then we do a bit of shopping.'

Leaning out at an impossible angle over the edge of the bridge he held up his open palm and gave a quick beckoning gesture. A smoking, blood-red geyser fountained towards him, spewing out a tumble of jerking bodies. As it hovered before them a hundred or so scorching beings bobbed like ping-pong balls on its cascading summit. One or two of the hardier ones took a break from screeching to gaze at the two figures on the bridge.

Archeous returned their stares with distaste.

'Is this meant to serve as an example of my punishment for failure?' he asked.

'What? Oh, no,' said Lucifer. 'This is nothing compared

to what you'll experience if you fail. No, these are your troops. Some of them, anyway.'

He repeated the gesture and another pillar erupted into the sky behind them with a cargo of howling humanity on its boiling surface. Now seven pillars of lava stretched towards the rolling clouds astride the bridge. Molten spume whipped off their waves, peppering Archeous' naked body. Sulphurous smoke swirled about him and squirmed up his nostrils into his lungs.

This irritated him less than the fact that Lucifer was quite unaffected by either the heat or the smoke.

'Time to pick 'n' choose,' smiled the angel.

He raised his arms as if to embrace the bobbing figures. Most of them managed to remain upright, sitting on the lava's surface. As they stared intently at the angel, their constant screams reduced to the occasional yelp, Lucifer's voice rose above the dull roar of the geyser.

'I need volunteers,' he called.

'What for?' one yelled.

'Bit of a dirty job, I'm afraid. No pay, find your own food, strong chance that you may not make it back.'

A mass of hands went up.

'What's in it for us?' gurgled one man. Unlike the others, he was standing, knee-deep, with his blistering knuckles resting on his peeling hips. He was the most muscular man that Archeous had ever seen. He appeared to be constructed largely of footballs. A constant stream of blood bubbled from a gaping blackened hole in his throat.

'Nothing much, Mr Savage. Death, if you're lucky. Back here if you're not.'

The man beetled his brows for a moment, struggled to maintain his balance and called, 'Yeah. All right.'

'Anyone else?'

Two more, sitting near the edge, raised their hands. One rose to his feet.

'OK,' said the prudent one.

'Oh, buggerrrrrr . . .' screamed the other as he toppled

over the edge and plummeted towards the swirling smoke. They watched as the dwindling figure disappeared from sight.

'Well?' said Lucifer.

In a moment the damned were bobbing grimly on scorching bottoms with their hands raised. The air was pregnant with the roar of tumbling lava punctuated by intermittent cries. Archeous looked on as the creatures waited patiently.

'Have they . . . done this sort of thing before?' he said.

'Oh, yes,' said the angel. 'As you've found out, that stuff about damnation being eternal is so much cobblers. There are openings if one is the least bit enterprising.'

'Even in this backwater slum . . . I never realized.'

'No one does. It's our secret: mine, yours . . .'

He swept out a hand across the abyss. A mass of bodies was sucked from the geyser, across the intervening space and placed with exact precision on the walkway of the bridge. Standing away from each other lest their skins stuck together, they grinned cold grins and watched Archeous hungrily.

'. . . and theirs,' smiled the angel.

12

AD 1987

With a prolonged scrabbling of key in lock and a gin-soaked belch, James Dimmot stumbled into his flat and slid along the passage wall until he arrived at his dingy bed-sitting room.

He reached through the open doorway, felt for the light switch and clicked it on.

The electricity was off.

Dragging off his raincoat, he began to rummage for some matches. After a few minutes the violent shuddering of his limbs served to remind him that his raincoat and carpet slippers had been the only clothes he was wearing.

'Laftewait,' he said and he peered round the room through drooping eyelids. In the snow-laden light from the street lamps shining through his curtains he made out the shadowy mess of his unmade bed and steered towards it. Pulling the thick eiderdown round his shoulders, he wandered to the sideboard, found the matches and, four matches later, brought alive the candle standing on top of his piano.

The room flickered reluctantly into life.

Dimmot sagged on to the piano stool.

What the hell've I been doing with myself?

Oh, yeah. Suicide.

He frowned.

Wha' went wrong?

The answer, mercifully, eluded him.

He sat slouched over the keyboard, thinking about nothing in particular. His black spiky hair hung damply over his forehead and he was vaguely aware that he smelt unsociable. A few scattered brain cells, bearing visions spanning two thousand years and encompassing the odd horrific experience flickered momentarily at the edge of his memory before snuffing out like distant stars in the night sky.

The dank cold of his unlit, unheated flat folded around him.

'Oh, balls,' he said.

He pulled the eiderdown closer and sat silently for another age. After a while his eyes focused on the keyboard dancing in the candlelight. He stretched out a finger and rested it gently on one of the notes. Middle C rang quietly under his finger and it was a few seconds before James Dimmot opened his eyes and gazed down in wonderment.

He pressed the note again and his eyes widened as it rang in his ear.

'Oh my God,' he whispered.

He tried a mellower note two octaves lower. As the sound reached his ears the sweat of terror broke out on his brow. He reached out and played a trembling chord and gasped as the sound resonated through every cell of his body. He stared in disbelief at the keyboard. He stared at his hand. He raised his eyes and stared at the opaque, shimmering reflection of himself in the polished wood of the piano.

The notes, the chords, were totally new to him. Old familiar shapes that he had played for over twenty years now sounded vibrant, shining like rays of sunlight through a vast cathedral window.

It seemed as though he had never heard those sounds before. An unbelievable urgency that had never been there for him sprang up like wild colour-bursting flowers.

And he heard something else.

He heard the echoes of Heaven and Hell. He heard the sounds of the cosmos. He stared at his reflection.

'What has happened to me?' he whispered. His haunted reflection stared back and said nothing. He gazed at the keyboard again and let his trembling fingers glide over the keys.

The music came to life, flowing, dancing and spiralling, resounding in his ears and deep into the heart of his mind. Every harmonic throbbed with the blood of its ancestral chords and brought forth new, even more subtle harmonies.

The room sang to Dimmot's creations.

His breathing came in sobs, in time to the pounding of his fingers. As the notes swirled to a climax his sobs became cries of ecstasy, anguish, ruthless courage. As the music softened and drifted mistily across lakes of Debussian quietness, the glistening, fluid tones caressed his inner eyes and brought tears of joy to a heart that had been joyless for years.

Dimmot played on through the early hours, oblivious to everything but the sounds, thoughts and feelings running through his mind. He didn't hear the banging on the wall from neighbours. He was quite untouched by the cold of his room and the wetness that had soaked through his slippers to assault his blue-veined feet. He was fired with a heat from within. He was also fortunate enough not to raise his head and glance at the reflection in the piano once more. Had he done so, the music born in his heart that night might have been strangled at birth. Behind him were three barely visible figures, existing simultaneously in his Reality and in another that had been and gone, touching only on his because both Realities were passing through the same place at the same time. A hazy Merlin, a Griswold and another Dimmot, as unaware of his existence as he was of theirs, were silently squabbling amongst themselves.

While the presence of the 'spectres' has no relevance in this scene and, in fact, belongs to the other Reality, it serves to tell us that we are dealing with many possibilities, and that nothing is immutable, especially when written on the fluid surface of Time.

Dimmot played on. As his rewritten Reality drifted away from the one he had previously occupied the figures faded and vanished, still blissfully ignorant of his presence.

As the first streak of morning light edged through his grey curtains, he realized that his fingers were burning with pain. Reluctantly he stopped.

'God, I need a fag,' he said, plucking his raincoat off the piano top and rummaging through the pockets. He had been forced to give up months ago for lack of money. His pockets contained nothing of use and nothing smokable, only a small, bedraggled paperback that Dimmot wasn't aware he owned. He dropped his mack on the floor and tossed the book on top of the piano. It slid to the edge and toppled out of sight down the back.

'Must be one somewhere,' he whined. 'Must be a goddam stogie round here somewhere, for Crissake!'

He wheeled round and leapt from the stool, catching his deadened legs by surprise and almost falling on his face. He reached the bed, dropped to his knees and peered underneath it. Seeing nothing in the dark he flapped his hand across the floor, feeling blindly for anything resembling a dog end.

He was still there at midday with his face pressed into the threadbare carpet and a gentle smile of hope on his lips, exhaustion etched across his features and his fingers an inch away from the only cigarette stub in the room.

13

AD 1987

Intermittent drips pinged and splopped into the dank water and the piles of rotting vegetation that lay at the bottom of the sewer twenty feet below London's busy evening streets.

Since he had lived with dripping water and had *been* a dank smell for most of his sixty years, the sole inhabitant of the sewer, a tramp whose name is not worth mentioning (since he won't have it for much longer) was unbothered by this.

He was fairly content. He had a home there and, although he sometimes missed companionship, he was, understandably, left in peace and to his own devices. Life was uneventful, except during the occasional rainstorm and the even less occasional visit by the sanitary department.

He swallowed the last slightly burnt mouthful of small

domestic creature that had wandered innocently into his domain two days earlier, with a trusting look in its eyes and no apparent regard for its tortoiseshell hide. He wiped his lips on his sleeve and lit a homemade cigar, made of cabbage leaves and spiced with herbs, courtesy of one of Soho's more distinguished dustbins. Digging into his pile of belongings he drew out a bottle containing a delicate blend of wines collected from the crates gracing the back alleys of several prestigious restaurants. He pulled his cardboard boxes firmly about him, swallowed deeply and puffed expansively.

He thought briefly about the family he'd never had, about the places he had never visited, about the man he'd have liked to have been. He would have liked to have been a man of means. He would have liked to have seen more of the world. He would have liked to have spent more time with his daydreams, but the distant slop of water against the curved walls interrupted both him and them. He peered into the darkness. At first he could see nothing.

Rats, he thought.

Although the rats normally showed no interest in him, wisely giving their attention to vegetation that couldn't fight back, he reached out and drew his heavy walking stick to his side. The noise of the water became more insistent and the familiar sound of a body walking knee-deep came to his ears. Round a bend in the tunnel a figure appeared. It was squat, stocky and, in the darkness, it appeared to be wearing several layers of clothing.

Bugger, thought the tramp. Bloody sewer inspector.

Cursing his cardboard overcoat, he eased himself as quietly as he could into the darker shadows and slid his cigar deep into the soggy silt nearby.

With a bit of luck he'd pass by. The tramp lay still, breathing as quietly as he could.

The figure came nearer, striding rhythmically through the water. It drew level with the tramp and stopped. It stood for a moment with its face turned up and the tramp thought uneasily that it was sniffing the air. He held his breath.

Slowly the figure turned towards him and he realized with horror that, as the creature was stark naked, the 'layers of clothing' were an integral part of its body. Its eyes appeared to be slightly luminous and they were filled with more hate than the tramp had ever seen. He reached for his stick and then the universe fell in on him. Before he could raise his arms to ward it off, the figure had shot from the water and covered the ten-foot space between them in one leap. The thing was on him, blotting out his vision of the dim walls and ceiling with its bulk, tearing at his meagre protection with unstoppable hands and going for his throat.

The tramp's scream echoed round the sewer walls and spiralled away into the darkness. His yellow woollen hat fell from his head and landed silently a few feet away. The leaden weight of the creature crushed him into the brick floor and the rough hands scraped past his throat as they reached out to grasp his ears. For a brief second the tramp wondered if he might get a reprieve. Then the creature pulled the tramp's face up to its own and its thick lips encircled his eye socket. With a snuffle and an obviously well-practised hooking motion of the tongue, the creature drew an explosive breath. A white-hot fire engulfed one side of the tramp's face and this time his scream filled the sewer to capacity for the twenty seconds it took the thing to savour and chew its prize and then to bite through the optic nerve in order to swallow it. As the creature lowered its head for a second time the tramp's terror found its way to his heart and put a stop to his suffering, but not before he realized with total certainty that the thing pinning him to the mud-covered brickwork was only on the hors d'oeuvres.

14

AD 570

The spirit of Rose Falworthy sat with her shimmering legs stretched along the branch of a sixth-century oak tree and her back against the cool, knurled trunk. On the ground beneath her sat two figures whom she had met only once, but would never forget. As is often the case with people who would give their lives for each other, these two were bickering.

Rose wasn't surprised.

'You knew this would happen if you dragged me away one day and returned me two days earlier! Why didn't you just bring Lancelot back to life?'

The little one, known throughout the world as Merlin the Enchanter, the epitome of all that is good and right, all that is loyal and true, compassionate and understanding, replied inaccurately, 'Fool, fool and thrice fool! Hast thou learned nothing from thy years with me? One doesn't bring people back to life. One doesn't reverse the course of history. One's only recourse is to guide the crucial events around such acts of destruction as thou saw fit to visit on Lancelot. *Twice.*'

'He asked for it. Twice,' replied Griswold.

'Thou art the pilot of destiny?' snorted the Enchanter.

'If Man's destiny depends on the acts of mere mortals defending their monarch's name against the slurs and actions of the treacherous, then you're damn right I am! am.'

From above Rose's position a squirrel scampered down the trunk and along the branch on which she sat, passing through her and sending a slight tremor through that tenuous field that links the material with the spiritual. Rose gave a little shudder and a smile as the squirrel shook itself and turned to stare quizzically in her direction.

'Gods,' sighed Merlin. 'Why can't mortal men keep their noses and their blades out of an Enchanter's business?'

'Why must wizards resort to deceit and subterfuge to achieve their ends?'

Rose, who had always been one to call a spade a spade, was beginning to like Griswold more by the second. She was eager to know just what was upsetting him.

'Dost thou know what really upsets me?' said Griswold. *'You gave me no choice in the matter. That's what upsets me.'*

'Wouldst thou have agreed if I had?'

'No, I wouldn't. You think that it's only big men who make history? History, for better or worse, is also made by small men like me.'

Rose wouldn't have called Griswold small by any stretch.

'What dost thou know of history?'

'You forget, Merlin, I've seen some of your history in its true light. I've been into the future. . .'

For a second the air around the two men shivered and crackled. Rose saw the Enchanter stiffen.

'Quiet, idiot,' he hissed. 'If anyone should hear of this—'

'Have no fear, Merlin?/*Don't worry*. Dost thou think I'm going to word it abroad that thou'st been steering me this way and that like a donkey on a rope? My needs are simple. *I want my body as it was, my thoughts straightened out and my reputation restored.'*

The squirrel returned along the branch, sniffed tentatively at the space occupied by Rose's toes and looked around for some other way to reach the tree trunk. Rose obligingly wafted off her branch on to the next one.

'What thou asks,' said Merlin, 'I will try to give thee in time. All I ask is that thou understands my position. My loyalty is to my king and thus to Mankind. My allegiance to thee must come second. That is the price I must pay for the privilege of serving both.'

'The price we must both pay, it seems,' said Griswold quietly.

'Indeed,' sighed Merlin. 'I am truly sorry, lad.'

Griswold squinted at the sky. 'How long must I be like this?'

'I know not,' said Merlin reluctantly. 'Possibly days. Mayhap . . . years.'

'*And there's nothing you can do about it?*'

'Nothing that I know of.'

The two men sat silently, each lost in his own thoughts. Rose, who had fought a number of lost causes when she was alive, was reluctant to interrupt those thoughts, but from what she had seen a few minutes ago in another Time she guessed that time was something none of them had right now. She swung her legs over the branch and executed a finely judged back somersault, landing cat-like near the two men. Merlin was on his feet instantly with his fingers splayed in her direction and his eyes ablaze.

'What demonry is this?' he hissed. Then his face lost a little of its colour. 'Oh, Gods. 'Tis thee.'

'That's right, old man, and you'd better put those fingers away before you do something silly with them.'

Griswold frowned at the Enchanter. '*Who on Earth are you talking to?*' he said.

'What? Oh . . .' snapped the wizard. Without taking his eyes off Rose or lowering his hand he waved the fingers of his other hand before Griswold's face. As he did so, the knight's eyes widened, then narrowed dangerously. He rolled away instinctively in anticipation of a possible blow and came to his feet with his sword drawn.

'Good move, Griswold. I'll remember that one,' said Rose approvingly.

'Do we know her?' said Griswold, carefully appraising Rose from two totally different points of view.

Merlin lowered his hands. His eyes resumed their normal ice-blue.

'Indeed we do,' he said thinly, 'although thou wast not in any condition to appreciate her when last we met.'

Rose Falworthy was dressed in a minimal two-piece costume of tanned leather, furry calf-length boots and a belt whose only function was to carry the sheath holding her long-bladed stiletto. The hilt of a heavy broadsword could be seen over her right shoulder and the end of the scabbard peeped out from behind her left buttock. Her auburn hair hung over one shoulder and almost touched her breast.

Griswold smiled a winsome smile that drew the livid scar on his cheek into a gentle pink ridge.

'*I wasn't?*' he said doubtfully.

Merlin smiled a faintly sick smile. 'Mistress Falworthy. This is a surprise. To what do we owe this . . . er . . .?'

'Try "pleasure",' suggested Rose.

'Indeed,' replied Merlin. 'I take it Uther sent thee.'

She wasn't sure why but something told her to choose her words very carefully.

'Uther *asked* me to come and find you. He needs you.'

'He's only been in power for a day and a half!'

'You're a bit out of date, dear. I've come from AD 4097. Uther has ruled the Earth and its peoples for nearly three hundred years.'

Her voice, though she wouldn't have admitted it had she realized, held more than a little pride. Griswold looked from one to the other, his frown deepening with each exchange.

'Ah,' said Merlin. 'And how is the old fool?'

Rose's lips tightened noticeably. 'His Majesty is fine,' she said. 'A little older. A little more tired than when you last saw him. A little more foolish,' she added. For a moment they held each other's gaze. Then Merlin nodded.

'And what does he need from me?'

While Griswold divided his time between trying to grasp

what they were talking about and gazing at the woman, Rose Falworthy explained that she had come at Uther's request to seek Merlin's help. Again, she felt instinctively the need for deviousness. Again she had no idea why.

'. . . diseases vanishing overnight . . .

'. . . no storms, no typhoons . . .

'. . . lands suddenly becoming fertile . . .

'. . . the climate generally improving . . .

'. . . Uther's worried. Says it's just not natural.'

'Nor is it. What else?'

'Well, over the last year women all over the world are beginning to have twins, triplets and such. Single babies are actually becoming a rarity.'

'Oh, Lord,' whispered Merlin.

'It's almost as if some kind of Messiah has at last come down to Earth,' said Rose. 'A divine power.'

'And,' said Griswold, 'does this divine power have a name?'

'Not yet,' said Rose. 'We haven't discovered the source.'

'Oh dear,' said the Enchanter.

A long silence ensued, punctuated by an icy full stop in the form of another, 'Oh dear.'

'You know what the source is?' said Griswold.

'There can only be one source,' said Merlin.

He turned and wandered off a few paces with his head hung in thought.

Griswold and Rose exchanged glances. Rose shrugged her shoulders, raised an eyebrow and gave a pout that said, 'No idea.' Griswold shook his head in concurrence. He also swallowed quite hard. They waited while Merlin paced between them as if unaware of their presence. Griswold watched him carefully and as he did so an old familiar tingle spread through his frame. The look on the Enchanter's face was one that Griswold had seen many times before. It almost invariably heralded the whistling of blades, the yelling of the outraged and that soggy splop of limbs hitting the ground. Only the touch of wariness in

Merlin's expression took the edge off Griswold's anticipation.

'Well? Who do we have to fight?' he asked.

Merlin stopped pacing and stared at the ground. Then he looked up and Griswold felt a stab of ice prick at his heart.

'I fear that our battle against the Forces of Darkness was not won after all,' said the Enchanter.

15

After Rose left, saying, 'I'll tell Uther you're on your way. And don't be late', Merlin and Griswold returned to the wizard's cottage.

'Hast thou eaten?' said Merlin as they climbed the last few yards.

'Nope,' said Griswold. The Enchanter fluttered his fingers and muttered for a bit and, by the time they reached the open door, the rich herbal aroma of soup was drifting out into the warm air. Inside the remarkably cool room a steaming cauldron bubbled gently in the fireplace, conveniently forgetting that a fire of some sort is normally required for such a moderately complex physico-chemical reaction. On the table two bowls of broth and some hunks of coarse bread were waiting. For a few moments they ate in silence. Then the Enchanter spoke.

'What dost thou remember of the last few days?'

Above his munching Griswold's frown brought his thick black eyebrows together, giving him a deceptively brutish look.

'Very little/Not a lot. S'all a bit of a mish-mash,' he mumbled. 'One moment I think that all's well and I've been here all the time, bedding maidens and brawling with the other knights. Then pictures of another world come to my eyes. I seem to phantomize . . .'

'Fantasize,' said Merlin.

'Fantasize. Just little pictures. No more. Creatures. Devils?'

The Enchanter nodded.

'And blood . . . also blood that would be blood if it was the right colour.' Griswold stopped his munching and licked his lips thoughtfully. '*And there is a man . . . not much of a man, yet . . . I owe him my life.*'

He sat there for a moment, staring into space, then scooped up another spoonful of soup.

'*And there was one hell of a lot of Evil about,*' he said, shovelling the soup into his mouth.

Merlin sighed. 'I had intended to keep such memories from thine sight, since they are the stuff of gossip and, therefore, legend. It would not do to give the very subjects of those legends warning of our recent machinations. However, it appears that the battle has been renewed whether we wish it or not. Therefore . . .'

As Griswold raised the spoon again to his lips, Merlin snapped his fingers before the knight's eyes. For a second Griswold stared intently back at him, his spoon poised before him. As his memories, carefully buried by Merlin only two days earlier, flooded to the surface of his mind, his eyes lit up. He saw himself amidst overwhelming odds with a double-edged axe in one hand and the small, spiky-haired Dimmot unconscious on his other arm. He saw a beautiful she-devil, Amanda, with her glowing skin and trembling lips. He saw a band of unEarthly minstrels playing terrible music that threatened to burst eardrums and he saw the awful demon Nemestis and his gruesome henchman Scarbald doing unbelievably evil things to Mankind. In an instant the whole story unfolded before him. Slowly a smile grew across his face and he pursed his lips around the spoon, drawing the warm liquid into the back of his throat where he let it lie to be savoured and swallowed.

'*So that's where she comes from,*' he mused.

Merlin's eyes narrowed. 'She. Who?'

'*Mistress Falworthy,*' grinned Griswold.

The Enchanter grimaced. 'She who, were she still able to do so, could talk for a week without needing to draw breath.'

'The very same,' said Griswold. He mopped up the last few drops of soup with his bread, stuffed it in his mouth and wiped his lips with the back of his hand. "*Twas truly delicious*/For a magician,' he said, 'you make a great cook.'

'For a man of singularly lewd perceptions,' replied Merlin, 'thou makest a fine couple.'

He spared the knight a brief but not unkind smile.

Griswold leaned back in his chair and stretched his arms contentedly.

'*So, where I was once one, now I am two.*'

'Until I find a way to cure thine condition,' said Merlin, staring intently at the parchments on the table. Not that he hoped to find a solution there. It simply gave him an excuse to avoid meeting Griswold's eyes.

'In the meantime,' said Griswold matter-of-factly, 'we have a mission and my being me and also myself would seem to be an advantage.'

Merlin looked up with a frown. 'Oh. How so?'

Griswold leaned forward on the table and, with a gesture of his chin, pointed to the crack running across it. Merlin acknowledged this with a shrug of his eyebrows and a thoughtful nod.

'Indeed, I wonder what other powers, manly or otherwise, thou might have inherited from this unique occurrence.'

'*What? Hast thou never come across this before?*/This can't be a first, surely?' said Griswold.

'It hasn't actually fallen within the compass of my experience,' said Merlin awkwardly. Despite his embarrassment, a germ of an idea began to niggle at his awareness. He could not quite bring it to focus and yet . . . a tiny thrill of anticipation flitted through his mind. He climbed to his feet. 'I'll be back in a moment,' he said, and disappeared into the back room.

He emerged a few moments later, holding an object about three feet long wrapped in a tatty piece of sacking. As he laid it on the table and unwrapped it the cloth fell apart in his hands and dust billowed around the room.

'Where on Earth has this been?' said Griswold, waving the dust away from his nostrils.

'In a place where no creature has ever dared to venture. A place known only to one man and protected by the most awesome magical powers ever known. A place—'

'Under your bed,' said Griswold.

'Under my bed.'

The last shred of sacking slid off the table and floated to the floor, raising another small cloud. The men stared at the object.

'It's a sword,' said Griswold before he could stop himself.

'Oh, wondrous day,' murmured the Enchanter. 'The lad surpasses himself.'

'I already have a sword,' sighed Griswold.

'Thou dost not have *this* one,' said Merlin.

'I do not need *this* one,' replied Griswold flatly.

The scabbard under its layer of dirt and dust was about as commonplace as one could imagine. Fashioned from a grey leathery hide, it was quite featureless and appeared to be too large for the weapon. The hand-guard of the sword was made of grey iron and the hilt was deep black with a dull, rather grubby stone set in its end.

'What dost thou think?' asked Merlin. His voice was unusually quiet.

'Is there any soup left?' said Griswold.

'Draw the sword.'

Griswold took the hilt in his hand, grasped the scabbard and withdrew the blade. It came out surprisingly easily for the blade itself was covered in dirt. The cutting edges were nicked in places and the blade was too blunt even to cut oneself accidentally.

'You want me to fight the forces of Evil with this?' said Griswold. He made it sound like an accusation.

'Quiet, fool,' hissed Merlin. 'Wait.'

Griswold waited. His eyes strayed towards the cauldron. He gazed up at the beams. He stood the sword on its point and twizzled it slowly back and forth round its axis.

'What are we waiting for?' he asked mildly.

'Destiny,' said the Enchanter.

'Oh, right. Whose?'

'Not whose. What's.' He nodded at the blade. 'Its.'

Griswold had known Merlin for many years and he recognized certain signs when he saw them. He started to lay the sword on the table and stand well back, but the Enchanter stopped him with a glare.

'Stop jiggling it about and hold it as it is meant to be held,' he snapped.

With a sigh Griswold gripped the sword and raised it in front of him. Something was about to happen. He suspected that it involved things glowing whitely, grubby gemstones bursting into multi-coloured lights and clapped-out sword blades shimmering until they became razor-sharp.

There would probably be some dramatic music too.

Not that he was complaining. Whenever things 'happened' in Merlin's presence, there was bound to be blood-curdling action and action-curdled blood. Griswold had never heard the word 'adrenalin' but, unlike men whose response to its body-trembling flow was blind panic, Griswold thrilled to the pump of it through his veins. He just wished that the old man would give him an inkling of what was going on.

He gripped the sword and waited. From a crack between blade and hand-guard a minute shape dislodged itself and floated, unnoticed, to the floor. The meatless skeleton of a

82

long-dead pond skater touched down without even raising a puff in the dust.

16

AD 1987

The small 'paperback' that Dimmot didn't know he owned lay wedged behind the piano, shaken but unharmed. It wondered if James Dimmot might come into the category of a Mist-Demon or some other entity that could change its shape at will. If not, then he was going to have one hell of a time crawling under the piano to learn the secrets that the paperback contained.

Three days later it was still there, having reached no conclusion.

S'bloody galling, it thought. There's nothing in my instructions about this.

It felt a growing sense of failure.

I could really do without this at this stage in my career, it thought despondently. You'd think they'd make allowances for idiots of Dimmot's calibre. I'd better have a word with the boss.

The manual, for such it was, focused its attention and put in a call to the nexus of multi-dimensional forces of which Time, space and mind are but a part and which pale to insignifance the magics and sorceries of all save that which created it. The answer came back immediately.

'*Yes?*' said the Book.

'This is Manual 13,017, extract from Appendix 8008A, pages one to—'

'*I know what you are,*' said the Book through the sub-ethereal layers of Reality. '*What do you want?*'

'Dimmot has lost me.'

'Pardon?'

'I'm stuck down the back of his piano. He doesn't even know I'm here.'

'Piano?'

'Yes.' The manual explained how Dimmot could create beauty out of disorder by organizing the natural harmonies of the cosmos into logical sequences of sounds on his 'piano', as he called it.

'I've been here three days,' it said.

'You haven't managed to attract his attention?'

'He's been as drunk as a skunk since he got back.'

'Ah.'

'Any ideas?'

'I have all the ideas, remember?'

'Sorry.'

'Don't worry. You're young. You've a lot to learn.'

The manual waited quietly for the Book to continue. It wished it had the power to move just a little. It was standing on its outer edge and its pages, which bore only a superficial resemblance to mere paper, were beginning to bend badly.

The Book finally spoke.

'I want you to imagine you are a small paper tube,' it said.

'Pardon?' said the manual.

'You are filled with shreds of vegetation and, this is the difficult part, James Dimmot finds you highly desirable.'

'Er, in what way?' asked the manual uneasily.

The Book, although a living entity in its own way, resided in dimensions which could loosely be called Timeless, and it was not given to that common trait of living entities known as impatience. However, there were limits.

'In any way you like,' it said shortly. 'As long as it has the desired effect.'

'Which is what?' asked the manual.

'Do you aspire to become an integral part of Man's

destiny?' said the Book. 'Or do you wish to remain a part of the Appendix for all Eternity?'

'How long am I meant to be?' said the manual.

'Seven centimetres long and half a centimetre across.'

'And that's all I need to do?'

'And let him know that you are there.'

'But I couldn't get through to him before. What makes y—?'

'Before,' said the Book, 'Dimmot didn't know that he needed you. He thinks he needs a thin paper tube full of vegetation. Therefore you will call to him in the way that a thin paper tube full of vegetation does and he will hear your call.'

A feeling of emptiness came over the manual and it knew it was now alone. It concentrated hard and imagined that it was rolling up and growing smaller and filling with some sort of plant life, although it could not imagine what form this was meant to take. After a few moments it called out to James Dimmot in the way it imagined small tubes of paper filled with plant life might do.

17

Dimmot awoke with a dull headache, a mouth like the bottom of a parrot's cage and a jerk that brought his head up against the bed frame with a crack. He climbed groggily out into the open with several one-syllable oaths dripping from his tongue. He crawled to the window, pulled the grey curtains apart and squinted out into the snow-bound streets. Heavy flakes were still falling from the leaden sky, adding to the blanket that had reduced the parked cars, the trees and the multitude of dustbins to a common round-humped, white-shrouded community of snow demons. Although it was midday the streets were sparsely populated with only the most determined office workers, the most well-paid street cleaners and the most drunken drunks. Dimmot glared at the snow. It reminded him of skiing and Christmases and such.

'Don't know why I bothered to wake up,' he grumbled.

Several minutes passed.

'Yes, I do!' he exclaimed. He looked around at the piano. 'S'one down the back,' he said.

Dimmot glared furiously at the dust and the eight-legged corpses rolling gently in the path of his heavy breathing.

'Bloody hernia and two slipped discs and what do I find? Not a ciggy in sight. Just some tatty old Mills and Boon.'

He picked up the manual and flung it across the room in disgust. It fluttered protesting on to the bed and slid under the sheet. Dimmot flopped against the wall with his hands resting on his knees.

No drink, no food, he thought miserably. No money, no prospects, no future. No friends, no women, no social life.

'And I'd give it all up for just one ciggy right now.' He sniggered humourlessly.

'I'm over here,' murmured the manual.

Dimmot looked up.

If I remember rightly, he thought, there was one over there.

He went to the bed, dragged the eiderdown about his naked body and felt gently among the tangled bed-sheets. Finding nothing except the ancient brown paperback, he flopped down on the bed.

'There are times when I could seriously contemplate suicide,' he said aloud. 'It's a miracle I haven't topped myself already.'

He stared out of the window. He stared up at the anaglypta peeling from the ceiling.

'*That* needs doing,' he added by way of understatement.

He picked up the manual and began to leaf through it idly. The pages were blank. 'This should be a bestseller on the dyslexic market.'

He looked at the front cover and a tremor of apprehension sent a shiver through him. Across the cover, written in some form of old English script, was the title *Thine Destiny in Thine Hand*. Underneath the title it was signed, 'To J.D. Kindest regards, M.'

'Who on Earth is M?'

James Dimmot glanced at the page again. This time the tremor fairly lumbered across his brain. The words faded and disappeared before his eyes, leaving nothing but a blank, pale buff-coloured page. He turned the page over and glanced inside.

'Oh, my God,' he said.

If the first page had him worried, this one improved on that to the power of about fifty. This time the words were slightly more explicit and much more confusing.

'James Dimmot, thou art a failure and unworthy of thy powers. We are about to change that.'

Dimmot looked about the room, as if expecting someone to poke their head round the door and shout, 'Ya hah. Fooled yuh!'

He turned back to the page in time to see the words following their predecessors into limbo.

18
AD 570

In the quiet of his bedroom Merlin listened to the sounds of the past. He was scouring through the memories that spanned a hundred and fifty adventurous, turmoil-ridden years. For all his complaints about his failing memory, the images of his childhood were as vivid as the events of yesterday.

He was searching for something and he didn't quite know what that something was. He did know that the only way to do it was to rerun the tape of his history until he reached the moment when a half-murmured phrase had drifted across his hearing, almost inaudibly, many years ago. He could not even remember when or where he'd heard it or what it pertained to, but it niggled in the way that thoughts do when you know that they are just what you are looking for.

The Enchanter's room was small, spartan and, being windowless, almost pitch-black but for the tiny crack of light peeping under the door. His only furniture was a bed and a small table on which stood a candle-holder containing a shapeless blob of wax and a charred wick. On the opposite wall hung a shelf bearing a very large book covered in some form of grey hide.

Merlin sat cross-legged on the bed. His mind was as still as a millpond. His breathing was as slow as a lake. Behind his closed eyelids hung a sepia-coloured screen and on it his life unfolded, second by second, to the accompaniment of a distant monologue summarizing, in a tinny monotone, each event as it occurred.

The voice was that of his father, Asmethyum.

'You are in your fourth year when I first make you aware that the power you feel cannot be felt by any other man, let alone a child . . .'

'. . . this is the time when you throw a tantrum and blast the branch off the oak tree at the bottom of the hill. You are only . . .'

'. . . six when you first encounter the Forces of Evil. Your will is tested and found wanting. But for my intervention . . .'

'. . . the spring of your seventh year, when I was discovered by the Forces of Darkness and had to depart for your safety . . .'

For an hour the Enchanter sat, playing the story of his life through his mind, unsmiling, unmoved, concentrating on the fragment of memory that might resolve his quandary. He was at one with each moment, as if he were there in body. The sounds, sights and smells unravelled and vanished as they were replaced by their successors. He recalled the taste of fear in the face of danger, the feeling of pain as the lances of Evil's mental anguish pierced his defences. Those impressions were part of his memories, controlled and diminished, but a part nevertheless.

'. . . you pledge your life to the good of Mankind . . .'

'. . . reach your full powers. You are but twenty years of—'

Merlin frowned.

No, he thought. This is not right.

'I have gone past it, I'm certain,' he said aloud. 'There is a sound that goes with it . . . and a movement. Rhythmic, like that of the sea but comforting. And the sound . . . a rumbling . . . no, a booming. A tide. A warm, comforting tide. Why and whence the tide?'

The silence that followed was wry and empty.

'What didst thou expect?' he mused. 'Some sort of assistance? Since when couldst thou rely on anyone but thineself?'

With surly determination he ploughed once more to his infancy, when a handful of words had begun to have meaning for him.

'Muh . . . muh . . . Duh . . . duh . . . daggen . . . doad . . . Merl'n . . . mummy . . .

'Daddy . . . Merlin . . . moon . . . Mars . . . Mercury . . . magic . . . darkness.'

*

89

'Passed it,' said the voice in his head.

'What?' said Merlin.

'You've gone past it,' said Asmethyum.

A shred of excitement flittered through Merlin's tiny frame. With childlike hesitation, he whispered, 'Art thou . . .?'

'Nope. I'm still back home, half a galaxy and a dozen dimensions distant. You're just recreating what our boffins call "the preprogrammed relevant responses" to the questions in your head. Sorry, son.'

'Oh,' murmured Merlin. Asmethyum's voice had sounded quite sincere. 'Then, perhaps,' growled the Enchanter, 'thou'd care to be more specific in thine preprogrammed relevant responses.'

'No need to get snotty, Merlin,' replied the ancient creature. 'You don't think it's easy for me, not ever knowing what's happening to you!'

'Art thou still living then?'

'Probably. What year have you there?'

'Year of our Lord AD 570,' said Merlin.

'In that case, yes,' said Asmethyum. 'What was your question again?'

'I don't *know* the question, only that thou appeared to have the answer.'

'Hmmph . . . hmmph . . .'

Some sort of Eternity went by as the mind behind the voice pondered.

Finally it said, 'The question was, "How do I and Griswold get to the year 4097 without arriving over a period of several centuries in pieces the size of a gnat's testicle?"'

'Very succinct. And the answer?'

'You go by dragon,' said Asmethyum.

'So *that's* what she meant.'

'She? She who?'

'The woman, Falworthy,' said Merlin.

*

90

Outside the Enchanter's cottage Griswold was going through a whole new learning experience. The tatty sword was still tatty. Its blade, which Griswold had discovered was engraved with a very faint E, was still blunt and its gemstone was, if anything, duller than ever.

The only change Griswold noticed was that now the sword talked to him.

'Execute an overhead block and bring me round to open up your opponent's left ribcage,' said Excalibur.

Dutifully Griswold raised his arm to ward off the imaginary blow and winced as the sword resisted his efforts and took its own path. It twisted in his hand to adopt an acute angle that was quite new to Griswold, and it cut through the air so quickly that his hand was dragged with it faster than he had ever moved it himself. With a twist and a hiss it slid back into the scabbard. The whole movement had taken less than a second. Griswold grasped his wrist and massaged it.

'Has it occurred to you that you don't need me?' he asked.

'I cannot function without a master,' said Excalibur. 'A weapon of itself has no purpose.'

'Then you need a better man than I.'

'You *are* a better man than you,' said the sword. 'You just need to reach your potential.'

'How?'

'Basic mechanics. You are centuries out of date with this wielding and swinging nonsense. Have you noticed anything unusual about me?'

'Apart from being a pain in the—'

'Apart from that.'

'No.'

'You haven't noticed that I'm nearly a foot shorter than the average double-edged sword. And I'm considerably lighter.'

'Well, yes . . .'

'Well, get your facts right first time, Griswold.'

Excalibur glinted dully in the evening sunlight.

'How about getting to the point?' snapped Griswold.

'Was that meant to be a joke?'

'No!'

'Good. The point will reveal itself in due course *if* you deign to do as you are told. We will block and sweep once more, slowly. I will show you what you are doing wrong.'

'Wrong! I've survived more than twenty years doing it wrong!'

'You have survived twenty years because your enemies were equally inept. Block and sweep, please.'

Griswold gripped Excalibur in both hands and raised it slowly until it was suspended horizontally above his head.

'Wrong,' said the sword. 'You fly in the face of natural laws. All you achieve by holding me thus is bruised hands and, more importantly, my cutting edge becomes damaged, my blade shattered possibly.'

'And my brain remains unmangled,' said Griswold tightly.

'There are more effective ways,' intoned Excalibur. 'Several, in fact. Now listen and do us both a considerable favour.'

'It's a long story,' said Asmethyum matter-of-factly. 'But, seeing as you've not got much time, I'll skip it and give you the bare facts.'

'Can I have a stretch first?' groaned Merlin. 'My legs are killing me.'

'You can, but I've no guarantee that you'll get me back if you break off now. If I remember rightly . . .'

A long pause stretched itself across Merlin's mind like a worm looking for its other end.

'Well?' he said.

'. . .'

'Come on. What dost thou remember rightly?'

'Oh, yes. Of course. Don't wake up. My place in your mind has become increasingly tenuous in your latter years.

If you return to consciousness now, you might never be able to recall me.'

The Enchanter resigned himself to his own aching legs and his father's obscure ramblings.

'Where were we?' said the ancient being.

'The dragon,' murmured Merlin.

'Dragon, dragon, dragon,' repeated Asmethyum. 'Drag . . . Ah. Here we are. Dragon, Dragonus Dragoni . . .'

He gave the distinct impression that he was reading from an encyclopaedia.

'. . . member of earliest reptilia. Common ancestor of several diverse species, most of whom are now extinct, including Tyrannosaurus Rex, Stegosaurus, Pterodactyl—'

'Is this relevant?' Merlin interrupted.

'Highly,' replied Asmethyum mildly. 'The dragon is the most ancient and noble of all creatures.'

Merlin said nothing, so Asmethyum continued.

'Long and short is, dragons are almost extinct, themselves. Might be completely so by the time you call me up.'

'I didn't call thee—'

'Anyway, just in case they *were* still about, and you needed one, which you appear to do, I left a sort of message in a bottle for you. Only pop to the surface if there wasn't any other option.'

'There isn't,' said Merlin.

'Quite right. Dragon's your only answer.'

'Well. Where *is* this dragon?'

'Where it usually is, Merlin! Picture it in y'mind. Gods, have you forgotten everything about deterministic visualization? Make the image appear and then you'll know where to look for it. The real one, that is.'

'Understood. So how is it that I could not find the location of thine message?'

'Heh, heh! You didn't look back far enough.'

'Ah.'

'I did it when you were no more than a finger's length in size and six weeks conceived. Pretty neat, aye?'

'Pretty neat. And dost thou have any more secrets from the womb that thou wouldst confide to me?' sighed the Enchanter.

'Go look for the dragon, my son,' said Asmethyum. 'And good luck.'

Before Merlin realized it, he was fully conscious and alone.

Briefly he yearned for that time long ago, when the tides of his mother's body had ebbed and flowed warmly around him and his father had dropped a bottle with a message into the waves.

19

AD 1993

King's Cross Station and the surrounding streets are alive with activity for twenty-four hours every day. In daylight hours the rush of taxis, buses and cars race past, creating a constant flow of noise punctuated by the occasional oath and exhortation from the less experienced, philosophical or courageous of their drivers.

During the hours between early evening and early morning the pace slows. The air sings to more blatant forms of exhortation laced with more explicit oaths. The screech and squeal of rubber on tarmac yields to the squeak of a different kind of rubber in the quieter thoroughfares and the furtive squeal from participants participating in history's oldest profession.

Such noises were currently wafting through the open window of a two-room habitation overlooking the short, cobbled road which lay behind King's Cross Station and which was named, with prophetic aptness, Clarence Passage. But the inhabitant of the room was completely indifferent to the noise.

Instead he bent to his task. Although his room was no more than ten feet by twelve, it was filled with components and instruments, many of which would be familiar to an indigenous observer, but which were put together so as to create a machine bearing very little resemblance to anything ever seen on Earth.

The inhabitant had been forced to remove the door to use every last inch of space. He had reconstructed it to open outwards. His landlord had found this particularly irksome at first and had, therefore, asked two gentlemen of his acquaintance to explain to the tenant that the landlord required the tenant to return the door to its original position and then to vacate the premises, both to be done within the next eight hours. When the two gentlemen did not return after three weeks had elapsed, the landlord approached the tenant with three more acquaintances, a renewed request and a crowbar. The tenant asked them to come in, showed them to the bathroom, and allowed the landlord to leave ten minutes later. The landlord agreed that the door could stay as it was. Furthermore, since the tenant could not afford to buy food, let alone pay his rent, the landlord thought it only fair to waive the latter. Similarly, he saw no particular reason to advise the authorities that the electricity needed for his tenant's crucial research was supplied through the line connected directly to the national grid by way of the lamp post just outside the building.

Instead he wandered through the streets for several days with a haunted look in his eyes before returning to King's Cross Station where he effectively prevented any trains from entering the station at Platform Two for the next three hours.

A fluid hum and a soft glow filled the room as the creature worked on. His eyes had relinquished their constant glare of hostility and replaced it with a contemplative gaze laced with cold purpose. He wore blue dungarees, from which he had cut three feet off the legs because they had once been worn by a man twice his height. He also wore a yellow woolly hat with which he always covered his ears. At the moment his feet were bare. He was now at the final stage of his labours, fine-tuning his creation, and his concentration was total. Now he would be 'humming', or rather snuffling, a little song that began, 'Heigh ho'. Now he would work in silence, his moist, grey tongue distending one stubbly cheek and threatening to pop from out between his enormous, grotesquely sensual lips.

In the centre of the room was the machine proper. It resembled, remotely, a Star Wars game in an amusement arcade. It had a seat, a console and it was surrounded by a protective cage, but it seemed to be less of a material thing than a collection of auras held together by interlocking gauzes. In the centre of the console lay a large crystal, rather tasteless and gaudy, which seemed to be waiting like a gross queen bee to be fed by the little streaks of light skittering through the air around it. The whole machine was held in suspension at a point three millimetres above the floor, a necessary precaution to prevent it from smashing through the floor boards to the basement four rooms below.

The creature worked on.

As the first streaks of dawn appeared, the night sounds became less promiscuous and more commercially orientated. He laid down his screwdriver, dug a filthy handkerchief from his pocket and flicked an imaginary speck of dust from the console.

The machine was finished and his confidence in his ability was complete. He felt no need to have a trial run. He was, after all, the longest-living gnome in the construction business.

He stared out of the window.

Not long now, he thought. Not long now, Dimmot.

The contemplative gaze faded and the familiar glare returned to his eyes, but with a colder, harsher edge to it.

But now it was time for a spot of breakfast. He tucked his handkerchief into his pocket and turned towards the bathroom.

His name was Scarbald.

20

AD 1987

It was another three weeks before James Dimmot dared to pick up the manual again. He immediately wished he hadn't. The pages he had already read remained blank, but on the next page new words appeared as if written by an invisible scribe. The book rustled in his trembling hands as the first few lines settled themselves comfortably on to the page.

'James Dimmot,' they read, 'by the time thou reads this, mine bones will have crumbled to dust many centuries since. Mine soul will have found a place to rest, I hope.'

Dimmot swallowed and read on.

'Meantimes, I leave thee a gift, from one friend to another. Thou didst once do mineself and others a great service and thou art deserving of a better fate than that for which thou art destined.'

How would you know? thought Dimmot uneasily. Although he was more than willing to put this hallucination down to the contents of the glass in his hand, a little tingle of Reality persisted in tugging at his mental trouser leg like a wary puppy.

'Thou wilt wonder how I know this,' went on the manual. 'Concern thyself not with such wondering, but read me throughout. Follow these words carefully and, one day, a far greater destiny will be thine.'

Already the words at the top of the page were beginning to vanish. Those that followed were dark and ominous and sort of gothic-looking. They seemed to imply dark, castley dungeons and things with levers and chains on.

'However,' they went, 'if thou strays from the path of the righteous, thine fate will be . . . fateful.'

Thanks, thought Dimmot. I don't need this crap.

He gulped the contents of his glass in one go, feeling the comforting burn slide down inside him, and once more tossed the manual across the room. It landed on the edge of the bed, slid (not ungratefully, since the sheets hadn't been changed in six months), on to the floor and lay open in the dust. Dimmot reached for his bottle and promptly forgot about it.

Which is as it should be. One shouldn't have to absorb too much of a totally alien concept in one go. He shambled to his piano, which still stood where he had pulled it away from the wall three weeks ago, and lowered himself on to the stool. His fingers slid lovingly across the keys and gradually organized themselves into a gentle melody, faintly reminiscent of a song that he had played many times over the years. But now it was accompanied by the unearthly harmonies that had captured his soul since his return from the Last Dark Age. Although the dreadful memories of that journey had been buried mercifully beyond his reach, the music he had experienced came creeping to the surface of his mind like a tiny tenacious root seeking the light of the sun. For Dimmot the song, or indeed any song, would never be the same.

Sometimes, he thought, I wonder where I get it from.

In the early February gloom the lonely, mercilessly beautiful notes of 'Blue Moon' crept out into the cold evening air.

21

AD 570

In the county of Sussex, just east of Horsham and west of Pease Pottage, is St Leonard's Forest. Within the forest are the Lily Beds, named thus because they are riddled with lilies of the valley. It is said that in the sixth century a fearsome dragon ruled the forest, terrorizing the neighbourhood, demanding virgin pâtés and generally making a nuisance of itself. St Leonard, a passing holy man, did stretch the bounds of credibility by entering the forest alone and emerging ten minutes later, claiming to have slain the dragon. He was, admittedly, well-bloodied and the story is that, wherever his blood fell, the lilies sprang up. And so they did, despite the ground being covered in thorn bushes.

As it happens, St Leonard apparently failed to deliver the goods, since rumours of hideous creatures lingered on well into the nineteenth century.

A rather loose translation from *Folklore,
Myths and Legends of Britain,*
published by Reader's Digest, 1973

The dragon was thirty feet long, its wingspan some forty feet from tip to tip. Draped around a jagged outcrop of rock in the centre of a forest clearing with the pearly glow from its scales throwing gentle shadows against the trees, it slept. Well, most of it slept. The quiet breath from two pairs of nostrils sent pungent cross-currents of air drifting across the clearing, adding a certain spice to the pervading smell of lily of the valley. The occasional sigh from the third pair of nostrils testified to the sheer, unmitigated boredom that was born of their owner's thirty-year spell of guard duty. There was nobody to talk to. All the things one had to think about one had thought about.

Ingrid, the middle head of the three, was by far the oldest, wisest and tiredest. Her large, red-tinted eyes had lost much of their sparkle. Her long slender neck was the original that had come with the body eight centuries ago. Wrinkled folds of skin hung from it and some of its scales were a little skew-whiff.

That she had only another five years of keeping watch while the other two slept was small consolation. She laid her chin on her claws and thought about nothing in particular.

The crack of a distant twig brought her head up slowly and ponderously. She stared without enthusiasm into the gloom. Rhon, the head on her right, and Liz on her left slept on. After a few moments the brush of metal against branch caught her ear. The long hair on her jaws and temples rose and reached out, testing the air for the nature of the intrusion. The sound stirred up old memories and Ingrid gave a sigh.

Armour, she thought. Recognize that sound anywhere.

Two tiny figures pushed their way through the undergrowth and waded through the lilies until they came to a halt before her. One was old with white whiskers and piercing blue eyes. He wore the plain robes of a magician. The other one with a bushy black beard carried a sword at his side and a shield on his arm. He was completely covered in chain-mail and plate.

Knew it, thought Ingrid.

The two figures looked up at her.

'*Is this the best you can come up with?*' said the larger one.

'A little respect for a noble creature would not come amiss,' hissed the other.

'Noble?' said the big knight. He pointed a gauntleted

hand at her. 'It is an affront to the very word. *It's completely knackered.'*

He seemed to be saying two things simultaneously.

Odd, thought Ingrid. Must be a new species. Looks remarkably . . . solid.

'When's it going to attack?' asked the big one.

'In her own good time.'

'How about if I go up and waggle my sword at it?'

'At her!'

'Her.'

'No.'

'Why?'

''Tis against the law.'

'What law!'

'Nature's law, fool! Dragons attack men. Men don't "waggle their swords" at dragons. 'Tis demeaning.'

'I wouldn't feel demeaned,' retorted the knight.

'For the dragon, fool!'

They stared at Ingrid in silence. Before she could stop it her mouth had stretched wide and she was drawing a deep breath. The big man stepped in front of the other with his shield raised. Ingrid finished the yawn and gave a weak cough. A thin trickle of smoke dribbled from her nostrils and hovered uncertainly as if wondering what to do next.

'*Good grief,*' grumbled the bushy one. '*This is embarrassing*/Do we have to go through with it? *Surely you can just tell it what you need without all this rigmarole.*'

'There are rituals to be observed,' replied the little one, stepping back into view. 'Procedures.'

He paused and added awkwardly, 'Traditions.'

Ingrid began to wonder if someone was under a misconception.

Then the big knight called the small man 'Merlin' and everything became clear.

The sun beat a dappled path through the glittering leaves and danced across the three figures residing in the lily bed.

Griswold had removed most of his armour and he sprawled on the warm ground, propped up on one elbow while Merlin sat cross-legged with his hands resting on his knees. Ingrid's body had unwrapped itself from the rock and was stretched out on its stomach with Ingrid's head hovering a few feet from the ground. Since Ingrid's head was as large as Griswold himself, the significance of its proximity was not lost on either of them. Ingrid had woken her other heads and they lay amongst the lilies carefully watching the two men.

'Those times are past, old friend,' Ingrid was saying. 'Such traditions have long disappeared from the Earth. In any case, dragons are a dying race. We haven't the numbers to spare on outmoded rituals that tend to result in our coming off second best. Modern weapons and all that. In fact, I'm given to understand that I might be the only dragon left. Only three-headed one, anyway.'

Merlin nodded sympathetically. 'And yet,' he said, 'men still feed off thy reputation and seek glory at the expense of thine auspicious name.'

'Mmm,' said Ingrid absently. 'Still, it's good to know that you and I do not have to come to blows this time.' She looked at Griswold. 'Especially blows dealt by him. He is a powerful-looking lad, Merlin. Reminds me of the warrior that helped bring this one' . . . She pointed with her chin towards Rhon, whose eyes were staring intently at Griswold . . .'into the world.'

Without taking his eyes from those of the youngest dragon-head Griswold said, 'How so?'

'Oh, about forty years back a young knight, bit younger than you, and I met up some distance to the west of here. Brash little devil, he was, but very hot on tradition, so we had a real old ding-dong. He managed to slice off my right-hand head just below the jaw. Rhon's predecessor. We were pretty furious as you can imagine.'

The two men nodded.

'Brave lad, I have to admit, but absolutely out of date in

his ideas. Anyway, as you know,' she said to Merlin, 'I can't fulfil my purpose without all my faculties, so a few months later this little rascal began to sprout.'

She glanced at Rhon once again. He had now abandoned his attempts to outstare Griswold and was concentrating his attention on Liz who had twined herself round Ingrid's neck to get a better view of the knight. It was apparent that Rhon probably spent most of his waking hours leering at Liz (which was all he could do when you think about it) or sneering at anything that crossed his field of vision.

'He seems to be a typically healthy youngster,' observed Merlin. 'If a little impractical in his desires. How fares his training?'

'To tell the truth, I haven't had the opportunity to test his skills before his last sleep period, but he's very bright. I don't doubt that he would be up to scratch already.' Ingrid gave the wizard a sideways glance. 'Why do you ask?' she said.

'Because we have need of thy services. I must make a journey of some considerable distance.'

'How considerable, old friend?'

'Two days' ride in miles, three thousand years in years,' said Merlin.

'A somewhat simplistic answer, but I get your meaning,' said Ingrid.

Griswold stirred impatiently and the young dragon-head turned sharply towards him.

'Hold your breath, Rhon,' murmured Ingrid. 'Or you'll find yourself sucking cinders.'

Rhon sneered. 'You'll only be happy when he shoves his sword up your nose, won't you? You can't trust humans any more than you can trust gnomes. You should know that.'

'Shut up,' intoned Ingrid. She turned again to Merlin. 'Where exactly do you need to go to?'

'Er, well. I hadn't actually thought of that,' replied

Merlin. 'I'd thought we'd reach the correct point in Time and then find the place from there.'

'Not as simple as that,' said Ingrid. 'That is not the dragon's *modus operandi*. The place that one travels to is as important as the Time, since that is the place that occupies a certain point in space at a certain point in Time. The farther one travels in Time, the more one needs to have a definite place to aim for. Without that, one could be a thousand miles, or years, off target.'

Merlin cast a quick glance at Griswold. The knight was watching him with a grin spread across his face.

'Well, of course. This is common knowledge.' The old lips gave a twitch and a slight tinge of colour appeared on Merlin's ears. 'The place is London. I trust thou knows where London is?'

Since Ingrid took great pride in her abilities she recognized it in others, even humans. She also knew what it felt like to have it mocked by inferiors.

'I know it, Merlin. You have a specific time in mind?'

'The year 4097.'

'Very precise,' smiled the dragon. 'I commend your diligence.'

The slight straightening of Merlin's thin shoulders and his barely perceptible nod of gratitude went unnoticed by Griswold and Rhon.

'Is that all thou needs to know?' said Merlin.

'Ideally I would require a specific Event,' said Ingrid.

Dragons have always known the secret of travelling through Time. They were born knowing it. It's only humans who haven't discovered it, which is why they call it a secret.

Humans were actually due to discover this secret around the thirtieth century when they should have been ready for it. The original formula, $E = MC^2$, was launched on its maiden voyage into the murky ocean of Global Consciousness by Asmethyum himself shortly before he planted the knowledge of the dragons into the mind of a magical foetus. The formula was meant to have started out as an insignificant little coracle, only blossoming into a full-sailed galleon on its arrival in the New World of Man's enlightenment. However, it was no more than a small frigate when, in AD 1905, it passed close to the land of one A. Einstein, a renegade thinker who was currently trying to launch a theory that would justify his beliefs about the nature of space and time. He jumped, as revolutionaries tend to do when they are in a hurry, aboard the first boat to come along. Shouting *'Eureka. Ich hab'es'*, he sailed into posterity by adapting the frigate to suit his beliefs and steering it, still not finished (in fact, still at the $E = MC^2$ stage) into waters which it was not equipped to enter. It went down in history, still known as $E = MC^2$, its full potential unreached, leaving Man unable to fathom the true nature of its original voyage.

Had Albert Einstein been born one thousand years later he might have discovered the principles of time travel instead of just coming up with some half-formed nonsense about energy and mass and stuff, and wasting a perfectly good formula on it in the process.

Thank heavens for dragons.

'What dost thou mean, a specific Event?' Merlin frowned.

'To complete the formula,' replied Ingrid patiently. '$E = MC^3$. Event = Moment in time $\times$ 3 Coordinates. The coordinates are the three-dimensional configuration giving an exact position in space, relating to an exact moment in Time.'

'I didn't realize it was that simple,' said Merlin drily. 'What sort of Event wouldst thou suggest?'

22

AD 4097!

It was time for Archeous to leave. His army of elite demons had been hand-picked down to the last man, woman and any-variation-you-care-to-name-in-between. They sat hunched and shrouded in silence. Archeous was reminded of the old war films showing rows of Special Services troops sitting in Dakotas waiting for the signal to throw themselves and their two hundred pounds of death-dealing equipment into the pitch-black night over enemy territory. No matter how long you've churned in the boiling pits of Hell, you never quite banish the trepidation that surrounds the idea of having your bits shot away. So the demons sat in silence, apart from the odd nervous fidget when steam puffed from splitting skin.

Archeous liked war films. He had spent much of his corpulent youth in the darkness of the local cinemas, revelling in the death and mayhem, the blood and the mud, the 'gore of war', as he liked to call it. Not that his only motive was homicidal voyeurism. Archeous' . . . Walter White's other reason for going to the cinema was to do with proximity to the opposite gender where the opportunity for maximum experimentation at minimum risk of recognition prevailed. Although the opposite gender were often less than willing to return Walter's advances, he was not overly concerned. He always had the silver screen with its blood-spattered, explosive, percussive . . . persuasive stimulation to sublimate a personal lust that was adaptable in terms of its outlets. When, occasionally, his fumbling overtures found a response, the music of scream, tank and field-gun provided a sublime orchestration to his part of the duet.

'As you can see,' said Lucifer, pointing at the purple sky, 'it'll be a bit of a squeeze.'

His beautiful white wings reflected the light from the evening sky in a soft mauvish pink and his face showed a little of his immense age as the long shadows of a low bleak-red sun slanted flatly across the rocky terrain. Lucifer, Archeous and his army had travelled overland for six weeks to reach this spot. Don't believe that stuff about Hell being infinite and demons breaking through the nearby dimensions into our Earthly world and all that.

Hell is like an apple pie.

It stands on the plate that we call our galaxy and every galaxy has its own Hell, its own pie. Like apple pies everywhere, it is round, relatively flat and steaming hot inside, although 'steaming' is putting it mildly. The only way to leave Hell is to reach the outer edge of the pie and go through the crack where the crust meets the rim of the plate.

'See where those clouds appear to be lying on the horizon?' said Lucifer.

Archeous stared myopically into the distance. The low, flat-bottomed clouds that dotted the sky with black disinterest appeared to get lower and lower as they neared the edge of the Netherworld, some two or three miles ahead.

'What of them?' said Archeous, pulling his red silk cloak tightly about him. He had never realized that there were parts of Hell that could actually be downright cold. He shivered and, for the very first time since arriving in Hell, he was thankful for the comforting warmth of a robe, although he would naturally have preferred something a little less gaudy, something in black or grey, perhaps. With pinstripes.

'Those clouds signal the very edge of our world,' Lucifer was saying. 'The outer reaches of Hell. All you have to do is squeeze under the clouds, drop down to the galaxy and head for Earth.'

'Seems a hell of a long way round,' said Archeous tightly. 'Why don't we take the direct route, like you do to Cygnus?'

'Because the direct route, as you call it, involves my dissolving into my constituent elements and reassembling myself at my destination. Do you fancy doing that?'

He gave Archeous a knowing smile.

'How am I expected to find the Earth when we leave here?'

Lucifer waved his hand to the silent, seated army. 'There are plenty of souls here who will guide you. Mr Savage!' he called.

From the edge of the crowd the creature known as Mr Savage rose to his feet. Archeous noticed that Mr Savage left a shallow pool of pinkish liquid on the ground.

'You're looking a lot better today, Mr Savage,' said Lucifer with a smile. The hole in Mr Savage's throat was almost closed up. Only a thin trickle, similar to the one on the ground, seeped from a small slit. He took a pace forward.

'Still a little anaemic, Lucifer, but getting better by the day.'

'Good to see, Mr Savage. Good to see.'

Lucifer turned to Archeous. 'Mr Savage was a platoon sergeant in the British Army on your world. Saw lots of action. Bit of a survivor. He and his lads . . . "copped it in the siege of Hong Kong", turn of the twentieth century, wasn't it?'

'S'right,' said Mr Savage. 'Twenty o two. Lost my whole platoon. Temporarily.'

'Sorry?' said Archeous. This was by way of a question. Archeous had never felt sorry for anyone else in his entire existence. It wasn't cost-effective.

'Mr Savage and his men were a little less than honourable in their dealings with the locals. In fact, they were destined for damnation from the day they were born.'

He gave Mr Savage a nod and the ex-sergeant called over his shoulder, 'Troopshun.'

From the sea of silent heads a score of isolated figures rose to their feet. They stood loosely, waiting. Mr Savage looked at Lucifer who gave a nod in return.

'P'toon fall in,' he said. The figures broke their stillness and came forward. Each one gave out the air of easy indifference that only the trained survivor of death is privy to. All the creatures sitting in their path shuffled aside to let them through. Only the fully fledged demons, whom nobody argued with, remained where they were and the soldiers sidled round them with nonchalant sneers. In a few moments the complete platoon stood before Lucifer and Archeous, if you allow for the odd leg or stomach that hadn't made the journey from Hong Kong to Hell. Lucifer appraised them fondly.

'These gentlemen will be your guides,' he told the demon. 'They've made the journey several times, including the last abortive effort of your predecessor, so they are well equipped to cope with both the travelling and its ensuing consequences.'

'They didn't cope with the consequences too successfully on the last trip,' observed Archeous caustically. 'Why should I think they'll do any better this time?'

The tremor that swept through both the platoon and the parts of the army that caught his remark was palpable. Mr Savage's lips drew back to reveal strong white teeth as he gave the demon a gentle, rather warm smile. His eyes glinted.

'Last time,' said Lucifer, 'they did not have my future successor to lead them.' He laid a featherlight hand on Archeous' shoulder. 'You'd best be on your way. Good luck and *au revoir*.'

Archeous walked towards the platoon.

'I'll lead the way until we reach the border,' he said.

'Then you and your men will accompany me as guides and personal guards. Is that clear?'

Mr Savage cast a fleeting glance towards the angel then nodded silently. Without another word Archeous strode past him and headed for the horizon.

Lucifer watched the demon thoughtfully for a moment. Then he spoke quietly.

'Mr Savage,' he said. 'A word in your shell-shocked before you go.'

23

AD 3000 . . . give or take

Ingrid swooped low over the English countryside, her heads swivelling slowly, her eyes idly scanning the terrain for signs of life. Her air speed was no more than forty miles per hour, but since she was travelling simultaneously through Time at around ten times the speed of light signs of life, and all other signs, were mere twinkles on a sun-flecked river.

The days and nights flashing by, twelve of each to the second, merged into a grey misty haze. The seasons skimmed past, changing the meadows and trees from summer green to autumn grey and winter white. The planet, shifting, living and dying, circled through its annual transformations with blinding regularity. Around the dragon-heads, sunlit cirrus and thunder-black nimbus clouds constantly burst into view, then boiled and vanished so quickly that the eyes could not register them.

To Merlin and Griswold, wedged firmly between the dragon's scaly shoulder blades, the view was decidedly stroboscopic.

'Thou seems to have a singularly casual approach to thine task,' called Merlin sourly.

The speed of Ingrid's path through ordinary space whipped up a wind that tore at their hair and clothes and brought blinding tears to their eyes. The *whoompp, whoompp* of her massive wings beat a pounding rhythm in their ears and the rolling motion of each beat lifted and dropped her body with nauseous predictability.

'I like to enjoy the view,' grinned Ingrid over her shoulder. The whiskers on her three jaws flicked and flapped over her necks and the not unpleasant smell of her smoky breath gusted past the nostrils of the two men. 'To tell the truth,' she called, 'we are having to take it more carefully now. We're in unknown territory. Timewise, that is.'

'How so?'

'We've never travelled this far before. We're nearing the . . . er?'

Ingrid turned her head enquiringly to her left.

'Thirty-first century,' said Liz.

'. . . thirty-first century. The year of the Last Trump approaches. If I understand you correctly, what lies beyond then is something that even you have been unable to foresee.'

'We only returned from there three days ago,' explained Merlin. 'I haven't had the time to devote to it.'

'No rest for the wicked, eh?'

'Or for the righteous,' said Merlin tightly. 'The year was 3797. How long will it take us to reach it?'

'Six hours, thirty,' rumbled Liz.

'Just over six hours,' said Ingrid. 'And another two hours to reach the Event, *if* that Event is when and where you say it will be.'

'It will be,' said Merlin with conviction.

He leaned over and glanced down at the ground, trying in vain to make some sense of the churning kaleidoscope of images below them. After a few seconds he sat back, screwed up his eyes and swallowed deeply.

'Wouldst thou care to enlighten us as to *where* we are right now?' he asked weakly.

Rhon, who had been squinting up at the scorching ring of fire that marked the sun flashing across the sky twelve times each second, turned his head to leer down at the tiny figure.

'We're coming to the country's capital. You *do* know where that is, I suppose?' he said.

'If thou means the stench-filled cesspit that calls itself London, I know it all too well and frequently.'

They had been flying for nearly twenty hours, during which Griswold had methodically geared himself to sleep every other hour. Merlin had dozed fitfully throughout. When he wasn't worrying about missing anything during the wondrous and probably unique experience, he was worrying about abusing his hostess's hospitality by shedding his last meal over her creaking, windswept scales.

Griswold, sitting behind him, found the Enchanter's discomfort too acute to resist.

'S'what comes of journeying hither and yon the easy way through your pin-holes in Time.' He grinned. 'If you made more use of your horse, you'd be used to a bumpy ride.'

When you spend a good deal of your time in the midst of brawls, mud-churned battlefields and cacophonous turmoil, you soon develop the technique of taking in what you need and filtering out what you don't. Griswold had quickly grown used to the bewildering array of images tumbling before his eyes. He sat easily in the groaning saddle of Ingrid's spine, carefully honing away at Excalibur with a whetstone.

'This shoddy dagger of yours will make a fine weapon,' he called, 'when I want to club a cabbage to death.'

'Still thy tongue, ingrate,' hissed Merlin. 'Thou knowest nothing of Excalibur's innate magicality.'

'Nope, I dost not. Nor does Excalibur by the look of it. I've been trying to sharpen its blade for two days.'

He leaned forward and slapped the flat of the blade on to Merlin's thin shoulder.

'See?'

The Enchanter reached up and grudgingly fingered the sword's cutting edge. It was as blunt as when he had first given it to Griswold. He lowered his hand and drew his cloak more tightly about him. Staring into the sky between the dragon's waving necks, he pondered, not for the first time, about the nature of Fate.

Thou givest me the means by which to reach an impossible destination, he thought sourly, then thou renders useless the one instrument that stands a hope of destroying mine enemy. Thine sense of humour is without equal.

Griswold raised the blade from his shoulder. 'Well,' he said. 'How is it that, of all the swords I've had, this "magical" blade is the only one that defies my stone?'

'It has been in the lake for many years,' said Merlin weakly. 'It needs time to . . . dry out.'

Before Griswold could think of a suitably irreverent reply, the Enchanter changed the subject. Leaning forward very carefully, he spoke into Ingrid's large tufted ear.

'I take it that, once thou reaches the Event I have decreed, setting down will present no difficulty.'

The dragon's wings slowed noticeably. The wind decreased and, below them, the passing of seconds and seasons quickly wound down from a grey blur to distinguishable changes in Nature's yearly colours.

'Time for a breather,' said the dragon. 'We'll coast for a while and rest on the wing.'

The massive wings ceased their beating and she glided on the thermals of Time flowing beneath.

'In answer to your question,' she said, 'setting down can present some difficulty. The trouble with trying to land from the past, down-wind so to speak, is that you can't see where you're landing because it hasn't happened. If you're not a skilled flyer, you could smash into any of the events leading up to the Event that you wish to reach,' Ingrid explained patiently. 'You might even knock *that* Event out of existence. Find yourself trying to land on something which isn't there any longer.'

Griswold lounged back with Excalibur resting across his knees. He had slipped the whetstone into his pocket and was gazing with renewed interest at the Earth below. The world had stopped whirling and across a summer-green meadow a tiny speck crawled with snail-like tenacity.

'On the other hand,' Ingrid was saying, 'if you come in from the future, you can see the Event clearly because it has already happened.'

Merlin's face cleared marginally. 'Ah. 'Tis plain, then, that thou must . . . circle round . . .?'

Ingrid nodded.

'. . . and make thine approach from the future!' Merlin grinned smugly.

Ingrid shook her head. The hair on her jaws and temples flowed up and down like marine flora.

'Would that it were that simple, old friend.'

Merlin scowled. 'It is for me,' he said evenly. 'Was,' he added. 'Why is it not that simple?'

'Time is its own master, as well you know, old friend. It heeds not the needs of men or dragons. It rushes on apace and never once slackens the speed of its passing. To approach it from the future is to . . .'

Ingrid faltered, trying to find a picture that would explain her meaning to the Enchanter.

'To try mounting a horse that's galloping straight towards *you*/thee,' said Griswold absently. The speck had a vaguely familiar look about it.

Merlin glared. 'Fool!' he said. 'What dost *thou*—'

'The lad's right, Merlin,' Ingrid interposed. 'To approach from the past is like running with the horse and trying to mount it blindfolded. To approach from the future is to see

114

the horse clearly as it bears down on you at an impractical speed.'

'Art thou telling me,' said Merlin grittily, 'at this stage in our journey, that thou canst be of no service to me?'

Ingrid turned her great head towards Griswold. 'What do you think?' she said.

'The craftsman whose skills are complete has no need to boast of them, even to little children,' replied Griswold. 'Since you see no need to boast to us . . .'

The shrug of his shoulders was reflected in Ingrid's dark, reptile eyes. She smiled a smoky smile.

'My skills are without equal, Merlin,' she said reassuringly. 'Indeed, they would be even if I were not the only one of my kind left.'

To Griswold's keen eyes the speck had become a man, barely visible against the greenery, galloping a horse of indeterminate colour across the countryside. He was the only sign of life on an otherwise totally unpopulated landscape.

'Have no fear, old friend,' said Ingrid to the Enchanter. 'We can take you to the time and place that you request and we can land you safely. Does that answer your question?'

'In part,' said the Enchanter. 'How dost thou propose to mount the horse that intends to stamp thee into the ground?'

Ingrid's teeth, none of which was less than nine inches long, glinted dully in the rapidly failing light.

'No bother. We hover,' she said.

'And what about getting us back?'

'Ah . . .'

The hesitation in her voice brought Griswold's eyes round with a start. He smiled at his brief feeling of alarm. He knew the feel of a good and loyal steed whenever he felt one beneath his buttocks, be it horse, mule, woman or indeed dragon. He turned back to watch the worm-slow progress of the figure below.

But it had vanished.

24

AD 1994

'It's chaos down there. You might as well stay in bed.'
Jazz FM, *Evening Standard* Sky Patrol,
somewhere over the M25 (1994)

Deep within the layers of his eiderdown quilt, James Dimmot tried to remember what life was like before he had become a musical success and a multimillionaire.

He used to drink less, eat less and think about women nearly as much. He didn't work anywhere near as hard before, but on the whole life in the old days was pretty foul.

No friends, no happiness, no purpose.

Nothing.

Now he had everything. Friends were always around, sleeping in one of his thirteen bedrooms, drinking his wines and lobbing the bottles through his windows into the Thames thirteen storeys below.

He peeped out from under the cover. One dull red eyeball swivelled, taking in the wide expanse of his bedroom, the Laura Ashley wallpaper, the plush curtains, the lush wall-to-wall Axminster.

'Who could wish f'more?' he mumbled. The eyeball blinked and, as if summoned by the action, its companion appeared beside it in the gloom. Together they peered up at the ceiling. Then they stared at nothing in particular while the brain behind them applied itself to summoning up the will power to drag the body out of bed. But the body wasn't taking calls right then. The eyeballs sunk beneath their lids. Only James Dimmot's mouth moved, rolling clumsily round the words that rarely failed to bring him back to life, sobriety or reality. He had picked them up about eight years ago, though he couldn't for the life of him remember where or when. *Reader's Digest* probably.

'Man's graidess' glorri,' he murmured, 'lies in the strength of his will.' He threw the cover off the bed, sat up and said firmly, 'Right, folks. It's show time.'

He ran his fingers through his hair, plucked the dictaphone from his bedside cabinet and steered his scrawny frame towards the en-suite shower.

By the time he had reached the door, he had booked two phone calls to the States and issued three orders to his secretary.

'Get the sound engineer to call me before nine and I want a full girls' choir for the Second Movement.'

Tossing the machine over his shoulder on to the bed with practised accuracy, he stepped into the shower and closed the door.

When he came out ten minutes later, the dictaphone had disappeared and his secretary had carried out two of his three orders from her office on the floor below. By the time James Dimmot entered her office, to which his was adjacent, she was scouring through her personal directory of contacts, looking for a supplier of choirs, female, ethereal symphonies for the enhancing of.

'I don't want any rubbish,' he said. 'They must be young, strident and devastatingly lovely down to the last one. Any dogs, kick'em out. How do I look?'

He was wearing a Royal Air Force greatcoat, which reached down to his ankles, a multi-coloured and multi-holed woollen scarf, green corduroy trousers and brown, open-toed sandals over bare feet.

'Do you really care?' asked Rosemary.

'About what you think?'

'No. How you look!'

'No, not really,' he said.

'Then don't ask.'

117

Dimmot had poached his secretary from one of his business acquaintances for three reasons. She was highly knowledgeable of, and experienced in, the music business. She was remarkably ugly and no source of distraction to Dimmot or any of his staff, except the most easily distracted and most easily fired. And she was named Rosemary. Only one man in the world was allowed to call her Rose.

'I knew someone called Rose, once,' Dimmot had told her. 'If I can call you Rose, the job's yours.'

Rose continued to scan the directory.

'Bugger off, Dimmot, and let me do my job,' she said.

'No chance of coffee? All right. I'll be at the Royal Fest, if you want me.'

He went into his office and came back with a small flat box very like a personal computer, shoved two earphones in his ears and pressed a switch. His head nodded vigorously. Giving Rose a flutter of fingers, he yelled, 'See you this afternoon!', and strode out conducting the unseen orchestra on his Walkman and giving a powerful impression of a man trying to wave away a swarm of hornets.

It could safely be said that James Dimmot was a self-made man. It could safely be said, simply because no one in the world, including James Dimmot, knew any better.

The fact is that the driving force behind his inspiration and his extraordinary degree of creativity came not from within him, but from a far distant source. One that couldn't be measured, unless one had access to instruments that worked in years as well as miles.

Centuries, actually.

When he walked into the Royal Festival Hall, the place was alive with activity. The stage was packed with unusual people doing unusual things to, for want of a better description, musical instruments.

The sounds, though quite uncoordinated and totally at

the mercy of the individual musicians, were, jointly and severally, magical.

As Dimmot walked briskly down the aisle towards the stage, one or two of the performers glanced up, gave various waves and returned to their music sheets. By the time Dimmot had reached the stage, every one of them was watching him carefully and in silence. Standing before the conductor's music stand, he turned off his Walkman, shoved it and the earphones into a voluminous pocket and slid the sleeves of his greatcoat up to his elbows, revealing thin, white forearms. He rummaged in another pocket, pulled out a pair of ancient, wire-rimmed glasses and set them on his nose.

He squinted at the music set out before him, gave a grunt of satisfaction and looked up.

'Hello,' he said to the members of the orchestra.

One hundred and fifty pairs of lungs relaxed quietly.

He was sober, drug-free and, temporarily at least, in control of his faculties.

Including his temper.

'Anybody got a baton?' said Dimmot.

Of all the musicians present in the Royal Festival Hall, only one was remotely aware of the true origin of Dimmot's inspirations, and that person wasn't actually James Dimmot.

Everyone believed that Dimmot was the creative genius behind the multi-rhythmed, incredibly complex themes and harmonic structures with their subtly shifting moods, heart-rending savagery and glorious climaxes. The squat, unspeaking creature who, in a flash of inspiration amounting to quantum proportions, called himself 'Mr Jones', knew better. He had heard those sounds before in another time and another place.

Mr Jones' eyes were permanently hidden behind enormous sunglasses and he wore a woolly hat pulled down to cover his ears. In the three years that he had been with the orchestra no one had ever seen him without his sunglasses and his woolly hat. Since every one of Dimmot's musicians was, as well as being a supreme artiste, thoroughly eccentric in character and dress, this was not considered unusual and no one had ever asked him to take them off.

He played a self-made instrument that didn't somehow lend itself to an accurate description. It was one of the few instruments in the world that one had to climb inside to play and it had a remarkably tasteless glass rock set in its centre. The sounds that it produced were so unEarthly as to give the impression that they emanated from a different dimension. This was a pretty accurate impression.

As Dimmot raised his baton the gnome rested his fingers on the console of his instrument. Dimmot's hand dropped and, as one man, the orchestra crashed into the opening chord of 'The Enchanter'. None of the instruments bore more than a passing resemblance to conventional instruments. While they observed the natural laws of sound and the usual methods of following those laws, they almost invariably appeared to have gone one step beyond those laws and methods.

As the first chords faded to give way to the initial bitter-sweet prelude, part of the 'string' section came in with a high tremulous keening which cut across itself to produce a shimmering sheet of sound like clingfilm hanging out in the sun. While there are normally thirteen different tones to choose from, the strings found tones between the tones and then more tones between those. Quarter tones, eighths and micro-tones, created by instruments whose multiple strings were interwoven and criss-crossed with more strings, vibrating in exquisite disharmony, pleading for resolution and the release from an agonizingly beautiful tension. Without ever rising above mezzo-forte the strings built up to an ear-rending degree of tension. Without being allowed to release the tension, they stopped, yielding abruptly to the bleak stridency of a single instrument.

A trumpet squeezed a thin, almost inaudible note out

into the cathedral silence. The note lingered above the orchestra, a solitary bird hovering high in the bluest sky. It wavered skilfully under the player's lips as he prepared to slide down the scale to where the timpani and woodwind were waiting to stir up a churning cauldron of thunder and screeching winds. Then the principal percussionist came in two bars early.

Ingrid was becoming rather concerned.

'Thirteen years and closing,' said Liz, peering into the blackness ahead. Ingrid nodded ponderously and turned her head to Rhon.

'Seven light hours and a bit to the left,' said Rhon uncertainly.

The dragon had slowed down to little more than light speed for the final approach and the Earth had suddenly fallen away out of sight, which was rather disturbing. Ingrid's instinctive guidance system could normally steer her through the swirling mists of Time even when the other two heads were working at half their capacity, but at this moment something was not quite right.

'Is something amiss?' squeaked a tiny voice behind her.

'Just lost track of the world. Nothing to worry about,' she replied.

'What is she talking about?' called Griswold.

''Tis nothing to worry about,' said Merlin.

'I'm not worried,' said Griswold. 'What did she mean by the world?'

'Big round ball. I'll explain one day.'

'If there is a "one day",' said Griswold.

He peered over the dragon's undulating back and saw only blackness where, minutes ago, there had been green fields and snow-filled passes.

Griswold stretched one aching leg, then the other, flexing his muscles vigorously to bring the life back into them. He slid Excalibur out of its sheath. The blackness, which seemed to begin where Ingrid's personal space ended, showed no signs of abating. Craning his neck to look over his shoulder, Griswold could just make out a dim glow, but since it was much farther away than he had ever experienced the distance meant nothing to him. All he knew was that the glow was where they had come from.

'It would be best to turn back and look for familiar ground before going on,' he suggested mildly.

'Don't be presumptuous, fool,' said Merlin. 'If that were necessary she would have done it.'

Without warning the movement of Ingrid's wings ceased and the undulations were no more than nauseous after-images.

'Hold on,' said the dragon. 'I'm going to turn back to find a landmark.' She gave Rhon a soulful stare. 'We seem to have got a little lost.'

She wheeled about, gracefully and silently, in a tight arc and straightened out to face the exact direction from which they had come. Since Merlin and Griswold were instantly disorientated by this manoeuvre, the dragon's consummate skill was lost on them. Griswold stared over Merlin's shoulder, but the distant glow was no longer in sight. He rose to his feet and balanced himself before staring round while Merlin scoured the area from the safety of his seat between Ingrid's dorsal scales.

'Dost see what I see?' said Griswold.

Merlin looked back sharply. 'No. What?'

'Nothing,' said Griswold.

Greatness had befallen James Dimmot and he did not know why, when or how, but he did know one thing.

He knew what to do with greatness.

'You're fired,' he snapped.

'Bullshit,' responded the drummer. 'You won't find a replacement for me in a year, never mind tonight.'

Dimmot slapped the baton on to the rostrum and shoved his hands into his overcoat pockets. He stared down at his sandals.

'You're fired anyway,' he said.

'Why?' said the drummer whose name, though imma-terial, was Kevin. When he stood up, which was rarely, he was six feet two inches tall, slimmer than when he sat down, which meant that he was scrawny, and he only washed when he shaved. He had a four-day stubble and he wore a leather flying helmet. Mention of Kevin here only serves to illustrate Dimmot's attitude to his own newly acquired power. Kevin's disappearance from this tale is unspectacular and imminent, but it's handy to get a picture of what we have here.

'Why are you firing me?' Kevin said in a voice that held a tinge of well-justified concern.

'Because I can,' said Dimmot.

When the rehearsal broke up an hour later, he raised his hand for silence, got it immediately and said crisply, 'I want you all back here, scrubbed and decent, two hours before the curtain goes up.'

Before anyone could raise an objection, he nodded to the four remaining drummers. Since he didn't know their names, and didn't care to, he pointed.

'You double up on Kevin's bass drum work. You take the seven-four beat on the snare. Kevin's effects, you. And you, forget the three-four pulse and make it a nine-eight with a six-eight across the bar every four bars.'

He stared coldly down at their barely concealed dismay.

'And get it right or you'll be out on the street with Kevin. Full dress rehearsal for everyone at six on the nose. Don't be high, legless or late. Particularly late.'

He jumped down from the rostrum and strode up the aisle with all eyes but two staring silently at his departing back. Sitting quietly between the cello-sthizers with his enormous grey eyes focused on the tiny screen held on his knees, Mr Jones smiled a leering smile.

But James Dimmot was oblivious to everything except the confusion that filled his thoughts. Firing the drummer had proved the extent of his power to everyone including himself. But he wasn't feeling nearly as great as he had been that morning.

25

AD 3097 minus two years and five months

To watch a three-headed dragon arguing with itself is quite an experience, especially when the argument starts to get, quite literally, a little heated.

'Skullion-brains!' screeched Merlin, throwing himself to one side and nearly toppling over the balustrade of Ingrid's dorsal fins. Catching a glimpse of nothing but blackness, he scrambled back, panting as the burst of flame that had skimmed past his left ear burnt itself out inches from Griswold's chest. Merlin looked round to see Griswold leaning back in alarm. The knight always treated fire with respect.

Fire knew no friends, no enemies and no fear, only hunger for anything in its path. There was nothing that could not be destroyed if the fire was hot enough.

'One of your less ridiculous spells wouldn't come amiss right now,' he growled. 'If you can't invoke your mighty powers to stop a childish squabble, perhaps you could protect us from their tantrums.'

Above them the three long necks swayed as Rhon and Liz roared smokily in each other's faces. Trying vainly to umpire and intervene simultaneously, Ingrid looked back over their shoulders and gave the Enchanter a helpless smile.

'You can't imagine how embarrassing this is,' she said.

The Enchanter nodded at Griswold glaring over his shoulder.

'I've had to put up with this one for over twenty years,' he replied by way of consolation.

'Lucky you, only having the one,' said Ingrid.

She ducked her head as a blast of flame leapt towards her.

'You cocky, jumped-up delinquent,' crackled Liz.

'Supercilious mare,' whooshed Rhon. 'You think you know it all. Why didn't *you* think about that?'

'About what?' asked Griswold.

'No idea,' said Merlin. He hated wasting his powers, but unless the argument waned soon someone was going to be frazzled. Ingrid had clearly lost some of her old authority since Rhon had come on to the scene.

Children don't have the respect they used to, he thought wryly. 'Tis time to make one's presence felt.

He whipped up a shimmering wall between himself, Griswold and the blazing nostrils. Then he did something which could be called disrespectful, but when you don't get respect from the youth of the day you're surely entitled to a modicum of spite. As Rhon entwined himself around Liz's neck and glared into her eyes, Merlin snapped his fingers. Instead of the blaze of smouldering vulgarities that Rhon had intended, a thin stream of water shot from his lips into Liz's snout. She shook her head, gave him a glare and tried to spit in his face.

Griswold gazed at her efforts in amazement.

'What are those?' he asked.

'Geraniums,' said Merlin.

'We don't appear to have moved yet,' observed Griswold.

Ingrid lay spread-eagled, hovering in mid-nothing. As she stretched her own neck high above the two men, the other heads were hanging under her chest as the eyes within them peered into the darkness for some sign of Reality. All sensation of movement had ceased an hour ago. Anything resembling a sense of direction had disappeared shortly after they had ceased to move. There was

125

no forwards, no backwards, no up or down. Only the faint pressure of buttocks on scales served to assure the two men that they would not drift off and float away into the depths of space and Time, and even that was not too reassuring. Everything was still with a stillness that could not be measured by any movement around them. They hung as a tiny winged oasis of life in an ocean of blackness.

They appeared to be in a space-Time doldrum.

Becalmed. In fact, it was nothing of the sort. It was just that Ingrid had stopped to reassess their position. To put it another way, they were lost.

'Pillock,' said Ingrid with feeling.

'Anyone can make a mistake,' grumbled Rhon.

'I blame myself,' sighed Ingrid. 'I should have taken more care to explain things to him.'

'What things?' said Merlin.

'Things like the vicissitudes of Man.'

Merlin shifted uncomfortably. 'Oh. How so?'

'Who else would divide the light and dark periods of time into days, weeks, months etc?' said Ingrid.

'And?'

'Only Man would break the natural flow of time into tiny segments dictated by whether or not his eyes could function fully or his mind stay awake. Nights. Days. I'm to blame. I always overestimate Man, as I suspect do you. I tend to forget his propensity for bending Reality when it really is unbendable.

'What is it that Man has so readily desecrated this time?'

'The flow of the moon, Merlin. Our path around the sun. He won't accept nature as it is. He has to create anomalies where there are none to keep his limited brain within the confines of his limited control.'

Griswold tapped the Enchanter on the shoulder with his sword.

'*What mystic gabbling talks the she-dragon?*/What's she going on about?'

Ingrid looked over Merlin's head at the knight.

'Leap years,' she said. 'I deal in days and nights. I convert them into years as I know them and pass the results to these two to set the course to our destination. They basically do the rest apart from the flying, which is back to me.'

She sighed a smoky sigh. The smoke, having no reason to dissipate, floated lazily about her heads until it was drawn back into her nostrils with each intake of breath.

'I've never had to teach a new head old tricks before. Didn't give the leap years a second thought.'

'What's a leap year?' asked Griswold evenly.

'A year and a day,' said Merlin.

'And?'

'I believe what she is *trying* to tell us is that we are in the right place in Time . . .'

Ingrid inclined her head sadly in agreement.

'. . . but at the wrong time.'

'How wrong?' said Griswold as if the knowledge might help him to resolve their plight.

'That's what I have been unable to work out,' she admitted. 'Doing a thing's one thing,' she added. 'Knowing how you do it is often another.'

Her big yellow eyes took on a glazed look and sporadic spurts of smoke puffed into space as she counted under her breath. For a few seconds she computed vainly, her brow furrowed with concentration.

'How many days are there in a year?' asked Griswold.

'What? Oh, er, three hundred and sixty-five.'

'And a leap year has an extra day.'

'Yes.'

'Why don't you shut up, little man?' hissed Rhon, swinging his head round and leering into Griswold's face. Griswold smiled back warmly and pointedly kept his hands away from the sword, while Liz appeared from the other side and eased herself between the two males.

'Be quiet, lad,' said Merlin sharply, 'and let her concentr—'

'Do these leap years occur often?' said the knight.

Ingrid gave a sigh. 'One in four,' she said patiently.

'And how many years have we travelled?' asked Griswold.

Ingrid told him. 'But, believe me, if I could work out where and when we were from such information, we could be on our way.'

'Did you say something about a month?'

'A month is thirty days long, give or take,' said Ingrid.

'Give or take?'

'It varies by a day, occasionally.'

'So we are two years and five months early,' said Griswold, 'give or take.'

'Are we?' said Ingrid.

26

AD 1994

At eight o'clock in the evening of 13 January 1994, James Dimmot tapped his baton sharply on the rostrum and the first performance of 'The Enchanter', a symphonic celebration of Man's battle against the Forces of Evil, began. The rehearsal had gone off with just enough hitches to give the orchestra a vital dose of adrenalin. As the opening bars resounded majestically both the musicians and the audience sensed that this was going to be a very special evening.

But James Dimmot, who had already fired someone for a minor mistake, did not share the feeling. Had he bothered to count he would not have been surprised to find that Kevin had been the five hundredth person he had fired in six years. Others had suffered Dimmot's indifference, his contempt and his abuse because of his obsession with the alien music that boiled within his mind. Even as his arms wove their commands and his eyes signalled instructions to his army of brilliant musical troops, he felt not the greatness of a leader but the treachery of a tyrant. As greatness wove its path through the wondrous harmonies and rhythms of his creating, James Dimmot felt very small. While the rolling arpeggios, the glistening strings, the soaring trumpets flowed about him, a tuneless lyric, no more than a single line, crept through his mind.

'Man's greatest glory lies in the strength of his will.'

And to hell with his humanity, thought Dimmot bitterly. He turned the page of the score, although it was not necessary since he knew it down to the last semiquaver. It had been born of an inner compulsion that had put aside all feelings and sensitivities other than those geared to the music inside him. People had taken second place to the music and now, just as he had reached the peak of his endeavours after six years, the glorious moment had grown ice cold.

I wish I could just have one crack at the bastard who came out with that stupid bloody saying, he thought.

'Stop!' commanded Merlin, stamping his foot sharply down on Ingrid's backbone. The dragon spread her wings in order to brake, which when you realize that they were in a Timeless, dimensionless, not to mention windless passage of limbo, was rather superfluous. She still managed to give a remarkable impression of a thirty-foot dragon skidding to a halt.

'What's the matter?' called Griswold, drawing Excalibur from its scabbard.

'What year did we just pass?' said Merlin to the dragon.

After a pause Ingrid replied, '3095. Why?'

The Enchanter rose to his feet and looked round. His face was ashen.

'It cannot be,' he whispered. Griswold rose behind him. 'Not across two thousand years.'

'What's amiss, Merlin?' Griswold asked.

'We have to make a detour,' said the Enchanter a trifle huskily.

Ignoring Griswold's groan of protest, he went on, 'There is someone who needs my help.'

'Well, if you require my sword, you'd better magic up something more effective than this lousy blade,' said Griswold.

'A sword will not be needed, lad,' said Merlin. 'Just a few well-chosen words.'

'Words!' groaned Griswold. 'You want to stop off on the way to saving Mankind to have a chat!'

'Er, is this really necessary?' said Ingrid. 'Changing our flight plan can cause all sorts of navigational problems.'

Merlin waggled his fingers with irritation. Objections appeared to be in season lately.

'We have two years and . . .'

'Five months,' murmured Griswold.

'. . . five months at our disposal,' said the Enchanter sourly. 'I'm sure thou canst spare me ten minutes.'

The orchestra rushed headlong towards the finish of the first movement. Behind the brass section ('brass' being a convenient word for categorizing all the instruments of varying metals that didn't actually contain much in the way of strings or reeds), Mr Jones lurked within the depths of his creation and gazed eagerly at the score. The symphony lasted for one hour and thirteen minutes, of which there were fifty-five to go. The final climax Dimmot considered to be the ultimate expression of Man's glorious will in the face of Evil. He always found it impossible to believe that he had found such inspiration within himself. He was convinced that he would never be able to better it and, as the first movement came to a close, an awful suspicion crossed his mind. The symphony that he had sweated blood over and had driven one hundred musicians to the peak of their abilities for was incomplete. It had strength. It had the power of good. It had triumph. It had true glory. It had everything but the one thing that would have made it worth the sweat and the blood and the driving, and James Dimmot, standing at the head of the greatest symphony orchestra in the world, conducting the most advanced, technically brilliant, emotionally commanding piece of music ever written, knew just what that one thing was.

So did Mr Jones. Sitting inside his machine, Mr Jones saw the look of understanding spread across James Dimmot's face and he smiled a smile of genuine happiness. It stretched muscles which weren't used to being stretched and caused him considerable pain, but this only caused him to smile more widely. Mr Jones, née Scarbald the gnome, once Nemestis the demon's right-hand man, knew that the essential difference between him and Dimmot was that Scarbald was alive. James Dimmot, realizing that his symphony had expressed everything but the living, breathing soul of James Dimmot, was in the process of dying. Scarbald's only regret was that Dimmot's living death would be so short-lived. In fifty-five minutes the final chords would rise to a crescendo and James Dimmot would know what black despair really meant. Only then would Scarbald give the gaudy stone a twist and thrust it deep into the core of the machine.

To an audience who is brought up on *Oliver*, weaned on *Starlight Express* and who eats *Cats* for breakfast, the theatrical effects which burst on to the performance of 'The Enchanter' were, putting it kindly, mediocre bordering on tatty. What they did for the unEarthly climax could have been done better by the Muppets.

Dimmot was less than pleased.

'Who the hell are you and what are you doing up there?' he yelled in mid-crescendo.

Griswold peered over Ingrid's dorsal scales at the upturned faces. Strangely none of the hundreds of worshippers seated round the raised dais made a move to rush out in blind panic. Only the priests or magicians gathered on the platform with their odd paraphernalia showed any signs of concern. Griswold gave the foreshortened Dimmot a wave.

'He hasn't changed,' he remarked. 'Are you sure we are eight years on in his life?'

'Of course,' said Merlin shortly. 'And I truly hope that he has changed. Stay here.'

Since Ingrid was hovering just below the ceiling of the Royal Festival Hall (with her heads and wingtips occasionally flowing through the nearby walls), Griswold felt no urge, other than curiosity, to disobey Merlin's instruction. The Enchanter stepped off and floated down to the level of the dais where he hovered, staring intently into Dimmot's face. The closing bars of music, which were not surprisingly a little shaky already, ground into silence. A hundred musicians and a thousand watchers watched with varying degrees of impatience and interest. Although the effect was amusing, neither the little man floating about on hidden wires nor the, let's face it, darling, totally unconvincing dragon was a patch on what a well-seasoned audience was expected to pay for. In fact, what began as a damn good concert looked like being thoroughly buggered up by cheap theatricals.

'Good morrow, James Dimmot,' said the Enchanter. 'You are in good health, I trust.'

'Do you know what you're doing to me?' snapped Dimmot. 'I want your name, mate, and I want to know who's paying you.'

From somewhere behind the orchestra a voice piped up, 'What's going on, Mr Dimmot?'

'Shuddup,' said Dimmot without turning. 'You!' he barked at the Enchanter. 'Name.'

His voice rang out across a silent hall. It was followed by the sound of Merlin clicking finger and thumb.

'Now dost thou know me?' he said quietly.

Dimmot's face paled and his jaw dropped simultaneously. 'You,' he gasped. 'I'd forgotten you.'

'In a manner of speaking,' Merlin agreed. 'And now thou hast remembered me.'

'Yes,' whispered Dimmot, his eyes alight.

He tossed his baton on to the rostrum and gazed up towards the ceiling.

'Was it that oaf Griswold I saw with you?'

'Indeed. Come,' said Merlin, holding out his hand.

Behind the string section Scarbald the gnome stirred uneasily. Give him anything to make with his hands and you would see an instant splash of genius, but when anything to do with shifting concepts hit the surface of his intellect it tended to land with a sludgy squelch. He bit his lip impatiently. The question of what to do lurched drunkenly through the back-alleys of his forebrain. His original plan had been to destroy the whole of Mankind in a blinding flash, but that was a few seconds ago when Merlin and Griswold had, to all intents, been dead for over a thousand years. Now . . .

Pleasant images floated through Scarbald's mind. Demonic beings were smiling and saying 'Well done, Scarbald' as he offered up the still-living bodies of the two men who had thwarted Evil's plan to destroy Mankind. Those images were followed by slightly less pleasant ones in which his spirit was hunted down by those same beings and roasted for all Eternity over an open fire because he had failed to deliver them alive.

He had less than six seconds to think fast, but since asking a gnome to think fast is like asking a sloth to break into a gallop, his chances of meeting this deadline were nil.

OK, so thinking was out. Scarbald switched over to instinct and slipped into the driving seat of his motivation, which was a consuming desire for vengeance. His eyes darted to the control panel of his creation. A loathing of men, blown to even greater proportions by his current frustration, demanded that he take the chance of a lifetime.

Merlin and Dimmot were three seconds away from escape and Ingrid was starting to increase her wing-speed. With the consummate skill that only comes without the inhibitions of thinking, Scarbald flicked his fingers over the keys, twisted the stone, plunged it into the core and flung himself out of the machine. Without pausing, he scrambled on to the shoulders of an adjacent trombaxophoonist and leapt on to the machine's domed roof. The audience stirred and watched this new development. Perhaps there was going to be some sort of death scene or a reincarnation or something. Or a surprise triumph of Evil over Good with the ugly little bugger taking over when the scruffy little good guy with the baton went to Heaven? It was becoming very confusing, not what you'd call good theatre by any stretch. Just as the phrase 'money back' was beginning to spread like a raging epidemic, Griswold reached down and hauled Dimmot up and Scarbald plumped himself down on the dome with his hands over his ears. One second later the stone, on a brilliantly engineered two-second timer, reached critical mass and released enough energy to vaporize the city for ten miles around. Half a second later Ingrid and her passengers flicked out of existence.

There is a scenario that appears to be fairly common throughout the known cosmos. It goes something like this:

Nasty creature (slime monster, vampire, evil dead person, etc) descends on innocent victim with intent to suck out brains, drain blood, eat alive. As sucking-out time becomes imminent and all appears lost, help arrives in the form of philanthropic barbarian, cynical renegade starship commander (complete with starship), or once-flaccid-muscled small-town waitress, now honed to anorexic wiriness by embittered guerrilla lifestyle and film director's sadistic work-out regime.

Thus is nasty creature almost thwarted. Hero reaches down, scoops up victim and displays rapidly vanishing rear-end with nasty creature hanging grimly on to tail of horse, white-hot boosters, back of battered pick-up truck.

Cut to close-up. Hero and victim's mutual sigh of relief is cut short by sight of creature trying to scramble aboard. Hero spends valuable seconds in convoluted lateral thinking, then persuades creature by ingenious and pathetically roundabout means to relinquish its grip and tumble over cliff, into black hole, lethal cesspit.

The only variation on this theme is decided by whether or not it's commercially viable to bring nasty creature back from Eternity. That's the cosmos all over. Perhaps that's what prompted someone to say 'All the world's a stage' even before 'Hollywood' and 'galactic warfare' were household words.

And it's always so predictable, isn't it?

Isn't it?

Merlin the Enchanter was tumbling dizzily, end over end, up and up towards the sky. Scarcely inches away a searing heat, borne on an earth-shattering explosion, roared after him. The sensation lasted for only a second before a grip of iron closed about his throat and he was jerked aside like a rabbit in the jaws of a terrier. The scorching wind tore past him, dragging at the folds of his cloak. In the same instant a barely registered thump sent a tremor through the surface beneath his feet. A total collapse of energy swept through his body and blackness overcame him. Then the blackness was wrapped in silence and all sensation ceased.

As Ingrid sideslipped sharply into the alleyway of an adjacent dimension, the blast of the explosion swept past her, taking with it the vaporized remnants of the Royal Festival Hall, the greatest musicians of the twentieth century and a thousand pretentious assortments of alcohol that had been pre-ordered for the interval.

Merlin, Griswold and Dimmot lay sprawled along the dragon's spine in a heap. When, after several minutes,

Griswold and Dimmot managed to summon the strength to sit up and look around, they saw nothing but the tranquility of another Reality. And endless space.

'Is he dead?' whispered Dimmot.

'It would seem so,' said Griswold grimly.

'Oh, God . . .'

'But that does not mean it *is* so. Merlin does not die easily.'

'He caught the full blast!'

'Blast?'

'Force, for Crissake! The explosion . . .'

'Quiet,' hissed Griswold. 'He stirs.'

You can say that again, thought Dimmot before he could stop himself.

Merlin's eyelids fluttered and opened, and he sat up unsteadily and peered about him.

'Are we well?' he muttered thickly.

'Well, we are,' grinned Griswold. 'How about you?'

'How the hell did you survive that explosion?' gasped Dimmot.

By way of reply the Enchanter reached out and gripped Griswold's wrist. He held the knight's hand up for inspection.

'This is how,' he said.

Dimmot gasped again. The back of Griswold's great hand was blistered and bloody. Shrivelled strands of flesh had peeled off to leave a moist, glistening patch the width of his fist.

Griswold shrugged. 'It'll heal,' he said.

Dimmot looked at the broad, craggy face. The eyes, serene yet at the same time intense, smiled back.

'You don't change, do you?' Dimmot grumbled.

'Should I?'

'Oh, no. Definitely, no.'

The Enchanter reached into the folds of his cloak, rummaged for a moment, then brought out a small

136

earthenware jar. He tossed it to the knight and turned to Ingrid.

'What happened?' he asked her.

Ingrid turned puzzled eyes in his direction. 'A sort of . . . volcano or something,' she said. Ingrid had never seen an explosion before. Arrows and the occasional ballista were the only propulsive dangers she had encountered.

(Whoever said that the ballista, or boulder-slinging catapult, was invented to knock down castle walls was talking through his rear-sight. The ballista was designed by the ancients when dragons were a common sight in the skies. Sort of anti-aircraft guns. The scoring rate was so low that it very nearly didn't last out the year that it was produced. It was only when castles were invented to protect people from the falling boulders that the true potential of the ballista was realized.)

'Was anyone hurt?' said Merlin.

'I didn't see,' replied the dragon. 'I ducked and hoped for the best. Who's this?'

She and the other heads craned to watch as James Dimmot shook his head, blinked and looked up into three pairs of large yellow eyes.

'I didn't think you creatures really existed,' he said.

'We almost don't,' said Ingrid.

'If I refuse to believe in you, will you disappear?'

'That's a rather puerile myth, I'm afraid.'

'Oh.'

Griswold was rubbing the contents of the jar into his injured hand. His face was expressionless except for a brief grimace of pain.

He nodded towards Dimmot and said, 'Now that you have him, what do we do with him?'

Dimmot glared. 'How about asking *him*?' he snapped and, managing somehow to ignore the interested stares of the dragon, he turned to Merlin. 'Do you realize I was in the middle of a performance when you lot blundered through the roof? What am I doing here, wherever this is, and why? What do you want from me?'

'So many questions. So few answers,' mused the Enchanter. He indicated the surrounding nothingness with a wave of his hand. 'Why thou, or any of us art here, exactly, I know not. Something untoward happened just as we left, the nature of which is beyond me. But as regards thee—' Merlin's face darkened. 'With thee I am displeased. Thine Wishing powers have blossomed as I intended, but thine mind is just as sour as when we last met. It is fortunate that Fate has conspired to bring us together again.'

He glared into Dimmot's eyes and Dimmot leaned back before his gaze.

'It is clear that thou still hast a long way to go.'

'Go where?'

Merlin's eyes flickered, but kept their colour.

'Back to the path of righteousness,' he hissed. 'At this time thou art little more than ribwash.'

'Hold on. That's a bit strong.'

'Strong! What dost thou know about strength, James Dimmot?'

Dimmot gulped. Reality was becoming like its usual self when one hangs around Enchanters for long enough. But in the haze that threatened to fill Dimmot's brain, a familiar rock stood out like a landmark.

'You once said that Man's greatest glory lies in the strength of his will,' he said accusingly. 'Well, I remembered that and I've tried to live by it.'

'Will alone is not enough, fool. Without compassion, what use is will?'

'But you said—'

'Said, said, said,' squeaked Merlin. 'Dost thou always listen to others instead of to thine own heart?'

Dimmot glanced towards Griswold. The knight gazed back impassively. He looked up at Ingrid, Rhon and Liz.

The old dragoness looked down with sympathy, the others simply with interest.

Dimmot was very conscious of the fact that he was the centre of attraction, but for all the wrong reasons. He was also very conscious that he was about to ask the Enchanter something that he had asked him once before.

'What do you want of me?' he whispered.

Some occurrences are destined to follow a set course from the moment that they are conceived. As sure as night follows day, they will ride off into a brilliant sunset with all their loose ends tied up and stuffed in their saddle bags. Some occurrences are fated never to fulfil their original destinies.

They have to wait until it stops raining.

Merlin's explanation to Dimmot, regarding a small, tatty book and the part that Dimmot was to play in the advancement of Man's powers, was never meant to be completed in a foreign dimension on the back of the only dragon in existence. Somehow the forces of nature would conspire to see that it wouldn't happen no matter how the odds were stacked in favour of it happening.

'Thou must . . .' The Enchanter's eyes widened as he stared past Dimmot and Griswold towards Ingrid's spiked tail trailing in her wake.

With his arms and legs wrapped about the dragon's tail, Scarbald the gnome was shinning towards them. He held a short metal rod between his teeth and a look of gnomish fury in his eyes. He had his woolly hat on.

Seeing the look on Merlin's face, Griswold whipped round with Excalibur unsheathed. 'You/*Thee*,' he snarled. '*How?*'

'*How?*' was not a question that Griswold normally asked, no matter how mystifying the circumstances. '*How?*' was the sort of question that could use up valuable sword-drawing time. '*How?*' was a bad habit, but since his sword was drawn and Scarbald was clearly unarmed except for the bit of metal in his mouth, Griswold allowed himself the luxury.

Dimmot was less than impressed.

'For Chrissakes, you oaf, don't waste time, kill him, kill the little bastard, cut his balls off, kill 'im, oh God, kill 'im,' he advised the knight.

'All in good time,' said Griswold. 'When he comes within reach.'

'He came within reach once before and nearly killed us both!' cried Dimmot. 'Merlin, frazzle him. Burn his balls off. Fry him.'

Scarbald had reached Ingrid's dorsal scales and was hauling himself quickly up her spine. A younger, more agile dragon might have been able to reach her own tail and pluck him off, but Ingrid's creaking joints couldn't quite make the round trip. Dimmot turned to see if Merlin was going to take his advice, but the Enchanter had made no move to do so.

'Leave it to the lad,' he said. 'My fingers are likely to harm our noble steed with their fire and lightning. Sir Griswold will see to it.'

They all watched as the gnome crawled closer until he was no more than ten feet away from Griswold. As he rose slowly and carefully to his feet and glared at them, a germ of a thought winkled its way through Dimmot's terror and slid down the steep shaft into his deepest recesses where it sought a memory. It was the memory of an uncontrolled talent that he had once had. In a more competent mind it would be the sort of tool that a wizard would give his staff for. In Dimmot's mind it was a recipe for disaster, mainly his. For this reason four days ago (eight years Dimmot time or fifteen centuries objective time, depending on how you look at it), Merlin the Enchanter had buried that talent deep down out of Dimmot's reach, until Dimmot was ready to use it.

Unfortunately, he was ready now.

Ignoring the pain in his hand, Griswold hefted his sword

casually. He never underestimated an opponent, but he could not see how the gnome could possibly get past him to reach Dimmot or Merlin. Then Scarbald snatched the rod from his teeth, pointed it at Griswold and squeezed. A black, silver-flecked beam zipped towards Griswold like an arrow. It was a hair's breadth away from his chest when Excalibur moved. Leaping from Griswold's hand, faster than one could see, it slammed against his chest, blocking the beam and sending Griswold tumbling into Merlin and Dimmot.

For a second time in five minutes they sprawled on their backs with their legs in the air as Ingrid lurched under the combined weight of their falling bodies. The beam spat and sparked and screamed off into space as Excalibur flew from Griswold's hand and spun out of reach. As Merlin tried to climb to his feet and Dimmot tried to tunnel through Ingrid's scales, Scarbald took aim again. Fighting down the temptation to jump out of the surrounding Time and leave all four men standing on nothing, nowhere and nowhen, Ingrid, Rhon and Liz ducked their heads and screwed up their eyes, their assorted snorts and squeals giving off clouds of acrid smoke. Dimmot reluctantly gave up his digging and looked round. Griswold lay dazed before him and Merlin was trying desperately to scramble from underneath him. Only Dimmot was able to rise and see Scarbald point the rod at him. Dimmot's fury became total and complete. As did his power.

'You ghastly little bastard,' he roared hoarsely. 'I Wish you'd just sod off back to the hell-hole you crawled out of!'

It really was a pity that Dimmot didn't think to add 'and never come back. Ever.' He would have saved Mankind a lot of aggravation in future years. Still, you know what it's like when you've just slammed the phone down and thought, Bugger, I wish I'd said that.

Instead, he vanished, leaving only the horrifying echo of his Wish fading in the Enchanter's ears.

'Oh, no,' whispered Merlin. 'Oh, no.'

As he scrambled up, his eyes relinquished their ice-blue hue to the multi-coloured flecks that signalled a potentially lethal loss of self-control. They stabbed through the space between himself and Scarbald, intent on skewering the gnome into the eternal blackness, but Scarbald was nowhere in sight. 'No,' said Merlin again, not a whisper this time but an animal snarl. Then he broke Rule One in the dragon-travel inflight manual. With his blazing eyes scanning the darkness, he lifted himself from Ingrid's back and dived into space. Gliding over her scales and dropping beneath her deep belly, he looked this way and that. Then he circled round behind her tail and alongside her flank before hovering in front of her, his face creased with anguish and fury, his fingers twitching dangerously.

'Where are they?' His voice echoed tonelessly.

The dragon looked down sadly, though not without a strong hint of relief on her faces.

'I cannot say,' she replied. 'I might be able to track them down, but I will need time. If you wish to abandon your journey . . .'

'No,' said the Enchanter firmly. 'The task ahead is, regrettably, more important than James Dimmot.'

Ingrid glanced anxiously at him. 'Merlin, you are jeopardizing your safety by leaving me in midflight. If we were to part company, you could be lost for all Eternity.'

Merlin nodded and glided back between the dragon's heads. He knelt down next to Griswold and ran his eyes over the knight's body searching for injuries. Over his shoulder he said, 'As soon as thou hast set us down at our destination, thou wilt return here and search for James Dimmot.'

'For how long?'

'Until thou finds him.'

Merlin gazed beyond the dragon's tail into the distant past of space and Time. He saw nothing but the blackness and, hanging loosely from a dorsal fin, a filthy, blackened, yellow woolly hat.

Scarbald the gnome had done as Dimmot had bidden him, not that he had a choice, since the power of Dimmot's Wish had become a force to be reckoned with. For one moment he balanced unsteadily on the back of the dragon. He saw the three dragon-heads waver and duck below the horizon of its humped back. Then, outlined against the blackness of space, James Dimmot, the man whose destruction he had been planning for eight long years, was standing and screaming incoherently at him. Despite his consuming hatred, Scarbald admitted a reluctant admiration for the creature in his ill-fitting monkey suit, unarmed and about to have his head blown off. Scarbald hesitated for a second, taking in Dimmot's performance with the eye of a connoisseur. It was one second too long.

Dimmot, the dragon, the sprawling figures of Scarbald's prey and the blackness of space vanished. Instead the dull lead-grey sky of Gnomedom filled his vision. He turned his head to see grey trees and houses and, glancing towards his toes, his own lead-grey body. He was home, empty-handed and stark naked. His disgust was only marginally outweighed by his fury. Someone was going to suffer the fires of Hell for this. He turned his pale eyes to the sky. Somewhere out there was the planet Earth.

Slowly and very deliberately he raised a clenched fist to the heavens.

27

AD 4096. Gnomedom

Grandeane sat at his low wooden table in contemplation. Nearby the fire blazed in a large alcove and the smoke disappeared through a hole in the cavern roof high above.

He gazed across the cavern at the snoring Scarbald, draped over a stone ledge.

'So that's why I haven't heard of you,' he said quietly. 'You've been away from Gnomedom for some time.'

Although the cavern was some forty feet across and twice as high, the great fire cast its heat easily to the far walls, adorning them with shuddering shadows of the sorcerer and his paraphernalia. Grandeane stared at the object he held lightly in his hand. It appeared to be no more than a square block of iron, but on closer inspection by an exceptionally adept pair of eyes, it would been seen to emit a tiny dull glow. The sorcerer stared at the block and a smile of icy cruelty stretched his thin lips across his tiny white teeth.

A sniffle and the sound of buttocks vibrating to the emission of ale-laden wind brought his gaze into focus. Scarbald belched, scratched his stomach and opened his eyes. As they alighted on Grandeane's face, the gnome's features hardened. He slid from the ledge, pulled down his rucked-up tunic and glided towards the sorcerer with his hands outstretched.

'Do you see this, little man?' said Grandeane, ignoring the gnome's barely controlled rage. Holding up the iron block, he swivelled it so that it caught the fire's light and bounced it dully over the gnome's crag-fissured face. For a second Scarbald hesitated and his eyes flicked to the block and back. Before he could renew his resolve to suck out the sorcerer's eyeballs, Grandeane had tossed the block towards him, saying, 'Key to planet Earth. Interested?'

The gnome caught the block deftly and reluctantly inspected it. He cast Grandeane a questioning look. Grandeane leaned back in his chair and clasped his fingers over his flat stomach.

'Embedded inside it there is a stone. Simple crystal actually, nothing special, except that it tells me the one vital piece of news that I've waited nearly four thousand years to hear.'

The gnome frowned. How did the greasy thin bastard know that? You couldn't see inside.

'I know this because, *a*, I'm far more powerful than you, your compatriots and any of your cretinous ancestors have ever come close to realizing,' said Grandeane. 'And, *b*, because an old wizard was stupid enough to reveal the nature of its powers and how they pertained to myself before I stole it from under his nose.'

His fingers executed a lascivious fandango and the block vanished from Scarbald's grasp, appearing simultaneously in Grandeane's hand. The gnome growled quietly, but didn't move another muscle, somehow indicating that he was not impressed by such party tricks.

'And what, you may ask, has this to do with a little craggy moron like you?' said Grandeane. He extended his arm, stretched his fingers and pulled the gnome across the floor towards him. This was no mean task since Scarbald was some twenty feet away. The gnome, with his arms windmilling and his bare feet trying to gouge into the rock to stop himself, staggered haltingly towards the sorcerer. When he was six inches from Grandeane's face and staring into the sorcerer's depthless eyes, he grudgingly admitted that he might just deign to be impressed. As he glared back, matching Grandeane's stare with his own, the black iron block rose up between the long, flared olfactory instrument and the pitted, multi-shadowed proboscis. Grandeane whispered over the hovering block.

'In a matter of days the glow from within this artefact will snuff out, quietly and without ceremony.'

The gnome's eyes flicked to the block and back to Grandeane, crossing and uncrossing as they did so.

'On that day certain forces will have run down and will thenceforth cease to exist. Then I will be free. Free to leave the incarceration that I have endured on your nauseous world these past millennia. Free to carry on where I left off. Free to return to Earth and to make it mine.'

The eyes that stared into Scarbald's took on a new quality and the gnome saw that Grandeane was looking straight through him, far into the distance. He gave a shudder and followed it up hastily with a sneer. He wondered briefly how far across the depths of space the sorcerer's gaze might be covering. Scarbald could not know, nor was it likely that he would understand, that the distant images dancing before Grandeane's blank eyes did not come from across the reaches of space. They originated from centuries long, long past.

For one whose life-span could be expected to encompass the best part of a thousand years, Scarbald had a rather stunted concept of the nature of Time. Time, if you are a gnome, is usually measured in the number of days since someone last crapped on you. Space is the amount of area that you take up while bludgeoning your crapper into mush. In fact, Grandeane and gnomes had some remarkably similar outlooks on life and, although Scarbald would never know how vast was the intellectual gap between them, he realized instinctively that he and Grandeane had much in common. He felt that it was time to acknowledge this. His belch was resounding, hot-breathed and, naturally, alcoholic. It wrapped itself round Grandeane's face, skirting his ears like an invading reconnaissance team, and rolled up the back of his neck. The sorcerer snapped back to the present, gasped for some clean air and, with his ears singing, flung the gnome across the cavern. He did this, of course, in true sorcerer style, without touching Scarbald physically, thus earning Grandeane Scarbald's accolade of cold hatred instead of just his, less prestigious, contempt.

Scrambling to his feet, the gnome attempted a grin with a touch of warmth to it, but his facial muscles were too set in their ways. Instead, he gave Grandeane a watery sneer which would have to suffice.

A log shifted and slipped in the fire, sending a shower of sparks and energetic young flames leaping towards the roof. Although the light and shade danced swiftly across the sorcerer's face, the set of his features remained unblinking and as solid as the lifeless rock surrounding them.

The gnome recognized unbending ruthlessness and sat down to wait.

'No, no, stunted throwback,' said the sorcerer. 'We have work to do. Off your bum and bring me those parchments. Please.'

With a nod of assent Scarbald rose to his feet and waddled into the darkened corner indicated. After a moment's fumbling and rustling, he came to the table and dumped an armful of scrolls in front of the sorcerer. Then he stood back and watched.

That's one I owe you, he thought blackly.

Grandeane gave him a knowing smile and delved into the scrolls. He glanced at one after another, his eyes piercing the dim light effortlessly. He tossed the unwanted scrolls aside, sorely testing Scarbald's temper by throwing several in his direction. One scroll that was unfortunate enough to have a life of its own bounced off the gnome's shoulder and fluttered wildly, trying to rise up to the shadowy safeness of the roof. With a snap, Scarbald's teeth closed on it and bit deeply. Then he spat it away and it slumped to the ground like a broken thrush. Grandeane glanced over briefly, saw the dead scroll and turned back to his task.

That's one I owe *you*, he thought coldly.

'Ah,' he said, holding up a nondescript parchment bound with a leather thong. He held it before him and did nothing. The gnome watched as the tightly bound knot unravelled itself and the thong slipped to the floor. The gnome's eyes flickered briefly with the tiniest glimmer of admiration. Grandeane spared him a cool glance.

'You haven't seen anything yet,' he said. 'What I did to you, what I did to this lifeless object, I can also do to men, to armies, to worlds.' He nodded towards the scroll in his hand. 'With the help of this little fellow here.'

He unwound it and held it at arm's length while he scanned the entire sheet in a few seconds. Scarbald managed to catch a glimpse of the symbols on it. He saw a circle in the centre of the page with four shapes in each corner. The shapes looked like men on horses. He caught a glimpse of the ruthless expressions drawn across their faces and he imagined the red of blood and the blackness of death, the grim whiteness of skin stretched across bleached bones, of sunken eyes and the green stench of death. He was surprised to see that none of these colours was in evidence. In the dim recesses of his cavernous brain a half-forgotten tale began to surface. Despite their fearsome expressions, he had the impression that, if they did jump out at you, they would shove a posy of flowers into your hand. They were depicted in a range of colours that he had never seen before. Had he been a native of a more colourful world than Gnomedom he would have recognized shades of pastel green, pink, lilac, gold filigree and silver lace. Had he been born of such a world, with a comparable set of legends, he might have found himself mumbling with the distaste of the disillusioned, 'What is this? The four Pansies of the Apocalypse?'

His eyes glazed as he attempted to wrestle with the logic of what he had seen. Then the snap of the scroll closing like a roller blind brought him back to his senses.

'Bother yourself not with the contents herein, little

cowpat feet,' intoned the sorcerer. 'Remember only this. Destruction is simple. Any man can destroy. Any half-decent wizard or magician can call up the powers of Death, War, Pestilence and Famine to eat out the hearts and souls of Mankind. But it takes a very special sort of man to create a better world from the energies of Evil. It takes a sorcerer of unique powers.'

He flashed his hand towards Scarbald and rent him asunder, gathering him together again before the gnome had even realized that his atoms had been momentarily scattered right across the cavern. As realization hit him, the gnome gave a great roar of rage and threw up nine pints of ale over the cavern floor. Grandeane watched him with unconcealed distaste. He drummed a rhythmic waltz pattern on the gnome's shuddering head with his scroll.

'It takes Me,' he said modestly.

28

Grandeane prided himself on a dedicated and professional attitude to his work, but he also prided himself on an ability to make do when necessary.

'Put your foot on that corner,' he commanded. 'Please.'

Scarbald, looking green about the gills and thus more colourful than he had for many years, dutifully slapped the four-toed slab that he called a foot on the flapping corner of the parchment, pinning it to the floor of the cavern. The other corners were held down by a stool, a spittoon and a six-inch dollop of molten rock. Scarbald was pretty sure that the rock had once been an unknown gnome with less respect than had been good for him. He couldn't be certain, but Grandeane's reputation with a loaded finger, and the little eyeish crevice peering malevolently out of the rock, made Scarbald's loins tingle with unease.

'Stand still, cretin, lest you tear the paper,' said Grandeane, adjusting his robe. With some degree of ceremony he picked up the iron block from the table and, holding it before him, glided across the floor to stand over the parchment. Scarbald could see the symbols on the paper clearly now and he had to admit that he felt a bit more at ease with the colours. The pastel pinks were more the colour of watered-down blood, the greens could have been the result of a severe head cold and the lilac bore a reassuring resemblance to the colour of disembowelled spleen. The golds were shot through with flecks of blood red and the silvers with streaks of black.

The Four Pansies looked decidedly more sadistic than when he had last seen them. The drone of Grandeane's voice, as he began to chant, interrupted Scarbald's meandering. The words were neither English nor Gnomish, but they had a power to attract the attention. Those words that didn't slither across the sorcerer's teeth like smooth-skinned serpents spat from his lips like yellow-eyed she-cats, or rumbled deep in his throat like the growl of a rabid wolverine. Scarbald listened despite himself and watched in wonder as the sorcerer altered. It was not a single discernible thing that Scarbald could put his stubby finger on, but in seconds Grandeane appeared to be a different person. Had Scarbald's intellect been up to it, he would have realized that it wasn't Grandeane who had changed, but that the sorcerer had simply upgraded the state of Reality around him to one in which his presence could find its full expression. One in which his personal brand of Evil would be lethally potent instead of as out of place as it had been for the last four thousand years.

The gnome watched in silence.

Grandeane continued for another ten minutes, never repeating himself and never faltering. Only when he stopped and murmured in his perfectly normal voice did

Scarbald notice that the feel of the space around him was different. It seemed to want to crackle, to twist and engulf him in coils of smoke and lightning. If he had ever seen a giant anaconda battling to the death with a live high-tension cable he would have been close to finding an accurate analogy.

'Ah,' breathed Grandeane. 'After all these years. Free.'

He smiled at Scarbald and held the iron block between finger and thumb.

'Its time has come and gone. The life within is snuffed, the power is no more. The one man who might have stood against me is long dead. Nothing can prevent my return and my dominion over the people of Earth.' He raised an eyebrow and leered gently at the gnome. 'Time for the fun to begin.'

Scarbald leered back, but the soles of his feet had become decidedly slippery on the stone floor.

'Now, little man. Watch, wonder and worship,' purred Grandeane.

The sorcerer raised a finger towards the roof. Scarbald's eyes swivelled and homed in reluctantly on the razor-sharp fingernail. He felt the urge to rise up on his toes preparatory to diving for cover, but the finger held his gaze and he knew beyond doubt that he was out of his league. A definite shift of balance had to be acknowledged.

At least for the present.

The finger lowered, dragging his eyes with it until he was staring down at the parchment with his neck muscles trembling.

'Move your toe slightly to your left,' murmured Grandeane, 'or you're likely to have a War on your hands.'

Scarbald moved the foot that was half covering the picture in his corner. The pale red creature on a dark red horse shook its head irritably and glared at him. Its horse snorted and pawed at the parchment. Scarbald grinned with delight. From the other corners the rider's companions rose up into miniature stances of vaguely

151

familiar creatures, each on a different coloured steed. One was a bone-white, underfed cadaver on a scrawny grey nag. One, the colour of putrid green meat with an unenviable display of sores on his face and bare legs, sat comfortably astride an equally diseased pale green horse, both clearly unconcerned about their condition. The last rider wore a tatty black robe and cowl and a Nazi officer's helmet, strapped under a chin which was, happily, hidden with the rest of his face from sight. Scarbald, whose understanding of mythology was outweighed only by his IQ, frowned. He had always believed that some things were common to all worlds. Even the long-lived gnomes had a fairly standard concept of Death. Although the bone structure was slightly different from, say, that of the Earthly Reaper, the basic idea was the same. No skin, see right through 'im, sharp instrument in one hand, bony horse (usually). If there *was* a scheme of things embracing a character who wielded a chainsaw and stood in the turret of a roaring, long-snouted chariot, Scarbald couldn't imagine it.

He jumped as Grandeane laid a hand on his bouldery shoulder.

'Time for these chaps to descend on the world of men. Watch.'

He opened his hand and let the iron block lie on his palm. With no warning the block crumbled into a small pile of dust that slipped through his fingers and floated toward the parchment. Each falling speck burst into a tiny glowing sun, a mere needle prick in size. As the rain of fine blazing droplets touched the parchment it smouldered, burst into flames and crackled furiously. A cloud of black acrid smoke blossomed towards the roof, engulfing the two men and searing its way up Scarbald's nostrils. He staggered back with his eyes streaming and his lungs on fire. Had he been able to stand and watch, he would have seen that the little planet was untouched by the flames, but the four figures were no longer fixed to the page. He would have seen the three horses whinny and rear on their hind legs celebrating their freedom, and the character in black execute a rather squeaky U-turn around the parchment's edge. He'd have seen the fire die as quickly as it had begun and the parchment disappear to leave the world floating in a square gap of black nothingness where the floor should have been. Had he stayed where he was he'd also have seen two-thirds of his foot go up in flames. Instead, he glimpsed through smouldering eyelashes, the charred leg of the stool, the half-melted spittoon spewing bubbling liquid and the molten rock flowing off the edge of the hole and tumbling into the abyss towards the tiny planet far below. Then the smoke swirled into a midair pin-hole and vanished and he turned his aching eyeballs up to see the sorcerer on one knee, talking softly. Scarbald crawled towards him with half a mind intent on murder and the other half tingling with curiosity. Grandeane gave him a wave. The pain and the last whiffs of smoke left him so quickly that he gasped.

'Come and look, dungeon brain,' intoned Grandeane. 'See what a doorway we have opened. Look upon those who will form the vanguard of our army.'

All Scarbald could see were four figures whom he could crush under one foot in one go. He sniffed doubtfully.

'Your scepticism is lamentable,' sighed Grandeane. 'Can't you recognize top-notch sorcery when you see it?'

Scarbald looked down at the figures and sneered. The figures looked back and began to grow. Had Scarbald not been a gnome he would have been terrified. As it was, he was quite disturbed. The tiny out-of-focus creatures rose before him, their every detail becoming sharper, every line and crevice deepening, every open sore shining, each eye glowing and becoming more piercing. Grandeane's thin lips stretched into a smile of delight as they stood before him, etched in the candlelight much starker than real life could manage, more like moving, breathing, thin-lined drawings, while Scarbald's nostrils cringed to the smells of putrid flesh, horses' breath and engine oil. The scrape of iron hooves, the crunching of ancient gears, the snorts and the breathing of men trying to control their steeds sounded in his ears.

He stared at them in fascination.

'These gentlemen are well known for their antisocial tendencies,' explained Grandeane, noting Scarbald's quizzical frown. 'Between them they can reduce a world to total desolation in a matter of weeks. They are in great demand in some quarters.'

Scarbald grinned.

'However,' continued Grandeane, 'their current mission, sponsored by me, is considerably more demanding. Theirs is not a mission of destruction, but of creation. Anyone can destroy, as you yourself well know. *This* gruesome bunch inflict pain, suffering and death, usually in that order, for one simple reason. That's their job. They were created to maintain the Balance. You've heard of the Balance, of course?'

The gnome gave a polite snigger, but it was clearly lacking in conviction.

'The Balance,' explained Grandeane, 'is that which permeates the whole of Creation. Right and Wrong. Order and Chaos. Good' . . . He straightened his robe and gazed casually at himself in the brass mirror by the fire . . . 'and Evil. Without one, the other is unthinkable. Without War, Famine, Death and Pestilence, Man would not value nor strive for peace, harmony, quality of life, stuff like that.'

Scarbald shrugged.

'Like the noble gnome, Mankind thrives on adversity. Take away adversity and what have you got?'

Scarbald nodded sagely.

Grandeane stiffened perceptibly and gave his fingers a somewhat irritable snap. The four figures froze conveniently while he continued an explanation that, in the circumstances, compared unfavourably with trying to swim through wet concrete. Describing a world free from adversity to a gnome is like trying to describe an octopus to a blind man. A gnome has nothing to compare such an idyllic world with. The closest he comes to universal harmony is when he, and five hundred others, rise to their feet as one gnome, roar a collective blood-curdling roar and hurtle down a hillside with a single intent.

'Take away adversity,' Grandeane muttered thinly, 'and you have nothing on which to hone the blade of aggression. Nothing to sharpen the instinct for survival. Nothing to unite the hearts and souls of the masses against the common foe.'

He peered questioningly into the gnome's eyes. Scarbald blinked and gave a yawn. The grinding of Grandeane's teeth slid like an undertow beneath the crackles of the dying fire. He snapped his fingers again and everyone jumped. The four figures jerked back to life. Without taking his eyes off the gnome's face, Grandeane gave them their orders.

'Go now, verminous riders. Descend upon the Earth and do your worst. And remember, if you do not act in accordance with the words to which you were bound on that scroll from which I have freed you, your demise will be instant, painless and quite devoid of the agony on which you thrive.'

Three horses whinnied. Three figures grinned deathly grins. The other would have done, but the effect was hidden in the black depths of his cowl. Instead he gripped the turret in thick knuckle-bones bearing the words 'mum' and 'dad' in blue tattoos, revved his engine and slewed round to drop deftly through the hole in the floor. The others dived after him, ignoring the usual physical restrictions made by a two-foot hole on three quarter-tons of horseflesh with riders attached. As sorcerer and gnome leaned forward and peered into the abyss, the four figures executed their perfectly controlled spirals towards the world of Man.

'In thirty Gnomedom days from now,' said Grandeane quietly, 'they will have done their work. The Earth will be ready, indeed waiting, for my arrival. An age-old plan will be on the brink of fulfilment. All it will require is a large dollop of adversity.'

He pointed melodramatically at Scarbald.

'You and yours,' he said. 'You have one month to amass your armies. We leave for Earth on' . . . He stared across the cavern at a strange wiry instrument revolving quietly in the corner . . . 'The third of the month.'

His small teeth gleamed in the firelight.

'For the Squabble to end all Squabbles. Go to bed, little man. You've got an early start in the morning.'

29

AD 4097. Earth

'You stupid buggers never learn,' Uther Pendragon roared impatiently as he swung his sword, slicing through his enemy's forearm to split open the belly behind it. Ignoring the flood of scarlet spilling on to the knee-deep snow, he spun round and fended off a heavy-clubbed blow to his head. Following through with a finesse that would have delighted the strictest fencing master, he thrust his sword hand into the startled face, extending his index finger to skewer a glaring eyeball on his fingernail. The man's screech of terror was cut off effectively as Uther's blade split his head in half from skull to clavicle.

In the heart of the Yorkshire Dales, the windswept canyon of Gordale Scar echoed to roars and screams as twenty men clad in ankle-length fur coats stumbled around in the snow, slicing, clubbing and skewering each other with unashamed relish. Uther and his four companions had walked into an ambush that a blind idiot in a coma would have spotted. In theory, they should be paying the price for such criminal disregard of basic strategies, such as

156

not following fifteen sets of footprints into a confined and unexplored area. However, since their casual attitude to their own demise was based on three very sound understandings, this tactic spoke more of Uther's innate battle-sense rather than sloppy soldiering.

Uther had amassed three hundred years of experience since he had died (plus another forty years beforehand) in all the aspects of warfare, from single combat to the command of horizon-spanning armies.

Furthermore, since Uther and his friends had been dead for several centuries, they were very nearly indestructible, short of being attacked by a sorcerer with a strong grudge or a bunch of exorcists.

Finally, King Uther still retained a shred of his old spiritual ability to pop back and forth in Time in the midst of such mayhem and carnage as he and his men thrived on. By slipping in and out of the present and hacking away liberally for a few seconds, he could reduce an opponent to manageable slices in no time at all. Uther never prolonged the process, for he considered himself a merciful man, so fierce whiskery warriors confronted with such an opponent would be terminated quickly and mercifully. A quick flourish would have ears, nose and scalp flying in different directions before the head was dislodged to join the other steaming pieces in the snow.

His philosophy could be summed up thus: 'The minute they get cocky, you've got 'em by the balls. No need to waste time hanging things out.'

While it was not the sort of motto you'd find on the wall of an SAS mess hall, it clearly worked for him. After three minutes' fighting eight of the enemy lay sprawled in the snow. The remaining men and their leader were separated from each other, and mostly stumbling backwards with looks of incredulity.

'Dammit, Wolfstone!' Uther bellowed as he struggled to dislodge his sword from the cloven head. 'Why don't you ever listen?'

He slammed a foot down on the recumbent chest and gave a heave, but the blade refused to budge.

'Screw you, Uther,' yelled Wolfstone Cusp above the howling wind. 'I'm not ready to die yet.'

Uther wrenched the blade back and forth but the head merely waggled with it, one remaining eye staring balefully into the leaden sky.

'Nobody wants you to die, you cretin,' snapped Uther. 'I came here to ask for your help.'

'In that case, why are you beating the living daylights out of my troops?'

'You saucy sod,' Uther said. '*You* started this fight.'

The commander lowered his battleaxe and raised a restraining hand towards his opponent.

'Hang on,' he said and waded through the snow towards the old king. His opponent, known inaccurately as Robin, was a slight athletic figure, dressed quite inappropriately in a green doublet and hose and wearing a little green hat with a silly purple feather in it. He looked around with a faintly embarrassed expression, then wandered off, waggling his flimsy sword in an attempt to persuade two opponents to take him on at once.

Above them the waterfall that had eroded its way through the wall of the canyon many centuries since now hung in icy suspension, untroubled by tourists and supremely unconcerned by the frenzied antics below. Wolfstone shouldered his way through the mayhem, strode up to Uther and took the sword gently from the royal hand. He gave a tug. The blade slid out with a squeak.

'You know you're really getting too old for this sort of thing,' Wolfstone said, handing it back. As if to prove him right, Uther gave a shudder and faded slightly. For a second the craggy rock face behind him could be seen clearly through him, mirroring the deep lines in his pained features. He stumbled and Wolfstone stepped forward quickly to catch him by the arm.

'See?' he said.

'Horseballs,' snapped the king, pushing off the other's hand. 'Nothing wrong with me. I can still give you the whopping of your life.'

'No, you can't,' said Wolfstone.

Uther shook his head to clear the muzziness from it. 'No, I can't,' he said. 'Call a halt, there's a good chap. We've got things to talk about.'

Wolfstone nodded and gave a piercing whistle.

'All right, lads. Knock it off,' he called.

Everyone halted in mid-strike and looked at their leaders for instructions. Uther slumped down on a nearby rock and raised a beckoning hand, so they lowered their weapons and gathered round.

'You all right, Uther?' asked one of the rebels with a frown.

'Of course he's not, you moron,' drawled Uther's sergeant, Belkin. 'He's knackered.'

Belkin was short by any standards, but what he lacked in height he made up for in attitude. He and Uther went back a long way. Over three thousand years.

The rebel looked away and concentrated on holding his water.

'It's just as well we stopped when we did,' said Wolfstone. 'While there's still enough of us left to talk.' He looked down sympathetically at the old king. 'And while you've some talk left in you.'

'I'll be all right in a minute,' said Uther. 'Always gets me like this. The life drains out of me in seconds for no reason. Very odd.'

'Most odd for a man who hasn't got any life in him,' observed Wolfstone.

'All right. The life-*force* then. Merlin used to say it was—'

'Say what *you* came to say,' said Wolfstone. He had no time for myths and old men's fancies. 'Before my men start getting impatient.'

The remaining rebels growled dutifully. Uther's men replied with 'Oh, yeahs?' and 'Come on thens'. Then someone mumbled 'Big girls' blouses', and everyone said, 'Yeah, well', and swapped baccy pouches. Once the first puffs of coarse, black smoke were snaking away on the wind, Wolfstone spoke again.

'Well, Uther. What's up?'

His piercing black eyes glared from within the punctured football with whiskers that he called a face. Wolfstone could point his eyes at you in the way that other men pointed accusing fingers.

Uther might have been impressed if he hadn't known Wolfstone since the rebel was a baby.

'Simple. The snow's starting to melt.'

The rebels' scraggy cigarettes poised and fluttered before half-open lips as they glanced uncertainly at each other. Seven brains of greatly varying IQs strove to absorb the old monarch's words. Uther's men nudged each other smugly as the rebels looked around them in blatant disbelief.

'Where?' asked Wolfstone.

'Everywhere. Wherever there is snow, that is.'

Just over a hundred years earlier Nature had staged a climatic, last-ditch rebellion against the near-fatal greenhouse effect. She saw it as Her global attempt at survival, but for once She'd made a right pig's ear of it. Large tracts of the planet had become snow-bound while others had remained untouched. From the depths of space, the Earth looked like a mouldy Christmas pudding partially covered in splodges of cream. To the people now living in the affected areas, snow and the way of life that came with it had always been around. They would have found it impossible to imagine anything different.

Wolfstone was more adaptable than most men. That, together with his innate compulsion to oppose authority, would make him an invaluable ally. As long as Uther could win him round.

'I don't know how or why it's happening,' he said. 'Neither do I know the reasons for certain other inexplicable things that have been occurring lately. I only know in my bones that it's not natural. Someone is *tampering*. Which is why I need your help.'

'To do what?'

'Ahm. I don't know. Yet. Not 'til I find out what's going on.'

'Yes?'

'And then . . .' said Uther uncertainly.

Everyone waited respectfully as the wind howled and the blinding snow built up on their furs. Uther heaved himself to his feet and, with some effort, stretched himself to his full height, which was some ten inches shorter than almost everyone else there.

'And then, Commander Wolfstone, there will be one hell of a fight. Global, if I'm any judge.'

A sigh of anticipation swept round the rapidly whitening crowd.

'Therefore,' he went on, 'we will need every warlord and leader the world can throw up. The British, of course. The Yanks. The Australians, I suppose. The Africans, the Japanese, even the Arabs. I've . . . we've been spending the last two months scouring the Earth, searching out all those contrary bastards who like a good fight. I've got several thousand bolshie miscreants like yourselves pulling their tribes together and preparing them for whatever it is we're up against.'

He was starting to enjoy himself.

'Any man, any mercenary, any military leader, chieftain, any man who rules the unruly, must be enlisted . . .'

Uther was aware that he was getting into slightly deep waters, but a vaguely remembered speech about filling up a breach, dear friends, was hovering at the edge of his memory and telling his instinct that it was time to go for broke. He raised his sword and thrust it towards the leaden skies.

'. . . to help Mankind in his hour of need!'

'To shovel snow?' said someone. 'Ouch.'

'You've got thirty days,' Uther continued. 'All the warlords you can muster are to meet at my place one month from today.'

'What about the world leaders . . .?' a rebel began.

'When the cause of these goings-on comes to light, those oiks who believe that they rule their own countries will become Man's biggest liability. I need men who need a cause.'

The look he gave each man was one of quiet desperation.

'We'd better get started then,' said Wolfstone.

Uther nodded. 'I've called a meeting of the nations' delegates to see if I can find out who, or what, is behind it all.' He cast a look around him. 'Right. Before we go, we'll help you bury your dead.'

Wolfstone scowled. 'Er . . . no, that's all right. We'll see to it,' he murmured.

'Oh?'

The rebels gazed casually into the distance and drew deeply on their cigarettes, releasing a flurry of sparks into the wind.

'Tradition,' went on Wolfstone. 'Tribal stuff, if you get my drift.

'Er . . . fancy a bit of lunch before you go?'

30

AD 4097

An hour before the Emergency World Conference was due to begin, Uther stepped out of the shower on the tenth floor of Camelonian Heights. The shower, a dry, sonic version which jiggled ethereal particles to bring a glow to even the most immaterial of cheeks, had invigorated him nicely. His 'body' felt almost alive every time he showered. It was at times like this that the old king would reluctantly acknowledge that the benefits of advanced technology beat an early morning dip in the moat, 'even though the latter was more likely to make a man of you'.

He padded across his artificial boarskin carpet, an embarrassing substitute for a commodity that had become extinct since his own time. It had been manufactured to his own specifications, and confirmed that what Uther had in style he more than lacked in taste. He opened his wardrobe doors and stepped in. The inside stretched away for one hundred yards and on either side was row upon row of rails holding 'suits'. No, we're not just talking bad taste now. We are talking gruesome. The various 'suits' represented people from almost every part of the world and a thousand different eras from the sixth century onwards. There were suits of armour, coronation robes, bearskin and loin cloths and horned-helmet-related apparel. There was an Honorary World Trade Union Leader's uniform, hardly used, and a President Schwarzenegger's suit in milk-white ('early twenty-first century'). There were two Far Eastern garments that Uther only wore when he had to negotiate International Agreements with 'those crafty buggers who haven't altered a bit since the Crusades'.

The inactive force-fields that were the wearers' 'bodies' hung inside the suits with distorted, cadaverous faces like creased and flaccid condoms.

Uther peered along the rows, scratching at his chin and trying to decide which 'suit' would fit the occasion and show him off to the best advantage.

'Right. Something aggressive.' He sniggered. 'I'm going to find out what's going on even if it means a spot of yelling.' Adding innocently, 'Much as I dislike pushing people around.'

He strode down the aisle peering left and right until he reached the back of the wardrobe.

'Hmm. Second opinion needed here,' he murmured. Placing his fists on his naked hips, he bawled at the top of his voice, 'ROSE!'

For a few moments nothing happened. Then the Queen of England and the Entire World walked through the wall and into the room.

'Your Majesty?' she said drily.

'You took y'time,' said the king.

'What do you want, Uther? I'm busy.'

Rose Falworthy was, by any standards, a striking woman. She had been in her late fifties when she had died in 1995. She was exceptionally fit at that time, having brought herself to peak condition with fencing, self-defence, weight-training and ten-mile swims, and she had retained her spiritual, slightly 'comfortable' but magnificent figure when her heart had gasped, 'Blow this for a ga—' and shuddered to a halt. Rose Falworthy was proud-bosomed, slinky at the hips and had bright green eyes which still shone with the lust for Afterlife. She was wearing a pastel coloured, gossamer-thin chiffon, just opaque enough to require one's visual impression to be augmented by one's imagination.

Uther gazed at her briefly and, getting control of himself, said, 'Need your advice, old girl. What to wear.'

'Who do you need to impress?'

'Everyone. More important, I need answers. Need to know what the devil's going on and why and, especially, who.'

'Then you don't want anything ostentatious. Down to earth, practical. Military.'

'My royal armour!'

'Bit too archaic.'

'My Saddam outfit?'

'You want them to take you seriously, don't you?'

'What then?' growled Uther irritably.

*

Uther was never at home in a 'suit'.

'Like washing your feet with your socks on,' he grumbled.

He would dearly have loved to get back to the early post-holocaust days when he had discovered how to get into the minds of men and control their bodies, their actions and their feelings.

Not having a living body can make the job of being World Monarch very difficult, when no one but a handful of clairvoyants, some cats and the odd dog are able to see you.

In the ten years following the Last Trump, Man was quite unaware that his monarch was scurrying all over the planet, trying vainly to get its inhabitants into some sort of order.

'Not much different from my first stint,' grumbled Uther.

Then, quite by accident, Uther found a way of making his presence felt. For those of us who aren't yet of a spiritual persuasion, or whose memory of our previous existences are a bit hazy, it should be noted that spirits can travel almost anywhere in space and Time, since neither of those dimensions present the sort of problems that they do to the living. There *are* areas which spirits are prevented from entering, either by Nature's laws or by certain rules of etiquette, but they are the stuff of other tales.

In the tenth year of Uther's 'reign', the monarch was nosing around in the mind of a high-ranking political figure, one Sir Jason Fenton-Fenton, an extremely success-ful businessman and entrepreneur. The chap had three things going for him. He had a great deal of power, a highly successful way with women and he had Rose Falworthy eating out of his hand. Or, he would have been if he had been aware of her existence. As it was, he was not privy to the spiritual world and Rose had to settle for worshipping him from afar. Her uncharacteristic infatuation, however, was enough to put Uther right out of the picture.

But, of course, this was not the first time Uther had had his advances rejected. Being as smitten as he had been over three thousand years earlier, he knew that a direct approach was useless. Uther would attempt to win his beloved over by subterfuge as he had done with Lady Igraine back in those medieval days of yore. Only this time he'd have to do it without Merlin's help.

He had sneaked into JFF's head not knowing what he'd find, but determined to make good use of it when he found it.

What he found was the key to the kingdom.

Sir Jason Fenton-Fenton was dictating to his secretary and, apart from a slight tickle in the hackle region of his snow-white, sickeningly thick hair, he was unaware of Uther's presence.

Ah, hah, my proud beauty! Uther just happened to be thinking. I'll have you sooner or later.

'Ah, hah, by proub ooty!' laughed Sir Jason Fenton-Fenton with a look of horror stretching his face to splitting point. 'Ah hab oo zooner o ladah.'

Although JFF's secretary was seventy-nine years of age and included amongst her ancestors several strains of hippopotamus, Uther was not a man to waste time on amazement.

In the Dark Ages amazement was one of life's luxuries. Usually the most short-lived.

Ah, hah, my proud beauty! he thought again.

'Ah, hah, my proud beauty!' sneered JFF with perfect diction.

Uther slid deftly into the saddle of his newly acquired steed, gathered up the reins and took off at a canter.

JFF raised a disdainful eyebrow and brushed his snow-white moustache. He swaggered towards his secretary, with a confident glint disguising the horror imprisoned in his head by Uther's new-found power. He leant over her, his neck muscles screaming as he tried to pull back. He placed his lips on hers and sweat broke out on his brow.

JFF slid his tongue between her unresisting teeth and his back spasmed as he tried to straighten up.

Uther Pendragon urged his horse into a gallop.

I love you, he thought with deliberation.

'I love you,' mumbled JFF with passion.

For the second time within four thousand years, Uther Pendragon's desires were about to make him world famous. And by the same token Uther maximized his good fortune to the full.

Three days later his queen spied JFF locked in a reluctant embrace underneath his secretary and on top of his vast leather-covered desk. The expression on JFF's face was similar to that which one would adopt if forced to chew a live toad.

If Rose ever guessed that the king had engineered the incident, she never let on.

Uther soon learned to control minds with tact and subtlety. If you can manipulate another mind gently, so that it is not aware you are doing so, it will readily believe that its actions are of its own making. This applies whether you do it by word of mouth, the raising of an eyebrow, or the more direct method of crawling inside it and cranking it up, tactfully and subtly, by hand. With practice and not too many casualties, Uther learnt to control men's minds and to use them to communicate with the whole of his kingdom. From then on, ruling the world became a piece of cake.

There was a downside, however.

In a sense, a whole line of monarchs came to rule the Earth for the next hundred years. In truth, Uther had to abandon each body as it began to flag and to migrate to a new one. In fact the one big disadvantage of this particular *modus operandi* was that Uther spent nearly as much spiritual energy in keeping his hosts moving as living beings do. After a hundred years he was visibly wilting, although he should have another thousand years of spiritual existence to go. The old king had grown even older before his time.

'You're a stubborn fool,' Rose had told him.

'I'm a monarch,' snapped Uther. 'Always have been. Always will be. I'm fit for nothing else.'

'You won't be fit for that soon. You must either abdicate or make your royal presence known by other means.'

Reluctantly Uther agreed. Having always used the bodies of big, strapping, handsome men, 'strictly in the interest of royal credibility, of course', he had enjoyed the many and varied perks that had been part of his kingly existence during the sixth century. Being a generous man, he was also unstinting with his favours to the ladies of his court in the thirty-ninth century.

So, in AD 3897, a hundred years almost to the day since his reign began, Uther decreed that the world's finest genetic scientists, spiritual investigators, computer experts and fashion designers stop whatever they were doing and come over to his place.

'I want a suit,' he commanded. 'The finest suit that ever was . . . No! I want a thousand suits. From all over the world and from every era since . . . Roman times. Get some historians down here.'

Every 'suit', he added, must be made to measure and perfect in every historical detail.

'You've got one year to perfect it . . . them.'

Rose Falworthy stopped halfway along the aisle and pointed the multi-ringed finger that was part of her chosen 'dress' for the convention.

'That one is perfect,' she said.

With a thankful nod of agreement, Uther wafted into the substance of the 'suit'. The particles of the force-field came alive at his presence and wrapped themselves dutifully about his spiritual aura. Uther settled himself comfortably and stepped back into the aisle. He strode to the nearest mirror and gazed with satisfaction at his reflection.

'Well done, old girl.' He smiled. 'Spot on.'

31

AD 4096. Gnomedom

Gnomes have a remarkable facility for finding the most interesting ways of sending their enemies through the Great Iron Doors of Death and into the eternal realms beyond. Even when scrambling, twisting and slashing indiscriminately their innate sadism can wriggle through the dense foliage of their survival instincts to reach the lucid pool of logic. While their bleeding bodies strike back with animal venom and their mouths continue to scream with insatiable lust, a tiny area in their already tiny brains peers with cold interest into that pool and perceives an age-old truth.

It is this:

Anyone can inflict a bloody death on anyone, but not everyone can make someone's death go on and on beyond the credible bounds of endurance. That requires artistry.

In the art of inflicting pain and breakage, gnomes are artists to a fault. They demonstrate the subtle sensitivity normally attributed to a flaccid-limbed grand chess master.

And why not? They spend many of their waking hours in practice. From the stance of their legs to the twist of the body, from the pull of the highly powered torso to the gentle flick of the stubby fingers, every atom of their bodies is trained and honed to the finest degree of control, just so that they may inflict pain and death over any period of time that they care to choose.

When the blood needs summoning up and the imitation of the tiger is required, gnomes are ready to a man. When the axes fall and clubs pound at the brain, gnomes swing into

*action with a grace and symmetry that a ballet dancer would
give his right leg for. Gnomes in battle are poetry in emotion.*

You can set your clock by a gnome in a killing mood.

*A casual shout of 'Two days, two hours and two minutes',
followed by a truncated coup de grâce, and you could wander
off to pick daisies, safe in the knowledge that the gnome's
victim would not move from his recumbent position until his
'time was come'. After two days, two hours and two minutes,
you could pop back on the dot and plant your bouquet into
his gaping chest just as he gives a shudder, mutters
'Ghaaagh', and goes permanently glazed about the eyes.*

Such is the artistry of gnomes.

Encyclopaedia Esoterica,
Early edition, AD 800 or so

'Scum. Cretins. Festerbrains! Lend me your ears.'
The voice of Scarbald's speaker, Crysius, trilled
through the grey Gnomedom air to pierce an arena full of
angry ears. By gnomish standards Crysius was a typical
orator, terribly high in verbal expertise and pitch, and
considerably lower in gnomeliness.

Not what you would call a gnome's gnome.

At the moment he was even less popular than usual for
he was committing the ultimate sacrilege. He hastened to
reassure five thousand murderously impatient spectators
plus the eighty or so gladiators who had been halted in
mid-carnage to listen to what he had to say.

'I come not to stop the games, but to praise them,' said
Crysius.

He glanced at Scarbald. Scarbald waxed into his version
of eloquence by shrugging his chin and Crysius continued
with impunity.

'The glory that gnomes do here lives after them. The
igominy of the losers is buried with their bones, and so it
should be, says Scarbald, for Scarbald is an honourable
gnome. Indeed, you are all honourable gnomes, waiting
with honourable patience to hear what I have to say. For

what have I . . . what has the honourable Scarbald to say that you know not already? That the games are the pinnacle of honour, that they epitomize the courage of the gnome . . .'

A rumble swept round the auditorium. Several sweaty gladiators raised their swords and growled menacingly. They liked the bit about 'scum, cretins, etc', but nobody was going to accuse them of 'epitomizing' in public.

Bugger, thought Crysius.

'They show us the courage of the gnome,' he amended.

A collective grunt confirmed that he was back on the right track.

'Who is Scarbald to criticize the wisdom of our noblest warriors in pitting their courage and their limbs against each other in this most honourable of pastimes?'

A ragged murmur of agreement wandered round the tiers.

'Who is he to wonder what on Gnomedom is the sense in decimating the numbers of our greatest warriors so that the masses, that's you, can observe courage and honour at its peak? Who is he to say, "Wouldn't it make much more sense if you yourselves could give that courage and that honour some meaning in the pursuit of a higher cause?"?'

The degree of disparity in the rejoinders indicated that, in IQ terms, Crysius had begun to sort the men from the boys. He drew himself up to his full three feet eight. It was time for him to deliver the greatest speech of his life. The speech that would stir the minds and hearts of the noblest and the lowliest of gnomes alike. A speech to summon up the most anaemic of bloods. A speech that no self-respecting gnome could resist.

'Who is he to say, "Wouldn't it make more sense if you got off your arses and went on an all-expenses-paid weekend to beat the living daylights out of Mankind?"?' he said.

32

AD 4097. Earth

The buzz of multi-tongued humanity rang round the vast World Community Conference Hall like the sound of frantic wasps in a jam jar.

The mighty, wall-spanning public address system echoed the noise and visual screens reflected the activity of twenty thousand delegates arriving from every corner of the globe.

Like each Annual World Conference that had been convened since its inception two hundred years earlier, it appeared to have all the makings of a shambles. Delegates were scrambling for seats. Some were scanning the screens for copies of the agenda. Those who were at a conference for the first time were searching for nonexistent interpreters.

But unlike any previous conference this one actually *was* a shambles, because this World Conference wasn't the annual one. The annual one had taken place six months ago. It had taken two and a half hours to convene instead of the usual fourteen days, and then everyone had adjourned to the bars and not come out until the fortnight was up.

This was an emergency conference and nobody knew how long it was going to take. The Japanese tourists had been herded out and the anti-tourist barriers were activated.

By the time it was due to start, delegates were still pouring in. The lawns surrounding the great transparent, multi-domed complex had been opened up as an emergency landing area and were covered with hundreds of private flying machines. The paths to the complex were dotted with scurrying figures in different national attire, clutching personal Id-computers and hoping to get into the hall before King Uther arrived with Rose.

'Now that you're all here,' said King Uther evenly, 'we'll make a start.'

Twenty thousand pairs of eyes peered towards the podium and video screens. Forty thousand ears listened attentively. Two hundred thousand fingers and thumbs hovered over twenty thousand Id-com keyboards.

The king wasted no time on preliminaries. He rose to his feet, cast a quick glance at the screens and put on his most monarchic expression.

'I've summoned you here today to discuss the miracles.'

As the PA system interpreted his words and the computer-aided screens reshaped his lips to reflect the translation into the common language of 'Earthspeak', a murmur swept round the hall.

Uther snapped his fingers and the assembly fell silent.

A hall-full of fingers poised expectantly.

'And until we have this cruddy matter tied up I don't want any more tidings on your Idlididdly thought transmitters leaving this hall.'

The hall bustled briefly as Id-coms were reluctantly switched off and put away.

Two or three hundred fingers remained poised.

'On pain of death,' murmured Uther casually.

In fact, Uther had seen enough of death when Man had nearly been extinguished three hundred years earlier. It had taken thirty years to clear the Earth's surface of the dead. Uther had not condemned anyone to death since his reign began, but as he now had a worldwide kingdom to run, he had to employ some effective method of persuasion. No sooner had he gained sufficient recognition from the Earth's population than he sent Belkin with a team of local researchers out into the kingdom to explore new methods of communicating with a race that was, after three

173

and a half thousand years, quite alien to a sixth-century monarch.

The research team scoured the books of history, investigated the events leading up to Man's near-demise and, after two years, came up with a set of ground rules, persuading royal subjects for the use of.

So now, when he said 'On pain of death', the camera cut to Rose Falworthy who looked up from the odd little activity in which she was engaged. From the multiple loudspeakers came the barely audible sound of a metal plate sliding down a wooden frame to stop with a peculiarly soggy thump. A single, significant frame from some ancient film about two cities flashed simultaneously on to the screens far below the conscious level of the delegates and Rose Falworthy returned to her activity. In psychological terms or, indeed, in the terms of magical lore, it would have been called planting a seed. In olden times it was called 'knitting'.

A tremor ran through the hall and the remaining fingers retreated, finding sanctuary in the comfort of warm laps.

Uther scowled with disgust.

Whatever happened to strength of personality and obedience to royal decrees? he thought, not for the first time. All this sublime . . . sublimbo . . . sneaking into the secret passages of men's minds instead of a good, honest frontal assault on the fortress of their wills was nothing short of demeaning. Oh, for the thunder of hooves over drawbridges, a hefty battering ram and the cry of men with the blood of battle boiling in their veins. Gods, how he missed Camelot.

He looked out across the silent hall.

'Two days ago,' he intoned, 'we received news of another spate of miracles. Tuberculosis has managed to vanish from the face of the Earth. The drought in Ethiopia has ended and they are now getting enough rain to ensure a decent harvest for the next ten years. Some old volcano called Krakatoa has seen fit to rise from the sea off the coast of

Java, but after a couple of quick puffs it has died out completely, according to experts' (Uther managed to make the words sound as if they were enclosed in inverted commas), 'and is rapidly becoming extremely fertile.' He paused. 'What else? Oh, yes. Nothing has disappeared into the Bermuda Triangle. What I want is answers,' he said. 'And I want them damn quick and, since you are aware that I've been about a bit, you know my views on miracles and the makers thereof. Therefore, before any of you shove your hands up and start talking about saints and gods and suchlike, you'd better be sure that you've got your facts straight.'

Several hands rose and Uther swept his eyes across the hall until they came to rest on one of the American delegates.

'Go on, Dwightenhower,' he said. 'And make it good.'

Justin Dwightenhower rose to his feet, slipped a thumb into the pocket of his waistcoat and, giving a nasal drawl to his carefully chosen words, he said, 'Yoh Majesty, Mister President. What we *have heah* is a sign. What we *have heah* is a portent. What we *have* heah . . .'

Is an idiot, thought Uther.

'. . . is a symbol of a New Age. An age in which Man shall rise and fulfil his destiny in accordance with the law of God.' He smiled warmly towards the cameras. 'Does it not say,' he went on, 'in Corinthians One, fifteen, verse fifty-two, "we will be changed in a flash, in the twinkling of an eye, at the last trumpet . . ."' Mr Dwightenhower drew back his shoulders and, beaming into the cameras, continued: '"For the trumpet will sound, the dead will be raised imperishable, and we will be changed . . . Death has been swallowed up in victory."'

'Dwightenhower,' said the king.

'Yoh Majesty?' said Justin Dwightenhower, turning his large face reluctantly from the cameras to the podium.

'Dwightenhower. Right now, I need your Second

Coming cobblers like I need a third hole in my bum,' observed the king.

'Sir,' replied Justin Dwightenhower. 'Yoh surely do not dispute the prophecies of the Holy Bible?'

The silence that filled the hall glistened with embarrassment. History is very flexible. Accommodating even. In the wake of the Last Trump, history had emerged confused, shell-shocked and prey to several groups of human predators who were waiting to scavenge off its mangled hide. The two major groups were the Believers in the Second Coming and the Advocates of Doubt.

Since the Second Coming had not yet succeeded the First, there was, naturally, an abundance of seers and omniscients who predicted that it would arrive sooner or later. They maintained that the Last Trump had been designed to prepare Man for the return of God to Earth (exact nature of manifestation to be advised). They were right in part. Man was certainly being prepared for something.

The Advocates of Doubt were marginally closer to the truth. The two groups spent a lot of time brawling in the name of their beliefs, unaware that those beliefs all stemmed from a common primeval knowledge, proving that some things never change.

'Mr Dwightenhower,' Uther said, 'I do not dispute one word of the Bible. On the contrary, I have it on good authority that the business with the trumpet is as valid as anything else therein.'

Justin Dwightenhower gave an approving smile.

'But that is the whole point,' went on Uther gravely. 'The assassin's blade cares not who it slays. The victim is decided by whose hand holds the sword.'

Seeing nothing but vacant expressions, Uther shook his head in wonderment.

'The prediction in the Bible,' he said slowly and distinctly as though addressing twenty thousand village idiots, 'came true. The trumpet call *was* sounded. We *were* changed' (sort of, he added under his breath). 'And what's more, death *was* swallowed up, but in *this* case it was the death of Mankind thwarted by Merlin the Enchanter when he turned defeat into victory. With my help,' he couldn't resist adding.

'Despite the blabberings and exhor-bloody-tations of your Second Comers, your New Christians, your Advocates of this, that and the other, *this* trumpet was not the instrument of God, even though the original technique was said to be His.'

He paused for effect, but got only a hall-full of blank looks.

'Since it *was* fairly well-publicized,' he went on with biting sarcasm, 'and since it was also a typically barbaric affair, it soon reached the ears of the nastier elements of society, one of those being Lucifer, the Devil, Prince of Darkness.'

The silence gave way to uneasy murmuring.

'And when Lucifer heard of it,' said Uther quietly, 'he said, "that'll do nicely", modernized the technique a bit and sent one of his lads down to Earth to repeat the trick on a global scale. Fortunately, his emissary, known to you as Nemestis, failed.'

Uther leaned forward and rested the hands of his 'suit' on the lectern before him. It was probably the best 'suit' for the occasion, since it was his Uther Pendragon 'suit'.

'No doubt, you can tell us which part of the original story I'm referring to, Mr Dwightenhower.'

'Er . . .' said Justin Dwightenhower lamely.

'Correct!' exclaimed the king. 'Joshua six, verses one to twenty.'

He favoured the American with an icy stare.

'Battle of Jericho,' he said. 'Don't talk to me about a Second Coming.'

33

*Despite numerous attempts to exclude James Dimmot from
the body of this work, that particular mortal was destined to
feature strongly in the destiny of Mankind. It is necessary,
therefore, to record further the nature of his Wishing power
and his contribution to these pages. However, his almost
schizophrenic inability to maintain the integrity of his beliefs
and the unpredictable nature of his power preclude the
possibility of a coherent or comprehensible synopsis.*

*It has been, in fact, almost impossible to keep track of the
stupid bugger.*

Encyclopaedia Esoterica

NB. Hold this page for 500 years hence, when we *might* just have
enough info for a worthwhile paragraph. Ed.

34

U ther laid his elbows on the candlelit banqueting table
in Pendragon Castle and rested his stubbly chin in his
hands. He stared mournfully at his select band of ten
leaders, fighters and heroes sitting silently on either side
of the long oak table. He glared angrily out of the window
at the early evening sun. Finally he let his eyes rest on
Rose Falworthy at the other end of the table. His features
flickered fitfully in the candlelight.

'How . . . when we had the cream of the world's public relations and communications experts, the elite of the nations' emissaries, the absolute cat's cobblers of the Phenomena Investigation herberts gathered together in that flaming conference hall . . . could they possibly come up with nothing?'

No one spoke.

'Nobody knows nothing! The whole world is being messed about by magical means as sure as my nose has hairs up it, and nobody knows nothing.'

His leaders, fighters, etc stirred impatiently. They could do without this maudlin nonsense when there was food on the table. They had their best ethereo-sensitive 'suits' on and their spiritual stomachs were itching to wrap themselves round as much of Uther's celebration meal as their hopefully short-lived sobriety would allow.

Just lately (meaning the last half-century or so), on the same day each year, the old fool would go into a depression that made the Devil's Punchbowl look like a bit of a rut. Last year it was about the myth of immortality being so much bog gas and anyway, to tell the truth, it'd be a blessed relief not to have to wake up to their ugly faces every day for the rest of Eternity. He used to be the soul of the party with his life and death jokes. Now, he'd kill a knees-up just by looking at it. This year, when they were having an ecological upslide, he'd decided that the miracles were the work of an *evil* force, would you believe?

They looked wearily up the crude wooden table at their monarch. They glanced warily down the table at his consort. Keeping their hands between their knees, they twiddled their great, callused thumbs under cover of the table. They couldn't believe that Uther was going to let the rest of the night go by like this, without at least getting rat-arsed. So, when his hand crept towards his untouched mug of mead, they sat forward expectantly. And, when he pinged his fingernail pensively against the rim of the mug, they ran their tongues hopefully over their dry lips. And,

179

when he dropped his hand on to the table and sighed angrily, everyone slumped back with a collective but cautious groan.

This celebration banquet was rapidly becoming the non-Event of the year.

'What I need,' murmured Uther, to himself more than anyone else, 'is someone who can see beyond the miracles to discover their source.'

While his leaders gave one another furtive 'here we go' glances and raised their eyes to the ceiling, Rose was less reticent. The hammering of her fingernails on the table warned of her fast-waning patience. The king was not oblivious. He brought his gaze back into focus and cast it down the table.

'I know, old girl. I know.'

He raised his hands helplessly in a singularly moving gesture for a man of his courage and kingly qualities. Apart from the peristaltic reaction to the smell of herb-laden meats and honey-rich mead wafting up the ethereo-sensitive nostrils of their 'suits', the leaders were singularly unmoved. Uther shrugged and waved a royal hand over the table.

'Oh, go on then, you insensitive buggers. Fill your faces,' he sighed.

With concerted cries of 'Ah haaargh!' and 'Parsthepig-yugreedy bastard' his loyal subjects threw themselves into a concentrated assault on the defenceless dishes. Once they were unleashed, there was virtually nothing that could stop them until they had licked the patterns from the plates.

Almost nothing.

The crash of Rose Falworthy's chair toppling backwards on to the stone floor would have been warning enough if there'd been time to heed it, but there wasn't. Before they could drop their food hurriedly on to their plates, Uther's consort reached out with both hands and gave two neigh-bouring heads a blinding slap.

'You misbegotten, self-centred, pig-ignorant, Neanderthal bunch of dump-trucks!' she screeched. 'Have you forgotten what day this is?'

There was a pause cloaked in shamefaced silence.

Slowly ten pairs of eyes looked up from looking down.

'Sorry, Ro . . . your highness. Sorry, Uther.'

Ten bodies rose to their feet, scraped back their chairs and reached for their mugs.

The tones of an ancient hymn rose tentatively from the warriors' lips, gathered pace and finally echoed raucously round the room.

> Happy Deathday to you.
> Happy Deathday to you,
> Happy Deathday,
> Dear Utheeeerrrrrrrrr . . .
> Happidethdaytyoupasthepigyugreedybastard.

It was two in the morning and the banqueting room was almost sort of empty.

The Queen of England and the Entire World had gone to the kitchens to organize coffee. Of Uther's warriors only five remained, sprawled in their 'suits' across the table or slouching open-mouthed in their chairs, not breathing because spirits don't need to breath and their 'suits' didn't need oxygen to function. Four of the others had wafted away to sleep off their hangovers. Their 'suits' lay over the table, staring out of deactivated eyeballs like four drink-riddled corpses. The chairs, plates and mugs over which the 'suits' lay were clothed with folds of sagging grey skin. The only sign that those 'suits' had been studiously eating their way through enough food for an entire army were the disturbing bulges in each abdominal area. The warrior known as Robin, not being one to resist the more pleasurable activities that followed a full-course meal, had popped upstairs, complete with 'suit', to the loo.

Uther sat brooding. He felt more indecisive than at any other time in his life, or his afterlife for that matter.

And more lonely.

He cocked an eye towards the window. Where are you when I need you, you old scrote, he thought sadly. I ran my whole kingdom on your say so, your prophecies and your wisdom. We were a good team.

He looked along the table at his heroes and sighed.

'What are you thinking about now?' said Rose, coming up behind him. She held a tray of steaming coffee mugs and plonked one on the table before him, looked at the sprawling bodies with disdain and planted herself in the chair next to him. 'Well?' she said.

'Fact is, old girl, I can't win this one. Can feel it in my water. Renegades, warlords and such is one thing. Miracles are the stuff of demons. Or gods.'

Rose stared at him narrowly. 'You're not beginning to believe that Messiah nonsense, are you?' she said.

Uther shrugged. Having realized that even immortality might have a limited duration, he was beginning to feel he could be forgiven for hedging his bets.

'Is that so bad?' he asked tiredly.

Rose gazed at him in alarm. 'Listen you,' she said thickly. 'Something unnatural's happening out there and anything that isn't natural is wrong, bad, evil. Soon it's going to burst like a ripe boil and you are the only one half capable of clearing up the mess.'

'But—'

'So stop feeling sorry for yourself and start behaving like a world leader. No, better still, start behaving like Uther Pendragon!' She reached out and placed her ghostly hand on his. 'Like the Uther Pendragon I used to know,' she added in a relatively small voice. She buried her words with her fears in the depths of her coffee mug and the two of them sat in silence for a while. Then Uther spoke.

'If I'm to behave like the Uther *I* used to know, I'll need my Enchanter.'

'He's been dead for over three thousand years,' said Rose.

'So have I,' replied Uther firmly. 'I'll send my heroes to look for him.'

'Your heroes are old like you, Your Majesty. They relied too much on their 'suits' for having a good time and enjoying a bloody fight. They couldn't manage a tuppenny bus ride into next week, let alone a trek across thousands of years. Besides . . .'

'What?'

'Not one of them could find a ferret if it was shoved down his leggings.'

'They're not that bad,' protested Uther. 'They're some of the greatest heroes of all Time.'

'Not *all* Time. Of their own times,' said Rose. 'None of them was around during your and Merlin's time except Belkin. They wouldn't know where or when to start. Anyway, it's academic.'

Uther gritted his teeth. She always used that phrase when they both knew he was just digging his heels in.

'They're twice the man your poncey Robin is,' he said sulkily.

Rose stiffened. We all have skeletons in our cupboards. Robin and Rose shared a cupboard between them. When Uther was searching for the spirits of heroes, leaders and fighters to aid Merlin in his battle against the demons of Nemestis, he had commanded Rose to use her clairvoyant powers to find Robin Hood and have him join Uther's band. While Rose had managed successfully to find most of the heroes that Uther asked for, Robin Hood eluded her. Since Uther had agreed to let her fight by his side only if she delivered the full set, Rose had resorted to a minor subterfuge.

Her conspirator, now tripping down the stone staircase from the upstairs loo was, to a fair degree, currently in his element. When he hadn't spent his time brawling with twentieth-century sailors in sleazy bars round the world, he had been spending much of his time in drunken revelry. When he wasn't brawling and revelling, he was seducing some of the loveliest women the world had to offer. When he wasn't doing any of those worthwhile things, he was leaping around in forests, market places and fortresses like Pendragon Castle with a flimsy sword in his hand and a rakish smile on his lips. Admittedly, the 'cold', 'dim' passageways of the old castles were cluttered with hot spotlights, filming equipment and vulgar cameramen, but even now the feel of flagstones under his feet and the ring of metal blades on pillars found a place in his affections.

The sound of a heated argument rolled up the stairs and caused him to pause in his stride.

'. . . poncey Robin . . .!'

'. . . he's the only one with enough brains . . .'

'. . . as much use as bum-hairs on a broadsword.'

Uther had never taken to him, thought Robin sadly. The king always tried to give him the rotten jobs, like looking after the horses when the fighting began. Uther had never trusted him either, though Robin had no complaints there since he'd always been here under false pretences anyway. Still, it would have been nice if he and Uther had got along. He admired the old man immensely. Had a lot of Robin's old mates in him, did Uther.

Bit of Spencer Tracy. Touch of Charlie Laughton. A lot of Durante.

He stepped quietly to the foot of the stairs and sidled towards the banqueting hall, keeping out of sight. Rose's voice strode out to meet him.

'He knows his history,' she said. 'He knows the country. He's still got the strength to travel through the centuries. He's ideal.'

'He's—'

'He's the only one who might possibly find Merlin for you.'

'No!'

'Don't you want to save the world?'

'Of course I do, woman!'

'Then call him and ask him.'

'Call him what?' bawled Uther. 'Call him Errol?!'

Oh, oh, thought Robin.

Rose's voice shook with indignation and shock as she said, 'You knew? How long have you known?'

'I've *always* known, woman. What do you think I used to do when I first died?'

No answer reached Robin's ears. (He couldn't quite think of himself as Errol any moĩe.) He listened with interest for Uther's explanation. It was ridiculously simple.

'I used to go to the pictures, same as you,' said Uther. 'In old London. Twentieth Century Fox, Warner Brothers, you name it, bloody Errol was in it!'

He's right, thought Robin.

'Robin Hood, Captain Blood, Sir Walter Howsyrfather. You couldn't miss him.'

True, thought Robin.

'I recognized the little runt as soon as I saw him.'

Oh, yeah? Well, why didn't you say anything at the time? thought Robin.

'Why didn't you say anything at the time?' said Rose.

A long silence ensued, then Uther mumbled something that Robin couldn't quite hear. From Rose's reply, he felt he could hazard a fair guess at what it was.

'Oh, you old silly,' said Rose. 'How on earth could you think that?'

Oh, thanks, thought Robin. His esteem, which had always been a bit on the shaky side despite his good looks, muscular physique, wit and devastating charm, sank to its knees. It would have remained there, but for Uther's next remark.

'Because he had everything I didn't,' he said. 'And he was so blasted good in every film he made. Truth is, old girl, I was jealous of him. If I hadn't been, I might have found meself wishing that *he* was my son instead of that skinned rabbit I begat.'

They talked some more and soon decided on a somewhat vague plan of action, but the main player in that plan was no longer listening. He had already crept away and was heading for the library where the archives, comprehensively cross-indexed, had a particularly large history section.

35

In AD 4097, Earth time, the invasion proper began. Grandeane the Sorcerer, using a relatively simple technique known in the occult world as 'The Moses System', opened up a mile-wide avenue in space-Time from Gnomedom to Earth. Not caring that he destroyed umpteen worlds and ploughed through several dimensions in the process, he thrust deep into the planet's crust and there made a vast encampment under the country known at that time as Inglande.

It was a land not unknown to him.

Encyclopaedia Esoterica,
AD 5008

'You will travel by night,' intoned Grandeane across the vast cavern. 'If you should chance to be spotted, neither you nor your observers will see the light of day.'

This was a statement of fact, backed up by the authority of one whose power can traverse the globe when necessary.

'When you are all secreted in the chosen spot, you will wait for a sign. Then you will emerge and do what you are so good at.'

'What will be the sign?' called out a really garrulous gnome.

'The sign shall be this,' said Grandeane without ceremony. 'The heavens will open and from the skies there will descend . . .'

The silent equivalent of 'Yes? Yes?' rang across the cavern.

'. . . rain by the bucketful.'

'Aaaghh,' signed the gnomes.

Every belly squirmed in anticipation. Stunted legs became weak-kneed. Grandeane smiled, comfortable in the knowledge that he had just pressed the button marked 'He's not God, but he'll certainly do.' Adding the icing to the cake, he said, 'And the rain shall not cease until the battle is won.'

You have gathered by now that the emotional aspects of a gnome's make-up are a little underdeveloped. To see a gnome showing any signs of gnomanity is less likely than seeing a smile spread across the face of a storm-swept cliff. Even Grandeane was caught by surprise at the sight of young gnomes weeping openly and older gnomes' chins quivering. A few of the really ancient gnomes sank to their knees, though Grandeane couldn't be completely certain whether this was out of worship or fragility. He turned to Scarbald, standing at his side, and raised his eyebrows.

'Good move, yes?'

Scarbald sneered back in admiration and jabbed his chin at the crowd.

'Quite right, little warrior,' smiled Grandeane. 'No time to waste on self-indulgence.'

He raised a hand and the clamour subsided.

'On your way, soldiers of Gnomedom. In one month from today we shall meet at the capital of this land and your place in history will be carved on the annals of Time itself. What's more, your little destinies will be fulfilled beyond your wildest nightmares.'

*

Imagine a sparkling waterfall cascading around you with vague Disney-type water droplets looking as though they were about to break into sickening, silvery smiles. The only sounds you hear are those of the world outside slowed down to baritone burps, and the wispy groans of protest from Realities crushed shoulder to shoulder like ponderous commuters in the rolling corridor of Time's locomotive. There is a smell of something wanting to catch fire and the air feels as if it should be oily but isn't. These are the confused analogies that leap into your mind when you are in that area of limbo between one dimension and the next.

'I could kill for a cup of tea,' murmured Archeous with unashamed honesty. Behind him sat his army of demons stretching like a swamp into the distant mists. Through the cascading curtain he could see shapes remotely resembling the trees, buildings and vehicles of Earth AD 4097. He was surprised to see how familiar they looked.

Two hours earlier Mr Savage and his platoon had slipped through the curtain into the world that Archeous was sworn to destroy, vanishing soundlessly with the skill of trained marines to reconnoitre before Archeous massed his attack. They had been gone an hour more than Archeous considered necessary.

'I bet they're lolling around with whores, and drinking and brawling like the morons they are,' said the demon. 'Or they've got themselves lost.'

Archeous hated soldiers, but then Archeous hated all men of violence. They had no class and lacked subtlety to a contemptible degree. The only thing they had going for them was that Archeous could use them to fulfil his needs. Never mind, he thought. When this business is resolved, they can go back to shovelling lava or whatever it is they do, if they don't get themselves killed first.

It occurred to him as he scratched his plump buttock that his ready agreement to the furry legs and hooves wasn't such a mystery. He was a Capricorn, ambitious, ruthless, a user of men and women, a loner, born to reach the top of the mountain.

A typical goat.

Baaa, he thought absently.

The curtain's shimmer became a shudder and it fragmented briefly as Mr Savage strode through it, dragging a snatch of sounds from the world of Man before the curtain closed behind him. Sparkling droplets showered Archeous' face and shoulders then faded, leaving him itching.

'Well?' he said.

'Yes, thank you,' said Mr Savage.

'Where did you get those?' asked the demon, looking at the webbing belts, boots and familiar items of twentieth-century combat gear adorning the man's powerful frame.

'War museum,' Mr Savage said. 'And my platoon *is* all safe and sound,' he added.

'Pleased to hear it,' said Archeous. 'Now, report on our strategic situation.'

Mr Savage smiled straight through him. 'Our strategic situation could be described as behind schedule,' he said.

Archeous stiffened and resisted the temptation to stamp his hoof.

'And what exactly does that mean?' he asked grittily.

'It means that you've arrived a bit late. They've started without you.'

36

AD 2500 and falling

The English countryside stretched as far as the eye could see, in that way that large fairly flat things do. It was green, lush and long-shadowed under a tiredly setting sun.

It was the sort of countryside that thrived nicely in the absence of Man, and it was doing so right now because Man had not set foot on this part of it for three centuries and had not dropped Coke cans over it for over two thousand years.

It lay quiet, serene and at rest.

But not waiting.

It is an illusion to suppose that countrysides, and their cousins the meadows, deserts and jungles and such lie waiting for anything. Whoever created that phrase should have his poetic licence revoked. Nature doesn't lie waiting, it gets on with growing and covering everything in greenery, or eroding and falling apart due to pressure of gravity and the weather.

The only thing it might consider waiting for is Man, and even then only for him to go away or die out, so it can get on with doing what it does best.

In fact, Man, being perverse by and contemptuous of Nature, was at that very moment not only *not* going away, but proving that he was still alive and well, by galloping across the countryside, regardless of both tranquility and a trail of sacrilegious divots spinning through the air in his wake.

Since the predictive faculties of this particular area of the countryside were limited to the seasons and the other foreseeables contributing to its survival, the imminent rampage of Man across its green and pleasant topography held no fears for it.

When the silence was shattered by the thunder and snort of a galloping horse, the local terrain hardly stirred. Rabbits raised their heads briefly. Sticklebacks continued to nose through the mud of gentle stream-beds and worms flowed with relentless patience through the soft spring earth.

When the hoofbeats clomped to a stop and the creak of leather, followed by an explosive, 'Bother! Missed again', crackled through the evening air, the countryside remained silent and unperturbed.

The man stood up in his stirrups, stared around him and sat down again with a thump.

'Damn, damn, damn,' he said without heat and in a cultured but potentially falsetto voice.

Robin, dressed in his usual green doublet and silly hat that looked like a small paper boat, blended in with the countryside as though he had been born to it, which he hadn't.

He gave a last glance about him, just failing to glimpse a great winged shadow skimming across the meadow behind him.

'Ah, well, Dobbin,' he said. 'No sense in wasting time. The sooner we get on, the sooner we find the Merlin chappie.'

Dobbin gave a snort that spoke volumes for his tolerance, wheeled around and headed back the way they had come, picking up speed at a rate that clearly belied his name.

37

The courtyard of Pendragon Castle was alive with activity, in the centre of which was a fuming Uther Pendragon.

'Where the devil *is* the dozy little runt?' he demanded at everyone in half a mile. 'Gods, can't I rely on anybody?'

He glared around at the stone battlements and up at the great slit-windowed turrets. The incongruity of a medieval castle standing in the middle of the glass and plasti-steel towers of forty-first-century London had not escaped him. Pendragon Castle, standing on the banks of the Thames since it was built by William the Conqueror, had survived all manner of wars and attempts to destroy it. It had been a part of Uther's life and afterlife for some three thousand years. When he became world ruler, he felt that he had a duty to save it from the ravages of time and tourists and he had promptly moved in. The old Tower of London wasn't exactly Camelot, but it would do.

'Belkin,' he bawled.

'Your Majesty.'

Uther turned to find his sergeant-at-arms standing at his elbow.

'Have you searched everywhere?'

'My men have scoured the castle and the grounds. We've put out an APB across the city on all audio, visual, mental and ethereal wavelengths.'

'Not too far, I hope.'

'Do me a favour, Uther,' said Belkin without heat. 'I ordered a restriction on broadcasts to a twenty-mile radius and ten days either way. He's nowhere to be found. And his horse is gone.'

Uther stared at Belkin for a second.

'Call off the search and get the queen,' he said. 'Quick.'

With a nod Belkin set off at a trot, shouldering his way through the platoon of guards searching the bushes and peering into the moat. There was a faint chance that Robin had wandered off in a drunken daze after the banquet and had stumbled into the black, ice-cold water. If they found his 'suit' floating on the surface they could safely surmise that his spirit was sprawled out in a nearby dimension, in which case he would come staggering back in a few hours looking like death.

Uther watched as Sergeant Belkin, his oldest and most faithful friend, next to Merlin, disappeared into the castle.

At the foot of a nearby wall, bathed in autumn sunlight, a very large grey cat twitched in its sleep.

After a few moments Belkin appeared with Rose Falworthy at his side. She was wearing her favourite 'dress', one that used up the very minimum of energy. This was not surprising since it could not have been more minimum. She wore a minuscule two-piece leather outfit with thigh-length boots and a belt to hold her broadsword. Uther glared as she approached.

'Your blasted Robin has disappeared,' he growled accusingly. 'What have you got to say to that, woman?'

'He is not *my* Robin,' hissed Rose. 'And what are you implying?'

Uther winced. Rose always managed to answer a searching question with a more searching question. They both glanced uncomfortably at Belkin, but he was peering dutifully in the other direction.

'I'm implying,' said Uther, waggling his fingers to indicate quotation marks, because he knew it annoyed her, 'that you've ignored my commands and sent the little toad to find Merlin.'

'What if I have? Are you going to let your misplaced pride jeopardize our one hope of finding him?'

'No, I'm not. Wasn't. I intended to bow to your wisdom and to give him clear instructions on how to get there.'

The cat, Arthur, gave a jerk and opened its eyes.

'*You've* sent him into a Timeless wilderness without directions or compass. *You've* scuppered our only hope.'

'For your information—' began Rose.

'I've got enough information! I've got all the information I need. Women! You can keep 'em.'

He turned to her in fury. Unnoticed, Arthur leapt to his feet with every hair standing on end and his eyes shining wildly.

'It's not my pride that's buggered us. It's your stubbornness. Your need to play queen.'

'Listen you . . .' said Rose, but before she could continue, a flash of grey tore across the courtyard, streaked between them, spat at nothing in particular and headed for the dark arches of the castle. They paused for a second to watch it go.

'Idiot,' murmured Uther.

Rose frowned. As cats go, Arthur was more of a brute-force merchant than a run-of-the-mill pussy cat. Rather than run away from shadows he would jump at them with both feet.

Not like him at all, she thought uneasily.

Then she felt a tremor in the depths of her stomach. No more than a slight dent in the fabric of Reality, as if someone was sliding a finger across a tightly stretched dimension and she was watching the bump moving across it from the other side of the fabric. In Rose's case, it wasn't so much a matter of watching as feeling. While her living body had been sensitive to the happenings of the supernatural, her spiritual body, free from physical encumbrance, was more so. And it was beginning to tingle in sympathy with something.

'. . . just have to hope that he's brighter than the average film idol.'

Uther's voice drifted sarcastically over her as if coming from a great distance. She refocused her eyes and peered out between the glass and steel towers of the city.

'There,' she said, pointing.

Uther and everyone within hearing distance squinted up at the sparse white clouds drifting across the pale blue backdrop of the sky. A shimmering knot of turbulence was heading towards the castle at enormous speed. The clouds near its path stirred and distorted slightly as it passed by. Then they resumed their shape as if the thing had not existed. As it got nearer, the apparently random writhing within it could be seen to be very rhythmic. Controlled. The watchers were struck by the impression of two great wings rising and falling.

The scrape of Rose's sword being unsheathed broke the silence. As she and Uther continued to watch, the men and women around them started to move uneasily towards the castle doors. A few of Uther's guards drew their guns and laser-blades, while the rest sidled hastily for cover. Without taking his eyes off the entity, Uther murmured to Rose, 'Get the lads.'

After a moment's hesitation she vanished and reappeared almost immediately.

'They're on their way,' she said. 'And *for* your information . . . in case I don't get a chance to tell you later, I've just come from Robin's room. There was an encyclopaedia on his bed, opened at M.'

Uther looked at her.

'For Merlin,' said Rose.

Uther nodded thoughtfully, gave Rose a shrug of apology and unsheathed his sword. The shape drew nearer, growing larger by the second. As he watched Uther was aware of the faint *splops* as his warriors appeared around him. Soon nine ghostly entities stood, grim-faced and suitless, at his side with their swords drawn. They waited while the traffic outside the castle screeched and ground to a halt.

I wonder, thought Uther. Is this the answer to our question? Is this the source of the miracles or, even yet, is it another form of miracle itself?

Deep within his ancient soul the king dared to ask the question that he'd once have sworn was beneath him to consider.

'Could this possibly be the Messiah?'

The shape was no more than half a mile away when it began to drop, a great squirming, light-distorting bubble swooping directly towards them.

The *whoomp*, *whoomp* of giant wings filled the air. Uther, Rose and the nine warriors raised their swords and waited. The beat of the wings grew deafening, smothering the cries and screams on the far side of the walls and the shapeless shape exploded into existence as if bursting through from another dimension. Bubbly debris fell from it and flashed away into the distance, leaving a creature hovering a hundred feet above them, an awesome creation, horned and winged with pearly scales glinting and smoke billowing from its nostrils. The sound of its wings had dropped to a barely audible *whooph*. The three pairs of eyes gazed down at the tiny creatures beneath. The tiny creatures prepared to fight their final battle.

'Are you Uther Pendragon?' called the creature through the pall of smoke.

'I am,' replied Uther in a clear, strong voice.

'I've got your wizard aboard. Sorry we're a bit late, what with diversions and trainee drivers. Sorry.'

Uther slapped his sword back in its sheath.

'Bloody typical,' he bawled. 'Y'don't see one for centuries, then three come along at once.'

Merlin, Uther, Griswold and Rose Falworthy, and the other bodies of assorted material-spiritual ratios, were tiny dots on the landscape when Ingrid flipped over and slipped into the next dimension. After a well-earned but short-lived break she would set about searching for the scruffy little man who, for some incomprehensible reason, meant a lot to Merlin. For the time being she'd hang around for a day or so.

'So you made it, then!' grinned Uther. 'And brought the young stallion of Camelot with you. Good to see you, Sir Griswold. Fit as ever?'

'Indeed, Your Majesty,' said Griswold with a smile. 'And you are looking . . .'

'Knackered's the word, but don't let the bags fool you.'

He pulled at his cheeks, giving a powerful impression of a depressed spaniel. Turning to Merlin he flung his arm round the Enchanter's shoulder and gave him a wild hug, not caring that his arm disappeared up to the elbow.

'By the gods, it's good to see you, you old relic. Only seems like a couple of days since we parted.'

'It was,' said Merlin drily.

'Come inside and have breakfast. Something came up this morning and we haven't eaten yet. We wondered where he'd got to. Now we know.'

'Who? Know what?' said Merlin.

196

Uther looked at him, his eyes bright and moist. 'Still as dizzy as ever, aren't you? You certainly know how to make an entrance.'

He strode off, leading the Enchanter towards the banqueting hall.

'Did *you* build that flying machine?' he said, cocking a thumb to the sky.

Rose and Griswold followed behind.

'I haven't seen him this pleased in years,' said Rose. 'That's one he owes Robin. Where *is* he by the way, do you know?'

'Who? Know what?' said Griswold.

Rose frowned. 'Never mind,' she said. 'He'll turn up. Are you well?' She eyed him up and down.

'My legs are stiff and my arse aches,' he replied indelicately. 'We've been travelling for some time.'

'Some three and a half thousand years,' said Rose, more for want of something to say. She had only seen Griswold once long ago and he had been in pretty poor shape. Bedraggled, to say the least. She wondered how many years he and Merlin had been back in Camelot before Robin had finally found them. Whatever the number, Griswold had improved considerably with them. He looked very *solid*.

'And what of thee, Mistress Falworthy/*What about you?* I trust that your return was uneventful?'

Return where? thought Rose.

'Why are you talking in that funny voice?' she said.

38

Uther stared morosely into the flames of the fire. 'That's when I realized I couldn't handle it without your help. I *had* intended to come and ask you myself,' he said sadly, 'but I can't go more than a fortnight without getting out of breath. So I was going to send her.' He pointed unceremoniously at Rose. 'Glad I didn't have to. No job for a woman.'

Griswold frowned. Some odd words had been spoken in the last hour or so. He glanced uneasily at Merlin and his unease turned to concern. The Enchanter's face was ashen. His eyes glowed alarmingly.

'Didn't have to?' he mouthed.

'Didn't have to,' confirmed Uther in a puzzled tone. 'No need. Wasn't necessary, was it? You're here, aren't you?'

Merlin darted a glance at Rose. She looked puzzled as well.

The ice blue of Merlin's eyes vanished and flashes of bright, blinding colours spat from between his eyelids.

Oh, oh, thought Griswold. He rose to his feet.

'What ails thee?/*What's the matter?*' he demanded.

The Enchanter glared at Rose intensely. 'Thou must go and get us. Now.'

'Go where? You're here,' said Rose.

'What're you talking about, you old fool?' warbled Uther. 'You're not having one of your turns, are you?'

His jaw dropped.

'Oh, gods. You are!'

Merlin's hair rose from his shoulders and flailed about

his face. His eyes watered and his cheeks shuddered. He was giving a convincing impression of having an epileptic fit while being sucked into a wind tunnel.

'Quickly, woman, before you completely change your mind,' he commanded.

'Do as he says,' snapped Uther. He hadn't the remotest idea what Merlin meant, but if Merlin said 'Do it' there was usually a damn good reason behind getting it done, particularly if it meant preventing a woman from changing her mind. For a moment Rose hesitated. Then, with a curt 'There'd better be a damn good reason for this', she vanished. Merlin's outline was fading and becoming smaller. Around them the air crackled and swirled impatiently as it tried to fill the space that Merlin was about to vacate. Things were beginning to get quite dramatic. What was happening to Griswold, however, was worse. At first he was rooted to the spot, unable to help the Enchanter. Then a ghostly arm reached out from his body and translucent fingers stretched towards Merlin, trying to grasp the thin wrist that was just out of reach. Uther stared in horror and then in wonder. From the waist up another misty Griswold, his face contorted with concentration, leaned towards Merlin's dwindling body. Hazy, callused fingers grabbed the little Enchanter's hand in a surprisingly solid grip and pulled him back. The eyes of the two men locked.

'How long canst thou hold on?' gasped Merlin.

'How long must I?' gritted the ghostly Griswold.

'I know not.'

'Then that's how long I will. Perhaps His Majesty could help.'

Uther snapped out of his immobility and started forward.

'No!' snarled Merlin. 'Stay back. If thou art sucked into this maelstrom thou wilt tip the balance against us.'

Uther stood back with alarm in his eyes. 'What is happening?' he growled.

As if in answer to his question the air turned into a gale. The curtains slapped frantically and strained to break from their rings. The candles spluttered and snuffed and the noise around broke into a screech. The solid Griswold began sliding across the floor and he flung his arms around a nearby pillar, while his ghostly torso was pulled in the other direction, his hand holding Merlin's in a grip of iron. His hair whipped about his faces stinging and almost blinding him. His grip on the pillar began to slip.

Then the wind stopped.

Merlin tumbled towards Griswold. Griswold the ghostly vanished into Griswold the solid. Griswold the solid thudded face first into the pillar and sank to the floor with a dazed grin and a smug 'We didit' dribbling from his squashed lips.

Rose Falworthy appeared. 'They're on their w—Oh,' she said.

'Indeed, "Oh", woman.'

Sparing Griswold a brief glance, Merlin the Enchanter turned and glared up at the proud, if momentarily confused, Rose.

'Dost thou know what thou nearly did? Hast thou a smidgeon of understanding in thy womanly brain?'

'Now you listen . . .' Rose's voice was dangerously low.

Uttering a cry which could easily have been mistaken for a yelp of pain, Merlin thrust his hand in her direction, closing his thumb and finger with a snap.

'No. You listen,' mimicked the Enchanter, though his tone, it must be admitted, held a degree of sympathy. Although she had some extraordinary powers for an ex-mortal, Rose couldn't be expected to comprehend the disaster that one can create when one decides not to do something that one has already done even though one hasn't technically done it yet. In fact, Merlin wasn't sure that he could explain in terms that she or Uther could understand. He held his hand before her with its finger and thumb still clamped together. Rose gave a grudging nod and Merlin opened his digits.

One should always give credit where due. Even with her lips held together, Rose still maintained her dignity. Uther, whose sense of dignity was closely related to his good taste, shoved a finger in his ear and swivelled it contentedly.

Two birds with one stone, he thought. *The old bugger's going to help me save the world and keep that woman in her place.* Uther was remarkably astute at misjudging how well-matched some people were.

'I'm listening,' said Rose.

'We both are,' Uther added with a grin.

'We all are,' mumbled Griswold from the foot of the pillar.

'Explain what that was about,' demanded Rose.

Merlin rubbed his wrist to bring the life back into it, took a breath to calm his nerves and explained.

Ten minutes later they all sat back and pondered possibilities. Uther's expression was only slightly more bemused than Rose's, but it was Rose who spoke first.

'So you were meant to be here yesterday. Yesterday evening to be precise, for the celebration of Uther's death-day. That was the Event that your dragon was . . . programmed for?'

'For want of a better word, yes,' said Merlin.

'And you were late because you had to stop off on the way?'

'Yes.'

'Why?'

'Why what?' asked Merlin uneasily. The truth would have to come out soon and there was little doubt that he would get no peace when the woman Falworthy had discovered that he had actually found James Dimmot and lost him again.

'Why did you have to stop off? And where?' insisted Rose.

'And when,' grinned Griswold helpfully. Merlin threw him a glance that would have blown Griswold's head off had it been loaded and went on quickly.

'More of that later, woman. Just remember that, had thou changed thine mind completely about going back to get me—'

'Us,' said Griswold.

'—us, thou would have altered the course of past history and future history.'

'And I'd have lost my wizard,' added Uther.

'For all time,' said Merlin quietly.

They stared at him.

'Really?' they said.

'Indeed. Coming or going, I would have been both and neither, trapped for Eternity, I believe, in a timeless limbo, though I cannot be sure.'

'And all because a woman chooses to change her mind,' mumbled Uther to himself. 'Sounds familiar.'

'I heard that,' hissed Rose.

'No offence, old girl,' said Uther hastily, but the damage, added to Rose's sense of guilt, which she would not have admitted to if she had been stretched over a wasp-infested rack, had been done.

She threw Uther a glance that clearly said 'I'll be in my room *if* you want me' and walked gracefully from the room, her air of regality diminished not one bit by the sight of her muscular buttocks disappearing out of the door.

'Amazing woman,' sighed Uther.

'Indeed,' agreed Merlin.

Bloody gorgeous, thought Griswold. To himself. Silently.

'She looks leaner than when we last met,' observed the wizard.

'Trains every day,' explained Uther with a touch of wryness. 'Seems to get younger as I get older.'

'That should be nothing new to thee,' noted Merlin.

Before Uther had quite grasped the implication, Merlin went on. 'We met Dimmot on the way here,' he said.

'Dimmot who?' said Uther with a frown.

'James Dimmot,' said Griswold, dragging his eyes away from the door.

'Never heard of him.'

'But—' began Merlin.

'It *has* been . . . three hundred years?' Griswold reminded him.

'Of course. Dimmot, Your Majesty. The miserable creature who did for Mankind what I, Merlin the Enchanter, could not. You found him for me, remember?'

'Oh, that little oik. Rose still speaks of him,' said Uther. 'As I remember, he did *you* a bit of a favour, young Griswold.'

'Indeed,' said Griswold.

'So where is he then?' asked the king. 'He'd be handy to have here right now.'

39

'Started without me?' muttered Archeous grittily. 'Is that supposed to be some sort of private soldier's joke?'

Mr Savage's eyes glittered. 'Beg to report, sir,' he said, 'that we have encountered open hostilities between what appear to be alien factions, occupying all major highways and surrounding all crucial emplacements throughout the capital. Bitter fighting has broken out and appears to be intensifying by the hour.'

'Which means?'

'The whole of London is knee-deep in gnomes beating the hell out of each other.'

'Gnomes?'

'Short and bandy, originating from Gnomedom, two hundred parsecs and three Realities west of here. Very ugly. Sir.'

'I know who or what. But how? Why?'

The sergeant shrugged his shoulders. 'That's academic. Fact is, they're here in force and all the signs are that they're not confined to the UK.'

'How do you know that?' said Archeous suspiciously. He wasn't wholly convinced that this mercenary bastard was telling the truth and he wasn't at all pleased with complications of any sort. He liked order and control. His orders and his control. Variables that might pose a threat to such made him irritable. When he became Prince of Darkness everything would be run on a rigidly tight rein.

'There are public video screens all over London on almost every large building,' said Mr Savage. 'What's happening out there is also happening in the USA, Europe, Asia, you name it.' He unslung a heavy (and by now outdated) rocket launcher from his shoulder and lowered it lovingly to the ground. He looked up and favoured Archeous with a mocking smile. 'I'd say the situation is a little out of control.'

Archeous felt the queasiness that overcomes you as you watch your fingers slipping from a greasy pole hundreds of feet above . . . anything. He swallowed and rubbed his palms discreetly on his furry legs.

'This isn't right. What about the locals? Is Man just standing around watching?'

Mr Savage paused before answering. He scratched his chin, apparently deep in thought.

'Man,' he said, managing to inject an air of ridicule into Archeous' choice of the word, 'seems to have dug in. Man is nowhere to be seen.'

'What?'

'Your enemy, your original enemy that is, has blended

with the landscape. Apart from one small community, we didn't spot a single human being all day. Just gnomes.'

'I don't believe it.'

Mr Savage shrugged again. He was in no rush to return to his old position. He and his platoon would happily stay here for ever, shooting anything that moved. They weren't fussy, Archeous thought furiously. He wasn't a strategist. He wasn't a soldier. He wasn't a fortune-teller either. He was a banker. For the first time since he had been in Hell the flame of ambition flickered with uncertainty. But somehow he felt that admitting to it might prove imprudent. Fatal, even.

He smiled a reasonably convincing smile, slapped his hands behind his back and turned to the sergeant.

'An interesting development, Mr Savage. What would you suggest, if you were in charge?'

Mr Savage glanced round to see the last of his men step through the curtain and shake a sheen of silver droplets from their clothes. He looked across the sea of demons sitting in silence.

Patient bastards, he thought without feeling.

'I would suggest that you find out what's happening from the only possible source of information at the present time.'

'Which is?'

'The small contingent who are still about.'

'And where can we find them?'

'They are holed up in the Tower of London.'

'Are you telling me the Tower of London is still standing?' said Archeous doubtfully. Mr Savage went on regardless.

'There are about thirty of them, give or take. The reason why they are still around is simple. The possibility of getting them to talk is not so simple.'

'Oh. Why?'

'Most of them have been dead for several thousand years,' said the sergeant.

'If you spent all your time talking in riddles, I'm surprised you and your platoon lived as long as you did,' snapped the demon.

Mr Savage's lips pursed rather dangerously. 'It's a recently acquired art,' he said tonelessly.

For a second they stood face to face and Archeous felt a thrill of alarm sweep up his thighs and glide across his navel. His mouth went dry. The low rumbling of the outside world crept into his ears. His eyes darted to the cascading curtain.

'How do you know this?' he said.

Mr Savage undid his grenade belt, dropped it carelessly beside the rocket launcher and sat down on a log. His men sat near at hand watching with expressions that varied from amusement to contained rage.

'We've met most of them before,' he said.

Archeous tapped his hoof irritably. 'When? Where?' he said.

Mr Savage gazed at the demon for a few seconds. Then his shoulders shook with silent laughter. 'Didn't Lucifer fill you in? The sloppy bastard.'

His men grinned, more at Archeous' discomfort than their sergeant's amusement. The civilian cretin had as much savvy as a stunted tree. What did he think they were doing here, sight-seeing? If you want to know what you're up against, you send in someone who can recognize the enemy. Each of the battle-hard men sitting around the demon had been in the front line three centuries before. Each one of them had got his arse kicked during the previous situation, the one that came to be known across the plains of Hell as the Night of the Last Trump. That was when they had followed Nemestis out of one Hell into another.

'The man who rules the Earth,' said the sergeant casually, 'is a long-dead monarch called Uther Pendragon. The story is that he was the original father of King Arthur of Camelot.'

206

'Rubbish,' said Archeous.

'Maybe,' said Mr Savage. 'Anyhow, he's easy to spot. He behaves like a king, spends most of his time wandering around with a sword in his hand and he likes his women.'

Archeous sneered with distaste. 'And he knows what's going on?' he found himself asking, and believing what this man told him. Something about Mr Savage said that he had no vested interest in lying because he feared nothing living, dead or in between. Three hundred years of swimming around in molten lava does that to a man.

Besides . . .

Archeous looked up at the sergeant and raised his eyebrows.

'He might know what's happening,' conceded Mr Savage. 'Anyway, he's the top man. With him in our hands, the masses of the world will be without a leader. He's worth having.'

Archeous nodded. 'How do we go about getting him?'

'Quietly and discreetly,' said Mr Savage. 'If we had only Man to deal with, we could go in mob-handed and wipe Him out. Whoever's managed to cover the planet with gnomes is a different matter.'

'Gnomes can be destroyed, surely,' said Archeous.

'The person that brought them here can replace those we destroy. Lucifer won't replace us.'

'Hmm,' said Archeous. 'So it's no good asking for volunteers.'

'Wrong strategy.'

'And this Uther likes women.'

'He's famous for it.'

Bastard, thought Archeous.

40

AD 1600 . . . more or less

The English countryside still stretched as far as the eye could see, which just shows how persistent countrysides can be.

Dobbin tossed his head irritably and flicked his tail at the bluebottles dawdling across his rump.

'Easy, old chap,' murmured Robin. 'We must be getting close by now.'

Yeah, right ho, thought Dobbin sourly. He pursed his lips and blew a raspberry, but it was the sloppy kind that horses do and it didn't convey his contempt for his rider at all. Robin patted him affectionately.

'All right, old boy. I know you're thirsty,' he said. 'We'll stop at the next inn.'

The road they were following was well built and fairly wide. It led straight across hill and vale and spoke of Roman origin. Robin and Dobbin continued, Robin looking for a sign telling him which era they were in and Dobbin toying with the idea of finding a low branch to gallop under. As they breasted a hill, the thatched roofs of a village met their eyes. Robin reined Dobbin to a halt and stood up in his stirrups.

'That looks fairly medieval,' said Robin. 'If we don't have any luck, we'll stop here for the night and you can eat and drink yourself silly.'

Which is just what you'll be doing, thought Dobbin, who wasn't too conversant with the limited possibilities open to people of a spiritual persuasion. By the same token, Robin wished that he had brought a 'suit' with him, in order to take advantage of the fleshly pleasures it allowed.

Then again, he might have been tempted to postpone doing what he had set out to do. The habits of a lifetime don't die just because we do. On the other hand, a 'suit' would have made things a damn sight easier. Trying to ask someone where you are when they can't see or hear you is a right setback and getting a sensible answer from cats and the odd dog is harder than getting rum from a banana.

They were half a mile from the village ambling gently down the hill when they heard the groan. They looked towards the source of the sound and saw a pair of soles sticking out from under the hedgerow. While Robin was a bit of a rogue when he was alive, he was not an unkind man.

He dismounted.

The man of the cloth was less than grateful.

'I di'n't need you prodding 'n' pulling at me,' he grumbled loudly. 'I was perfeckly happy where I was.'

He took a pull at the flagon in his delicate, long-fingered hand and scratched at his spiky black hair. They were sitting side by side in the shade of the hedgerow, while Dobbin grazed with ill-concealed impatience nearby. The man's clerical robes were earth-stained and grubby.

'You didn't sound too happy, old boy,' said Robin carefully. He had known people who were able to see spirits when they'd had a few, but this man had something more about him than just a fleeting perceptiveness.

And he looked familiar.

The chaplain turned his head jerkily towards Robin.

'Y' know what? You look familiar to me,' he said and he frowned. Then he sniggered. 'Love the hat,' he said.

'Thank you,' said Robin drily. 'Can you tell me what year this is?'

'Yes.'

'. . .?'

'S'sixteen hundred 'n' sumfin.'

'You don't sound seventeenth century to me,' said Robin suspiciously.

'How perceptive.'

'Then what are you doing here? Now?'

The clerical man took another long pull at the flagon and gave a deep, resounding belch.

'Wish I bloody knew. One minute we were being shot at. Next minute I was lying starkers in a field 'bout a mile from here.'

'We?'

'Me 'n' Merlin. And Griswold, of course.'

'Oh,' said Robin.

41

'By St George, he's got it,' said Excalibur. 'Now, do it again.'

Griswold's range of emotions was not what you'd call extensive. It ran from unashamed tenderness towards small, defenceless creatures and it finished somewhere around all-out severity when faced with cruelty. Had there been any spectators around right now Griswold would not have let them see what we are witnessing, but there were only the surrounding bushes and the high stone walls of the Tower of London.

'That's amazing,' he warbled excitedly. 'I never knew you could do that with a sword. Did you teach this to Arthur?'

'Indeed,' said Excalibur.

'Now I know why he's considered invincible,' said Griswold happily.

'Simply ahead of his Time, thanks to me. Again, please.'

210

Grinning like a child, Griswold went through his new routine once more. With the lighter, more wieldy Excalibur, he was able to do things that were impossible with the five-foot broadsword he was used to. But with Excalibur's training, Griswold's understanding of true swordplay and the resulting skills he was learning took on a completely new meaning. He saw now what the sword meant when it spoke of 'letting your enemy destroy himself'. No more hacking away and hoping you could hold your armour-clad body up for longer than the other bloke, or trying to carve through his chain-mail before your fingers seized up.

As if reading his thoughts, the sword said, 'Armour, yours that is, is now a thing of the past. Save for protection from the odd arrow, your iron-wear is nothing more than an encumbrance. Speed is all. Armour will avail you nothing against the enemy's stallion or a well-aimed broadaxe and certainly not against any propulsive weapon that the warriors of this barbaric world would use. But speed and the skills I teach you will prevail against anything that comes at you. One more time, a little slower. There is a minor fault you must correct.'

Griswold had been practising for over an hour with no signs of fatigue. His feet had worn grooves in the dried earth where he turned and side-stepped, but he was not even breathing hard. He felt he had enough energy for ten men. In fact, he had acquired enough for two.

Literally.

'Having no armour surely makes things easier,' he said.

'So does having no need for armour,' replied the sword.

'Perhaps,' said Griswold jokingly, 'I'll be able to do without you soon.'

'Practise,' said Excalibur.

Griswold raised his hand as Excalibur had taught him and parried an imaginary downward blow. Instead of presenting the blade square on in true knightly fashion, he angled the sword so that a blow would slide down his blade and catch on the hand-guard. Then he let his sword hand drop as if yielding to the enemy's blade, guiding it past his head until his own sword could roll over it and smash it to the ground under its own momentum. His free hand swept round and delivered a crushing blow to a fictitious head. In the average warrior's arsenal, this ancient technique would have been effective. The sound of Griswold's hand whistling through the air could be heard fifty yards away, and Excalibur knew that it had found a man worthy of its teaching.

'That was reasonable,' it said. 'Now sheath me and we'll continue.'

Griswold slid the sword into the scabbard, flexed his fingers eagerly and waited. Just then a tiny tremor of alarm slithered across his awareness, but since he hadn't yet got used to his heightened sensitivity he put it down to excitement.

'It's time to practise with the other hand,' said Excalibur.

'I can't. I'm right-handed.'

'You're also left-handed. You just need more practice.'

'Why?'

'For the time when your right arm hangs broken and useless at your side,' whispered Excalibur.

Griswold nodded. 'Oak hay,' he said.

He would have liked to say more, but the woman who appeared from behind the bushes made words somewhat inadequate.

'Oh, oh,' murmured Excalibur in muffled tones.

'Shut up,' said Griswold. His teeth flashed into view from beneath his whiskers as his face broke into a grin. *'Good morrow, my lady,'* he said.

'Hallo, mister,' smiled the woman. She was wearing, just, a white dress that swept down to the ground and her eyes shone with promise.

'Dost th—do you have a name, my lady?'

'I am Esme,' she said huskily.

''Tis a most beautiful name, yet it does not do thee

justice.' She looked at him. 'You are very young,' she said uncertainly.

'Pardon?'

'Draw me,' whispered Excalibur urgently.

'Why?' said Griswold, but the sword's reply was wasted on him. The poison in the three-inch dart flooded into the back of his neck and sent him slumping to the ground with every muscle powerless and his mind spinning into oblivion.

As Griswold hit the ground and lay still, another figure strolled out from behind the bushes.

'As Mankinds go, he's one hell of a specimen,' said Esme, staring down at him. She relaxed her concentration and let her body melt back into its natural shape. The dress vanished. She grew four inches taller and the colour returned to her cheeks; in fact, to all of her. She placed her hands on her smooth-haired hips and gave Griswold a gentle nudge with her boot. The leg that disappeared into the boot had the shape and length that women would kill for. The twitch of her long, smooth tail was not an angry twitch.

The other creature tucked a blow-pipe into the belt at her waist. She was shorter by a foot, but what she lacked in height she made up for in menace. Her long blonde hair hung to her shoulders like a lion's mane, which wasn't inappropriate since her face and eyes were distinctly catty. She didn't have a tail, though.

'Shove your eyeballs back, madam, and help me carry him,' she hissed. 'Hurry, before we are seen.'

They grabbed an end apiece and lifted him easily with animal strength, though neither of them was strictly animal or woman.

'He's very . . . *solid*,' said the taller one.

'He's a man!' replied the catty one. Her name was Hannah.

'Indeed, he is, madam,' said Esme.

Thirty minutes later they stood before a short human-looking creature with three strands of hair slicked across his head. He was dressed in a red cloak designed for a larger man and he had furry legs that were designed for a shorter man. Griswold squinted at him through sedated eyes.

'Aren't you supposed to have horns?' he mumbled.

'He's awake!' snapped Archeous.

'He's stronger than we thought,' said Hannah.

'Much,' added Esme.

'He shouldn't be awake yet, you idiots,' said Archeous coldly, glaring at Griswold.

'And, no, I'm not,' he added.

Griswold tried to move, but he found that his hands were bound by thongs designed to cut them off at the wrists if he struggled.

'Y'don't look like much of a demon to me,' he said groggily.

Archeous glanced at the women, straightened up as far as possible and tried to pull his stomach in without anyone noticing.

'And you don't look like much of a monarch to me,' he said.

'S'not surprising . . .' began Griswold before something told him to stop.

The demon sniggered. 'You'll look even less like one with your head in your hands and your bowels all over the countryside.'

Griswold saw that the demon had a thin sheen of moisture on his upper lip.

'I imagine so,' he said.

He stared round the room, overdoing the bleariness as much as possible. Excalibur, still in its sheath, stood in a corner. Archeous followed his gaze.

'Your tatty sword is of no use to you. You'd be torn to shreds before you could reach it.'

Griswold glanced at the two women. 'Indeed,' he said. The dizziness had completely dispelled, but it made sense to keep that to himself. 'What is it you want from me?' he asked.

'For now, I want to know what's going on. Where is Mankind hiding? Why are there gnomes everywhere? Did you bring them here to protect you? And how did you know I was coming?'

Griswold's eyes narrowed as his mind raced. This man was definitely not responsible for the miracles. If not, then who?

'If I don't answer your questions, what then?'

'Then your head will roll all the sooner. The whole world will see you and know you can't even lead a sing-song. Then they will despair. Then I . . . we will strike.'

'Strike?'

'Strike.'

'Why me?' said Griswold.

'Oh, for God's sake. It's common strategy, isn't it? Leaderless troops. Headless armies. Good grief, Pendragon, do I have to spell it out to you?'

'Of course not,' said Griswold. 'Silly of me.'

42

Rose and Uther left Merlin to meditate on the facts and surmises they had given him. With luck and his powers working together, he hoped to discover the source of the phenomena that were besetting the planet.

Griswold had trotted off to play with his sword.

'So much for your Messiah,' said Rose scornfully as they strolled beside the bank of the moat. When Uther took over the castle, the first thing he had insisted on was that the moat be redug and refilled with thirty-ninth-century technology from the Thames.

'What use is a moat your enemies can gallop through?' he had roared. 'Buggerall, I'd say. Fill it up.'

Now he sighed. His sense of purpose had diminished with his flagging sense of self during the last few years.

'We all have need of a god of sorts, old girl,' he replied. 'To tell the truth, that old fool back there is the closest anyone has ever come to something worth worshipping. Apart from y'self, of cour—'

'Shut it, Uther. I know where my place is in your heart.'

She linked her arm through his and gave it a squeeze. Uther nodded gratefully.

'You're still number one where my lips and loins are concerned,' he said.

'Well, that's something I suppose,' said Rose.

The moon has had many unlikely tales attributed to it. The sun and the planets have also suffered diverse speculations regarding their powers to influence the course of men's lives and the acidity of their vapours, but the moon has suffered more allegations than any other celestial body known to Man. And with good reason, since most of the allegations are true. The bits about the green cheese and the B52 are a little far-fetched, but the tales concerning love and lunatics are pretty well on target. It's all to do with the tides of Man, the ebb and flow, the electro-magnetic neuro-chemical comings and goings that respond to the gravitational electro-magnetic comings and goings that can raise ten million tons of ocean water a hundred feet into the skies each month.

Ask any wizard, werewolf or schizophrenic. The moon is a powerful influence on us all.

And it is so predictable.

A half-decent wizard can tell you what people will be up to in the next twenty-four hours or the next month by tuning his mind and body into the fluctuating forces exerted by the moon.

An Enchanter, on the other hand, can actually predict what people may be *thinking*, because an Enchanter can open up his soul to the moon.

Any over-sensitive person will tell you that the turbulence caused by the moon's influence on your inner tides can drive you mad. Fortunately, most of us aren't that sensitive, but then most of us aren't Enchanter material.

The particular mind that lay between the thin white ears of Merlin sifted and sorted, rearranged and made little quantum leaps while the Enchanter sat cross-legged, his body barely two levels above death itself. Facts, figures, dates, events and Events were herded into groups, scrutinized, locked together or reherded. Impressions were tried on for size, held up to the light of inspiration or placed alongside conclusions to see if they looked right together.

Soon trends began to suggest themselves to him. Projections lanced out from the light that filled his brain, striking into the darkest regions of conjecture that lie in the future and lurk in the unknown past. A picture was forming. At first it appeared in its grossest form, a mere mess of shadowy colours. Then it became clearer, more definite in outline as the moon swept its brush of logic across the canvas of Merlin's mind. Every stroke left not one line, not one colour, but an array of each as the Enchanter added the hues of his life's experiences to those drawn by the Earth's orbiting sister.

Soon the picture was complete. Before him hung a vision of the future, colourful, alive and vibrant. It was edged with black and spattered with blood and the future that it depicted was imminent. In the centre stood a man, no less at the mercy of the lunar forces than any of us, but who could contain and control those forces so that he was master of himself while most others were slaves. He was a cadaverous creature with a thin smile and delicate hands. He was the only man who could fit into such a picture.

Merlin's deathly white lips curled. He stared with hatred at the face of Grandeane the Sorcerer. Beside him was another figure. It was impossible to identify, since it was no more than a hazy blob, but Merlin knew roughly what sort of creature it would be: small, unusually gnarled and horrible, a fitting complement to Grandeane's height and grandeur. A creature who would enhance the sorcerer's ego. Grandeane liked small people around him, preferably ones who would show him the sort of blind adoration usually attributed to born-again religious nuts.

Merlin's lips twitched. It was over three thousand years since he and Grandeane had last clashed, when the sorcerer had come within a whisker of destroying him in mortal combat. Grandeane's one mistake had been due to his abiding weakness. He had given Merlin one last chance to acknowledge Grandeane as the true master of wizardry, greater than Merlin and all others put together. Therefore Merlin was to drop to his knees and worship Grandeane. Merlin had willingly knelt before him, but only to catch him off guard and unleash a power that would send him spinning through the wall of Reality to banishment for as long as he lived. How Grandeane had survived and escaped from . . . where was it?

The Enchanter's brow creased imperceptibly.

Ah, yes. Gnomedom. The world so suited to Grandeane's taste, where death was a way of life. The Planet of Squabbles where mindless violence was god and cowardice the one and only deadly sin.

A rough picture of Grandeane's imaginary companion formed itself in Merlin's mind. Large eyes full of hatred for anything that moved, craggy hands too big for its arms and shapeless feet, so named only because they were located at the bottom of its legs.

A gnome. Another gnome.

I have a formidable task before me, James Dimmot, thought Merlin. Before I can come for thee, I must complete it and my chances of surviving are small. But my will is strong and I swear to thee that no gnome who crosses my path shall survive to set the rafters of his alehouse ringing with the tale.

He began to disperse the picture in his mind before returning to consciousness. Grandeane's present location was unknown to him, but this was not important. Merlin knew that the sorcerer would soon reveal himself to the world, though in what way it was impossible to tell. His tactics were ingenious and diverse, but he was not a man to hide his light for long. The picture began to fade under Merlin's instructions, then it wavered and remained before him shimmering. As he stared into the scene, the gnome shuffled off, stage left, to do some typical gnomish thing like clubbing something to pulp. But Grandeane remained, despite Merlin's attempts to dispel him. For a second Grandeane seemed to be thinking, as if unsure of something, before his face lit up and he turned to look straight out of Merlin's mind into his closed eyes.

'Of course,' said Grandeane as understanding dawned. 'I am being observed. But by whom? A man of considerable powers, I believe. And I can feel your hate, yet it is not a gnomish hate.'

Grandeane squinted out of the picture of carnage and death and he smiled with genuine delight.

'Merlin,' he said. 'I didn't dare to hope that you'd still be around on my return. Yet, here you are.'

'Thou wilt have cause to regret my presence,' hissed the Enchanter.

'Mmm. Doubt it, Merlin. I won't make the same mistake again.'

'Thou'll have no chance to make any mistakes once we meet,' said Merlin. 'That is, if thou hast the courage to face me.'

Grandeane's lips still smiled but it was a smile of cruelty.

'Oh, we will face each other, Enchanter,' he intoned. 'But there is much I wish to do first. The Earth and its people are to be mine for the taking. Then, when that is done, I shall destroy you before the eyes of all Mankind. Merlin the Enchanter, epitome of goodness and right, shall perish at the hand of me, the "Messiah". The reputation you have so carefully nurtured over the centuries shall be shredded and rewoven until you are seen as the Devil incarnate. I'm glad you came. You owe me one.'

'Where are you?' whispered Merlin.

'Actually I'm not that far away. Next door, if you really want to know.'

'I'll be right over.'

'No, you won't,' grinned Grandeane. 'I'm not receiving visitors today.'

Before Merlin could protest, the picture faded, leaving him alone and feeling helpless. Desperately, he scoured through his mind for signs of Grandeane's whereabouts, but the sorcerer had covered his tracks with consummate ease.

Ten minutes later Merlin rose to his feet, shivered and went to tell his monarch to muster his troops.

43

Sir Griswold des Arbres found himself in a somewhat unique position. It was not one he had ever adopted before and it required considerable concentration to prevent himself from losing his balance and toppling on to the floor.

'Have you girls known each other long?' he asked with genuine interest.

Hannah flicked the hair from her smooth, furry

shoulders and replied, 'None of your business, mister. Just keep your mind on what you're doing.'

'I'd find it a lot easier if you'd untie my hands,' said Griswold.

'We'd find it far more difficult if we did.'

Her silky thigh curled round his and pulled it firmly towards her. The soft fur covering her body from neck to ankles was warm against his naked body.

'I feel ashamed that I can't do you justice like this,' he mumbled as her enormous red lips pecked at his.

The voice of the other female floated to his ears.

'You're doing just fine as you are, mister.'

Her six-fingered hands caressed his cheeks and ears and her body, soft and lightly scaled, moved contentedly. The slender long legs had a rippling quality that matched the languid gaze of her yellow eyes.

Griswold had to admire Archeous' taste. The knight had known many types of execution, including some meted out by himself with sword, lance or bare hands, and he had seen Merlin visit destruction on villains in a hundred different ways. This was something else.

'You don't *really* think you can pleasure me to death?'

'Not at all. The pleasure will be all ours, Uther. Then, when you're exhausted beyond help, you will die by other means.'

'Which ones?'

'You'll see. Don't stop.'

For some reason the bed was very large. It could, at a guess, accommodate over a hundred people.

'It's quiet tonight,' mumbled Griswold through lips that were not so much being kissed as engulfed.

'Shuddup and concentrate,' ordered Hannah.

For a moment Griswold thought she intended to suffocate him. Then, realizing that it would be premature in the circumstances, he jerked his head back and spluttered, 'You have a lot to learn about pacing yourself, my lady. If I had the time—'

'Forget it. We must do as Archeous commands.'

'Any chance of a reprieve for good behaviour?'

'Sorry,' groaned Hannah.

'More's the pity,' moaned Esme.

''Tis a waste, isn't it?' grunted Griswold.

'I want peace and quiet,' Merlin told Uther and Rose. 'I expect to be leaving you shortly and might be gone some time. I have to find a man. In the meantime, Your Majesty, I suggest you get in touch with this Wolfman—'

'Wolfstone,' said Uther.

'—and his warriors. I fear that the day of reckoning is closer than you suspected. You'll do well to muster them as soon as possible.' Adding to himself, Though I fear they will be little more than gnome fodder if my efforts are fruitless.

Reluctantly, he said, 'Summon Griswold and tell him I expect him to stay by your side until I return.'

Uther turned to Rose and raised his eyebrows in request. She picked up her sword and dagger belt from the chair and slipped them on.

'Leave it to me,' she said. 'I'll find him.'

As the door closed behind them, Merlin wondered briefly if this might be the last time he ever saw them. He sat down on the stone floor, pulled a stick of evil-smelling candle wax from the folds of his cloak and drew a potent, if somewhat ragged, circle around himself. He closed his eyes.

Hannah sat back on her haunches and glared at Griswold venomously.

'What was *that* supposed to be?' she demanded.

'Sorry,' said Griswold. 'I can't be everywhere at once. Not like this, anyway.'

He held out his hands and gave an apologetic shrug of his eyebrows. Esme, who had less cause for complaint, stretched with delight. Her long, slender frame quivered uncontrollably and her tongue flicked between her lips.

'Oh, Uther! That was heavenly, 'scuse my language.' She peered over Griswold's shoulder at the other woman's expression. 'But there's definitely room for improvement,' she added hastily.

Griswold craned his neck. 'Indeed,' he said. 'Unless, Mistress Hannah, you are more easily satisfied than Esme is.'

'As it happens, I'm not! It'll take much more than you, human. You'll never know how much I can take.'

'And,' sighed Griswold, 'you'll never know how much I can give.'

Beneath the Enchanter's closed eyelids a glow of energy began to spread. It seeped into the banqueting hall where he sat alone. All other creatures had been prohibited from entering until Merlin decreed it. Beneath his bony buttocks the stone floor, smooth and shiny from centuries of footwear, faintly reflected the dull red light shimmering about the Enchanter's features. The curtains behind him trembled. Merlin's lips moved soundlessly and, as such, the words that he spoke would only be heard by one other living creature in Creation.

> I call thee here from the depths of time.
> I command thy presence within these walls.
> I order thee, wherever thou be,
> To ride the tides that will carry thee here,
> To drift on the winds that blow through these halls,
> And cross the path of one,
> Whose existence prevails because of thee.
> I am the Good, I am the Bad.
> I hold the Balance here within,
> And, so I call thy presence to me,
> Thou Demon of Hell, BEGETTER OF SIN!

The last of Merlin's words rose to a roar. A wind howled through the windows and the great free-standing candlesticks crashed to the floor. Spinning across the room, the oak dining stools skimmed past Merlin's head, missing him by fractions. The banqueting table shuddered under the force of the gale. The wind became a hollow roar. The circle that Merlin had drawn on the floor, and in which he now sat, crackled and distorted about him.

For long, agonizing seconds the Enchanter waited, hoping grimly that this most daunting of spells would bring forth the terrible entity that he had sought to command. Above the roar, above the howl of the wind, came the reply from the epitome of Evil, the incarnation of all that men dread.

'You might say, "please",' said the Prince of Darkness.

'Both of us?' sneered Hannah. 'You must be joking.'

Griswold threw Esme a questioning glance and said nothing.

'S'worth a try,' mumbled Esme hopefully.

'Nobody asked you, you slut,' growled Hannah. Her blue cat's eyes glared at Griswold.

'All right.'

She leaned over him and began to untie the ropes on his wrists. Her tight, muscular breasts brushed against his back.

Twice.

'Just to prove you wrong, understand? You'll be begging to stop soon. And then your demise will be as undignified, as humiliating and as sweet as possible.'

Griswold nodded solemnly.

'And, Uther . . . if you try to run . . .' She drew back her lips, exposing two upper canines each an inch long . . . 'I'll sink these into your neck and drain every last drop of blood from your . . . beautiful body. Consider the results of your performance as a matter of life or death. Temporary, of course.'

I'll worry about life or death later, thought Griswold. Right now there's honour at stake.

'After the first ten thousand years, you've seen it all, done it all, even got the hair shirt,' sighed Lucifer sadly. 'The rest of Eternity starts to get somewhat boring.'

He leaned forward in Uther's great oak dining chair and poured himself another flagon of the monarch's thick, red wine. His eyebrows rose.

'Are you sure you won't . . . ?'

Merlin raised a hand, careful to refuse without seeming dismissive. Sitting still and upright at Lucifer's side, he waited while the Prince of Darkness took a long gulp and went on, 'Trouble with Mankind is it's so predictable. Half of it's good, half of it's bad and the rest is all shades in between.'

When Merlin didn't reply, Lucifer gave him a long inquisitive stare.

'I know why you asked me here,' he said. 'You're involved in this present business, here on Earth. You don't really think you can whop me, do you?'

Merlin relaxed his shoulders and leaned forward to look into Lucifer's eyes. It was like gazing into an endless tunnel. Lucifer's face seemed to go back and back, as if it was a thousand miles deep and terribly, terribly timeless. For a fleeting moment the Enchanter felt a twinge of pity.

Lucifer caught his expression and smiled. 'Goes with the territory,' he said.

'Is the territory worth it?' said Merlin.

Lucifer sat back in his chair. 'Nope. I can't say that it is.'

'And so thou intends to destroy the territory,' said Merlin evenly.

Lucifer gave him a pained look. 'Oh, Merlin. As analogies go, that one is not worthy of you. Have you been talking to Archeous?'

'That pleasure is yet to come, which is why I commanded thine presence.'

Lucifer smiled warmly. 'Go on, then,' he said.

'Thine motive poses a question. Thou hast made one attempt to destroy Mankind.'

'Ably thwarted by yourself,' said Lucifer lightly.

'And, three hundred years later thou art trying again.'

Lucifer said nothing, but raised the flagon to his lips. Merlin waited until the angel had replaced it on the table, then he went on.

'Why?' he said.

'This time it's different,' Lucifer said.

'What is?'

'My motive.'

'How so?'

'As I took moderate pains to explain to old Archeous, I intend to resume my original place in the scheme of things. The job I had before I . . . fell from grace.'

Merlin stared at him narrowly. 'And what makes thou think that thou'll be allowed back?' he said.

'Oh, I'll have no bother there,' said Lucifer and gave a vague wave towards the window, 'once this business is finished with.'

'Thine logic leaves something to be desired,' murmured the Enchanter.

'How's that?'

'Thou art hardly likely to be allowed back into thine previous employment after destroying thine previous employer's cosseted creation.'

In the dim candlelight, Lucifer's eyes glittered with amusement. The great white wings arched cathedral-like above his head to hang down over the arms of his chair, the tips brushing the stone floor. His muscular arms with their thick snaking veins rested lightly on the table's edge.

'If I didn't know better, I'd begin to think you had some inkling of the truth. The Ultimate Truth, that is.'

'I am but a mortal man,' said Merlin.

'And I am not,' replied Lucifer. 'I am solid, living flesh only by definition. I who can visit destruction on whole worlds, complete star systems, if necessary; I, who epitomize a million years' worth of human evil. I'm not a mortal man. And you know why, don't you, Merlin the Enchanter?'

'Yes,' said Merlin. 'I do.'

After a moment's silence Lucifer said, 'I learned a new trick the other day. Well, when I say "the other day" . . .'

Merlin nodded understandingly.

'I learned how to go to sleep, after a fashion.'

'Oh?' Merlin looked up with concern.

'Mmm.' Lucifer nodded, his eyes dimly alight for a second. 'I was on my way to one of the worlds right on the edge of the galaxy. Fair old trip, so I had a couple of seconds to ponder on the way. And, just for the hell of it, I thought I'd see what happens when you stay in a wave particle state instead of reassembling straight away, like you do when the journey is instantaneous. Have you ever tried spinning it out?'

'No,' Merlin said.

'Anyway,' Lucifer went on, 'I found that I could stay like it for quite a while, and do you know what? I'm pretty certain it's just like being asleep.'

'Or being dead,' said Merlin. He sounded disturbed and Lucifer shook his head.

''Fraid not,' he said. 'I can't keep it up any more than a mortal can sleep for ever. I'll wake up whether I want to or not.'

'Let's hope that will always be the case.'

'*You* hope what you want,' said Lucifer. 'If I don't get back to my old position, I'm going to keep trying until I can sleep for all Eternity.'

44

Griswold slid carefully to the edge of the bed and eased himself into an upright position on to the floor. With the grace of a large cat that was only just recovering from a night on the tiles, he slunk across the room, gathered Excalibur and his clothes as he went, and slipped out through the door. The light click of the latch did nothing to interrupt the gentle snores of the two creatures behind him.

Easing his legs into his leggings, he glanced up and down the corridor. The only feature was a door-shaped sheet of blue mist on one wall. He slipped his tunic and shoes on, went over to it and touched it carefully with one finger. The mist yielded as his finger sunk into it.

'Which floor would you like?' said a voice.

Griswold spun round into a crouch and tugged at Excalibur. His hand skidded off the hilt as the sword remained fast in the scabbard.

'I've heard of overreacting . . .' it murmured. The corridor was empty. Behind him the voice came again.

'Which floor would you like?' it said disinterestedly.

Griswold's eyes narrowed. 'Which floors have you got?' he said.

The mist remained silent. Griswold got the distinct impression that it was saying something along the lines of 'good grief'. He looked along the corridor again, unsure which way to go.

'Are you the mist that takes men hither and yon?' he said.

'Probably. Which floor would you like?'

'I need to leave the building.'

'Yes?'

'I suspect,' said Griswold evenly, 'that the way out of here would be situated somewhere on the ground.'

'Ground floor. Certainly. Step in.'

Griswold weighed up the possibilities for a second, decided that the mist was unbiased and thrust his head through it. On the other side was a small featureless room with walls, floor and ceiling composed of more mist, only this mist was pink. It was large enough to hold only four people. He stepped into the elevator. With just the barest impression of movement, absolutely nothing happened.

'I hope you're not going to pull that stunt too often,' said Griswold to Excalibur.

'I saw no point in being waved about when it was quite apparent there was no cause for alarm,' observed the sword. 'You're just wasting energy.'

'Let me be the judge of that,' said Griswold. 'You're supposed to be at my command, not me at yours.'

'Please yourself,' said Excalibur.

When nothing continued to happen for several seconds, he stepped forwards into blue mist. The blue changed to pink and a voice from nowhere said, 'No sir/madam. This way, if you please.'

Griswold looked round. The wall behind him was pulsating gently. He stepped carefully through it on to the street and into the middle of a pitched battle. A tide of dirty black-grey waves ebbed and flowed fitfully, crashing against the cliff face of the grey, sky-touching buildings that stretched the length of the street. The screeches of triumph and anguish cut through the air. The bellows of rage and pain thundered between the walls. A mass of ghastly waist-high creatures was heaving to and fro, every last one intent on clubbing anything else into a lifeless pulp. There seemed to be no way of distinguishing one side from the other. None of them appeared to be too concerned about Griswold's appearance, since they went about their mayhem without giving him so much as a glance.

I don't believe it, he thought. I'm being ignored by gnomes!

He couldn't help feeling a bit miffed, but before his indignation could turn to anger he noticed that, although every gnome was armed with a grim assortment of blades, not one of them had drawn sword or dagger. The air was filled with thuds, but no squelches.

Something's very wrong here, he thought.

He strode towards the two nearest creatures and grabbed them by their throats. Since the one whose head was being smashed methodically against the wall had ceased to show any interest in things, Griswold let it fall to the ground and lifted the other one up with one hand.

'What is occurring here?' he yelled above the din. Instead of either answering him or trying to brain him with its iron-studded club, the gnome squirmed desperately in an attempt to fling himself back into the fray. Its great, pale eyes glared eagerly at the heaving mass and gave no indication that the knight even existed. Griswold tucked it under his arm and strode back through the mist. Inside, his ears were greeted by a welcome silence. He set the gnome down, snatched the club from its hand and pinned it against the pink-misted wall.

'I ask you again, cretin. What is going on out there? Who is doing what to who?'

The creature hissed at him. A string of barely intelligible words spewed from its lips on the crest of an appallingly astringent breath and broke over Griswold's craggy face.

'Practice,' it mouthed. 'Gorra practise, muss practise, carn destroy if don bloody practise!'

It aimed a stubby-legged kick at Griswold's groin and reached for his eyes with its filthy nails. Griswold warded off the kick with his knee and held the gnome at arm's length so that its fingers scrabbled only inches from his face. Twisting its grotesque head from side to side, the gnome snapped at his arm and Griswold tightened his hold on its throat until the pocked, grey features began to take on a purplish tinge. It sucked in a deep breath and spat a stream of yellow oily fluid at him. Griswold wiped his face with the back of his hand and grinned at the gnome.

'There's no stopping you, is there, little man?'

'Bas'ard,' snarled the gnome.

Griswold realized that he was not going to get an answer by using standard man-to-man tactics. He let go of the club, turned the creature upside down and dropped to one knee. Throwing it on to its stomach, he raised his hand above his head and brought it down with a resounding crack.

'OWWW! Worra bloody 'ellsat?!' it squeaked, a sound almost unheard in Gnomedom.

'*That*,' grunted Griswold, 'is a spank, guaranteed to dispel the strongest woman's tantrums, and this . . .'

THWACK!

'. . . is another one.'

'S'undinified,' squealed the gnome.

'S'right,' said Griswold. 'What is the fighting about?'

'Toad turds,' snarled the gnome.

THWACK!

'All right,' the gnome spat over its shoulder. 'You assed for't. Now I'm goin' to tell yo whether yo lige it o' not!'

Griswold stared down at the gnome with alarm spreading across his face.

'You're not going to scare me, are you?'

'Scare yo? I' gonna terrfie yo!' It glared up through what it would prudently term 'tears of consuming rage'. 'Yo know wot we doin' out there? We trainin'.'

Sniffle.

'Training?' whispered Griswold, wide-eyed. 'For what?'

'We gonn beat the hell out of Mankin'.'

'You mean, you're all on the same side? That's terrifying.'

The gnome slid from Griswold's unresisting grip and

planted its feet firmly on the floor. It stuck its fists on its hips and leered through its tears.

'Isn' id?' it said.

Griswold picked up the club and handed it back. 'You'd better get on with it then,' he said solemnly.

The gnome swept the club from Griswold's hand and turned for the door. Then it paused, looked back at the knight and nodded.

'Right,' it said and vanished.

Griswold paused in thought for a second. 'Is there any other way out of here?' he asked the door.

'My sensors tell me that there are life-forms on all sides of the building. They appear to be universally aggressive.'

'What does that mean?'

'It means no.'

'Thank you. Then take me to the battlements.'

'What does that mean?'

'It means "roof".'

'Thank you. Going up.'

The view from the roof was even more impressive than from the ground and the noise had a different quality about it. The sounds of battle, when heard from above, are quite different than when heard at ground level. You get a more panoramic sound, more quadrophonic, you might say. The cracking of bones two hundred yards away can be heard as clearly as that immediately below, being unshielded by the press of grunting bodies around you. You also hear them more objectively, since your mind is not distracted by terror, or the need to adopt methods of survival, or the possibility of failing to hold on to your bowel contents.

Although Griswold did not succumb to negative distractions, there were times when he could appreciate the advantages of an aural overview.

This was one of those times.

The building stood apart from the sprawling tenements on either side. It was eighty feet tall with a low stone wall skirting its perimeter. Griswold took no more than twenty seconds to trot round it and assess the situation below. As he did so, a sound completely out of place amidst the screams and gurgles came to his ears. A sing-song voice rang out across the field of battle.

'Wonderful. Wonderful! Go to it, my little ones,' it called.

A hundred yards down the street, amidst the flashing neons, a massive video screen, fixed to the top of the ancient Canary Wharf Tower, displayed a tall, cadaverous figure. Seated on a throne with a long black staff in one hand, his image gazed out across the battle as if he could actually see it, exhorting and encouraging every gnome to keep on until he was the last one standing. Even at that distance, Griswold recognized the robes of a magician and the smile of a tyrant.

'Grandeane,' he murmured grimly to Excalibur.

'Manipulator of men. Destroyer of Worlds,' quoted the sword. 'I know him well.'

'If we could get to him, perhaps the slaughter to come could be averted,' said Griswold hopefully.

Peering over the edge, he looked around for a gap in the fighting, but there was no part of the landscape that wasn't covered in gnomes. He moved away from the wall and sat down on the roof to think. Two plans came to mind.

(a) He could join the battle and try to escape, or kill the sorcerer and every gnome in sight.

(b) He could wait until the battle ended or until it got dark or until one particularly adept gnome had defeated every other gnome in sight.

Or there was plan (c).

The ache in his legs had faded to a mild stiffness and the sounds and sights of battle had breathed new life into his body. Stepping into the blue mist of the elevator, he clasped his fingers together, stretched each of his muscles in turn and gave the machine an order.

'Women's quarters,' he said.

45

Still AD 1600 . . . more or less

'I've seen all your films,' said Dimmot. 'No. Tell a lie. Missed the one where you did the song and dance in the barroom.'

'Ah, yes.'

'Liked to have seen that.'

'It *was* one of my favourites,' admitted Robin shyly.

The coolness of the evening was settling around them and Dimmot had sobered up, more or less.

'Can I call you Errol?' he said.

'Robin'll be fine. You never know who might be listening.'

'True,' said Dimmot with a puzzled frown. 'Were you really as randy as you were meant to be?'

'Afraid not, old sport. Wish I'd been half as bad as the papers made out. Only just got into second gear by the time I died.'

'I know the feeling.' Dimmot looked at Robin for a moment. 'Your horse isn't dead, is he?'

'No more than you are, Jimmy.'

'James. Yet he's come from the future. How?'

'He's with me,' said Robin simply.

Dimmot thought for a moment longer. 'I really would like to go home,' he said. 'Back to London, 1993.'

Robin eyed him briefly, but with pity. 'Sorry, old chap. I'm going in the other direction.'

'You'll get there a lot quicker with my help,' Dimmot said very quietly.

*

'I've been looking everywhere for you, Griswold,' said Rose.

She had spent half a day scouring round searching the grounds for Griswold only to find that he had managed to get himself lost in a nearby dimension. Now she found two women with him who were obviously not locals.

Griswold had them eating out of his hand and Rose had a fair idea of how he had managed it.

'What are you doing here?' she asked him.

Griswold beamed a disarming smile at her and Rose's knees grew warm.

'We are about to meet the top man. These ladies have agreed to take me.'

'I'll bet they have.'

'And you?'

'What?' said Rose half hopefully.

'Why are you here?' smiled Griswold.

'Oh. Uther's ord . . . request. He wants me to stay close to you, dear, and wipe your bottom for you.'

'Then you won't mind if the trip is a bit of a squeeze, will you?' said Griswold.

46

Ranged along one horizon ten score buglers raised their instruments to their lips, ready to signal the first charge. Spanning one side of the plain from edge to edge a vast horde of grey, stunted gnomes prepared to drive their spurs into the shivering flanks of their ponies, flying horses and pterosaurs.

On the opposite side of the plain ten score demons crouched, waiting to leap up and screech in traditional demon manner. A milling army of demons hovered and twittered, pawing at the ground and glaring impatiently at their commanders. In their midst Mr Savage and his platoon sat smoking, cigarettes, that is, and waiting with the patience of the dead.

Grandeane and Archeous surveyed the scene with smug satisfaction. From their position at the top of the high steel tower that Grandeane had created out of the air, they could see across the whole landscape.

'At last the battle may commence,' said the sorcerer.

Without waiting for the demon's agreement, Grandeane lifted his hand for both armies to see. Two lines of commanders raised their arms in turn. Two hundred buglers raised their horns. Two hundred screechers raised their heads.

'Wait a minute,' said Archeous.

'What?'

'There's something we need to discuss.'

With a sigh Grandeane signalled everyone to hold fire. The commanders lowered their hands. The buglers lowered their bugles. The screechers relaxed their larynxes. Two mass groans of annoyance floated across the plain and mingled at the foot of the tower.

'What is it, demon?'

'Archeous,' said Archeous. 'And it's this. When this battle is over and the victors are . . . victorious. Should you, by some remote chance, come out on top, I require your written . . .'

'Written!'

'. . . agreement on two points. One, that you will take no more than one hundred years to satiate your lust for bloodshed on this planet. And, two, that you will call me personally to oversee the final conflict.'

'Good grief. You've got one hell of a nerve.'

'Well, I would have, wouldn't I?' retorted Archeous, unwittingly mouthing the only joke he had ever made in his lives.

'And if I don't agree?' asked the sorcerer.

'I'll be forced to call in reinforcements.'

'You'll cut your own throat. Lucifer won't stand for it.'

'Lucifer will see my side of things.'

Grandeane chewed his lips and scraped a hand across his chin. He knew that the demon was not bluffing. Archeous had unlimited backup if he needed it and Lucifer was one person that even Grandeane didn't want to answer to. However, there were possibilities here. Although he was convinced that his gnomes would win hands down, a contingency plan was always, well, handy.

'All right.' He nodded.

'Good,' said Archeous. 'Now—'

Grandeane held up a hand imperiously. 'But, if *you* win, by some miracle of God—'

'Hardly. Go on,' said Archeous.

'I want *your* written agreement that you will stretch Man's final death throes over a period of at least five hundred years . . .'

'You are *joking*, of course.'

'. . . and that I may be present at the final conflict. Furthermore, should I win, I may have at least five hundred years in which to decimate the Earth.'

Archeous stared out at the two armies ranged on either side of him. They could wait while negotiations took place. There was no doubt about the outcome of the battle in his mind.

Still . . .

'Impossible,' he said.

'Why?'

'Because Lucifer gave me one hundred years, maximum.'

'I thought Lucifer would see your side of things,' leered Grandeane.

Archeous shrugged a noncommittal shrug. 'I might be able to stretch it a little,' he said carefully.

'See!'

'If you're prepared to reduce your terms.'

'Certainly,' said Grandeane. 'Four hundred.'

'Two.'

'Three fifty.'

'Two fifty.'

'Three hundred.'

'Either way?'

'Done.'

The sorcerer reached into the air, plucked a blank sheet of parchment and waved his hands before it. Archeous squinted at the words that appeared, nodded and both men signed where it said, 'We, the undersigned . . .'

'Let the battle comm—' they chorused.

The screech of something squeezing rapidly through several very tight dimensions at once interrupted them in mid-sentence. A streak of grey light sped across the darkening sky, dipped towards the plain and hurtled groundwards, flattening out at the last second. It glided softly to earth like an experienced parachutist. In its wake came a dull roar, broken by a series of *pflopps*, similar to the clamping of indignant lips, as the dimensions snapped back to their normal shapes. A growl of alarm went up from both camps and everyone bobbed about, peering over each other's shoulders to see what had landed. Grandeane and Archeous leaned over the parapet of the tower and peered down. The streak formed into a blob and then into the shape of a man.

It shook its head to clear it of time-lag, glanced around at the military hordes and squinted up at the tower.

''Morrow/*Good afternoon*,' said Griswold.

'What on Earth?' said Archeous.

'Who on Earth?' said Grandeane.

'Would you like a clue?' said Griswold. 'How about knight of the Round Table, defender of the realm, destroyer of Evil/*and practising swain to interesting and diverse ladies*?'

'Ah,' said Archeous and he made a mental note to

interview at length two members of his female staff who had obviously been lying down on the job.

Grandeane, who was not at his best when left in the dark, said coolly, 'Do you know this idiot who purports to be some knight from the Dark Ages?'

'Of course,' said Archeous smugly. He always liked to have the edge.

'Well, is he of any consequence, or can we get on with the battle?'

The sounds of gnomes and demons losing their patience drifted across the plain.

Archeous paused, relishing the moment. As he had no waistcoat or braces, he tucked his thumbs under his armpits.

'Grandeane, meet King Uther, Monarch of All the World,' he announced. 'Thick as a brick,' he added in a stage whisper.

'By "thick", I take it you mean solid,' said Grandeane thoughtfully. 'He's . . . certainly that. King Uther, you say?'

'That's right.'

He stared down at Griswold. 'You are a colleague of King Arthur?'

'Indeed/Yes. *And you must be that evil bastard Grandeane.*'

'You are a little out of your usual territory, Sir Knight. Why are you here?'

'Because you are there,' said Griswold casually.

Archeous tapped his hooves impatiently on the steel floor. A brief tinge of unease clutched at his loins.

'For goodness' sake, destroy him,' he snapped, flapping his hands impatiently. 'Do that trick with lightning or whatever.'

Grandeane gave a chuckle that oozed ominously. 'Why crush the moth when you can watch it throwing itself into the flame?'

'In that case, let's get on with the battle.'

The demon raised his hand to the two armies. 'He'll be ploughed under in the first charge. He's nothing.'

A sigh of contentment went up as the commanders raised their hands, buglers raised their bugles and screechers . . .

'On the contrary,' murmured Grandeane. 'I believe that he might be *something*, although I can tell you from personal experience that one person he is not, is Uther Pendragon.'

He grasped Archeous' hand and gently pulled it down. The commanders dropped their hands in disgust, the buglers tossed their bugles over their shoulders and the screechers, uttering two hundred equivalents of 'bloody 'ell', flopped down on the grass and set about exploring each other for lice. Ignoring a melting glance, Grandeane smiled and leaned over the parapet. He called down to Griswold who had drawn his sword and was loping towards the base of the tower.

'Sir Knight!'

Griswold skidded to a halt.

'What?'

'Your appearance was an impressive bit of wizardry. Not the stuff of a lowly knight, would you say?'

'Not so much wizardry as demonry,' said Griswold with a smile. 'Female demonry,' he added.

Lucky bastard, thought Archeous, born Walter White. Memories of stinging cheeks and the words 'Filthy little sod' in the darkness of the Odeon Cinema filled his head.

If it kills me, I'm going to foreclose your assets before closing time.

Grandeane, oblivious to the demon's fury, went on.

'Since you are, as you say, there because I am here, it would follow that your mode of transport from Arthur's era and your apparent omniscience are jointly the work of an old acquaintance of mine.'

'Correct,' Griswold called back.

'What acquaintance?' snapped Archeous.

'A man to whom I owe a great deal,' whispered the sorcerer. He turned and looked deep into, or perhaps through, Archeous' eyes. The demon gave a shudder of apprehension.

By God, he's as terrifying as Lucifer, he thought.

'And where is the Enchanter at this moment, Sir . . .?'

'Griswold,' said Griswold. 'And I wish I knew.'

'Enchanter?' said Archeous. 'You surely don't mean *Merlin* the Enchanter.'

'The same,' replied Grandeane with a disturbing glint in his grey eyes.

'But how?'

'I don't know. I only know that I have an old score to settle.'

'You and I both. Except that mine must take priority.'

'Oh, no!'

'In the name of Lucifer!' growled Archeous.

'To Hell with Lucifer!' snapped Grandeane. 'Merlin must be mine.'

'No!' Archeous' clenched fist pounded the parapet and his voice carried across the plain.

In both camps warriors rose to their feet and pricked up their ears.

No matter where you go in the cosmos, there's nothing like listening to the blokes at the top squabbling to put a smile on your face before you go into battle.

47

Rose Falworthy gritted her teeth and squeezed a little harder. Locked under her powerful arms the heads of Hannah and Esme were turning greyish.

'Do you know what you've done, you stupid cows?' she asked them. 'You've let him go without me.'

'Glugwerpbb,' they said for want of something more apt.

'Precisely,' said Rose. 'Now, tell me where he's gone.'

She released the pressure just enough to allow a reply, as long as it came in fairly thin words.

'He's gone to find Archeous and Grandeane the Sorcerer.'

'Archeous. Who's he?'

'Our master. Lucifer's servant. Nemestis' successor.'

'Is Grandeane working for Lucifer, too?'

'No. He's nothing to do with us. Their alliance is just temporary.'

'Alliance! What alliance?'

'Archeous' soldiers located the sorcerer and he offered Archeous some sort of deal.'

Rose Falworthy's eyes narrowed.

'Then Griswold'll need all the help he can get, whether he wants it or not. Show me where he is.'

They rolled their eyes at her.

'You *do* want to breathe again, don't you?'

'Griswold? Who the hell's Griswold?' croaked Hannah.

48

'Well now,' said Grandeane, 'since it appears that you cannot help us with Merlin's whereabouts, the next best thing is for you to die.'

'Perhaps. Perhaps not,' replied Griswold. 'Where is your . . . champion? I don't see anyone worthy of my blade.'

'Even in the face of death, you sneer. My admiration for you is boundless.'

'Death is nothing. Your admiration is even less.'

The light breeze of evening wafted across the plain. The knight's whiskers stirred and his dark unruly hair caressed his massive shoulders. His eyes glinted with contempt and Grandeane's constant calmness yielded for an instant. His slender fingers trembled with the desire to hurl a sheet of black, flesh-consuming ectoplasm around the knight. His eyes twitched uncontrollably, aching to see Griswold thrown to the ground with the skin peeling from his bones and the scream of terror gurgling in his throat.

Only the will that had enabled him to survive against the most horrendous odds for so many centuries kept his hands at his side and his eyes from watching the feast that they craved. Instead he smiled paper thinly and called out, 'Hold on. I'll be right down.'

And he was.

'Most impressive,' said Griswold absently, as the sorcerer materialized at his side.

'You've not seen anything yet, my friend,' said Grandeane. He lowered his eyelids and sank into the depths of his mind wherein lay the source of his powers.

Griswold waited with Excalibur held loosely in his powerful fingers.

As the sorcerer began to intone the spell that would call up whatever creature he had in mind, the breeze dropped and silence covered the plain. Every creature was quite still. Every eye was on the knight.

'You know what you have to do,' murmured Excalibur. 'Your skill is complete. You are on your own.'

'I know,' said Griswold.

Only the low monotone of Grandeane's voice rolled across the heather, barely audible, yet piercing every ear and stirring every heart with trepidation. Every heart but one.

'I bid thee come forth, little one. Bring with thee thine mirror-being. Enter my dimension, prepared for blood, yearning for the screams of fear, desirous of the crack of limbs and the spill of life on to the yielding ground.'

Griswold watched through narrowed eyes.

The sorcerer raised his arms towards the darkening sky. From his fingertips trickles of smoke curled and drifted to the ground. They lay in two loose clouds at his feet, building gradually until they were a foot deep, black against the surrounding heather. Grandeane's voice rose in volume and his words came faster.

'Arise from thine rest, oh creature and brother. Fill thine black soul with thoughts of Evil, thine heart with lust, thine limbs with the power of death. Come forth and destroy he who would presume to challenge thee.'

He whirled his hands above his head and brought them together with a crack of thunder. In an instant the whole plain lit up with a blinding white flash and every creature staggered back clasping its hands over its eyes.

Griswold whipped his head away from the light, shutting his eyes to avoid the glare, but not before it had scorched through his eyelids and brought brilliant flashes bounding across his vision, obscuring everything from his sight.

'Your sense of honour is clearly boundless, sorcerer,' he

roared. 'You, who would have others fight your fights against those already stricken.'

He tried to open one eye, but the light persisted. The crack of thunder died away, leaving only the sound of a hundred thousand men, gnomes and demons groaning with pain and fear.

Then another sound rose through the universal anguish. The low, laboured sound of breathing, husky and gurgling, as if from ponderous, heavy-limbed animals, drifted over the ground towards him. Peering through the tiniest crack in his eyelids, Griswold saw that Grandeane was no longer alone. On either side of the slender figure were two . . . shapes.

Manlike, possibly, in that they had arms and legs. And heads, after a fashion. Both were squat and cumbersome, stooped over with great fists reaching almost to the ground. Their shoulders were larger than Griswold's head, their legs as thick as his waist. Had Griswold known anything about the dawn of history, he would have called them positively Neanderthal, except that Neanderthal man was never thought to have been twelve feet tall.

As his vision cleared his hopes rose.

'They seem to be too heavy for their own good,' he whispered to Excalibur.

'Do not be deceived,' replied the sword. 'They've got a lot of growing to do.'

'I see what you mean,' Griswold sighed.

The man-shapes rose from their semi-crouching position and rose to their full height, their clumsiness falling from them like snow from a sunlit roof. Griswold dropped his head back and stared up at them.

'Are these demons?' he asked.

'Trolls,' said Excalibur. 'Not gifted with supernatural powers, but nevertheless . . .'

'Still a temporary setback,' said Griswold.

'Temporary might be an understatement.'

'In that case, the sooner we engage them the sooner we will defeat them.'

Grandeane's voice carried across the intervening gap.

'Since I can afford to be magnanimous, Sir Knight, I will give you the choice of which weapons they use to slay you. Name it and it shall be done.'

'Snowballs?' suggested Griswold.

'I see. In that case, yours shall be a slow and interesting death.'

He gave a casual flourish and in the hand of each troll appeared a proportionately large sword.

'It might be prudent at this stage to discuss tactics,' suggested Excalibur.

'I can only think of one,' said Griswold.

'Me, too.'

'Well, since running like hell is out of the question, we'd better stay and fight.'

Griswold gripped the sword firmly in his hands and edged slowly forward. Grandeane folded his arms across his chest and strolled out of the field of battle. All round them warriors stepped back, which was odd since they were at least a hundred yards away already. They then concentrated on resisting the temptation to keep on stepping until they reached the horizon. Griswold circled warily. A plan was forming in his mind and he hoped he could conceal his intentions from the sorcerer long enough to bring it off. If he could manoeuvre himself close enough to take a swipe at Grandeane he could finish the whole business in one go.

'Don't even think it, Griswold,' called the sorcerer lightly.

So be it, thought Griswold. We'll have to do this the hard way.

He continued to circle, keeping one troll between himself and the other one. This is a standard tactic and can be effective in normal circumstances. However, it only works when one's opponents are of solid disposition and are inclined to get in each other's way in the heat of battle. It tends to fall down when they drift through each other's personal space, regardless of the fact that they are both occupying it simultaneously. Before he had realized what had happened they had descended on him in a sort of controlled tangle and were lashing out from both sides. Their laboured breathing had given way to eager grunts and their movements had become alarmingly fast and accurate. Griswold fell back, barely fending off their blows and finding no time to strike any of his own. Thinking that he was possibly fighting his last fight, he threw himself to the side and rolled away, coming to his feet in a manner that would have brought a smile to Rose's lips.

This is no time . . . he thought harshly. Ah!

A picture flashed into his mind. That contrary woman nearly changing her mind, Merlin almost killed as a consequence, Griswold doing something unthinkable in order to save him.

Divide and conquer!

Perhaps he could do it again. If he could just gain a little time to bring his mind to bear. If he could just grasp that feeling that he'd had when Merlin nearly copped it. He took a breath, gave a roar of fury and charged. Trolls might be faster than legend gives them credit for and they might be pretty effective with swords, but it's all instinctive. On the intellectual front, they are pretty slack. Limited, really. They are used to people running away, usually screaming. They don't have to form any new synaptic links in their thinking. They always react instinctively. Therefore several seconds elapsed before they could formulate a survival-related response to the fairly unique phenomenon of a very little creature dashing towards them, waving a very little sword. And shouting.

They frowned. They looked at each other. They were toying with the idea of frowning again when the fiery agony from two severed toes reached their brains and told them that it might be time to enrol on a refresher course in basic combat psychology.

They sat down with two soft thumps and stared at the fountains of red fluid pumping on to the heather.

As Grandeane strode up to them with an expression that might possibly melt granite, Griswold skipped away and concentrated furiously.

'Do we have a problem?' asked the sorcerer mildly.

The trolls pointed.

'Loog wod he dub to our tobe,' said one.

'Day wone dob bleebin,' said the other.

'An day blubby erd.'

The sorcerer threw Griswold a glance. 'If I stop the bleeding . . .'

'An der paib.'

'. . . and the pain, will you get on and finish the job?' he said.

Tightly.

'Yeb,' said one eagerly.

'Yeb,' said the other keenly.

'Very well. Nothing a little cauterizing can't cure.'

Grandeane pointed and released two thin streams of fire. And two trolls made trollish history by actually considering something. That is, whether to vent their feelings versus the chance of receiving more cauterization than was needed to seal up their toes.

Deciding that it would be prudent not to scream at the tops of their voices, they wisely played down the searing agony by screeching with appreciative laughter.

'Oh, thab won'erful. Thab marvlus. Oh, thag you, master! Ah, ha haa!'

'Oh bliss. Hebben. Sheah hebben. Ha haaah. Thags, master.'

Across the plain a legion of warriors stirred uneasily, poised and ready to dive for cover. Unnoticed, Griswold strove to bring his minds under control.

'What exactly are you trying to do?' asked Excalibur quietly.

'That depends partly on thee/*That's largely down to*

248

you,' replied Griswold. *'If you're as timeless as you claim, then we're back in business.'*

He glanced at Grandeane. The sorcerer raised an eyebrow at the trolls and they stood up, gave their feet an experimental stamp and grinned with genuine thanks.

A sigh of relief rolled across the plain like a Mexican wave.

'Now, may the battle continue?' asked Grandeane.

'Yeb.'

'OK.'

'Griswold?'

Griswold waved in agreement and beckoned to the trolls.

Their footsteps shook the ground as they pounded towards him and they swung their swords with renewed vigour, jostling to strike the first blow. The two blades descended simultaneously on each side of his head and it was clear to everyone, including Griswold, that he could not avoid both blows at once.

So he didn't.

A collective gasp went up. One Griswold had raised his sword at an acute angle to guide the troll's sword past his head and straight into the ground. Another Griswold, stemming from the same legs and body, had parried the other troll's sword with a sword of his own and had swung his fist to smack it into the groin six feet below the startled face. As one troll struggled to pull his sword from the earth, the other staggered back clutching at the fire in his belly and giving a tiny high-pitched squeak.

Both Griswolds had lost some of their . . . solidity.

Grandeane gave a chuckle of astonishment.

'By the gods, young Griswold. You are full of surprises. Whence come your powers? From wizardry or what?'

'From leading a double life,' replied Griswold calmly.

'Indeed? Well, I must admit it will be a shame to end your lives. Both of them.'

'I agree. Therefore, I will forgo that pleasure,' said

Griswold. He turned to the trolls. 'Would you like to talk about this?'

'Er . . .'

'No, they wouldn't!' said Grandeane. He had the distinct feeling that he might lose a grip of the situation if he wasn't careful. 'Get on with it!'

The trolls glanced at each other, reluctantly lifted their swords and charged.

Things became a bit of a blur. Everyone who spoke about it afterwards seemed to have a different version of what happened.

Some said that, while there were three men fighting, occasionally there seemed to be four. Or three and a half. Or any one of a dozen permutations. As Griswold twisted and turned, parrying and thrusting, another arm would . . . sprout from his body.

Others said that a third leg would appear from Griswold's buttocks, driving his body out of reach of a lethal blow or thrusting the foot into an unprotected knee. At times there seemed to be two slightly hazy Griswolds occupying the same space, separate but not quite.

Still others would have sworn that, each time a third hand appeared, it was holding another Excalibur.

The exchange lasted no more than a few minutes before the trolls fell to the ground, their swords discarded. One was holding his head in his hands. The other clasped a broken arm. Grandeane glared down at them.

'For goodness' sake, stop snivelling,' he hissed.

'Bud, id's so 'mbarrasing.'

'I fill such a foll.'

'You are fools! Both of you.'

The sorcerer turned to Griswold, who seemed to be trying to gather himself together.

'Destroy them,' he said tonelessly.

'I've defeated them. No one said anything about killing them.'

A pregnant silence hung over the plain.

'You cannot defeat them and not kill them. It's not done.'

'I'm doing it,' replied Griswold.

The silence gave way to an ominous rumble. The trolls glanced at each other hopefully. Grandeane frowned.

'But you are a warrior. Warriors kill people.' He waved a hand around him. 'We're about to indulge in nonstop bloodshed. We're going to have a whale of a time. It's the way of things. It's the way of demons, gnomes and men alike.'

Griswold had assumed his singularly solid appearance. He raised his voice to carry across the battleground to the farthest ears.

'*This* man does not kill the slaves of tyrants,' he said.

'But that's what they're for. They'll understand.'

Griswold considered for a second before his face lit up.

'Oh. I see.' He turned to the trolls. 'You *do* understand, don't you?'

The trolls shook their heads, one very carefully.

'Oh. You'd rather live, then?'

Both trolls nodded eagerly and, with a lift of his eyebrows and a shrug of his shoulders, Griswold slid Excalibur into its scabbard. Before Grandeane could protest further, a ragged, somewhat exploratory cheer went up from both armies. One or two warriors tentatively raised their fists in salute. Griswold waved a hand in acknowledgement and nodded his thanks.

'You're too noble for your own good, young man,' said a voice behind him. Griswold grinned and turned to see Rose Falworthy standing there with her sword drawn. 'Do you intend to take on both armies or just one at a time?' she sneered.

Griswold's smile faded. He wasn't used to sarcasm from a woman until after he had refused her his favours.

'I hadn't planned that far,' he said.

'It's as well I arrived when I did, then, isn't it?'

'Oh, yes? And what does an ex-serving wench think she's going to do to save Mankind?'

Before Rose could think of a suitably scathing reply, a shadow loomed over them.

'S'cuse mi,' said one of the trolls apologetically and he pointed a thumb towards the tower. 'You're wanted,' he said.

They looked up to see that Grandeane had reappeared at the top of the tower. He and Archeous were staring down at them, one with eyes of ice, the other with eyes ablaze.

'Sir Griswold, good lady,' said the sorcerer, 'your presence has turned out to be somewhat of an embarrassment. Since you, Sir Knight, have managed to gain a certain degree of prestige by your unreasonably civilized gesture, I am reluctant to frazzle or dismember you in front of my admiring followers.' He inclined his head towards Archeous. 'My colleague and I are about to engage in a bloody battle to the death. Not ours personally, of course, but it's important that both sides go at it hammer and tongs without the distraction of doubting my godliness and his demonic omnipotence. Therefore, what say we reach an agreement?'

Rose tossed her hair back over her shoulder. 'If it means you coming down here and having your guts scattered over the hills, then we agree,' she shouted.

'Ah, woman's logic. Can't beat it, aye, Sir Griswold?'

Griswold nodded and shrugged his eyebrows.

'No, dear lady. Better than that. Clearly, if you pop off and leave us to it, at the end of the day there will only be half of us for you to contend with. Though the outcome is academic, you understand, in theory we would all benefit. What say?'

Across the plains, on the hills and in the valleys, a hundred thousand creatures waited in silence. So far, this had been a moderately interesting day, but it needed rounding off. They couldn't help feeling it would be a bit of an anticlimax if those two at centre stage just wandered off and left them to it. The bushy one was quite a character and the woman had a certain something.

They waited.

Griswold and Rose each held out for as long as they could, then said simultaneously, 'Well. What do you think?'

By way of an answer they gazed impassively at each other for while. Smiles spread across their faces and from Griswold's scabbard came a muffled, 'Oh, oh.'

As their two swords flashed in the sunlight and Griswold and Rose turned to cover each other's backs, the hills rang with cheers and Grandeane, not being one to waste time on regrets, smiled, raised his hand and flicked his fingers at the sky.

Archeous, not being one to waste time on regrets, raised his hand and screamed, 'Kill!'

A horde of demons, gnomes and long-dead soldiers swarmed on to the plain.

The sky began to darken.

It does that a lot.

This time it began to rain.

49

AD 4097 *and* AD 570

There is a matrix of multi-dimensional forces of which space, Time and mind are but a part, and before which pale to insignificance the magics and sorceries of all save that which created it. At its centre exists the sum total of all knowledge, all myths, all legends pertaining to Mankind's reason for existence, to his fight against those forces who seek to destroy the Balance, and to his ultimate destiny.

Those who have been to that place are few. Those who have returned are even less.

'Welcome, Merlin,' whispered the Book. 'Are you well?'

'Indeed,' mumbled Merlin painfully. 'Thou doesn't make it any easier to reach thee, dost thou?'

'The rules don't change, Merlin the Enchanter, and you'd be the last one to wish it otherwise.'

'Thou couldst do with a dusting,' noted Merlin sourly.

'You've been gone for some time,' agreed the Book. 'The manual you asked for has returned to the matrix. It appeared very pleased with itself. It seems that you may have accomplished your task.'

'I know not. The idiot Dimmot vanished before I had time to judge the extent of his current powers.'

'By whose hand did he vanish?'

'By his own, who dost thou think? And another was spirited away at that time. An evil one.'

'Then Dimmot's power must be considerable. It seems highly likely that you succeeded in your aim.'

'So thou doesn't know for sure?'

'That information has not been entered in my matrix yet,' said the Book.

'Just a thought,' said Merlin.

'But that is not why you are here.'

'No. There is another who eludes me,' said Merlin. 'One who is capable of infinite cruelty.'

'Name?'

'Grandeane. You should find him under "Sorcerer".'

'Thank you,' said the Book stonily. 'Perhaps you would care to furnish me with more details.'

'He was born about seventy years before I was. His powers were at their height and he was aiming for world dominance by the time I was eighty. It was only by good fortune that I was able to defeat him. I managed to

254

incarcerate him before his ignominy became common knowledge. For that reason I fear that thou will have little information on him.'

'On the contrary, Merlin. Your father, Asmethyum, was very thorough, particularly in recording the events in which you featured. Give me a minute.'

Merlin gave a metaphorical nod, since his body functions had dropped far below the level where he had any control over them.

He waited, alone with his thoughts. The cold of the dungeon in which he sat, deep below the Tower of London, did not reach him. The clammy dampness of its walls failed to affect him. The echoes of a thousand tortured creatures whose souls still wandered therein did not touch him, for his own soul was on a different level of existence in a place that was spaceless and Timeless. Only one other entity existed there, a vast store of understanding that manifested itself in the one form that men, only a few men, could comprehend.

After an immeasurable moment, the Book spoke without preamble.

'Grandeane, sorcerer, born AD 350. Between the years AD 500 and 520, he aspired to build an empire on Earth and the nearby planets. His attempts were courageously thwarted by one Merl—'

'Yes, yes, yes,' growled Merlin. 'Clearly common knowledge, very interesting. What else?'

'There is no need,' said the Book, 'for tetchiness. Let me see. Mmm . . . Oh, yes, Gnomedom. Awful place. Ah!'

'Ah?'

'That's where the entry finishes. Ergo, Grandeane is probably on the world of Gnomedom. It's not my place to conjecture, of course, or to imagine, but I would assume that your sorcerer must have died many years since on that ghastly planet.'

'Really?' said Merlin.

'Do I detect a note of scepticism?'

'Canst thou tell me no more?'

'Is there more?'

'Who knows?' sighed the Enchanter, preparing to return to consciousness. 'The information hasn't been entered in thine matrix yet.'

'Sarcasm does not become you, Merlin. Kindly stay a moment longer. I'll see what I can find.'

Merlin remained where and when he was while the Book scanned its pages. The Enchanter had a distinct impression that it was muttering 'Pom, pom, pom, pom' to itself.

'Ah. Here we are,' it said at last. 'How odd.'

'What?'

'There is a reference here under "Sir Lancelot du Lac".'

'Yes?'

'Quote: "Knight of the Round Table, etc, etc, whose exploits, notably the confrontation with the sorcerer Grandeane and his erstwhile ally, Archeous, were often mistakenly accredited to the mythical knight Sir Griswold des Arbres." Unquote.'

'Archeous! Who in Heaven's name is Archeous?'

'Er, Archeous. Archeous. Pom, pom, pom . . . Oh.'

'Well?' sighed Merlin.

'"Who in the name of Hell?" would be more apt,' said the Book. 'Archeous is a demon. In fact, he is Nemestis' replacement. It seems you were right for the wrong reason. Lucifer has renewed the battle after all. There's not much to go on, yet,' said the Book. 'Of course, this Archeous will come to light in Time.'

'I don't *have* the Time.'

'I wish I could be of more help,' said the Book, but its words hung in the space no longer occupied by the Enchanter.

He had left the Book lying on the bed in his own cottage and he was heading back to London.

Perhaps a bit of clarification is needed here. When Merlin pops out for a trip through space and time, he always does the ultimate chub 'n' lock job, based on the premise that if you can't see it you can't burgle it. So he renders his home invisible to men's senses and impervious to their assaults. While Camelot Castle may crumble and fall, the Enchanter's cottage will stand through Eternity, or until Merlin returns whichever is the sooner. Thus do vandals fail to desecrate it. Thus do motorways curve inexplicably round its location.

Thus does it stand, Timeless and unobserved. On a shelf in the bedroom lies the Book gathering dust, a regular thesaurus of cosmic Events, characters, plots and intrigues. Since it, too, is Timeless, it can easily be opened by the right man with the right key in the right place, no matter what Time it is.

The Book paused for a moment uncertainly. People didn't usually leave its company without taking their leave. They rarely left without its permission. It pondered for an immeasurable Time.

Then *'You might have said thank you,'* it said.

When Merlin reached London, he would embark on a search for the one man who could lead him to his quarry. He could not be sure whether Griswold would still be alive when he arrived, or whether Man would have been condemned to eternal Hell by Grandeane's dreadful magic, but as long as there was still one able cell in his body Merlin the Enchanter would search and, when he found, he would move the very heavens before he gave in.

He knew for a certainty that he would never find Grandeane himself. The man had many awesome powers and he had little to fear from anything living, yet he had still gone to great lengths to learn such spells as would render him untraceable. Even Merlin, whose powers could transcend space and Time, could not locate Grandeane once the sorcerer had covered his tracks. Worlds might move aside at his passing, dimensions might split asunder, but by the time a pursuer arrived all trace of Grandeane's presence would be gone.

The sorcerer was very hot on insurance.

However.

Merlin wondered if Grandeane had thought about third-party cover.

50

Gnomes love rain. If there is one thing they that they enjoy more than a Squabble, it's a Squabble in the rain. The reasons for this are many, but it all boils down to size. When you are three feet tall, built like a cement toadstool and you have feet that could carry you safely across a swamp, fighting on waterlogged ground cuts everyone down to the same size: yours. If you can keep your feet when all about you are losing theirs, you will stand a good chance of becoming the only man standing. Gnomes adore rain. They write songs about it. They even sing in it. But even gnomes would admit that you can have too much of a good thing.

As the hordes poured on to the plain, the rain poured on to the hordes. In seconds the ground, the hills and a million yelling bodies were soaked and visibility was marginally more than two arm-lengths. Yelling was rapidly becoming a lost cause beneath the thundering downpour and bumping into things began to occupy a good deal of both sides' time. Beneath the tower, Griswold and Rose peered through the stair rods and waited for the first of the enemy to appear. From the distance the sounds of a battle of sorts met their ears.

'Not *me*, you stupid hap'erth. I'm on your side!'

'Well, get out from under my feet, you twit.'

'Snuffle, grunt, grouch!'

'Oh, yeah, grubble, sneer, what y' gunna . . .?'

'There's one, Serg! Damn, where's he gone?'

'Where've *you* gone?'

'I'm over here. Aargh! My flippin' toe.'

Griswold shook the hair from his eyes. 'Stay close,' he hissed to Rose.

'I'm not going anywhere, sonny,' said Rose. 'You'll need me here to look after you.'

'I'm going for the tower,' replied Griswold. 'If nothing else perhaps I can do some damage there.'

'Go on, then. I'll meet you at the top.'

Behind him the air crackled and, when he looked round, the woman was gone. It didn't occur to him to envy Rose her ethereality. If anyone had tried to persuade him right then to take up time shares in immortality he would probably have said something like, 'I'll stick to what I do best.'

He sprinted for the steps of the tower. Behind him, drowned by the noise of the rain and the shouts of the confused, came the 'clumpity clump' of four enormous feet.

Up in the tower a bit of a row was going on. Rose watched silently as the two figures compared their interpretations of an updated Geneva Convention.

'Unfair?' Grandeane sniggered in disbelief. 'How can it be unfair? This is war. All's fair and whatever . . .' he trailed off, shaking his head.

Archeous began to wave his arms animatedly. 'We have a contract. Signed. In writing.'

He was acutely aware of how silly he was beginning to sound, but he felt that he was watching his future slip away. The invasion that would have set him up for afterlife should have been a pushover. Now it had all the makings of a takeover. Archeous was also aware that Mr Savage had been right. Lucifer had not given Archeous enough input, either by way of information or of weaponry. A slight tingle crawled up his spine. It was the sort of tingle that could have saved Caesar from a premature end if he had been a bit more on his toes.

Grandeane leaned on the rail overlooking the battle and, without turning round, said, 'There's only one rule in war, little goaty creature. That is win, don't lose.'

'Making it rain is cheating,' whined Archeous. 'You don't win by cheating.'

'I do,' said Grandeane. He looked up at the clouds. 'Time to see what's going on,' he said. He straightened up, raised his hands to the sky and made a little placating gesture. In moments the sound of the rain decreased and the clamour of a rather sloppy battle could be heard more clearly. As visibility increased the extent of the chaos became evident. The rain was still heavy, but now one could see from horizon to horizon. Grandeane and Archeous (and Rose) gazed out over the plain. Where there wasn't water there was mud. Two soggy brown gashes, each half a mile wide, marked the paths of the marauding armies from the opposite horizons. Around the tower, as far as the eye bothered to look, a carpet of waterlogged warriors stood about, looking round and toying with their weapons. All the flying creatures had been beaten to the ground by the downpour and lay spread over the earth, and the slower-moving ground-troops, like soaked handkerchiefs. The only casualties were those trodden into the mud in the rush. It looked suspiciously like there might be a colossal anticlimax in the offing.

Unseen by the sorcerer, Griswold paused at the base of the tower. He looked around to see a listless lack of carnage and two mud-splattered trolls staring down at him.

'What do you want?' he said.

'Er . . .' said one.

'Uhm . . .' said the other.

'Ford you mide lige a hand,' said the first one.

'Could be fatal,' said Griswold.

'Could be worse,' said the trolls.

They smiled sheepishly.

'Lose that tower,' said Griswold.

Archeous stared across the plain and gave Grandeane a glare.

'Well, you've really put a damper on things,' he said and made a mental note of Grandeane and Lucifer under 'people to see to before the lights finally go out'.

'Now what?' he said shortly.

'Now we get on with the battle,' smiled Grandeane. 'My lads beat your lads and Earth is mine for the taking.'

'You'd make a marvellous Lucifer,' murmured Archeous sourly.

'Don't think he isn't on my list,' said the sorcerer and he snapped his fingers.

A minor disturbance occurred in the centre of the room. The air distorted, swirled a little and, with a velvety *floop* sound, a large casket appeared in the centre of the floor. With an emotionless creak, the lid rose. Archeous drew back in alarm.

'What are you doing?' he gasped. 'What's in there?'

Grandeane leaned over and peered in. 'Well, there's chicken, pickled onions, pork pies, selection of cheeses. What do you fancy?'

'What?' said Archeous weakly.

'You don't want to watch the battle on an empty stomach, do you?'

And Grandeane looked round at Rose who was gazing wide-eyed with surprise.

'Perhaps the lady would care to join us,' he said.

If Rose was shocked by his awareness of her presence, she didn't have time to show it. The floor heaved beneath them and, with a scream of protesting metal, the tower buckled at the base and toppled majestically to the ground.

51

By the time the tower had splashed into the thick grey mud, its three occupants had departed, leaving it empty.

Grandeane had whipped off to the nearest hillside where he sat down under an instant, erect-it-y'self (if you're a sorcerer, that is) awning complete with table, two loungers and a bottle of Gnomedom '38, 'a little fat in the legs, but with a dry agreeable un-Gnomish aftertaste'.

Archeous had let the tower fall from under him and was making a gentle descent to Earth with the hole where his heart once was throbbing with anger and his eyes peeled for Mr Savage.

Rose for some reason had decided to wait until the very last moment before flinging herself from the structure and going into a superb rolling breakfall. She wasn't really sure why she did it, but then women are unusual creatures, especially women who wear swords.

And roll around in mud.

And do things to impress younger men.

Perhaps they are not so unusual.

She came to her feet with so much mud dripping from her aura (which was only half a wavelength away from being fairly solid), that it outlined the contours of her figure in a glistening sheen. Drawing her sword, she looked round for the cause of the tower's collapse. Griswold was coming towards her and, apart from the two trolls who were watching her intently with their arms around each other's shoulders, everyone else was getting back into the swing. Squelches and thuds were starting to pick up nicely.

The screams began to assume a satisfyingly high-pitched quality.

'You should bathe in mud more often,' shouted Griswold above the noise. 'It becomes you.'

Rose glared back at him. 'Did you shove the tower over?' she demanded.

'Not me personally. Are you all right?'

'If I'd been alive, you could have killed me!'

'Where's the sorcerer?' asked Griswold.

Rose glanced round and pointed. 'There's Grandeane. That thing giving an impression of a dying duck in flight is Archeous.'

'Right. You take care of Archeous. I'm going to finish off Grandeane once and for all.'

Rose gazed at him in astonishment. 'You're not real, d'you know that?' she said.

'I feel real,' said Griswold. 'Quite solid, in fact.'

'You won't be solid if you take on Grandeane. He's got more power in one brain cell than you've got in your two.'

Griswold looked up the hill to where Grandeane was pouring himself another glass of '38 and made a mental note to ask the Enchanter what a brain cell was.

'Perhaps a bit of help from Merlin might not come amiss,' he said. 'Do you know where he is?'

Rose shook her head.

'Then I've no time to waste,' said Griswold. 'See to the duck.'

And he sprinted off towards the sorcerer, swerving between the struggling warriors and gathering speed until his legs became a rapidly receding blur. Rose stared after him for a moment, then turned an imposing glare on the trolls.

'He's going to need all the help he can get,' she said meaningfully.

'Oag hay.'

'We're on our way.'

They turned as one and shot off after Griswold, leaving two streaks of grey smoke weaving through the crowds behind them.

Rose looked up at the descending Archeous.

'Right, sunshine,' she murmured. 'You want to invade my Uther's kingdom, you have to get past me.'

Not far away, at a point three and a half feet above the ground, a small patch of air creaked and wavered, rather like clingfilm being stretched out of shape.

Griswold took the slope of the hill in his stride and powered towards Grandeane with the trolls close on his heels. Most of the fighting was far behind him. While he was still half a mile away, Grandeane glanced up. His face took on an expression of delight.

'Jolly good, Sir Knight. You don't hang about, do you?'

He pointed two fingers and a bolt of something nasty flashed through the air, tearing up a jagged canyon inches in front of Griswold. It was easily twenty feet across and terminally deep. And it was too close for Griswold to avoid.

'Oh, oh,' murmured Excalibur, but Griswold wasn't so easily deterred. In the three paces that he had left, he increased his speed and drove himself into the air. He sailed across the gap and came down running.

The trolls threw themselves after him, hit the ground in a smoky tangle, scrambled free of each other and stumbled on. Grandeane clapped his hands.

'Bravo, Sir Knight! Bravo,' he chortled. 'Try this one.'

With a faint flash, a great squat creature made only of bones stood blocking Griswold's path with a club the size of a tree trunk raised over its head. Griswold swerved to his right drawing off the blow to come, then veered to his left. As the club thudded into the earth, he let loose a punch with his bare fist which struck the creature's breastbone, shattering it and sending bones hurtling off in every direction.

'Ah, well,' called Grandeane, 'worth a go, if only for the entertainment value. You're getting a bit too close for comfort, Griswold. It's coup de grâce time, I'm afraid.'

He made an odd gesture with one hand and then pointed his thumb at Griswold. Griswold ran on, ready to duck, dive or do whatever the sorcerer's mode of attack demanded. Behind him the trolls groaned in alarm.

'Oh, no!'

'Nod dad blubby trig again!'

Griswold managed two more paces before one pair of smoky arms engulfed his head while another pair wrapped themselves round his legs and brought him crashing down. As he hit the ground a ragged golden streak glittered through the space he had just vacated. He had never seen barbed wire, but the way in which this weapon tore into a troll's shoulder and left a shredded gully of flesh in its wake told Griswold that, as a weapon, it had potential.

He tried to rise.

'No,' chorused the trolls.

'He'be only jus begun.'

They rose to their feet and closed up, shielding Griswold from the sorcerer's aim.

'Stay dowb,' said one, which was rather unnecessary as the other one was resting his foot on Griswold's chest. Another streak crackled and tore through trollish ribs, spraying Griswold with blood and smoke. The troll staggered.

'Bas'ard,' he roared.

Up the hill, Grandeane was starting to become annoyed. He wasn't used to rebellion.

'Stand aside, fools,' he snapped.

'*You* stand aside,' came the reply which was pretty stupid, even for a troll. Under his foot, Griswold squirmed and fumed.

'Let me rise/*get your damn foot off me*,' he growled. As

if in answer to his command, the foot rose, but only because its owner was sent reeling with strands of gold wrapped round his head and shoulders. For a moment he remained upright, like a tinsel-covered christmas tree with smoking blood rolling down his arms. Then he crashed to the ground with a cry.

Half a mile down the slope, the patch of warped space paused. It appeared to hesitate and look around. Then it skimmed over the plain towards Sir Griswold des Arbres. Little rhythmic bulges appeared underneath it and one could imagine invisible feet running over a suspended sheet of rubber.

By the time Griswold had risen to his feet, both trolls were covered in the terrible strands. As they tightened and cut into the trolls' skin, bloodied smoke dribbled from their giant frames. With imploring stares, the trolls began to disperse.

'We're off, Giswol,' said one.

'Goo' luck, Giswol,' said the other.

'Keep yo' head down,' they choroused and, with their faces contorting in agony, they dissolved into a grey misty heap. It spread across the ground, lapped briefly at Griswold's ankles then seeped into the heather. Griswold turned to stare at Grandeane through eyes that blazed. He threw a glance at the remaining dribble of smoke, gripped Excalibur and raced up the hill once more.

Archeous hit the earth solidly, sank up to his ankles and spent several seconds dragging his hooves free. He looked up to see a woman staring down at him. She was built like an Amazon and held the promise of an incredible experience in her green eyes. She also held the biggest sword that Archeous had ever seen.

'What do you want?' he snapped.

'You, ducky,' said Rose, raising the sword.

Archeous glared and they circled each other warily. Rose wasn't ready to skewer the demon before she had tried to find out what he was up to, and Archeous wasn't too sure about how he should handle Rose. She was easily a foot taller than he and obviously as fit as Hell, even for a spirit. Her sword wasn't something you could ignore either.

But she was only a woman.

Archeous', née Walter White's, opinion of women was only slightly jaundiced by the manner in which the long and shallow relationship with his wife had ended. Walter had engineered the 'voluntary' redundancy of his assistant manager, who immediately lapsed into a widely predicted breakdown. Two days later Florence White popped round to the depressed bachelor's semi to offer sympathy and homemade pickles, and she never came back. Up to that time Archeous' opinion of women had been simply one of derision.

'Who the Devil *are* you?' He frowned.

'Rose Falworthy, you little tyke. Consort to Uther Pendragon and the one who's going to dice your podgy carcass into chips.'

And she effectively dispelled Walter White's lifelong contempt by slicing up the next two protagonists who staggered too close to her blade.

Archeous licked his lips.

'Savage!' he yelled.

The next few moments were a turning point in his lives. He realized, somewhat belatedly, that first impressions, or even lifelong ones, should always be open to change. As the flat of Rose's hand spun his head through one hundred and eighty-five degrees, the snarl that came from her lips was completely and exquisitely womanly. The fist that lifted him from the ground by his chest hairs and the guttural, 'You're calling *me* a savage?', had all the femininity of Mike Tyson just before the referee steps in.

Archeous the demon embarked on the most one-sided

and painfully besotted love affair of his lives. Also short-lived.

'I'm sorry,' he whimpered. 'I wasn't referring to you.'

Rose brought his face to within kissing distance.

'Up the hill,' she said. 'Now.'

'Isn't this pleasant?' cried Grandeane happily. 'All together, watching the toings and froings of the masses as they hack each other to pieces. Marvellous!'

He laid back in his chair and gazed at the battle which had spread across the plain and was now at full pitch. Both armies had been totally routed when rain stopped play and any hope of regrouping was long past, not that anyone down there seemed to mind. The dull explosions of ancient military weapons occasionally disturbed the relative peace of hand-to-hand fighting whilst peppering the skies with bits of gnome and demon alike.

'That must be some of your lot,' said Grandeane to Archeous. 'My lads wouldn't resort to such crudities. Explosives must be a new experience for you, Sir Griswold.'

Griswold said nothing. After Rose had joined him to spend several minutes trying to cut their way through the sorcerer's invisible defences, and Excalibur had advised them that it was futile, Griswold simply watched patiently and waited for his chance. Rose waited with considerably less patience, making her feelings plain to all around her.

'. . . not worthy of being called a man . . .'

'. . . I've known eunuchs with more balls . . .'

'. . . back-street wizard . . .'

'My only regret,' said Grandeane, as if Rose did not exist, 'is that Master Merlin cannot be with us to witness my victory *and* the demise of you people when the battle is over.'

'Fear not, sorcerer,' said a thin, distant voice in his ear. 'I am here and thou wilt have more cause to regret mine presence than mine absence.'

The four of them could see what appeared to be a small disturbance of air inches from Grandeane's face. The sorcerer smiled.

'Merlin! You never fail to amaze me. I'd have sworn that I'd covered my tracks. How did you find me?'

'I didn't. I found him.' A slight, finger-like protrusion in the air pointed at the grinning Griswold. 'He led me to thee. Now, lower thine shield and face me like a man.'

'Ahm. I think not, Merlin. You'd only cause trouble. We're having much too good a time to let you spoil it, aren't we, friends?'

The Enchanter's voice rose, but it still couldn't get above a tinny echo to bridge the gap between their two dimensions.

'I command thee, Grandeane, as thine victor and incarcerator in times past, let me in. Or dost thou tremble at the thought of what my powers will do to thee?'

Oh, oh, thought Griswold. He never learns. He looked at Grandeane and knew that events were about to take a slight turn. Grandeane's face told him so.

'You talk of power, Enchanter,' said Grandeane. 'You who cannot break through my simple shield. I'll show you power.'

His smile faded and his eyebrows rose to meet over the bridge of his nose. He held his hands out flat before him. Archeous, speechless up to now, croaked. 'What are you doing?'

Ignoring him, Grandeane turned his hands up and over until they touched palm to palm. Down on the plain two great strips of earth, both half a mile long, rose up with a mass of bodies between them. As the screaming figures tumbled and fell, the strips crashed together like giant waves, smashing into a million blood-stained clods and falling back to Earth.

'No!' squeaked the little patch of air. 'I don't believe it.'

'You still doubt the extent of my powers!' cried Grandeane in delight. 'Good! I'm thrilled. When Merlin the

Enchanter doubts what he sees with his own eyes, it must be pretty impressive.'

He raised his arms as if he was about to conduct an orchestra.

'Let me demonstrate further. Only too pleased, as you know.' He paused thoughtfully. 'Let's see. Ah yes. Try this on for size,' he said and his hands began their terrible work.

The ground heaved around him, tremors spreading away from his small island of stillness. Soon the whole plain rose and fell beneath the warring armies, throwing them to the ground or heaving up and buckling their knees under them. At one moment a thousand men, gnomes and demons milled about in a fierce clash. In the next, as Griswold, Rose and Archeous watched in horror, the plain dropped beneath them and they fell like a congealed mess into the ground a hundred feet below.

Grandeane gave the distorted patch of air a smile.

'Good, huh?'

He swept an arm across his body and, with the shrill screech of grinding rocks, a rift full of struggling creatures folded in on itself then erupted to become a high outcrop of solid granite. The creatures could not be seen, but the rock displayed some suspicious little ridges. Merlin, in his cell of air, shuddered and turned on the sorcerer.

'Stop!' he squeaked. 'I command it!'

All fighting had ceased. Every creature still able to rise was scrambling to its feet and heading for the hills to escape from the insane landscape. But Grandeane would not let anyone escape. As they got close to the horizon the slopes rose up and folded over them, crushing and engulfing. Copses of trees wavered and vanished only to appear somewhere else, either half buried in the hills or ablaze with blood-red flames.

The sorcerer threw back his head and roared with laughter.

'What wonderful stuff power is, aye, Enchanter?' he

yelled above the screams and the rumbling of the ground. 'Even your puny powers must have made you feel like God.'

'Thou art not Godly,' screeched Merlin. 'Thou art not even worthy of the name "sorcerer". Thou art merely a wart on the skin of Reality to be burnt off and forgotten.'

'No!' roared Grandeane. His hands flashed and the rocks half a mile distant exploded in flames.

'No!' he roared again and, scooping his hand, he gouged a great valley out of the plain.

'I am a god. I am THE GOD!!'

'Thou art nothing more than a child with a toy meant for a man,' hissed Merlin. 'For all thy powers thou canst not destroy the one that thou fears most, the one that thou most dreads. Thou canst not destroy me!'

Grandeane froze in mid-flourish. The terrain froze with him. The only sounds were the cries of the injured and the roars of the enraged. The sorcerer's head turned very slowly like that of a scrawny reptile, and his eyes bored into the patch of air.

'You really think that?' he whispered.

Merlin said in a voice dry with contempt, 'Compared with thee, I am the essence of magic. I am life to thine death. I am light to thine darkness. Thou art merely the word. I am the deed.'

Grandeane's eyes flickered from the Enchanter's space to see the creatures across the plain picking themselves up and sidling towards the horizon.

'Thine army is no more. Thine gnomes will no longer succumb to thy pretensions to Godliness,' said Merlin quietly. 'As it was once before, so it is again. Just thee and me.'

Grandeane's voice trembled. 'So be it. Prepare to die, Enchanter.'

He flicked a finger and sent a flash of fire into Merlin's space, but it seared through the air and found no target. Merlin's bubble had vanished, reappearing almost instantly some yards to the right. Grandeane's lips drew back in a sneer of impatience. 'I see,' he said, and loosed another crackling streak at the Enchanter. Again the patch of air that was Merlin ducked out of the present to reappear in another place. Grandeane frowned.

'So. You do not retaliate, wizard,' he said. 'I do believe your powers are so meagre that you can only resort to cowardly comings and goings.'

'Fear not, Grandeane, for thou art a god, remember. My comings and goings cannot be an obstacle to thee with such awesome tricks at thy command. Unless, of course, thou lacks the simple ability to find me. Or the courage.'

Grandeane looked about him. His troops had turned away. His token enemy, the demons, had too little fight left in them. The people of Earth, innocently going about their lives on the real Earth, only next door, would not even know of his presence unless he started again from scratch. And that he could not do until Merlin, the ever-present thorn in his side, was plucked out. Taking a long, deep and silent breath, the sorcerer opened up his evil senses and let them scan through Time and space for the one soul that could not help but shine like a beacon.

'Ah,' he said as his inner eyes caught a glimpse of soular flame. He gave a flick of his wrist and whipped his cloak around Archeous. Before the demon had time to be terrified, he was drawn into the copious folds like a fly into a spider's cocoon. With the crack of air rushing to fill a man-sized vacuum, the space they had occupied became empty. Only a wisp of black smoke and the faint smell, not dissimilar to that of burnt armpits, remained.

52

They reappeared in a woodland clearing. It was no more than fifty feet across and at the other end stood Merlin the Enchanter with his arms spread wide. The Enchanter's body was glowing with a pink fire which lit up the forest and cast dancing grey shadows amongst the trees. His eyes were ice blue and staring. Grandeane looked about him. No one else, apart from Archeous, was in sight.

'What is this?' he called. 'Does the wondrous Merlin offer himself as a sacrifice? Is his compassion for Man so deep that he would give of himself to save a few low-life goblins and dregs from the slopes of Hell?'

'All men deserve to die,' replied Merlin, 'which is why they do. But they should not die on the whim of a despot, nor in the manner that gives him the most pleasure.'

'And you intend to prevent that?' the sorcerer sneered. 'You are powerless to stop me.'

'Indeed, that much has become clear,' said Merlin.

The glow around his body was starting to fade. He lowered his arms tiredly.

'But I offer thee a bargain.'

Grandeane stared at him in amazement, then burst into laughter. Archeous stood by his side, looking from one man to the other. His eye twitched nervously and the sheen on his lip was not as enthusiastic as it had been in the past. Archeous was fairly certain that, one way or the other, this would be his last day on Earth. The forest echoed to the sorcerer's laughter while Merlin stood silently before him.

'What bargain can you offer me?' the sorcerer chortled. 'You have nothing to bargain with.'

Merlin's shoulders sagged a little and his body wavered. Grandeane gave a casual flourish and sat down on the throne that appeared beneath him.

'I can do anything,' he said. With a lowering gesture of his palm he made Merlin stagger and all but drop to his knees.

'Clearly thou canst show contempt,' grunted Merlin. 'Canst thou also show compassion?'

'Of course,' said Grandeane, 'when it suits me.'

'And when is that?'

Grandeane stared thoughtfully at Merlin for a moment. The Enchanter was looking ancient. The old spark of defiance was no more than an ember. Gone was the fire that reflected Merlin's passion for everything living.

Everything good, that is.

The sorcerer smiled a thin smile. His superiority was beyond doubt. He had nothing to fear from this little man who had only bested him once by luck. His revenge would be prolonged and all the sweeter for its prolonging.

'When the price is right,' he said.

Merlin nodded wearily. 'Then I offer thee a price. If thou agrees, I will be no further impediment to thee.'

'Which means?'

'In return for thine word that thou'll treat Mankind with mercy during thine reign, I will leave this world and this time, and I will swear never to return.'

Grandeane pursed his lips. 'Hmm,' he murmured. 'A tempting possibility, old man. Give me a few moments.'

'Don't listen,' said Archeous in a tremulous whisper. 'He's playing for Time.'

'He doesn't *have* any Time, idiot. He doesn't have anything.'

He leaned back in his seat and closed his eyes as if in thought. When he opened them again Merlin was standing as motionless as before. If Grandeane was disappointed that the Enchanter wasn't fidgeting, he made no sign. Instead he tapped his finger on his thumb as if knocking the ash from a cigar, and with each tap Merlin jerked and fought to retain his balance.

Grandeane said, 'Let me see if I have this correctly. You cannot defeat me. You cannot command me. All you can do is jump out of hiding occasionally and snap at my ankles like a frustrated terrier, unless, of course, I destroy you this instant. And you offer me a deal?'

Merlin said nothing, but swayed slightly and his eyelids drooped. The energy was draining from him, together with his spirit. Grandeane sighed, savouring his triumph.

'You have no deal, Merlin,' he said. 'You are beaten. I have a world to regain. Time for you to die.'

The Enchanter sagged and dropped to one knee, his face contorted with pain and anguish.

'Then my triumph will outshine thine own, since there is no one here to tell how thou defeated Merlin the Enchanter . . .'

Merlin was fighting for breath. His face was ashen and his limbs were shaking.

'. . . the greatest magician in history,' he whispered.

With his smile becoming disturbingly expansive, Grandeane rose from his throne.

'Your vanity is beyond belief,' he laughed. 'Indeed, it is even greater than my own. Well, it is about to be pricked.'

'Wait a minute,' gasped Archeous. 'I'm here. I can tell the gnomes. And the cretins of Hell. Even Lucifer himself.'

'Don't be silly,' said Grandeane. 'You carry as much clout as a sponge battleaxe. Besides you won't exactly be around much longer.'

He described a circle in the air and, thrusting his hand in, he made a grab and dragged a grim grey figure out by its throat. In its eyes was a look of fury. Grandeane beamed happily.

'Scarbald,' he said. 'I believe you two have met before.'

The gnome cast a look at Merlin and his fingers twitched.

275

He scuttled towards the Enchanter with his hands outstretched and spittle cascading from his lips. Before he had gone ten paces, he was pulled up short, with his legs paddling, and dragged back to Grandeane's side.

'No, no, no, little ugly one. You are here merely to observe and record.' He patted Scarbald's sweating cranium. 'For posterity. Now stand and watch. Are you ready to die, Merlin?'

'It seems that I have no choice.'

Merlin's head hung and his body shuddered with the effort of kneeling.

'One last request,' said Grandeane.

'I have none.'

'Not *you*, you old fool. *Me*. Kindly raise your head and look me in the eyes. I wish to remember the shame of defeat in your gaze.'

'And if I don't?'

'I will extend your dying until you do.'

With a sigh the Enchanter raised his head. He stared with glazed eyes at the sorcerer.

'Tyrant,' he gasped. 'Whatever my fate at thine hands, thou'lt never subdue the people of this world. Their spirit is beyond thine power to break.'

Grandeane laughed. 'Their spirit is the last thing I wish to break, old man. As long as their spirit lasts, they will fight and go on fighting. I will quietly guide their actions. I will watch with glee as they fight themselves almost to extinction. And, when the remnants look upon their shattered world and see what they believe they have done to themselves, they will say, "Where is the one who brought us the miracles? Perhaps he can save us from ourselves."'

He swept his fist in an arc that sent Merlin staggering on to his back.

'Then I will step into view and offer my services for the good of Mankind. I will help Him to create a wondrous new world, free from torment (temporarily), and I will give him a destiny.'

Merlin rose unsteadily to his feet with a splash of blood spread across his lips.

'Man already has a destiny, thou bag of scum, and it is far beyond thine powers to alter that destiny,' he said.

Grandeane's face creased with anger. 'You are a fool, Merlin,' he gritted. 'I'm not interested in Man's ultimate destiny. That can take whatever course it wishes. I want only to rule the Earth and its people while I still live. When I'm dead, Man can thrive or succumb as he wishes. I will not care.'

Without further ado, except to favour Merlin with a final victorious leer, Grandeane stabbed one finger towards him. The crack of thunder resounded through the forest and a blinding flash etched the space-black shadows of beings and trees on the sparkling backdrop. Before the sound had died away, Scarbald was scrambling through the thick smoke towards the spot where Merlin had stood. His eyes were alight and a new thought had crystalized with remarkable lucidity in the mire of his mind. It ran along the lines of, 'One down and two to go'. He came to a halt and stared ahead. A scorched tunnel nearly six feet in diameter stretched away into the trees. A few wisps of smoke drifted lazily among the branches. Merlin the Enchanter was gone. Scarbald turned and leered joyfully at the sorcerer, but his joy was not reflected in Grandeane's features. Instead there was fear in Grandeane's eyes as they darted from the tunnel to the surrounding trees.

'Snuffle?' said Scarbald.

What could be wrong? Almighty flash, big burnt hole, no wizard. QED.

Since only Grandeane had heard, in the final fraction before his magic had struck its target, the words of Merlin the Enchanter, Scarbald could be forgiven for a natural mistake. Instead of fear or resignation, the ice-blue eyes and porcelain features had come alive and looked back at

Grandeane with a mixture of triumph and cold cruelty. In that fraction the Enchanter had said to Grandeane, Thus I deal with the enemies of Mankind. In that instant Merlin had said, This time my victory is for ever. The words that he actually used were, 'I've changed my mind.'

Grandeane looked about him. He called out, 'If you've survived my powers, why don't you show yourself?'

Scarbald looked around, confused.

Archeous looked around, terrified.

'Are you still afraid, wizard? If your triumph is so conclusive, why do you not face me?'

Only the stillness of the forest answered him. Then the sound of the breeze drifted through the trees. It grew steadily to become a biting wind and Grandeane knew that it was Time to leave. Ignoring Archeous and Scarbald, he summoned his powers and tried to leap out of the clearing, past the plain and back to the safety of Gnomedom. His powers were not sufficient, for a greater force was at work, but it was not actually the power of Merlin the Enchanter. Unable to jump out of the present, Grandeane turned to run into the forest. The wind became a gale, whipping his cloak to shreds and slashing the branches into his face. Sorcerer, demon and gnome staggered against the gale and, before the slit-eyed gazes of Archeous and Scarbald, Grandeane began to grow smaller. For Archeous and Scarbald to describe the effect with any accuracy, they would have had to come across an epileptic fit *and* a wind tunnel. As the sorcerer's feet and legs stretched away into the vast distance and disappeared into what seemed to be an infinitely deep and awfully black hole, Grandeane arched his back and twisted his terrified features to the demon. He reached out a rapidly diminishing hand.

'Help me!' he screamed.

53

'Damn,' snapped Griswold.

He turned to Rose.

'Find him for me,' he commanded.

'And then what?' she replied. 'You go bumbling in, you get in everyone's way and you screw up what little chance of victory Merlin has!'

Griswold glared at her and she returned his glare with sympathy.

'He can't afford distractions,' she said.

'Damn,' said Griswold again and, slamming Excalibur into its sheath, he sat down to wait. Rose dropped on to her haunches beside him. She looked at his deceptively passive features.

'If the others reappear alone, we'll search for Merlin. You and I.'

If Rose expected gratitude, she was disappointed. The look Griswold gave her was one of ruthless purpose.

'After I've killed the sorcerer,' he said quietly.

The voice of Mr Savage brought them to their feet.

'You won't be around to kill anyone, matey.'

He was flanked by the five of his remaining troops who were still, more or less, in one piece. Each one had a weapon trained on the lone knight. Griswold cursed himself for being caught unaware, whipped Excalibur into the sunlight and rose on his toes. Unseen by the soldiers, the spirit of Rose Falworthy unsheathed her blade a fraction later.

'Freeze, Griswold,' said Mr Savage lazily. 'Unless you think you can survive a direct hit from a bazooka.'

Griswold glanced at the tube-shaped object resting on Mr Savage's shoulder.

So that's what it looks like, he thought with disdain.

'Your club is hardly a match for my blade,' he said.

'You don't *club* people with it,' groaned Rose. 'You blow them to pieces.'

Griswold stared at the bazooka. 'You blow through it?'

Mr Savage grinned with delight. You have to admire a bloke who's standing there alone with six gun barrels pointing at his belly and he tells you to 'blow through it'.

'Mr Griswold. You're beautiful,' he said.

'Just Griswold,' said Griswold. He held up Excalibur. 'Are we going to talk or fight?'

'Neither, I'm afraid,' said Mr Savage. 'You are going to die.'

He lowered the bazooka to the ground and rested it gently against his thigh. He anticipated staying on Earth for some considerable time, fighting off humans and gnomes for years to come. Anti-tank shells weren't growing on trees in this particular era.

'OK, lads,' he said. 'Aim.'

Five guns nestled into shoulders. Griswold frowned. The last time someone had pointed a harmless-looking tube at him, it had knocked him senseless.

'What are our chances?' he murmured.

'Slim,' answered Excalibur. 'I might manage to stop two or three, but five is too many.'

'So I need to cut down the odds.'

'You'd best be quick.'

And Griswold was. Very quick. As the air split with the crack of gunfire, he leapt high, well over his own height. Five bullets whistled underneath him, but he realized that he had adopted a bad strategy. Having gone up, his path was, predictably, straight down. Griswold could skewer a rabbit with a dagger at thirty feet, if the rabbit stayed on course. Griswold wasn't about to veer off course.

The first slug of the second round threatened to hit him

in the chest and would have taken out eight square inches of backbone. The second would have mangled intestine and spleen. Instead they smacked into Excalibur's blade and dropped to the ground while Griswold fell to Earth, already staggering from their force. His fingers stung and his chest began to drip blood where the sword had nicked it. Instinctively he let himself fall and roll. Two more shots passed over him and Excalibur blocked a third, smacking Griswold round the ear as it did so.

'Ow! Thanks,' he growled.

'Keep moving,' said the sword urgently, but there was no longer any need to.

'Hold your fire,' called Mr Savage. 'By God, Griswold, you're one hell of a man. It really grieves me that you've got to go.' He turned to the man on his right. 'Staines,' he said. 'Spray him.'

Corporal Staines lowered his rifle and brought up a shorter, stubbier weapon. If he'd had the opportunity to use it, this particular branch of the story would definitely have become a bloody stump. No amount of jumping about could save Griswold from an ancient M16 machine gun. Corporal Staines smiled a nicotine smile, released the safety catch and slumped to the ground in thirty horizontal slices, fifty-two if you count twos for the legs and threes for the body and arms, not that anyone was counting, least of all Corporal Staines. Before too much else could happen, the man on his left sprang twenty simultaneous leaks.

As no one was paying Griswold attention any longer, he leaned on his sword and watched with interest. For a brief moment Rose would appear. There would be the odd blur as she jumped in and out of the present, slicing away as she did so. Then a soldier would drop to the ground in lumps. Griswold had witnessed the outcome of this tactic once before, but he hadn't been able to see the people doing it, they being spiritual and he being of limited perception in that area.

So that's how she does it, he thought as the last of Mr Savage's men merged chunkily with the countryside.

'Griswold, I'm really disappointed in you. You're just a friggin' magician, that's all,' said Mr Savage, raising his bazooka once more. 'Well, magic your way out of this.'

And, before Rose could reach him or Griswold could duck, he squeezed the trigger.

There is a trick that goes something like this: hold your left thumb in your right hand . . . oh, you've heard of it, haven't you? And you saw the result.

In front of Griswold a patch of air shimmered and squeaked a tiny 'no!'. From the shimmer two silvery, see-through hands appeared. The tips of their thumbs and forefingers touched to form the sort of diamond shape that wizards try to jump through. It's just as well that a bazooka shell is only three and a half inches in diameter or it would have ploughed through the fingers and turned Sir Griswold into a much-travelled ex-knight. Instead it flashed cleanly through the diamond and into the woodland scene contained within. There was a terminal yelp from the shimmer and a muffled explosion. With a creak and the scream of clingfilm under intense stress, the shimmer split open. Merlin the Enchanter burst out and tumbled through the air. He cannoned into Mr Savage, sending him sprawling. Before the soldier could rise, Griswold was standing over him with Excalibur pressing into his throat. A pall of white smoke hung in the air and all ears rang in the wake of the detonations. Merlin staggered to his feet and glared at Griswold.

'Fool, fool and thrice fool,' he said hoarsely. 'Does thou always have to bite off more than thou canst chew?'

Griswold glanced at the bazooka rolling down the hill. He had a feeling that, between the first bang and the second, he'd missed something.

'I'm meant to fear an iron tube that breathes smoke and thunder!' he growled. 'What sort of mouthful is that?'

'The sort that could render thee asunder,' screeched the Enchanter. 'Fool,' he added.

Mr Savage lay with the sword wavering dangerously near his carotid artery, while the two men squabbled above him. Out of the corner of his eye he caught a slight movement. Clambering up the hill came a wave of gnomes, each with the appearance of a gnome who was prepared to fight to the last gnome.

Mr Savage coughed politely. Merlin and Griswold looked down at him.

'There's no chance of you letting me go,' he said.

He made it sound like a military assessment. His voice held no trace of pleading.

'No,' said Merlin.

'I have a mission to complete. Lucifer will give me Hell if I fail.'

'Thou *hast* failed. I stand between thee and the demise of Mankind.'

Mr Savage sniggered. 'You're about as well informed as Archeous,' he said. 'My job's not to destroy Mankind. I'm supposed to kill that fat, hairy idiot.'

Rose and Griswold stared at the soldier in amazement.

Unnoticed, the gnomes were closing fast. Merlin pondered on Mr Savage's words for a moment.

'Ah,' he said. 'I understand.'

'I thought you would,' said Mr Savage. 'Well?'

Merlin waved Mr Savage to his feet. 'I canst not release thee, since by thy very nature thou remainst a threat to Man, even should Archeous fall.'

'If Archeous survives, I'm destined to return to the lava pits. I don't intend that to happen.'

'Archeous does not survive,' said Merlin mysteriously. 'Indeed, his fate is a direct result of thine actions. Thou hast my word.'

Mr Savage straightened up and stared Merlin quizzically in the eye for a few moments. Eventually he said, 'Your word's good enough. Now I'm going to run down the hill, jump over those little cretins and be of no further threat to you. All right?'

'All right,' said Merlin quietly.

Mr Savage gave Merlin a brief salute and said to Griswold, 'I was right after all. You *are* a hell of a man.'

He glanced at the remains of his platoon, then turned and loped down the hill. As he approached the scrambling horde, he plucked at the objects hanging from his webbing. There was the dull glimmer of the blades, then with a roar Mr Savage leapt over the heads of the leading gnomes and disappeared from view. For three seconds precisely the flash of swords and the screeches of gnomes filled the air. Then three explosions went off simultaneously, and flashing swords and gnomes filled the air. Then all was silent.

'By the gods,' murmured Griswold. 'What demonry was that?'

'The bazooka's little cousins,' said Rose. 'Hand grenades.'

Her eyes were moist with tears.

'That man had guts,' she said thoughtlessly.

54

As the blackness closed over Grandeane's dwindling head and shrunk to the size of a pin-hole, an awkward silence followed. Archeous and Scarbald eyed each other with tentative appraisal. It's one thing to join forces with one enemy in order to batter a third into gruel. It's something completely different to allow your mutual enemy to come to a horrible end simply by doing nothing. The first method always results in feelings of great camaraderie from a job well done. The second leaves everyone feeling embarrassed.

Archeous scuffled his hooves and looked at the ground. Scarbald shuffled his cowpats and stared belligerently at the trees. Then Archeous the bank manager spoke.

'In the absence of a suitable replacement required to get us out of here, I will take charge. You will search for the exit and report directly to me.'

Scarbald the gnome replied. He sent a stream of fluid sparkling across the clearing to strike Archeous between his bulbous nipples. The demon stared down at his chest and back at the gnome. The feeling of outrage barely had time to crystallize in Walter White's brain as the familiar whistle of a military projectile sounded in the still air.

The explosion sent Scarbald tumbling end-over-end with his eardrums shrieking until he smacked face first into a stalwart tree trunk and came to a stop. He looked up through two swiftly swelling eyelids to find that Archeous had gone. In the demon's place a small blackened crater lay smoking and, above it, the nearby trees had acquired some colourful and untree-like appendages.

Scarbald stood motionless for quite a while, while some aggravated gnomish cellular activity took place in his mind.

Before the crater, made by a remarkably fortuitous bazooka shell, had stopped smoking, Scarbald had shuffled the recent events into a workable scenario from which he could formulate his plans for the future.

Scarbald the rejector, betrayer and inconvenience to others, sat down to think.

Or, rather, to make those awesome, inspiring quantum leaps of the imagination that only a truly creative mind can make.

By no stretch could Scarbald be called the Albert Einstein of Gnomedom. Logical thinking was to Scarbald like crossing a tightrope would be to a frog. He couldn't walk, he'd just have to jump.

So Scarbald sat down to jump.

Er . . . Tried it on me own . . . ballsup . . . tried (reluctantly) taking orders . . . ballsup . . . ergo . . . er . . . go . . . go forth and . . . multiply . . . tried it . . . ballsup . . . what's left . . . try *giving* orders . . . who to, don't know anyone who'll listen . . . well, make 'em . . . make 'em . . . make 'em.

Make 'em.

Scarbald was not known as the greatest living gnome in the construction business for nothing. He could make almost anything out of almost anything.

He could make an ally.

A buddy.

Someone who would obey him and help him in his quest.

He cast an eye towards the glistening leaves. With a graceless leap, he scaled the nearest tree and scrambled along the branches scraping up the scattered pieces of flesh and viscera and tucking them into his tunic.

In a few moments the memory of the fat, hairy-legged little person had merged indistinguishably with all the other non-Scarbald creatures that the gnome had never really known. After all, one shouldn't waste valuable brain cells on anything that was not called James Dimmot. The image of Dimmot and the thought of what he would do when they met again brought the faint sneer that passed for a gnomish smile back to Scarbald's thick lips.

Snuffle, oh, snuffle.

55

Overhead the clouds were doing very uncloudlike things. Whites, greys, blacks and the blood red of evening cumulus tumbled about each other before halting completely in mid-flight and reversing like massive smoking dodgem cars. Some changed shape in seconds into cloudy spirals and grid-like edifices floating on the currents like giant magic carpets. The crackles of lightning ceased in mid-crack and recommenced, as if being chopped in half by an invisible scythe. The wind, galing across the flickering terrain, would stop and start and the trees would straighten and bow in unison with it.

'Now what's happening?' yelled Griswold above the noise.

'I know not,' shouted Merlin, 'but I suspect that Grandeane has left a legacy of chaos in his wake.'

As if to prove him correct, the sky opened and, amidst the brilliant beams of the sun, four tiny figures appeared high in the sky. They were riding steeds of some description, though it was difficult to see them clearly.

'Look,' cried Merlin, pointing.

'Are they any part of this?' shouted Griswold.

Merlin squinted and his face darkened. 'They are the cause of this,' he said. 'With Grandeane's demise, they are free to do what they do best instead of that which they were commanded to do.'

'Which was what?'

'Which was to create the miracles. 'Twill give them ecstatic pleasure to undo the good that they have done before they return to their origins.'

'Then we must stop them,' said Griswold.

'Indeed,' said Merlin, not moving.

Griswold looked at him for a moment. He looked up at the figures. They were scooting across the sky in a ragged formation, swooping lower with each second. The one in the chariot was managing to trail a stream of smoke behind him.

Odd sort of horse, thought Griswold. He could just make out their different colours and shapes. They had the look of warriors, knights on horseback.

Easy pickings.

'Magic me a horse,' he said. 'One that flies.'

Merlin gave him a scathing glance. 'I do not *magic* horses.' He scowled. 'I am not a back-street wizard, you know.'

'Well, do something Enchanting,' snapped Griswold. 'And make it quick!'

'A most sensible suggestion, but I fear that I am at a loss.'

'You've just destroyed the most potent force on Earth, by the mere fact of changing your mind,' observed Griswold with notable sarcasm.

'Precisely. I am what thou sees fit to refer to as "knackered".'

'Pardon?'

'My powers are depleted. I need to rest and replenish them.'

The wind lashed at their faces and they were finding it difficult to stand. Around them the rocks creaked ominously. Griswold was becoming irritable. He had the greatest Enchanter on Earth on one hand and the most powerful sword in history in the other, and neither was of the slightest use to him.

'Well, if you can't help, surely you must know someone who can.'

'Not in this day and age,' said the Enchanter.

Merlin stared up at the sky. The figures were only a few

hundred feet above the groaning Earth, swooping across the tumble-shadowed countryside on their snorting steeds. Merlin could make out the grins of evil spread across the faces and the vulture-like craning of their necks as they scoured the planet's surface.

'Dammit,' snapped Merlin. Time was running out. The four horsemen were heading away towards the horizon.

'Dammit's no use. If *you* can't reach them, then I must. I'd better be going before they disappear from sight,' said Griswold, slapping Excalibur into its sheath.

Merlin stared at him in astonishment. 'Going?' he said weakly.

'I can get up a fair turn of speed now, if you haven't noticed. If my luck holds, I might catch them as they land.'

Griswold had long since buried the word 'impossible' in the same deep hole as 'give up' and 'forget it, it can't be done'.

The wind and the clouds began to settle noticeably as the figures grew smaller, but the turbulence followed them as if their very presence dictated that everything around them be in a state of pandemonium. Griswold turned and was about to break into a sprint.

'Wait,' cried Merlin.

He laid his small hand on Griswold's forearm.

'There may be a way,' he said.

War, Famine, Pestilence and Death are not your run-of-the-mill unnecessary evils. Not random hit-and-run drivers, as you might say. They are artists. Thinking man's catastrophes. They have a job to do and they do it well. The fact that they relish it is not the point. Without them the Earth would be overrun by healthy, loving, well-fed humanity and would creak under the weight of shining knights and do-gooders fighting the forces of Evil and living to ripe old ages.

There has to be a Balance.

Messrs W., F., P. and D. (especially D.) see that there is, occasional tiffs and tossing of curls notwithstanding.

'This is the Time for war,' rumbled War. 'The Time to drive the aliens from the Earth and let Mankind fight amongst himself for a new order.'

'Rubbish,' squeaked Pestilence. 'The whole of the planet is now virtually free of disease, thanks to me. Time for depressions, herpes and piles.'

W., D. and F. weren't too sure about the piles, but they were not going to be sidetracked.

'Nonsense,' moaned Famine dolefully. 'This green and pleasant planet is ripe for starving. Time to dry out the pastures, parch the plains. Time to cancel rainfall.'

'Leave the rain alone,' screeched Pestilence. 'Disease thrives in the rain.'

'Disease is mucky, you foul pus bag,' groaned Famine. 'What we want's good clean starvation. Nice and tidy. White bones gleaming in the sunlight. Stuff like that.'

'Where's the art in that?' roared War. 'No. Blood, bits and pieces. Great armies, nineteen to the dozen. Maximum mayhem in small timescales. That's where it's at.'

Death scowled stonily from beneath his cowl.

Shut up, he thought. The others ignored him. He wasn't the most popular member of the group. To tell the truth, he lost most of his credibility when he flogged his old Harley-Davidson to buy that clapped-out Panzer. Hardly conducive to the image of immortality. Didn't deserve his helmet.

The skies opened before their headlong flight and the snorting of horsey nostrils and the slapping of saddlery on flanks was underscored by the continual whine of the wind as they plunged onwards towards the Tower of London, home of Uther Pendragon.

It was all of thirty seconds before they realized that they were not alone.

'Ah, hah,' stormed War. 'Bandit at twelve o'clock!'

They looked up to see the green underbelly of a fair-sized dragon looming above them.

'Don't see many of them these days,' sighed Famine. 'Thought they were extinct.'

'Looks remarkably healthy to me,' puked Pestilence with distaste.

Ingrid side-slipped and glided alongside them, evoking a chorus of nervous whinnies. The dragons' taste for fresh horsemeat was common knowledge among horses. Its three heads turned towards them and its long tail flowed gracefully in its wake.

It's wings *whoomphed* rhythmically.

'Wodyuh want?' thundered War quietly.

A small figure stepped into view from between the massive wings.

'I want you to return to where you belong and leave Mankind alone,' called Griswold.

The four creatures glanced at each other.

'Hop it!' War bellowed and, feeling that something more was required, 'Or I'll declare Me on you,' he added.

War hadn't made many mistakes in his life. The odd error that had opposing factions signing peace treaties all over the place and living happily ever after. The occasional last stand where every creature except for the general's dim-witted horse was killed and there was no one left to fight another day. Nothing that could give rise to ridicule. But now he had made a big mistake. Another figure stepped into view.

'You jumped-up little fist-fight,' screeched Rose Falworthy. 'You dare to threaten us? Draw your sword, you scurvy bastard. Let's see what your guts are made of before teatime.'

War glanced at Griswold.

'She's known for her subtlety,' Griswold explained. 'Are you going to call off your attack?'

'No,' came the chorus.

'But we will postpone it just long enough to cancel you

out,' yelled War. They broke formation and wheeled off in four different directions to vanish into the clouds.

'Damn,' said Griswold. He rapped Excalibur on Ingrid's scales. 'Follow the one in the armour,' he commanded.

'No!' snapped Rose.

Although she had been too young to help in World War Two, her knowledge of aerial warfare was far more comprehensive than Griswold's. Kenneth More and Errol had seen to that.

'Head for the clouds and start climbing,' she said.

For a crucial moment Ingrid faltered as she swivelled her heads to look down at Griswold. Griswold looked at Rose. Rose glared back. 'Make for the clouds,' said the knight.

'And be quick,' added Rose.

'Hang on,' said Ingrid and, before they quite had time to obey, she accelerated, ears pinned back and wings biting into the air like giant oars. Seconds later four enemy fighters zoomed out of the clouds from different directions with nostrils snorting, swords whistling and chainsaw buzzing. They sliced through the sky, churning it into a blinding cyclone that caught up the clouds and sucked them into a black and white swirl of thundering destruction. With the whinnies of the horses, the whine of the chainsaw and the roar of an ancient tank echoing in their wake, they tore round in ever-decreasing circles until their separate outlines blurred into an indistinguishable image.

Then they screamed to a stop and looked round sheepishly. The sky became still.

'Where'd they go?' rumbled War.

'Er. Don't know,' said Famine thinly.

'God, how embarrassing,' hissed Pestilence.

Death just nodded. His skull was paler than usual and his helmet had slipped over one eye.

'I feel like death,' he murmured, laying his forearms on the edge of the turret. He was about to rest his head on his hands when the silence was shattered. From out of the sun, faster than the speed of sound, Ingrid came with all three heads craning forward and three pairs of nostrils blazing. A loose scale broke free and whistled past, missing Death by inches. As the dragon swept by, three sheets of flame spewed across the sky, but Ingrid's aim left a lot to be desired.

All that got singed were Griswold's whiskers.

'Not me, idiots,' he growled from his prone position behind Ingrid's necks. 'Them!'

'Sorry,' said Ingrid breathlessly. 'Wind speed.' She swung round and rose up under the horses, intent on melting the shoes off their hooves, but her body floundered and she came to a halt.

'What's amiss/*What's up?*' called Griswold.

'Run out of steam,' groaned Ingrid. 'Too old. I'm not going to make it.'

The indignant voice of Rose Falworthy cut through the air.

'Don't you dare give up!'

She scrambled to her feet, shoved Griswold aside and gave the dragon's neck a belt with the flat of her sword.

'Do you hear me?' she said. 'You're only as old as you want to be.'

She threw an arm round Ingrid's neck and shinned up it, using just her legs and her free hand. Above her, the four horsemen looked down with interest (except for Death whose cheekbones had taken on a Pestilent-green hue). Below her, Griswold gazed in admiration at the rippling muscularity of her ascending buttocks. As she reached the level of Ingrid's ears he sighed contentedly and took a fresh grip on the hilt of his sword. The harsh laughter of War fell upon their ears.

'What's up, you clapped-out old warhorse?' he thundered. 'Lost your puff?'

Ingrid wheezed painfully while Rhon and Liz hovered on either side urging her to get a move on, because right now they were sitting ducks.

'Sorry,' she said hoarsely. 'Can't make it.'

'Horse crap,' hissed Rose in the dragon's ear. 'You're not going to let a bunch of egotistic macho-heads drive you out of the skies. This is your domain.' She grabbed a tuft of Ingrid's hair and gave it a yank. 'Come on,' she said. 'You're a woman. Use your head.'

Ingrid turned large, doleful eyes towards Griswold.

Griswold grinned at her. 'You'd better do it,' he said. 'And fast.'

'Oh, all right. Climb down.'

As Rose dropped on to the dragon's back, the four creatures above began to spiral towards them. What happened next was a little confusing. Rose and Griswold never did quite grasp the nature of it. Throwing a wing across her foreheads, Ingrid gave a cry of anguish.

'Oh,' she cried smokily.

'Ah,' she gasped. 'I am done. Finished. Doomed.'

'What!' cried Rose and Griswold together.

'I cannot go on,' intoned Ingrid. Her other wing flapped feebly and she began to lose altitude. War closed in fast.

'What're you up to?' he rumbled impatiently.

'I am beaten,' replied Ingrid. 'I am no match for your manly power.'

Not being particularly conversant with the finer points of his art, vis-à-vis that men did the fighting and women the bawling, War didn't quite know what response was required.

'Yeah, well,' he murmured. Without taking his eyes off her, he said quietly, 'What do I do now?'

'Ask her to surrender,' hissed Pestilence.

'Or die,' added Death.

'Oh. Right. Er, surrender or die,' War roared tentatively.

Griswold couldn't help feeling that things were getting slightly out of control. His control, anyway.

'What are you up to?' he whispered.

'If I can't get you to them, I'll have to deliver them to you,' said Ingrid. She turned her eyes towards War and fluttered her lashes at him. 'Sorry. Can't do either. You'll have to catch me,' she said.

Wrapping her wings tightly about her, she enclosed Griswold and Rose in dim green light and dropped out of the sky like a stone. Over her shoulder she called out, 'You lousy excuse for a dim-witted foot soldier.'

War stared at her dwindling back-end in disbelief.

'Did you hear that?' he demanded. With three concerted yells of rage and a very quiet 'It'll end in tears, I know it', they plunged after her. While Griswold and Rose struggled vainly to see what was happening, Ingrid whistled Earthwards with more loose scales rattling themselves free and her tail snapping in the wind. She picked up speed and became a green blur.

Griswold's muffled voice squeezed out from under the dragon's wing.

'What the hell's she up to?'

'Looks like suicide,' replied Excalibur doubtfully. 'Battle fatigue, perhaps.'

'There hasn't *been* a battle,' observed Griswold.

'Well, I'm sure she knows what she's doing,' said Excalibur.

Griswold recognized a fait accompli even though he had never heard of it. When you are five thousand feet above the Earth and lacking the inflight luxury of your own personal wings, a philosophical approach to life is very handy. And when physical action was beyond the bounds of possibility, Griswold could be remarkably philosophical. Rose Falworthy was less passively inclined.

'Don't just lie there, moron. Do something,' she ordered.

'Suggestions?' said Griswold.

'Use your bloody sword, you idiot. Cut her wings off.'

'She's on our side,' Griswold reminded her.

'We can't stay here 'til she ploughs into the ground,' said Rose.

'*I* have little choice,' smiled Griswold in the dim light. 'You can spirit yourself out of here any time you wish.'

'I'm not leaving without you,' said Rose.

The whistle of the wind had increased to a howl and was threatening to become a screech as Ingrid hurtled down with the four horsemen seconds behind her. The throaty roar of Death's engine was segmented by shrill neighs and the desperate flapping of leather on horseflesh.

'You can't escape,' bellowed War. 'You're as good as dead.'

That's for me to decide, thought Death. The others ignored him. The green of the English countryside rose rapidly to meet them. If Griswold had been able to see that they were plunging towards it at such a blinding rate, he might have been a little more concerned. All he needed was the chance to wield his sword and to visit grief upon the Forces of Evil. His brief moment of thought on the subject was interrupted as the muffled chatter of dragons squeezed through the whistle and rattle of wind and scales.

'Two eight zero by eight seven five by nine six nine,' Liz was saying.

'Three days, six hours and twenty-seven minutes,' added Rhon.

'Seconds?' asked Ingrid.

'Not needed. More than enough time,' replied Rhon.

'If you're sure,' said Ingrid doubtfully.

'Look! If you can do better, jolly well—'

'All right, dear. No need to snap. On my mark . . .'

Rose leaned over and placed her hand on Griswold's arm. 'What are they doing?' she said.

Griswold shrugged. The wind was shrieking now and Ingrid's whole body was shuddering as if it might begin breaking apart. Her wings began to lose their grip and to slide apart. Then a crashing blow racked through her body, evoking a cry of agony from her three throats. For a moment Griswold could see the grey shapes of the four creatures through the thin film of the dragon's wings. One

296

of them was raising his immense sword to strike a second blow. The one in the chariot was closing in with a weird, screaming blade in one hand. As Griswold struggled to free his arms, streaks of red wind-swept fluid covered the leathery canopy, blocking out the light and the view.

'Dammit, dragon! Give me room to fight,' he snarled.

'No time,' croaked Ingrid. 'Three, two, one. Now!'

They were fifty feet from the ground when Ingrid vanished with an ear-splitting SPLOPK.

When you aren't ruled by the law of gravity, the word 'down' has no more meaning than the word 'plummet'. You don't go 'up' or 'down'. You go 'from' or 'towards', 'past' or, perhaps, 'through'. And when you are travelling as fast as W., F., P. and D. were, and you are intent only on catching the dragon in front of you, the blinding realization that you're going to need a good two hundred feet braking distance comes as a bit of a shock. Six red-veined eyes widened in collective terror and lips drew back from stained teeth to utter the words, 'Oh, buggerrr!!', as War, Famine and Pestilence approached Earth at a speed that could be called downright unhealthy.

Death just sped on.

Next door, dimension-wise, the people of London went about their daily business of commuting, making money and helping to run King Uther's empire. They swayed, glassy-eyed, through the tunnels beneath the city's streets and they spewed out on to the ancient history-ridden concrete of the world's capital. They rose in metal elevators, avoiding eye contact, 'morning'd their way to the coffee machines and carried their coffees and Id-coms to their desks.

They began their day's work.

At eleven thirty-seven a.m. the people of London were beset by a brief dose of Reality. A dragon, green, complete with wings, scales and three heads, burst noisily out of nowhere two hundred feet above the city and dived towards the Earth at an alarming speed. It flattened out, glided between the tall, windowed buildings and soared up towards the sun, followed closely by a small, black-cloaked figure in an asthmatic Panzer tank. They climbed for a few seconds before vanishing. Only a stream of tiny blood-red droplets and a thin streak of black smoke were left, both of which rapidly dispersed in the morning sky.

That evening and for the next few days local TV and hologram stations broadcast conflicting versions of the incident, but since dragons do not exist and private jetters and power-pack merchants were always bombing down the airways the incident quickly faded from the public's interest. The only Earthly records kept of it were on a few Id-coms, where they were subsequently erased or slapped deep in the international archives.

And in *The Encyclopaedia Esoterica*, where they were not erased.

Ingrid exploded into view two hundred feet above the spot where she had just disappeared. Death, the only one of the four who was not bound by the ties of Time, was yards behind her, so busy straining to slice her tail off that he didn't realize he was on his own. He gripped his chainsaw in one bony fist and leaned out from his tank at a suicidal angle, even for him, with his weapon scything wildly from side to side. As he barrel-rolled over Ingrid's spine he caught a glimpse of War, Famine and Pestilence entwined in a splattered heap on the Earth below. His concentration faltered briefly and a smug, rather deathly grin spread briefly across his skull, revealing his bleached white teeth. Then, before he could quite manage to say 'amateurs', a spiked scaly tail snapped over and rammed the word down his throat into his turret.

Ten seconds later the gruel that was War, Famine, Pestilence and horsemeat was liberally garnished with shattered bones and ancient tank tracks.

As Ingrid cut her power and silently glided in to land,

the army of King Uther rode over the hill, ready to do
battle, despite the sad loss of their monarch.

56

Sergeant Belkin dropped from his horse, took a small
bag from the saddle horn and strode hesitantly towards
the Queen of England and the Entire World. Silently, he
handed her the bag and stood back. Rose looked around at
Wolfstone and the mounted warriors behind him and they
avoided her eyes.

'Is this what I think it is?' she said.

'I believe it is, ma'am,' Belkin replied.

'You're late,' said Rose.

Belkin pointed at the bag with his chin and his moisten-
ing eyes and Rose nodded and wandered off with the bag
clasped to her breast. Merlin and Belkin watched her go.

'What happened?' said Merlin quietly.

Belkin briefly explained about the 'suit' of Uther Pendragon which had finally drained the old king beyond help.
He pointed at the bag in Rose's hands.

'The body was willing, but the spirit was too weak.
Where is the enemy?'

'Destroyed,' said Merlin.

'By your hand?'

'Of course. Who else's?'

'So our headlong return and my king's demise were both
in vain.'

Merlin looked into Belkin's eyes and the small sergeant
returned his gaze. For a moment King Uther's two most
faithful servants shared a loss beyond grief. Then the
Enchanter gave Belkin the gift of purpose.

'Not so, Sergeant. The land is awash with the lackeys of Evil. There is still much fighting to be done, Evil to be purged and a monarch to be avenged.'

Belkin creased his brow in thought for a long moment while Wolfstone and the army waited in silence.

'What of her?' said the sergeant, indicating Rose Falworthy. She stood silently with her back to them and the bag containing the 'suit' of Uther held to her cheek.

'She will make a fine monarch,' said Merlin, catching Griswold's eye and inclining his head towards the queen.

The big knight strolled after her, leaving the others to their awkward mourning and their half-hearted suggestions for the battle strategy during the next hundred years.

'Are you all right?' Griswold asked, standing beside her. Rose gazed out across the plain at the sun, now sinking bloodily to the hills.

'It was his own stupid fault,' she said. 'Him and his "suits".'

When Griswold didn't answer she looked round to see him frowning. She explained about the 'suits'.

'When I was a boy,' said Griswold, 'I would put on the heaviest suit in the armoury. I'd wear it all day. I'd train in it, ride in it, even rest in it. It drained my strength, but with each day I grew stronger.'

'Did it drain your spirit?'

'No.'

'Well, stop talking like a prat.'

'Oak hay. Is there anything I can do?'

'Bring him back.'

In the grounds of the Tower of London, Ingrid waited patiently for Merlin to come out from the dark-shadowed castle. She spread her wings and flexed them like a giant butterfly in the sun. While Liz stretched her head lazily out on the grass, Rhon glared impatiently at the courtiers, warriors, Griswold and Belkin.

'I say we go without him,' he snarled smokily. Ingrid favoured him with a scathing glance.

'We go when they are ready to leave. Not before.'

In the banqueting hall the warmth of the day yielded to the coolness of impassive stone all around and underfoot. Merlin the Enchanter and Rose Falworthy sat at the table with the bag containing Uther's 'suit' between them. They remained silent for some time, reluctant to part company, as if their parting would put the final seal on Uther's death. Merlin knew that, in leaving this place and this time, he would leave a large part of himself behind, possibly too much to recover. Uther, like his son Arthur, had been a point of focus in the Enchanter's lifelong commitment to Mankind and, even after the old king's bodily demise, the fact that his spirit lived on had sustained Merlin's resolve and his sense of purpose. Now, with the task of seeking out James Dimmot before him and Uther's world on the verge of turmoil, Merlin was dismayed to find that his will to survive and fight on was so diminished. He had never realized how much he needed a god of some sort to sustain him.

He gave a deep sigh.

'We must be on our way, Your Majesty.'

'Rose,' said Rose sternly.

'Mistress Rose. I fear that our task is impossible' (even had I the will to pursue it to its conclusion, he thought to himself) 'but the sooner we start, the sooner we accomplish the impossible.'

'That's a noble and courageous sentiment, Merlin,' said Rose with a sad smile. 'Wordsworth?'

'No,' replied the Enchanter. 'Griswold.'

'Might have known. He's a bit on the casual side, but he's smart and gutsy.'

'Indeed,' said Merlin.

'Make a fine monarch,' said Rose.

Merlin stiffened. 'He lacks vision,' he said shortly.

'What's vision got to do with it?' said Rose. 'Uther had as much vision as a telly without a tube.'

'Kindly do not speak ill of the king,' Merlin whispered. His eyes sparked with flecks of red and orange.

'Now look—!' began Rose.

Merlin rose to his feet. 'Surely thou dost not question the judgement and wisdom of the man who ruled the world for three hundred years and never once faltered from his duty?' His lips trembled. 'Thou dares to even suggest that he was not the greatest monarch of all time?'

'Listen, you—' said Rose.

'*What d'you mean "was"?*' squeaked a very small voice from within the bag.

57

Very little is known about the soul, such as its being the direct link between Man and the cosmos that He was created to protect. We all know that the soul lives for ever.

Most of us know that a soul owner's spirit lives on for a while after his body dies. Deep down we even know why, don't we?

The spirit's job is to keep the soul from wandering off and getting lost before a replacement body (with its own built-in spirit) is ready. Hell, as well as containing all the evil buggers and all the oddballs who sold their souls for dubious rewards, has a fair quota of lost souls whose current spirits had died before a suitable new body had been born. (Which is why it's a pretty good investment to keep up your spirits while your body is still alive.)

In theory a suitable body usually comes off the production line within weeks, what with Mankind being highly motivated in the job of manufacturing more Mankinds. In practice, souls such as those of Merlin, Uther Pendragon and other exceptional mortals, might have to wait years, or even centuries, for a compatible body.

'Thine soul,' smiled Merlin, 'is a creature of instinct. It knows not that the ill-conceived vehicles in which it presided over these last centuries were aught else than that created by the natural order of things.'

The soul of Uther Pendragon lay within its new body (with built-in spirit) and sighed contentedly. Even the Enchanter's convoluted verbals could not get up its nose as they had at times in the past. This might have been because the new body and spirit were by nature less volatile than the old ones.

'Pardon?' it said patiently.

'What he is trying to say,' said Rose thinly, 'is that it couldn't tell the difference between a real body and those dumb-arse tailor-man "suits" of yours!'

The old mouth of Uther Pendragon would have said something like 'Gruntfuttocks!' or 'All right, woman! Steady on.'

The new one just smiled.

'Which is why,' continued Merlin, 'thine soul lay around happily inside those "suits" while thine spirit worked itself into an early grave.'

Uther leaned back in his chair and attempted to plant his feet nonchalantly on an imaginary ledge two feet above the ground. He picked himself up off the stone floor and sat back down. Having a solid living body after all these centuries was going to take some getting used to. He threw Rose a cautious glance and spread his arms expansively.

'Well, old girl. What d'you think?'

Rose's feelings were mixed. She saw before her a powerful, muscular, not to say vibrant frame. The manner in which it lounged in its chair, the sensuous play of its large callused fingers, that look in its eyes, all held a degree of animal promise that made the old Uther seem like a rampant bus. In normal circumstances Rose would have been wearing a smug smile and feeling a tingle of anticipation in places where . . . well, in places. But since there are certain areas in which living bodies and spiritual entities can never quite get it together, Rose considered that a degree of desperation was in order.

'Merlin,' she said grittily. 'You got him into this. Now get me into it!'

'Sorry,' said the Enchanter.

EPILOGUE

AD 4097 . . . a couple of weeks later

In the greenish glow of the room that is not a room, Lucifer, Prince of Darkness, is talking to the demon, Nemestis, still locked in the glass tomb. Lucifer is unconcerned that his words fall on deaf ears.

'What a cock-up, aye, old chap? My own fault, I suppose.'

He taps his fingernails absently on the glass.

'It would have been a good time to swap ends, too. Wind of Change behind us, Mankind on the verge of a magical revolution. We'd have been playing downhill all the way.'

Lucifer sucks his cheeks in and makes little sucking noises. For a brief moment he looks like a million-year-old goldfish.

'Still, we had a good first half. Man had really hit rock bottom, morality-wise. We didn't do too badly, you and I. We scored a few.'

Nemestis says nothing.

'Trouble is, I didn't allow for last-minute variables like, wotsisname, Grumpy, Grundy? . . . whoever. If your heart's not in it, you do tend to miss the finer details and that's the sort of thing God hates.'

He stares deep into Nemestis' opaque eyes.

'The Old Man won't let me swap jobs, knowing that I've skimped on the details lately. Very hot on details, he is. So.' He gives the demon a rueful smile. 'You're stuck with me for another . . . God knows how long.'

He purses his lips and his beautiful wings swing gracefully in the green glowing light as he turns to leave the room.

'Think I'll try and get some sleep.'
Nemestis stares sightlessly ahead.

It was not just coincidence that, just as Man was about to make the evolutionary leap denied him for so long, the planet Earth was invaded by not one aggressor but two.

Nor was it coincidental that both invaders had quite different motives.

Up to the early thirty-ninth century, the power of White Magic had been suppressed by the Forces of Evil for over two thousand years. With the defeat of Lucifer's emissary, Nemestis, the hold was broken. Magicians began to emerge, wizards to awaken, sorcerers to sally tentatively forth. As the century progressed, Earth became riddled with wild magic waiting to be tamed and brought under Man's control. In the wake of the invasion, however, the planet was also crawling with the remnants of two vast and belligerent armies. Demons, gnomes and living dead abounded, leaderless and uncontrolled. They brought terror. They procreated and thrived. Earth became a world of occult turbulence, where the night was a dangerous place to be and the stuff of both grim fairy tales and horror stories walked the streets.

And wherever the evil ones smelt the sweet smell of enchantment, there did they go to devour and absorb.

It seemed that the infant magic would never be allowed to reach maturity. If the stars were not to be forever beyond the infant's reach, magic must be protected and nurtured.

Unfortunately, the one person with the power to accomplish this was not even aware of his potential.

And, not surprisingly, nobody else of that era was even aware of his existence, since he didn't actually exist in that era.

And, quite typically, he was, at the time when he was most needed, riding off in the opposite direction from that of his destiny and from the one man who could help him to fulfil it.

Encyclopaedia Esoterica

AD 1400, more or less

Tthe countryside cowered beneath the onslaught of
wind and rain. Above it tumbling leaden clouds spat
forks of lightning into its flanks. Below it earthworms left
their flooded passages and came up for air. Sticklebacks
sank to the muddy bottoms of their streams and waited.

Eric Pennyfeather sat on his cart, oblivious of the
weather conditions, him being eighty-eight years of age
and never missed a day's work in his life. He squinted up
at the sky.

Gonna get wuss in next day an' erarf, he thought. Then
sun'll be out in time for t'market.

He pulled the hood of his garment over his head and
lifted his whip to flick it at his horse's rump. The clatter of
hooves made him turn round. A monk rode up on an
irritable-looking stallion. His rosary bounced about his
nose, indicating that he was no horseman. This view was
endorsed by the fact that he didn't seem able to stay in the
saddle, because he was sitting behind it.

"Morrow, good sir,' he said breathlessly.

Eric Pennyfeather squinted uncertainly. He might swear
later that both the monk and his horse were bone-dry as
they approached, even though there was no cover for miles
around. As they became soaked within seconds, the old
man put it down to the fact that his eyesight might not be
what it used to.

'Arternoon, father,' he said.

'Where are you bound?' said the monk genially.

'Colchester village.' Eric Pennyfeather pointed.

'Ah. That's a fine mare you have,' said the monk
amiably.

Eric Pennyfeather stared at him.

'What, er . . . What year would you say this is?' said
the monk casually.

''Tis the year of our Lord, fourteen hundred and . . . something, father.'

'Very good, sir. You're obviously an educated man. Well, we must be getting on. We've still a long way to go.'

And the monk muttered something to his horse that sounded like, 'Told you, didn't I? "Only fifty years to go," you said. Bloody miles out!'

Then, without even taking up the reins, he wheeled his horse, which he called 'Honestly Robin!', and galloped off into the teeth of the oncoming storm.

Ingrid sweeps upwards into the purple evening, wheels once across the sky and heads for her next destination. Her passengers do not know if they will reach that destination or if they will find their quarry when they do reach it. From their positions between the dragon's protective dorsal scales, Merlin and Griswold look out over the city and then settle back to make the best of what will be a long and tiring journey.

Merlin is drained and pale. Shortly before they departed, he performed a most demanding spell. Before long, he must set out to find the man who will soon be needed to fight all manner of Evil in the world of Uther and Rose Falworthy. If only that fool will stay in one place long enough to be found.

The Enchanter scowls.

Why, he thinks bitterly, of all the beings that nature has created, does it fall to that idiot, Dimmot, to become the guardian of Man's destiny? Why does the most potent power to exist in the minds of men have to reside in such an elusive and irritating pile of ribwash?

Griswold is also very, very tired but, in an odd way, he is content. He has had a brief, albeit distant glimpse of immortality and he has found it wanting. There is something very precious in mortality, just as there is in having an honest blade with no special powers.

You know where you stand when you stand on your own two feet. Especially when you've only got two.

Rose, Uther and Sergeant Belkin sit astride their horses, watching the sky long after the dragon is out of sight. The king is unable to speak of his old friend with whom he will never again share a scathing word or a moment of warmth. So he turns to his sergeant and spreads his arms for inspection.

'Well, old friend. This is a turn-up for the scrolls, eh? What d'you think?'

Belkin eyes him critically. 'A novel reminder of your roots, Your Majesty. While you live thus, so lives Camelot and all that it conveys.'

'By God, Belkin, you're a poetic little sod, aren't you? I never realized. Come on.'

They wheel their horses about and gallop noisily through the still evening to the Tower of London.

'Bed as soon as we get in, old girl,' calls the king to Rose Falworthy. 'We've got a heavy day for the next hundred years or so.'

Rose doesn't answer immediately. She knows that Uther's soul is talking as though he is going to live for ever. The awful truth is that Uther hasn't quite grasped the implications of his new body's mortality. Rose knows that she will be around long after this Uther has turned to dust.

At last she shouts back, 'You'll be wanting your cocoa when we get in, then.'

'Indeed.'

Rose chokes back a tear. 'I'll make it while you see to the horses.'

Uther Pendragon gives her a winsome smile that stretches the livid scar on his cheek into a gentle pink ridge.

'Oak hay, old girl,' he says.

CRITICAL WAVE

THE EUROPEAN SCIENCE FICTION & FANTASY REVIEW

"CRITICAL WAVE is the most consistently interesting and intelligent review on the sf scene."
- Michael Moorcock.

"One of the best of the business journals... I never miss a copy..." - Bruce Sterling.

"Intelligent and informative, one of my key sources of news, reviews and comments." - Stephen Baxter.

"I don't feel informed until I've read it."
- Ramsey Campbell.

"Don't waver - get WAVE!" - Brian W Aldiss.

CRITICAL WAVE is published six times per year and has established a reputation for hard-hitting news coverage, perceptive essays on the state of the genre and incisive reviews of the latest books, comics and movies. Regular features include publishing news, portfolios by Europe's leading sf and fantasy artists, extensive club, comic mart and convention listings, interviews with prominent authors and editors, fiction market reports, fanzine and magazine reviews and convention reports.

Previous contributors have included: MICHAEL MOORCOCK, IAIN BANKS, CLIVE BARKER, LISA TUTTLE, BOB SHAW, COLIN GREENLAND, DAVID LANGFORD, ROBERT HOLDSTOCK, GARRY KILWORTH, SHAUN HUTSON, DAVID WINGROVE, TERRY PRATCHETT, RAMSEY CAMPBELL, LARRY NIVEN, BRIAN W ALDISS, ANNE GAY, STEPHEN BAXTER, RAYMOND FEIST, CHRIS CLAREMONT and STORM CONSTANTINE.

A six issue subscription costs only eight pounds and fifty pence or a sample copy one pound and ninety-five pence; these rates only apply to the UK, overseas readers should contact the address below for further details. Cheques or postal orders should be made payable to "Critical Wave Publications" and sent to: M Tudor, 845 Alum Rock Road, Birmingham, B8 2AG. Please allow 30 days for delivery.

Also available in VGSF

Prices correct at time of going to press (October 1994)

Merlin and the Last Trump

COLLIN WEBBER

Sir Griswold wasn't sorry about bumping off Lancelot. After all, the sanctimonious prat had asked for it. But he couldn't fathom all the fuss Merlin was making about it.

The demise of one vainglorious knight couldn't be that important, could it?

Evidently it could. And it was to throw Griswold into an adventure involving walking castles, talking boxes, demons that lived in 'cans', and the deadliest enemy humanity had ever had to face. Not to mention the band who were about to play the Last Trump.

'Goes at a cracking pace. Recommended for anyone with a warped sense of humour' – Mary Gentle

'Some delightfully quirky twists, punchlines and dramatic effects, [that] often brought a smile even to my notoriously cruel and thin lips. Watch for what he does next!' – Dave Langford

£4.99   0 575 05718 1

Blood and Honour

SIMON R. GREEN

A travelling player down on his luck accepts a job impersonating a prince. Unknowingly, he is plunged into a world where the Real and Unreal meet, where ghosts, apparitions and spies prove to be deadly; a world where all his theatrical skills are required, just to stay alive.

'A good book, a good read and fun . . .' – *Vector*

£4.99   0 575 05545 6

Down Among the Dead Men

SIMON R. GREEN

There is a part of the Forest where it is always night, where the tall trees bow together to shut out the light. Men call it the Darkwood, and in living memory its denizens have threatened the Forest Land. Now the scars are slowly healing – until, in a clearing near the Darkwood's boundary, something buried deep beneath the earth begins to wake from its foul dreams . . .

£4.99   0 575 05620 7

Shadows Fall

SIMON R. GREEN

You won't find Shadows Fall on any map, but it will be there for you if you need it badly enough. It's a place where all stories find their ending, all quests are concluded and every lost soul finds its way home at last. Strange people and stranger creatures walk the sprawling streets and there are doors that can take you anywhere, to lands that no longer exist and worlds that someday might.

But now Shadows Fall is under double threat – from a killer who strikes randomly, again and again; and from a bunch of fanatics who want this elephants' graveyard of the supernatural wiped out – and have the means to do it.

The town has just one night to save itself . . .

SHADOWS FALL

The town where dreams go – *to die*

£5.99   0 575 05711 4

Eric

TERRY PRATCHETT

Eric is the Discworld's only demonology hacker. Pity he's not very good at it.

All he wants is his three wishes granted. Nothing fancy – to be immortal, rule the world, have the most beautiful woman in the world fall madly in love with him, the usual stuff.

But instead of a tractable demon, he calls up Rincewind, probably the most incompetent wizard in the universe, and the extremely *in*tractable and hostile form of travel accessory known as the Luggage.

With them on his side, Eric's in for a ride through space and time that is bound to make him wish (quite fervently) again – this time that he'd never been born.

£3.99   0 575 05191 4

Mort
A Discworld Big Comic

TERRY PRATCHETT
Illustrated by Graham Higgins

Death wanted some personal time.

He hired an apprentice.

Unfortunately, he chose Mort.

Being Death's apprentice is a *good* job. Board and lodging, free use of company horse, and you don't even need time off for your grandmother's funeral. Looking like a skeleton is not compulsory, either.

And you meet lots of interesting people. Although, of course, not for very long.

All in all, it's a job for life. Well, nearly. It would have been if Mort had remembered that he wasn't supposed to rescue princesses. After that it all began to go dead wrong...

The best-selling Discworld books have always been said to have a particularly graphic quality even before they had pictures, and now author Terry Pratchett is pleased to present *Mort* as A Big Comic, specially rewritten by Terry Pratchett and illustrated in the spirit of Discworld by Graham Higgins. Read it and reap.

£7.99   0 575 05699 1

New Worlds

Edited by David Garnett
Afterword by Michael Moorcock

Britain's most celebrated science fiction anthology: cutting edge science fiction stories and comment from some of the best writers around, including World Fantasy Award winners Robert Holdstock and Garry Kilworth.

'The avant-guardian of experiment in the nineties' – *The Times*

'The best ever . . . the range of fiction is impressive . . . all that can be done within the wide realm of speculative fiction in the 1990s' – Norman Spinrad *Asimov's SF Magazine*

'The Real Thing . . . a non-stop literary meltdown of massive proportions . . . a spectacular trumpeting of the new wave of literary might crashing onto the shoreline of today' – *New Pathways*

'The stories are powerful . . . Garnett has lost nothing of his touch as a perceptive editor . . . well worth buying' – Orson Scott Card, *The Magazine of Fantasy & Science Fiction*

'The hippest coolest zine of all time is back!' – *SF Eye*

New Worlds 4   £6.99   0 575 05147 7

Cloud Castles

MICHAEL SCOTT ROHAN

The Spiral: where past and present meet, where myth and legend infiltrate the mundane world, where Hy Brasil and Babylon are a short voyage away from Liverpool or Hamburg – via the cloud archipelagos.

You can't always find it – but it can always find you. And when it once again calls lonely business-man Steve Fisher he discovers that in the heart of hi-tech Europe a denizen from the dawn of time is reaching out to ensnare one of humanity's most sacred emblems. If it succeeds an apocalyptic struggle that has raged for millennia will be resolved – and a new, eternal dark age will begin.

Cloud Castles is fantasy on the grand scale, sweeping across Europe's past and present in a dramatic, panoramic story – a magnificent novel from the bestselling author of the *Winter of the World* trilogy.

£4.99   0 575 05778 5

Popes and Phantoms

JOHN WHITBOURN

From his villa in Capri, Admiral Slovo looks back on a past full of dark magic, corruption, and random violence: as a brigand on the high seas, or as emissary to the Borgias, or even Mr Fix-it to the Pope, Slovo has lived life to the hilt – but now it is time to pay . . .

'A masterly sense of fantastic landscape and baroque plotting, with the added bonus of a rounded cast of exotic characters' – *The Dark Side*

'Wreaks stylish havoc on Renaissance Italy' – *Time Out*

'Everything you never knew about history but were afraid might be true. Machiavelli, the Borgias, Martin Luther – what is *really* down there in the crypt of St Peter's – at last, secrets buried for centuries brought to light! Don't wait for the Illuminati cover-up, buy it now!' – Colin Greenland, author of *Take Back Plenty*

£5.99   0 575 05763 7

Bill, the Galactic Hero
HARRY HARRISON

Acclaimed as science fiction's answer to *Catch-22*, *Bill, the Galactic Hero* is a hilariously satirical sf novel that explodes sf clichés by the shuttle-load.

'Simply *the* funniest science fiction book ever written' – Terry Pratchett

£3.99   0 575 04701 1

The Weird Colonial Boy
PAUL VOERMANS

Nigel is a drongo – a wittering, spot-faced pillock whose only, lonely passions are music (it's 1978 and the Sex Pistols are riding high), sex (unconsummated) and tropical fish.

Then one of his fish finds its way into another dimension (don't ask) and Nigel follows it . . .

'A wild comic romp' – *New Statesman*

£4.99   0 575 05715 7